LIKE the BREAK of DAWN

#1 LASS OF LEGEND SERIES

BY BREE WOLF

Like the Break of Dawn by Bree Wolf

Published by WOLF Publishing UG

Text by Bree Wolf
Cover Art by Victoria Cooper
Ebook ISBN: 978-3-98536-190-8
Paperback ISBN: 978-3-98536-223-3
Hardcover ISBN: 978-3-98536-224-0

Also by Bree Wolf

Lass of Legend

Whisked centuries into the past, fiery Scottish lass Yvaine MacKinnear finds herself entangled in a bloody feud between rival clans. While struggling to reconcile her identity and resist her clan's political plots, she falls desperately for enemy warrior Caelen MacCarmaig. Torn between her home and a new life with Caelen--prophesied in the old legends of her people--she races to alter the course of history.

With betrayals, passion, and destiny colliding, Yvaine and Caelen fight to forge peace between the warring clans; yet conspiring forces threaten everything.

#1 Like the Break of Dawn

#2 By the Grey Light of Morning

#3 In the Coming of Tomorrow

LIKE the BREAK of DAWN

Prologue

MacKinnear Island, Scotland 1785 (or a variation thereof)
Sixteen Years Earlier

The wee lassie's feet ached as she trudged ever onward, each step taking her farther away from the comfort of familiar sounds and smells. The vast sky stretched endlessly above her, day and night blending together in a seemingly never-ending cycle. Lost and alone, she searched for something, anything that might break through the fog of confusion that filled her young mind. Her thoughts were muddled, her memories distorted like ripples on a lake after a stone is thrown in, as though they had been torn and ripped and then put back together in ways that made no sense to her three-year-old mind.

The grief her little heart carried was like a mountain, so heavy it threatened to crush her. Everywhere she looked there was no one—just the green of the woods and the distant blue sky. The air was thick with sadness and salt, but she took a deep breath anyway as she stumbled on. In her half-forgotten dreams, the girl remembered the sea; the rolling waves, the cool water, her hair drenched in salty spray—none of it made sense. Her mind harbored nothing but blurry images, echoing those first moments when sorrow had taken root in her heart, since the very beginning of her journey.

And with that thought of sorrow, she staggered onward through the thicket of the rugged hills, her bare feet sore and aching. Her clothes hung from her body like rags, soiled by dirt and leaves with her tangled red hair sticking to the layers of mud caked on her skin. Hunger gnawed at her insides as if she had swallowed shards of glass, searing her throat in pain. Her head spun, and her tongue felt dry and cracked like she had been gulping up sand.

The harrowing sounds that had been ringing in her ears for days still echoed, and she knew something darkly sinister had befallen her and...

Oh, she could not quite grasp the images that spun through her head. And although her memories were fogged with dread, she felt certain that she had not always been alone. Aye, she had known love, still felt its echo like a soothing calm that held the overwhelming fear at bay... however tenuously it did so.

As she stumbled out of the woods, the sun beat down on her, hot and unforgiving, and she fell to the rough ground, her feet bloodied and aching. Yet the smell of the sea still filled her nostrils, stirring a longing in her heart that she could not explain.

And then, as if in answer to her silent plea, the neigh of horses filled the air.

Startled, the wee lassie jerked her head up and saw two men galloping toward her. Though they bore a striking resemblance, one had a kind face lined with wrinkles befitting his age while the other was much younger with disheveled hair that matched his bewildered expression. They reined in their horses when they spotted her, surprise evident on their faces.

The girl stared back at them mutely, confusion clouding her mind; no words would fall from her tongue. The two riders exchanged silent glances before the dark-haired man dismounted his horse and knelt before her. He smiled warmly, his green eyes twinkling with compassion and understanding as he spoke words that sounded familiar but carried no meaning in that moment; still, somehow the lass felt comforted by them all the same.

He reached out his hand to help her stand up, and without hesitation, she took it.

"Do ye have a name, wee lassie?" the man asked, gently lifting her into his arms. His green eyes studied her face, and the lass saw his brows draw down and sadness overshadow his eyes.

Aye, sorrow echoed in the lass's own heart as well, and she leaned into him, resting her head upon his shoulder. Her eyes closed, and she felt her mind drift away. The moment before a black void engulfed her, though, strong arms wrapped around her, promising safety and care.

The lass drifted back into wakefulness to the sound of voices, a steady rhythm that seemed familiar yet distant, like a song she had heard in a dream and could not quite recall. She blinked her eyes open and found herself still in the arms of the dark-haired man, now seated atop a large horse.

Beside them rode the younger man—or rather a lad—from before, and his eyes often strayed to her, the same wrinkled expression upon his face the lass had seen come to the man's upon seeing her. "Is she all right?" the lad asked then shifted his gaze from her to the man who held her so tightly.

The lass could feel the man's chest move with a deep sigh, his arms still holding her. "She doesna seem to be injured beyond a few bruises and scrapes," he murmured softly. "But she's in need of water and food. We needa get her home to yer mother." And with that, he dug his heels into the horse's side and sent them bounding forward, his arms holding her safely.

As they rode, the lass drifted in and out of consciousness. Each time her eyes blinked open, the world around her had changed. Villages passed them by in a blur of stones and thatched roofs while in the distance she could make out an imposing castle with flags and banners flapping in the wind and walls so high they seemed to reach into the clouds. Each thundering hoof beat drew them closer to the castle until they found their way through a village that sat nestled at its feet near the coast.

The air around her thickened with salt, and seagulls circled overhead as if leading them onward. The tempestuous sea lurked nearby, reminding her of lapping waves and the soothing sway of the water.

The man guided his mount through the village, its people stopping to gaze at them in curiosity. The occasional greeting was called out, and although vague images of fear and danger lingered in the back of the lass's head, there was nothing of that in the faces of the people they passed. Instead, she saw a kind of warmth and understanding that quelled the fear and loneliness in her little heart.

When they arrived at the castle, they found the courtyard bustling with activity, and the lass's eyes widened at the noise.

"Heather!" the man holding her called out. "Someone fetch my wife!" Then he dismounted, carefully cradling the girl against his broad chest, and hurried toward a large door, the lad upon his heels. The lass glimpsed his face over the man's shoulder and wondered about the expression she saw there. He seemed worried and yet watchful, the look in his eyes almost fierce; and in that moment, the lass understood that the lad would not leave her side but watch over her.

A small smile graced her lips, and she closed her eyes, once more feeling the soft pull of something far away.

On a slow blink, a woman appeared in the lass's vision, dainty like a fairy and with eyes as blue as a summer's sky. She stood in the doorway, and her jaw dropped as she beheld them, an audible gasp escaping her lips. Two boys rushed up behind her, one almost as old as the one who had come with the man and the other younger, reminding the lass of herself. "Duncan," the woman called out to the lad who had arrived with them. "See to yer brothers." She nodded toward the two younger boys, brushing a motherly hand over their heads.

Then her gaze returned to the wee lassie, and her expression now, too, echoed the sorrow that still rested in the lass's heart. "Aiden, what's happened?" the woman exclaimed, hastening toward them with a fierce protectiveness in her summer blue eyes, and snatched the lass out of the man's arms without a moment of hesitation.

"We found her out near the glen," the man named Aiden explained as they climbed the steps to the large door and then rushed inside. "No one was with her." Aiden met the woman's eyes. "Heather, she hasna said a word."

The woman named Heather nodded, her lips pressing into a tight line. "It makes no difference now," she murmured then smiled down at the lass. "Dunna worry, wee lassie. Ye're safe with us. I'll look after ye."

In a flurry of images, the lass's world changed again. She felt her throat soothed by cooling water and her belly's ache eased by the taste of warm bread and hearty broth. Gentle water washed away the grime that clung to her skin, relieving the itch on her scalp and calming the stinging of the scratches on her arms and legs. Her bruised feet were bandaged, and she was wrapped in a soft garment.

And throughout it all, there was the woman's gentle gaze and protective embrace that reminded her of someone from... before.

The lass could not quite recall; yet she felt drawn to the woman named Heather in a way that she could not explain. She felt safe here, and despite the vague images of fear and danger that lingered in the back of her mind, she could not help but feel as if she was finally... home.

Chapter One
FAMILY

MacKinnear Island, Scotland 1801 (or a variation thereof)
Sixteen Years Later

The wind was blowing fiercely across the Scottish countryside as Yvaine, daughter of Clan MacKinnear, walked determinedly down the path leading to the castle. She had been out late, much later than she should have been, truth be told, and she knew her family would be beyond themselves with concern. Not that there was any need for concern as Yvaine had never found herself in a situation she could not handle. Her family, however, tended to disregard that fact, often treating her as though she were still a wee lassie and not a grown woman.

The castle loomed before her, its towers stretching into the night sky. Yvaine took a deep breath, taking solace in the weight of the bow and arrows strapped to her back, and marched up the steps to the entrance, ready to face her family.

The great hall of the MacKinnear castle stood tall, its ceiling towering above Yvaine and its walls filled with tapestries and ancient weapons. The torches burning on the walls cast shadows on the ground in front of her, and a large fire crackled in the enormous stone hearth, a slow deep sound in this large chamber. Yvaine's heart drummed in her chest, as she placed one foot in front of the other, silently approaching her parents as well as her three elder brothers.

While Yvaine's mother was bustling about the room, her face drawn in worry, her father stood by the fire, looking grave; as justified as Yvaine felt, she could not help but feel a pinch of regret at seeing them thus. Her brothers—Duncan, Keir, and Magnus—all turned toward her as she approached. Anger was etched into Duncan's face, and Yvaine thought to hear him growling something unflattering under his breath. Magnus, though, appeared almost unaware of her presence, his nose as always buried in a book, his feet propped up as he nestled in a cushioned armchair. Keir was the only one who looked as though on the brink of a smile despite the way he was currently shaking his head at her.

Lifting her head, Yvaine brushed a fiery-red curl behind her ear and faced her family, unwilling to show guilt. After all, she did not *feel* guilty. No, indeed, she did not. They ought to have known that she was fine. Was she not always? Did she not always return without so much as a scratch on her?

Still, meeting her parents' gaze, Yvaine felt her cheeks flush, and she cursed under her breath. "Good evening."

With her hands on her hips, her mother fixed her with a glare. "Yvaine! We have been so worried about ye! Where have ye been?"

Yvaine opened her mouth to explain, but her father beat her to it.

"Yvaine, we dunna expect ye to sit at home all day long, embroidering cushions and..." Her father shrugged, clearly lost for words, and Yvaine had a hard time holding back a giggle at the thought of her embroidering. "Do we not grant ye the freedom to explore on yer own?" His gaze was once again serious, and it held hers until she nodded. "Why then can ye not grant us the small mercy of returning home before night falls?"

Yvaine bit her lip and nodded. "I'm sorry," she admitted grudgingly. "I shouldna have stayed out so late. I ken. I ken. I... didna mean to. I simply..."

"Lost track of time?" Duncan finished for her, his arms crossed and his gaze hard. Indeed, he would make a fierce clan leader one day; Yvaine was certain of that.

Still, he was her brother, and she had never felt intimidated by his bear-like stature, remembering only too well how he had carried her around on his shoulders when she had been a wee lassie.

"As though it never happens to ye." Glaring at him, Yvaine had to lift her chin to hold his gaze, annoyed with his height, nonetheless. Indeed, it was hard to stare down someone with righteous indignation when that person was at least three heads taller than her. "How come ye get to go out as long as ye please while I have to be home by nightfall?"

Duncan leaned down to her, the movement making him seem taller still. "Because I'm ten years older than ye, lass, and because—"

"And because ye're a man," Yvaine snapped, hands on her hips now. "That's what ye were going to say, isna it?"

Duncan sighed, his anger dissipating. "Aye, lass. Ye ken how 'tis. We have to protect our own."

Yvaine rolled her eyes. "I can protect myself."

"I ken ye can, lass," Keir chimed in, his voice light. "But we all worry about ye. Ye're our sister, after all."

Yvaine softened at her brother's words. "I ken that, Keir. I simply... I hate being treated like a bairn."

"Aye, well, ye canna have it both ways, Yvaine," her father said sternly, though there was a hint of amusement in his eyes. "Ye're our daughter, and we will always worry about ye. But we do trust ye, too." Deep down, Yvaine knew his words to be true. After all, had she not gone exploring all her life? With her parents' blessing no less?

Yvaine nodded, feeling a sense of relief wash over her. "I ken ye do, and I promise to be more careful in the future." She gleaned at her parents sheepishly. "I'll try to make it back before nightfall."

"Thank ye." Her mother bustled over, wrapping her arm around her. "I ken ye dunna worry us on purpose but..." She heaved a deep sigh, furrows upon her forehead as she looked at Yvaine, her gaze lingering. "Ye'll ken what this feels like once ye have bairns of yer own. 'Tis not easy to worry all the time."

"Then dunna worry," Yvaine exclaimed with a grin. "There's no need to worry after all. I assure ye."

While Duncan rolled his eyes, Keir chuckled. "Ye'll be the death of us one day."

Their mother glared at Keir, a touch of fear in her eyes as though his words might tempt fate. "Now, come and have something to eat." She tucked a red curl behind Yvaine's ear. "Ye must be starved."

With a contented sigh, Yvaine followed her parents and brothers into the kitchen where they shared a late supper before Yvaine bid them all goodnight. As she began her ascent up the winding stairs, a wave of contentment washed over her. There was something comforting and familiar about the soft hum of voices that echoed through the ancient castle, like companions following her up the stairs.

As she passed the upper landing, she saw her grandmother sitting in a cushioned chair near the window. She was a slight woman with dark hair and traces of silver running through it, her hands resting in her lap and a calm look on her face.

"Ah, there's my girl," her grandmother said with a twinkle in her eye, her English accent still revealing her as a duke's daughter even after all her years in the Highlands. "Where have you been this day?"

Yvaine smiled. "I explored the southern coast of the island." She paused for a moment before adding with a mischievous grin, "And I didna get back until after nightfall."

Her grandmother chuckled softly and shook her head. "You have such an adventurous spirit! I remember feeling that same longing for adventure when I was young." She leaned forward and placed her wrinkled hand on Yvaine's arm. "Be careful out there, my dear, but never stop exploring."

Yvaine nodded solemnly before continuing up the stairs to her chamber with a smile on her face and her grandmother's wise words ringing in her ears. Her mind still clung to the thrill of sneaking around and exploring the countryside, climbing the cliffs to the south, stalking deer in the woods or swimming in the lake beyond the glen. Indeed, it was a feeling Yvaine could never quite shake, a feeling of being alive and free. And she knew, deep down, that she would never stop seeking it out.

Chapter Two
LEGENDS

Seated in the great hall of her clan, Yvaine watched as a lively band played traditional Celtic music. She smiled as people clapped along and couples danced in circles, their feet tapping out a rhythm on the stone floor. But Yvaine's eyes were drawn to her beloved grandmother seated by the fire, her gnarled hands weaving a story about two rival clans who had fought over the same land centuries ago. The old woman's warm eyes sparkled like two stars in the night sky, and she beamed with joy as everyone gathered around to listen.

Silence fell over the hall, the only sounds echoing in Yvaine's ears the crackling fire in the hearth and the hushed breaths of those waiting expectantly to hear the retelling of an old legend. "Beyond the waves, near the coast," her grandmother began, her soft voice carrying easily around the grand hall, "there lived two clans, the MacLeòirs and the MacCarmaigs. For many years, they had been at war, a terrible feud the cause of strife and death."

With a sigh, Yvaine swept her gaze around the hall, her eyes lingering upon many beloved faces. Like herself, her parents and her brothers, too—especially Magnus with his love for history—adored Lady Adele's stories. Though an Englishwoman by birth, she had fallen in love with Yvaine's grandfather long ago and followed him to Scotland. Today, she was a Scot at heart, belonging to the land like thistle and heather.

Seated beside Keir, Yvaine listened intently, as the words of her grandmother's story wove a tale of battles, courage, and justice. It was a story of how one day, in the midst of all the fighting, a mysterious woman named Yvaine had appeared as though out of nowhere.

Yvaine had always loved this part, for she had been named after the mysterious Yvaine of long ago. To her parents, it had seemed fitting because she, too, had appeared as though out of thin air, as though the Fey had dropped her at their feet, as though they had meant for her to be their daughter.

"No one knew where she had come from," her grandmother continued, her eyes sparkling as they swept the hall and then came to rest upon Yvaine. "Some said she was the MacLeòir clan chief's lost daughter while others were convinced the Fey had sent her, being displeased with the quarrels between the two clans."

The faces around the hall shone with fascination even though the story was well-known. Yet it was a favorite, for it spoke of a light to be found even in the darkest of nights.

"The son of the MacCarmaig's chief fell in love with Yvaine," her grandmother winked at her, and Yvaine felt Keir elbow her playfully, "and together, they fought to end the feud."

Joy danced over everyone's faces as they lived and breathed the legend of Yvaine and Caelen. "Yet their fathers refused to listen to reason," her grandmother continued, her voice now heavy with regret and sadness, and Yvaine could all but feel those very emotions draping themselves over the hall like a blanket in winter. "They continued their hatred, determined to fight one another. Even a peace summit called by the two lovers ended in bloodshed, for there was a traitor hiding in their midst." With her eyes full of sorrow, Yvaine's grandmother shook her head, her shoulders slumped. "Aye, blood was spilled that day, that of the guilty and that of the innocent alike."

Unfortunately, as the legend of Yvaine and Caelen had been told and re-told, passed down through generations of MacKinnears, some details had been lost, among them the reason for why the summit had ended the way it had as well as the identity of the one who had caused the rift.

Still, there had been a silver lining, for the Yvaine of old and her beloved Caelen had not surrendered in the face of the clan chiefs's unforgiving refusal to end the feud. Nay, they had stood strong and tall, determined to save their people even if the feud were not to end. And so, they had gathered those willing to turn over a new leaf and left the mainland. They had made their way to the Fey Isles that today's Yvaine had called home for as long as she could remember. And there, they had begun again, founding a new clan by the name of MacKinnear.

"To them, the island was an ancient place," her grandmother continued, secrets twinkling in her eyes as though she knew more than she was willing to share, "steeped in myth and legend. Its rolling hills and meadows were alive with the sound of birdsong, and its forests were home to all manner of wild creatures." Her gaze drifted to the tall windows behind which the beauty of MacKinnear Island lay hidden in darkness. "Yet most importantly, it was a place of peace—which was precisely what the two lovers sought."

Yvaine loved the way her grandmother told this old legend, her voice reverberating with pride, the look in her old eyes full of memory as though she had seen these times herself. "Despite the chiefs' refusal to see reason, Yvaine and Caelen declared a truce and called for their people to join them on the island if they wished. Some answered their summons immediately while others followed more slowly as word spread of the chance for a new beginning in this peaceful place."

Often had Yvaine imagined these beginnings of her people, picturing them constructing their homes from stones found in the nearby riverbeds, with many hands pitching in to help with whatever task needed completing. Everyone had worked together, forging strong bonds among them all in the process. And eventually, this new clan made up of different people from different origins had turned into a vibrant community full of laughter and shared knowledge—a safe haven for those seeking refuge from the harshness of mainland life. And when trouble came knocking at their door—whether it be natural disaster or man-made ill will—the people of Clan MacKinnear had stood together—and did so to this day—

unafraid and undeterred by any adversity that threatened their newfound home.

As Yvaine's grandmother finished the tale, the hall was filled with awed silence, and Yvaine saw eyes misted with tears at the reminder of bravery and courage of these two clans as well as the sorrow of their fate. She closed her eyes, imagining the people who had come before her and the rocky path they had walked... and she was grateful, determined to follow in their footsteps and stand up for what was right.

As the night drew to an end, the people dispersed, intent on seeking out their beds, wide yawns stretching over most faces. A warm hand on her shoulder pulled Yvaine from her thoughts, and she opened her eyes to find her brother Keir standing beside her. He smiled at her warmly as he offered his arm, and Yvaine accepted it gratefully, allowing him to lead her from the great hall.

"Yer name was well chosen," Keir remarked as they walked down the hallway together, "for ye clearly possess the same daring spirit as the Yvaine from the legend."

Yvaine smiled and squeezed his arm gently in response. "I'll take that as a compliment," she said with a chuckle.

Keir pulled to a halt then and sought her gaze, his own suddenly overshadowed by concern. "However, we shouldna forget that it took both Caelen and Yvaine to make peace." His eyes looked deep into hers. "Sometimes we all need help, and there's no shame in asking for it."

Yvaine sighed. "Aye, I ken," she replied, squeezing his hand. "I promise I'll take care. Ye dunna have to worry."

Keir chuckled in wry amusement. "Says the lass who almost drowned in the lake because she believed herself a selkie."

"I was five at the time!" Yvaine retorted with indignation.

"Who nearly got herself skewered by a wild boar when she was seven?"

"I thought it was a deer!"

Keir shook his head in amused exasperation. "And then there was the time ye decided to climb the highest tree in the forest and ended up stuck halfway up for hours."

Yvaine groaned. "Ye dunna have to list every foolish thing I've done," she said with a sigh, burying her face in her hands.

"Ah, but I do," Keir replied with a fond smile as he placed an arm around her shoulders and gave her an affectionate squeeze. "For one day, should ye ever be tempted to wander off on another grand adventure without me, I shall have these tales at the ready to remind ye of why sometimes it pays to be cautious."

Yvaine heaved a deep sigh, casting her older brother a rather indulgent look. Aye, she could not be angry with him, for he was right, the oaf! And deep down, she loved how he worried for her because... it meant he cared.

Deeply.

And that was a precious gift!

Chapter Three

ANOTHER ADVENTURE

The following day, Yvaine was already busy making plans to go exploring again. She thought of the places her grandmother had told her about, the stories she had heard from Mrs. Murray, the chieftain's ancient housekeeper, and the travelers who occasionally came to their island. Eager to be off, Yvaine took extra care to pack supplies for the journey. She filled her bag with food, water skins, and a blanket before strapping her bow and arrows to her back and heading out, her long hair braided down her back. Half-way down the stairs to the courtyard, though, she paused, remembering her family's words of concern and caution.

With a heavy sigh, Yvaine turned back around and headed into the library where she found Magnus, his nose stuck in a book—as always. Though only two years her senior, Yvaine had little in common with her youngest brother. Oh, she loved him dearly; oddly enough, though, his clear blue eyes only ever sparkled when he was absorbed in a world far away, his heart never leading him out the door, daring him to seek out adventure. "Would ye like to go riding with me?" Yvaine inquired, her foot tapping impatiently, certain of Magnus's answer.

His chin rose, and his gaze needed a moment before it focused upon her. "Mmh?"

"Outside," Yvaine reminded him, nodding her head toward the tall windows, the bright sunlight sparkling like diamonds in the stained-glass. "Let's go for a ride!"

Magnus's jaw dropped, his gaze fixed on her as though she had just suggested they try jumping off the cliffs to see if they could fly. "Well, I..."

"Never mind," Yvaine interrupted, giving him a warm smile. That befuddled expression upon his face was endearing, and she had never been able to be furious with him. Duncan? Certainly. Keir? Upon occasion. Magnus? Never. "I'll see ye when I get back," she called, waving over her shoulder as she headed out the door.

Yvaine made her way to the stables, the smell of hay and horses already wafting in the air. She took a deep breath, feeling an overwhelming sense of peace wash over her. Her eyes scanned the stalls until they finally landed upon Keir, who was busy brushing down a bay horse.

As she drew closer, she noticed how skittish the horse was, tossing its head anxiously. Still, a smile claimed her features as she watched her brother work, his movements gentle yet firm. She could see why the horses trusted him so much; he had an innate understanding of them that only those who truly cared about animals had.

"Keir," Yvaine called out softly, not wanting to startle either him or the horse.

He turned toward her, surprise flashing across his face before it softened into a warm smile. "Yvaine! What brings ye here?"

"I thought I'd go for a ride," Yvaine replied as she walked over to where he stood beside the gelding's stall. "What about ye? I didna think ye'd be here."

Keir nodded at the reddish-brown gelding, his mane and tail a deep black, and said, "Aye, this is Scout—we are to get to know one another today." He ran his hand along Scout's neck affectionately. "Are we not?" Then he turned back to Yvaine with a rueful smile. "Unfortunately, today, I canna come with ye—but Duncan should be down by the harbor if ye're looking for company."

Yvaine sighed before nodding and wishing Keir luck with Scout. She knew better than anyone how difficult it could be to work with horses—especially when they were still getting used to humans being around them.

And so, she continued on her way, stopping at the last stall to saddle her own rust-colored mare. As she tightened the girth, the mare shifted, snorting softly in anticipation. Yvaine threw a quick glance over her shoulder and smiled; Keir had already left with Scout, his arm draped protectively around the horse's neck as he whispered words of encouragement.

Having finished saddling her mare and attaching her bag, Yvaine stepped into the stirrup and swung herself up onto her back. The mare shifted beneath her, eager to be off—but Yvaine held her steady, patting her neck gently until she settled down again.

By the time Yvaine approached the docks, the sun warming her skin as she rode, she could hear voices shouting orders and the clanking of metal against wood as the merchant ship was unloaded. She spotted Duncan standing on a small platform overseeing the operation, his expression serious and focused. He glanced up briefly when he caught sight of her, waving her over with a nod of his head.

As Yvaine dismounted from her horse and walked to where he stood, she could see that he looked tired—but still handsome and commanding in his blue woolen tunic and leather breeches. "Hello," Yvaine called out softly as she reached him.

Duncan smiled in greeting, though it seemed forced. "Yvaine," he said gruffly before apologizing for not being able to ride out with her. "We've got a full load today—I canna leave until 'tis done."

Yvaine nodded before turning back to look out at the harbor. It was breathtakingly beautiful here; the sea sparkled like diamonds beneath the sun's rays while seagulls glided through the air gracefully, their cries echoing off into the distance. It was moments like these that reminded Yvaine why she loved living here so much; it truly felt like home, the one place where she belonged. Still, the need to explore burned fiercely in her veins, and she could not wait to be off.

She turned back to Duncan with a smile on her face. "Until later then."

"Not too late, though," Duncan reminded her with a stern expression, his blue eyes drilling into her. "Ye hear me, Yvaine? Dunna make me come after ye and drag ye back home."

Yvaine laughed, lifting her brows challengingly. Oh, Duncan, like no other, often annoyed her—enraged her, to be honest—with that overbearing protectiveness of his. However, he meant well; she knew that. Sometimes she simply forgot. "I'll do my best," Yvaine replied as she rode off, guiding her mare away from the harbor. Her brother's growled words nothing but a faint murmur upon the breeze.

Yvaine rode south, the wind in her hair and the sun on her face. She felt energized and alive, like a new person—and she was determined to make the most of this day. Curse her brothers!

After a good bit of riding, she came across a small path that led up into the hills, and she followed it until it wound its way to the highest cliffs overlooking the sea.

Here, she paused to take in the beauty before her—waves crashing against jagged rocks below while seagulls cawed loudly overhead. This was truly breathtaking! She could feel herself being drawn farther and farther into this magical place. Yet as Yvaine looked out at the horizon, she remembered what she had glimpsed here a few days before. A part of her still argued that it had merely been a trick of light. After all, fairy tales and legends were only for children. It had been years since Yvaine had stopped believing the many stories that constantly flowed from Mrs. Murray's lips. Still, when she reached the clifftop, inching forward to peer over the edge into the depths below, Yvaine felt the breath lodge in her throat.

There it was again.

Just below the surface.

Something... glimmering... and shifting?

Could it be true? Yvaine could not help but wonder if there was any truth to these tales after all as she squinted against the bright sunlight shimmering on the waves below. And yet again, something caught her eye—something glistening in the waters below her!

Yvaine's heart raced with excitement, and in her mind, she heard Mrs. Murray's voice whisper the story of the sea serpent that was rumored to live in a cave beneath the island, protecting their clan today just as it had these past hundreds of years. "It canna possibly..."

Yvaine murmured, stunned by the sight before her eyes. What she glimpsed could not truly be an enormous serpent, could it? Doubt remained, and Yvaine squinted her eyes yet again, trying to see whatever it was that hid beneath the waves. Unfortunately, it proved elusive, always remaining beneath the surface, never quite revealing itself.

"I have to see it," Yvaine murmured to the wind as the sound of the waves below crashing against the rocks filled her ears. Slowly, she made her way down from the cliffs, which barred her view of the sea below. From the south side of the island, the sea was inaccessible and always had been.

Still…

Large rocks stood in Yvaine's way, the sound of the sea upon their other side taunting her, urging her onward. A wild thicket grew at their base, and Yvaine wondered…

Never having been a stranger to exploring the most inaccessible of places, Yvaine stepped forward. She had never shied away from a challenge, and she would not start now. If there truly was something to be found, then she would be the one to discover it. And so, with that in mind, she crawled into the thicket, pushing her way through the dense foliage. It was damp and dark, and the farther she went, the thicker it seemed to become. Twigs caught in her hair and on her dress, and at one point, the bow on her back got so entangled that she wondered if she would ever be able to free herself. Eventually though—miraculously—Yvaine reached the rock wall and felt her hands moving over the rough stone.

And there it was.

Just as she had hoped.

An opening in the rock.

"A tunnel," Yvaine breathed, excitement speeding up her heart. Unable to keep still, she crouched farther down and peered into it. Her eyes, though, met only darkness, and it sent an icy shiver across her skin.

"Dunna be a coward," Yvaine reprimanded herself and then crawled into the tunnel, not daring to think on the wisdom of that choice. She followed the tunnel downward, feeling the cold stone beneath her hands, the sounds of the sea growing louder and louder until eventually Yvaine found herself at the tunnel's end.

For a moment, the bright sunlight blinded her, and she blinked her eyes as she sat back, lifting her hand to her forehead. Then slowly, everything came back into focus, and she found herself at the edge of the sea.

The waters were calm here, lapping gently against the shoreline, and Yvaine spotted a few scattered shells on the small rock ledge where she sat and an occasional seagull or two that flew overhead. She breathed in deeply, taking in the sight before her eyes.

A small island—miniscule, truly—nestled into the curved shoreline of MacKinnear Island. Yvaine had already seen it from above. Now, though, it seemed almost within reach.

Her gaze shifted and settled upon the gently moving sea, and her eyes grew wide when she spotted the soft shimmering of a serpent's scales beneath the waves.

For a moment, Yvaine was certain her heart would stop. She all but expected the creature to lift its head above the waters and...

... peer at her?

... perhaps devour her?

No, that was unlikely. After all, in each and every one of Mrs. Murray's stories, the serpent was friendly. At least, to those dwelling on MacKinnear Island.

Inching closer to the water's edge, Yvaine peered at it more closely, suddenly struck by the fact that it did not seem to move.

At all.

Indeed, it was only the movement of the waves that conjured the illusion of a snake shifting beneath the water's surface.

Mustering her courage, Yvaine reached out a tentative hand. When her fingertips touched the cold waters, she drew in a trembling breath. "Dunna be a coward," she reminded herself once more and then thrust her hand into the sea, her breath instantly lodging in her throat.

Nothing happened.

She felt nothing save for the cool waters, and nothing touched her or—heaven forbid—bit off her hand. And so, Yvaine inched forward a bit more, her hand sinking in deeper until...

"Rock?" Yvaine murmured as her fingertips brushed the smooth and rather solid *something* beneath the softly shifting waves. Disappointment stabbed her heart in that moment, and her gaze shifted, followed the path of the serpent, its long body stretching from MacKinnear Island all the way to the small speck of land in the bay. "Not a creature," Yvaine murmured, her hand still exploring the smooth stone below, "but... a... a path?"

Yvaine's heart leaped with sudden excitement, and she stood, her eyes scanning the waters. *A path!* This was not a serpent at all but a path that led from MacKinnear Island to the small island in the bay. What a discovery! A path to the island that was so close yet seemed so far away. A path she was now determined to take.

With a deep breath, Yvaine stepped out into the water, carefully setting her feet on the submerged cobblestone path. It was not deep, the water only reaching up to her ankles. Yet it soaked her skirts, and as she carefully made her way across, Yvaine could feel icy fingers trailing up her legs. Despite the warmth of the air, the water was freezing, and Yvaine was shivering by the time she reached the other side.

On the small island, she found only a tall rock formation at its center and more wild-growing plant life surrounding it like a defensive wall, as though trying to keep out intruders. Still, there was something about this place that captivated Yvaine in a way she could not explain. The air here was different—fresher—like it had been untouched by man for years. As the sun shone brightly above, Yvaine felt as if time had suddenly stilled around her as if this place existed outside of reality and time itself.

Awed by this moment, she breathed in deeply and then pushed her way into the thicket, cursing as her bow and arrows snagged on twigs and vines. Her view was almost obstructed, and yet Yvaine knew she could not stop. Whatever lay ahead, she needed to know what it was.

Finally, she reached the tall rock, jutting out into the sky, as though it strove to reach the heavens. It seemed to draw her in, her limbs humming with some unknown force, urging her onward.

Yvaine took another step toward it but tripped over something on the ground. At first, she thought it to be a root. Then, though, she paused, her eyes narrowing as she kneeled down to inspect it. "'Tis made of metal," Yvaine murmured, gently fingering the small iron ring. It moved from side to side but seemed firmly attached to the ground. She pulled on it but nothing happened. Shifting position, Yvaine put all her weight into it and pulled once more. This time, it seemed that whatever the ring was attached to shifted ever so slightly. "I'm standing on it," Yvaine breathed as realization dawned. "'Tis a door! A trap door in the ground!"

Quickly, her hands worked to uncover it, digging it free and pushing aside the dirt. Her heart beat painfully against her ribs and her breath came fast as she stared at the next step of her adventure. Never would Yvaine have thought that this day would turn out like this!

Wrapping her hands around the iron ring, Yvaine pulled with all her might. Slowly, aggravatingly slowly, the door began to rise, a small gap appearing. Leaning backward, Yvaine pulled harder, her teeth gritted together as she strained with the weight. Then, finally, the door gave in and fell back, landing on her right foot with a dull thud.

Yvaine cringed, but the pain only lasted a moment.

Excitement surged through Yvaine's veins as she peered down into the darkness, wondering what lay hidden down there.

Treasure?

An old pirate hideaway?

Something... unfathomable?

Taking a deep breath of courage, Yvaine descended into the depths of this unknown place, feeling an intense sense of anticipation as to what secrets may lay hidden beneath the island.

Her heart raced as she followed the tunnel; her hands running along the damp walls. She could feel something calling to her, a strange energy that seemed to be emanating from somewhere deeper still. Her steps quickened despite the darkness that surrounded her, and she squinted her eyes, trying to make out what lay ahead but saw only blackness. With her hands upon the walls for guidance, Yvaine moved onward, not daring to stop as fear began crawling up her spine.

Oh, her family would surely disapprove, and they were probably right to do so. Yet...

Yvaine simply could not stop. Her feet carried her onward even when she stumbled in the dark and almost lost her balance. If she was hurt down here, no one would ever find her. Indeed, it was a chilling thought.

Yet it quickly slipped from Yvaine's mind when her eyes glimpsed a faint light coming from up ahead. It could not be daylight, could it? After all, the tunnel was gently sloping downward.

Not up.

And then the tunnel made a sharp turn, and suddenly, it was there before her; a small cavern bathed in a soft light. Yet the light did not come from a hole in the ceiling but seemed to emanate from a small pool of water in its center.

The sight of it filled Yvaine with awe and wonderment. She had never seen anything like this before and yet, something about it felt strangely familiar.

A sudden touch of fear gripped her heart, and the faint echo of a wee lassie's cries drifted through her mind, like a memory long forgotten but not lost. Tentatively, she stepped forward, feeling the cool air wrap around her like a blanket of protection. The walls of the cavern were smooth and glistened with thousands of tiny droplets of water that seemed to sparkle in the faint light.

With wide eyes, Yvaine ventured farther into the cavern and soon realized that it was a dead end; there was nothing else here but the pool at its center. No items of any kind that might have been left behind by another visitor. No drawings upon the walls whispering of—

Yvaine jarred to a halt when her gaze fell upon the faint shimmer of something etched into the rock wall. At first, she could not quite make it out. Then, though, her eyes widened when her mind recognized the cuts as letters, stringing them together to form a word.

A name.

Yvaine.

An icy shiver raced down Yvaine's back as she stared at the carved name. Her name. And for a moment, she wondered if she had ever been here before. "Nay, it canna be." Perhaps though...

"The Yvaine of our legend," Yvaine murmured into the stillness, her mind drawn back to the story her grandmother's words had weaved the night before. Her hands reached out tentatively, and she traced her fingertips across the small indentations made by a blade of some sort.

Yvaine smiled, enchanted by the thought that the legendary Yvaine might have stood in this very spot centuries ago.

Once her eyes had seen their fill, Yvaine cautiously made her way toward the small pool of water, drawn to it as though something were beckoning her closer still. Small waves rolled across its surface, and Yvaine frowned, wondering how that could be possible. The water glistened and gleamed, illuminating the small cavern with its strange, ethereal light. "How can this be?" Yvaine murmured, entranced, reaching out to touch it.

The moment her fingers brushed against its surface, dizziness engulfed her as if something were trying to take hold of her. A strange energy seemed to surge through her veins, and she gasped, fighting to remain conscious as the world around her began to spin. She felt herself fall forward into the water before blackness engulfed her.

Chapter Four

ONE SMALL STEP

Yvaine awoke to find herself lying on the hard, rocky ground, surrounded by a pale, ethereal light. She blinked in confusion, trying to make sense of what had just happened. Her mind felt foggy and heavy but slowly memories began returning; the tunnel, the pool of water... the strange sensation that had taken over her body.

As she sat up, Yvaine noticed that the walls of the cavern were now illuminated with a faint blue light that seemed to be coming from all directions at once. The droplets of water still sparkled like stars, though they now shone with a brighter intensity than before and seemed almost alive in their movements.

The pool at its center was even more entrancing; its waters now glowed with an unearthly hue and small tendrils of light swirled around it like tiny creatures dancing in joyous celebration. Yvaine's heart raced as she realized that this place was truly magical; there was no other explanation for it! She could feel its power radiating throughout her body and knew without a doubt that something extraordinary had taken place here this day. Mrs. Murray had been right!

All of a sudden, Yvaine felt an almost desperate need to speak with the ancient housekeeper, her mind reeling with all she had seen, all she had experienced. Was it possible that Mrs. Murray knew about this? This island? This cavern? This pool?

If anyone knew, it was her.

Pushing to her feet, Yvaine stilled when she noticed a tunnel leading off to one side. Nay, this was not the tunnel she had followed before, was it?

To confirm, Yvaine craned her neck and spotted the one that had guided her here over her shoulder. "But..." she murmured, staring at the shadowed tunnel ahead of her. "Was this here before? Did I overlook it?" She stepped closer. "'Twas a dead end, wasna it?" She nodded, searching her memory. "'Twas. Then how...?"

She drew to a sudden halt when her gaze swept over the rock wall —now bare of any writing. The name that had been etched into the stone before was gone... as though it had never been. No trace left of it.

Rubbing her eyes, Yvaine blinked then looked again, but the name had not reappeared. Indeed, this was a strange day, and for a moment, Yvaine wondered if she was dreaming if her mind had conjured all of this and she would awake any moment now and laugh at herself.

When nothing of the kind happened, Yvaine stepped forward, carefully leaning into the new tunnel. Again, darkness met her, and yet she could hear the soft rushing of waves echo toward her ears. Did this tunnel lead back to the sea? Was it perhaps... the submerged path she had walked to reach the island? "Perhaps 'tis more than a path. Perhaps 'tis a tunnel as well."

Taking a deep breath, Yvaine moved forward, wondering what lay ahead of her. Her muscles tensed as darkness engulfed her, and yet her heart beat fiercely in her chest, excited at this discovery. How was it that no one knew about this?

As Yvaine made her way through the winding tunnel, she felt as though she were being led home; the sound of water nearby kept her company and gave her comfort. The tunnel went on a while before curving upward, and Yvaine felt relieved when she realized that it was taking her closer and closer to the surface. Would she come up somewhere on MacKinnear Island?

Finally, after what seemed like an eternity, Yvaine emerged not into the light of day but into a room with stone walls. It was dark but no longer pitch-black, for through cracks up ahead, light filtered in.

Yvaine cautiously made her way forward, her hands outstretched, her heart once more beating wildly. Her fingertips explored the surface, only to find that it was not the cool, rough texture of stone but rather a sturdy and varied quality of wood. Her index finger felt splinters and grains, hard surfaces, and softer curves. As she brushed her fingers over the wood, Yvaine heard a soft creaking sound as if the wood had not been touched in a long time.

Sighing, she leaned against it, catching her breath when the wall suddenly moved. It swung outward, its hinges creaking in protest, and Yvaine stumbled out into another chamber, this one made of stone. Light filtered in from a doorway, and she realized that the wooden wall was indeed a shelf, guarding the passage out into the tunnel.

Yvaine smiled. "'Tis amazing!" she breathed in awe, wondering yet again how no one knew this was here. Did Mrs. Murray perhaps? "Oh, that old dragon! How dare she keep this a secret?"

Craning her neck, Yvaine wondered if perhaps she was back in MacKinnear Castle. It seemed like the only explanation. After all, there was no other stone-built structure like it anywhere else on the island. Indeed, the walls were too thick to belong to a cottage or church.

A touch of unease sidled down Yvaine's back as she crossed the chamber and stepped out through the doorway. It was almost eerily quiet. Not a sound beyond the faint echo of the wind and rolling waves drifted to her ears. She could not hear a single voice call out.

Approaching a spiral staircase that led upward, Yvaine listened, her muscles tense. She slowly ascended, her gaze fixed upon the promise of daylight, its light slowly emerging and dancing upon the stone walls. And then she stepped out into a long hallway, her hands now trembling even though she could not say why.

"Hello?" Yvaine called tentatively yet the only answer to reach her ears was the soft trill of a bird.

Quick steps carried her onward, fear now gripping her limbs, and she stumbled into the great hall through a side entrance. "Hello? Where are ye? I—" Her voice broke off as her eyes took in the once-grand chamber where she had sat only the night before listening to her grandmother's retelling of an old legend.

Only now, it lay in ruins; the walls were crumbling, and the floor was scattered with debris. The tapestries which had adorned its walls were nothing but tattered rags, their colors faded from time and neglect. Even the grand fireplace in the center of the room had been reduced to ashes and dust. The large staircase leading up to the second floor nothing more than a pile of rubble, and cobwebs hung from every corner. Yvaine felt a chill run through her body as she realized that the castle looked as though it had been deserted long ago. Yet she could almost hear the echo of laughter that had filled this place only this morning.

Yvaine took a few steps forward, feeling lost in time and space. Despite its ruinous state, she knew where she was—this was indeed her home!

This was MacKinnear Castle.

Only... it was not.

Not truly.

Confusion filled Yvaine's heart as she stood in the ruins of her home. If only these walls could speak of all they had seen and heard. "Hello?" Yvaine called out again; and again, only silence met her. "Where are ye all?"

As tears streamed down her face, her feet carried her through the arched doorway and out of the castle's large oak doors. For a moment, the sun stung her eyes, and Yvaine blinked her lashes to focus her sight. Yet when it cleared, her heart broke yet again as her gaze swept over the landscape.

The outer wall of the castle was missing in parts, leaving gaping holes that allowed her to see down into the valley beyond, and what remained of it was crumbling and worn. Where there had once been a bustling village and harbor, now not even ruins remained. In fact, it almost looked as though they had never been.

Vanished without a trace.

Heavy sobs tore from Yvaine's throat as she stared at the destruction around her. Nothing made sense. Was she perhaps lost in a dream after all? A nightmare? Where had everyone gone? What had happened here?

Blindly, Yvaine searched the castle, every chamber, every nook and cranny. Yet she found nothing and no one, only destruction. "How is this possible? How...?" Swallowing hard, Yvaine stared at the crumbling outer wall, for it looked as though the holes had been torn into it a long time ago.

Only this morning, the wall had been in perfect condition.

Glimpsing the clifftop, Yvaine turned toward it, her feet running now, carrying her away from the place that had once made her feel safe and loved but now only broke her heart. Perhaps up there, she could see something that would... explain?

Yvaine prayed that somehow the world would right itself again; yet when she found herself on the clifftop, the very place where her adventure had begun that morning, her heart sank.

MacKinnear Island looked as it always had. Only the castle now lay in ruins and the village and harbor seemed to have been wiped from the earth. "Are all the other villages gone, too?" Yvaine murmured to the wind, her hands balled into fists against the panic that raged in her heart. "Where are ye?" she screamed to the wind. "Where did ye all go? What happened here?"

Only there was no answer, and Yvaine sank to her knees and wept.

Chapter Five

A BLOOD FEUD

With large strides, Caelen MacCarmaig, tall and broad of shoulder, strode down the seemingly endless corridor that led to the great hall of MacCarmaig Castle. His heart beat forcefully in his chest as he considered the words he needed to speak to his father and clan chief. Indeed, one wrong word could lead to even more bloodshed, for the MacCarmaigs and the MacLeòirs had been locked in a bloody feud for many years now.

As he stepped into the great hall, Caelen's right hand came to rest upon the handle of his broadsword, his muscles suddenly tense. His face remained stern; yet he did not doubt that his blue eyes betrayed a hint of anxiety as he saw his father standing at the other end of the vast room.

The man had graying hair, and yet his large frame gave off an aura of strength that had been honed from years of battle. He had been a formidable fighter in his younger days and still kept up his strength even now in old age. Caelen had inherited much of his own strength from his father, including a powerful arm for wielding a blade and an unyielding spirit that refused to surrender even when all seemed lost.

Their eyes met, and Caelen bowed his head in respect and deference. Caelen wore a deep green tunic over leather armor that had seen its fair share of battle, and upon his hip was strapped not only his broadsword but also a dagger or two. A cloak hung loosely around his shoulders, made from fine wool dyed in shades of blue and grey—colors that spoke to his noble heritage. His boots clacked against the stone floor as he approached, and in spite of their differences, Caelen could not help but feel pride swell within him at seeing how far he and his father had both come since those days when they used to spar together on these very grounds.

His father, Graham MacCarmaig, exchanged a meaningful look with his brother Angus, Caelen's uncle and Lachlan's father, and then he looked upon his son with an expression that was difficult to decipher. After what felt like an eternity, he finally spoke: "Welcome home, Son."

"Thank ye, Father." Caelen inclined his head in greeting, his gaze briefly drawn to his uncle before he glanced at the window through which the early morning sun streamed in like the sea rolling onto the land in waves. Most days, the large windows allowed in no more than a weak light that struggled to compete with the ever-present smoke from the fire. Was this perhaps a good omen?

Caelen's gaze shifted to the walls covered in tapestries that showed a history of their homeland stretching back centuries. Warriors, kings, and battles, both lost and won; these images told a story of a proud people and their struggles through time. A heavy sigh left Caelen's lips as the sound of the fire crackling in the hearth filled the silent hall, and he wondered if peace would ever be theirs.

Finally, his father spoke, his voice a low rumble. "What news do ye bring?"

Caelen straightened his back, determined not to be swayed by his father's impressive presence. "It appears the MacLeòir Clan plans to travel to the Fey Isles."

His father scowled, his right brow arching challengingly at the word *travel*. He glanced at his brother once more, who stood with his arms crossed, an eternal scowl upon his face. "What proof do ye have of this?"

"My scouts have seen their ships being prepared."

The MacCarmaig chief nodded slowly, anger etched into his face. "'Tis serious, indeed. We must prepare for battle."

Caelen's muscles tensed. "Battle, Father? Isna it possible that they merely wish to travel there to pay tribute to the spirits of the island?"

To the west of the mainland, a small group of islands sat in the churning sea, rumored to be inhabited by the Fey, their presence nothing to be perceived by human eyes. Still, men who dared travel there spoke of a chorus of whispered voices that hummed and echoed on the wind, a gentle and calming chorus that swayed the trees and brush like the waves of an ocean. Indeed, the island was whispered to be alive with enchantment, an old and powerful magic that was beyond human reach.

His uncle's gaze narrowed, his lips curling into a snarl, and Caelen's hopes for a peaceful solution plummeted. "Nonsense! They seek its power, and we would be fools to allow them to seize it."

Caelen gripped his sword handle harder. "What power, Father?" he dared inquire then shifted his gaze to his father. "Despite the whispers, the stories and rumors, the Fey—if indeed they dwell there—have never seen fit to bestow any sort of power on anyone." He held his father's gaze, willing him to listen, to heed his words. "Ye ken that to be true, Father. There's no power there. The MacLeòirs have nothing to gain from traveling there, and we have nothing to gain from preventing them."

His father's face hardened. Then he slammed his fist down on the large banquet table, and Caelen felt a chill run through him. "Ye dunna ken what ye speak of, Caelen! I willna have them lay claim to that island! Ye will take yer men to sea and ensure they are kept away!"

Caelen felt his heart sink as he bowed his head in defeat. He knew there was no use arguing with his father or his uncle. There never had been. For as long as Caelen could remember, the brothers' hatred of the MacLeòirs had been his daily bread. Caelen had been told it had all begun with a dispute about land and an accusation of a cattle raid, yet Caelen had always wondered if these reasons were true.

If these reasons were the ones that had set them on this bloody path.

With heavy steps, Caelen left the great hall, loathe to prepare himself and his men for battle against the MacLeòirs yet again. Every instinct told him that a piece of land was not reason enough to risk bloodshed. After all, what was to be gained?

As he walked away, disappointment washed over him that his words had gone unheard by the chief; perhaps if he had been able to make his father understand, there could have been another way forward without bloodshed or violence. But such was his life, forever the son, groomed to be leader one day, but with no power to choose his clan's path.

Caelen's heart pounded with an almost overwhelming sense of doom. How much longer was this hatred to continue? And how many more of his people would die for it?

Just then, as if to answer his silent musings, Caelen heard a voice calling out to him. He turned and saw his younger sister Gwyneth standing in the corridor.

Against the dim light of the corridor, Gwyneth's form appeared almost ethereal, her features soft and pale, her eyes glistening in the shadows. She wore a cream-colored dress that rippled in the slight breeze, her hands clasped in front of her. There was an air of innocence and hopefulness about her that seemed to shine even in the darkness. Yet her blue eyes widened with concern as she beheld him. "Caelen," she said softly, "Why do ye look so angry?"

Caelen sighed heavily and looked away. "I seek peace for our people," he replied quietly. "And yet Father..." He bowed his head, wishing he could right the world for his people, for his sister. "If only he would listen..."

Gwyneth's eyes dropped to the tips of her slippered feet, her voice barely audible above the hums and echoes of the wind outside. "Perhaps my marriage will bring peace," she whispered timidly, a soft blush chasing away the paleness of her skin. With a trembling hand, she brushed a curl of her chestnut-brown tresses behind her ear, her gaze brave and yet fearful as she met Caelen's eyes, and the expression upon her face clearly showed how much she dreaded this union of convenience.

Caelen's heart broke for his sister, and he wished with all his heart that he could help her escape this fate. He had already done his utmost to reason with their father, appealing to his heart, reminding him that Gwyneth deserved happiness. Yet his efforts had been in vain.

In a matter of weeks, Gwyneth would come of age and then she would be married to Malcolm Morganach, chief to Clan Morganach. Not only was the man rumored to possess a most foul disposition, but his countenance had been destroyed by a fire years ago, as though to match his outside to his inside. Indeed, Caelen feared for his sister's well-being. Always had she been a gentle creature, her spirit bright and joyful but easily crushed.

Their father, however, did not care, his sole focus that of strengthening their clan, of allying it with the Morganachs.

Gently, Caelen took Gwyneth's hands in his own and gave them a tender squeeze before letting go. "Whatever may happen, I shall stand by ye," he murmured softly. "Always. Never doubt that."

Gwyneth surged into his arms, her own squeezing his ribs in a surprisingly powerful way.

Caelen chuckled then looked down into her wide blue eyes. "Ye're stronger than ye ken, Gwyn. Ye needa believe in yerself."

Blinking back tears, his sister nodded, though, her eyes remained doubtful.

"I must be off," Caelen growled under his breath. "But I shall return before..." His gaze held hers, saying all that was needed, for his tongue could not.

Nodding, Gwyneth stepped back. "Be careful, Brother. I canna live this life without ye." She gave him a brave smile before hurrying away, her spirit's gentle glow quickly swallowed by the shadows of the corridor.

Caelen stood and watched as she vanished from sight, heading toward an uncertain future, and he wished...

Oh, he wished for a great many things!

If only...

Chapter Six
ON THE FEY ISLES

Yvaine awoke with a start, her eyes snapping open to adjust to the darkness of the ruins around her. She blinked, disoriented, and then the memories and pain of her nightmare flooded back into her mind. She curled up into a ball, tears streaming down her face, as she remembered her family, her people, her home—and how it had all been taken away from her. She had thought it to be a dream, a nightmare—but now she realized that it had been all too real.

With a heavy heart, Yvaine rose from her resting place and slowly meandered her way through the ruins as she had the day before. She had no idea what she was looking for, but she was drawn to the sadness and despair of her surroundings. It was like a wound that refused to heal, a wound she could not help but poke and prod, renewing the pain as her thoughts circled around the question she feared the most: was her family dead?

Her stomach churned, demanding nourishment, and yet every part of Yvaine felt numb, her heart aching so fiercely that she feared it might stop. Blindly, her feet carried her out of the castle ruins where she had slept the night before, exhaustion closing her eyes as darkness had fallen over the island, and out across the wide expanse of grass-land. She walked and walked as the sun shone down upon her, warming her body despite the icy chill in her heart. Her feet began to ache, and yet Yvaine continued on, her mind barely taking note of the trees that now graced her view, forest creatures scuttling around her, their calls and trills like echoes of another life.

"Is it ye?"

Jarred from her trance-like state, Yvaine spun around at the soft sound, her eyes going wide as they fell upon a young woman. She stood no more than a few paces away, her hair so light it almost seemed devoid of color and her sky-blue eyes gazing at Yvaine as though she did not quite believe her presence here.

Yvaine swallowed hard, stunned to see another person upon the island after finding it deserted the day before. "Who are ye? Where did ye come from?"

The young woman smiled at her, her features kind, the simple linen dress she wore a simple white, a dark cloak draped over her slim shoulders. "My name is Catriona, and I've been waiting for ye to return."

Confused, Yvaine stared at her, her mind still too overwhelmed, unable to make sense of the world around her.

Slowly, the young woman approached, the wind teasing her streaming pale-blond hair. "The Fey sent ye away many years ago to protect ye," she whispered in a strangely awe-inspiring voice. "But now, ye're needed here. The time has come."

Yvaine's hands trembled as the wind chased a chill down her back. "The time? The time for what?" she croaked, her throat dry and sore, her mind overwhelmed with questions. "Who are ye? What...?" She swept her eyes over the horizon, MacKinnear Castle—or its ruins—outlined against the bright blue sky in the distance. "What happened here? Where...?" Yvaine's voice broke. "Where is my family?"

A shadow fell over the young woman's face as she reached out a hand, placing it upon Yvaine's arm in a gesture of comfort. "I ken yer heart is heavy and that ye must feel lost." A compassionate smile graced her lips. "Yet ye were brought back for a reason, to set things right."

"Brought back?" Yvaine asked with a frown. "What do ye mean? Brought back from where?" Her mind reeled with everything that had happened, and more than anything she simply wanted to go home. For once, her heart did not long for another adventure.

The woman stepped closer and took Yvaine's hands in her own. "From the time ye call home," she said softly, her words only adding confusion instead of clearing it up. "But ye belong here, and ye were always meant to return."

Perplexed, Yvaine shook her head. From *the time* ye call home? Had she truly just said that? Why time? Yet before she could ask more questions, the woman's expression changed. "Listen," she said urgently, turning her head toward the coast of the island.

At first, Yvaine heard only the wind's whispers and the crashing of waves against the coastline. Then, slowly, a distant chorus of men's voices began to waft to her ears, their words indecipherable from such a great distance. Yet the cacophony was growing stronger with every passing second.

"Ye must find a man named Caelen," the woman said quickly, looking directly at Yvaine. "He will guide ye on yer quest."

"Quest?" Yvaine croaked, staring at the young woman. "What...?"

"Dunna fear, all will be revealed to ye in time."

Another shout cut through the sunlit day, and Yvaine whipped around, her heart hammering in her chest. After the silence of the previous day, her body felt overwhelmed by the sudden presence of others. "What are ye saying? Who is Cae—?"

As Yvaine turned back around, the young woman had disappeared, the spot where she had stood only a moment earlier empty, as if she had never been there at all. Yvaine stood in shock, unsure of what had just happened. She looked out to sea, and then back to where the woman had been—but she was still gone.

Trembling like a leaf, Yvaine sank down onto the grassy ground, her limbs weak and her mind spinning. She could still hear the distant echo of men's voice, and yet it was the young woman's words that drifted through her mind.

Caelen?

Of course, it was a common enough name, and Yvaine had known two or three Caelens throughout her young life. Yet her first thought always went to Caelen from the ancient legends. Always had Yvaine loved these stories about bravery and courage, about loyalty and respect. After all, she herself had been named after the woman who had been Caelen's love.

The wind that blew across the island felt chilling, raising goosebumps upon Yvaine's skin, and her gaze swept toward the horizon and the ruins of her home. Aye, Mrs. Murray as well as her grandmother had told her often enough how Yvaine and Caelen had come to this island long ago, restoring an ancient castle to new splendor and making it the home of their people. Could this be the ancient castle?

Yvaine buried her face in her hands, her heart and mind overtaxed by a thought that slowly drifted into the realm of consciousness.

From *the time* ye call home? Was that not what the pale-haired woman—Catriona—had said? She had spoken not of a *place* Yvaine called home but a *time*. "How is this possible?" Yvaine murmured, her voice carried away upon the strong breeze that tugged on her red curls. "How can this be?" Had she truly come from another time?

It seemed unfathomable.

Chapter Seven
UNINHABITED

The smell of the sea was heavy in the air as Caelen and his men sailed across the churning water. The wind whipped his cloak around him, reminding him of the urgency of his mission, and the sky darkened as though in foreboding. He had been tasked by his father to travel to the Fey Isles, and he knew he must not fail in his quest no matter his own thoughts on the matter. Just or not, he had to obey his father, his chief.

And despite Caelen's apprehension, the sight of the Fey Isles in the distance was welcome after their long journey to the coast. It had been overshadowed by stories of old, and more than one night, his men had sat around the fire, speaking of the ghosts that haunted the island. Caelen had laughed, disliking the idea that something unseen held such power over the world. Yet he had felt a shiver in his bones as well and wondered if he had angered the Fey by disputing their existence. Indeed, his father had warned him, whispering words of caution as Caelen had bid him farewell in the courtyard. "The Fey Isles are a place of great power, and great danger. You must go there with courage in your heart and never falter."

As their boats drew closer to the shoreline, Caelen could see that his father had not been wrong—there was a strange power in the air, something ancient and powerful. He could feel it like a presence nearby, watching them, urging them to keep their heads down and be careful. Caelen signaled for his men to stay low and quiet, and they did so without hesitation, the expression upon their faces tense.

Once they arrived, Caelen would need to ensure that his men made it off the boats and onto the island without being detected, and his gaze swept over the place in more detail. He could make out the old ruins to the south, dense forest and hills covering the land.

His boat finally came upon the beach, and Caelen took a deep breath before hopping out into the surf. His eyes widened as he took in the sight of the island around him—dark trees cloaking hillsides, old crumbling ruins surrounded by an ominous mist that seemed to hang in the air like a veil. He had heard stories about this mysterious place since he had been a lad, but now that he was here it felt truly otherworldly. Was it merely his imagination? Would he have felt like this if no one had ever spoken to him of the Fey?

Keeping quiet, Caelen led his men up onto dry land and they followed his footsteps cautiously toward their destination—an old castle said to have been built by an ancient people centuries ago. As they drew closer, Caelen could see that there were indeed signs of habitation on top of one of the hills near the clifftop—crumbling walls and ancient towers that still stood despite their age. Caelen motioned for his men to stay hidden behind trees then turned to his cousin Lachlan and his oldest friend Fergus. "We shall split up," he commanded in a hushed tone, his gaze occasionally sweeping the shoreline, wondering where the MacLeòirs were. Could they already be on the island? "Lachlan," Caelen said to his rough-handed, burly cousin, "head farther south."

Lachlan nodded, his expression stern and his gaze narrowed as he slipped away and then disappeared into the woods.

"Fergus." Caelen nodded to his even-tempered childhood friend. Still crouched low, Fergus moved closer to Caelen, his dark hair pulled back from his face. "Go north, and keep a wary eye."

"Aye," Fergus agreed, and his gaze narrowed inquisitively. "And where will ye go?"

"To the ruins," Caelen replied, suspecting that the MacLeòirs would seek to claim the ancient keep if they were to make it to the island. Indeed, according to legend, many men had attempted to reach this island, only for their courage to fail them long before setting foot upon its shores.

Fey or no, 'tis a strange place, Caelen thought as he and his remaining men crept into the ruins, eyes wide as they looked for any signs of the enemy clan. The structure was ancient and crumbling, but Caelen could still make out what seemed to be walls and towers from a bygone era.

The wind blew fiercely around them, carrying with it a strange murmur like that of a thousand voices whispering secrets in the night. Caelen shivered, feeling a chill travel down his spine despite himself. His mind argued that it was nothing but the wind; yet a part of him could not shake the sense of trespassing upon sacred ground. Indeed, in this moment, the ancient legends certainly seemed to be true. Did the Fey have their hands in this place?

As they moved farther into the ruins, the whispers grew louder and more distinct as though they were warnings to turn back, threats of what would happen should they remain. Despite his unease, Caelen pressed on, determined to discover what lay within these walls—if anything at all. Then a howl echoed to his ears from a distance—was it coming from one of the MacLeòir scouts? He motioned for his men to stay hidden as he peered around a corner, but all he saw were shadows as the sun hid behind gray storm clouds.

With his sword drawn, Caelen skirted the ruins, signaling to his men to remain alert, his own attention focused on every rock, every blade of grass, every clump of moss. Yet despite the whispers upon the wind, they discovered no one.

Nothing.

Exhaling deeply, Caelen smiled in relief and sheathed his sword. Yet just as he was about to gather his men, his cousin's voice split through the air with urgent intensity.

Lachlan had found something.

Chapter Eight
ANOTHER TIME

Fog clouded Yvaine's mind like a protective shield, like a mist clinging to her hair and skin. She sat slumped upon the ground, her fingers absentmindedly toying with a blade of grass as her eyes stared into nothing. "I wish to go home," she murmured, desperately trying to avoid the thought that she was now separated from her home, from those she loved by an impenetrable barrier of time. Indeed, it could not be!

The air around her was still and silent; the only sound her own steady breath. And yet the skies had darkened, and as Yvaine looked up, her focus slipping from her inner turmoil to the distant sound of rolling thunder. "Aye, it looks like rain," she murmured on a sigh. Then she pushed onto her feet, still weary and her heart burdened; yet an old instinct gave her strength, reminding her that she could not simply remain here, out in the open with a storm upon the horizon. Nay, she had to return to the ruins, find shelter and—

Suddenly, a large shape emerged from the woods ahead, and Yvaine froze, her heart pounding in her chest. Instinctively, her hands reached for her bow and arrows, only to find them absent. Had she left them behind in the cavern? Or the ruins? Or... the other time? The thought pierced through her like a dagger, and she cursed her lack of foresight.

She cursed her hunger for adventure, her need to push forward into the unknown. In fact, she cursed the very day she had first glimpsed the small speck of land nestled in the southern bay of MacKinnear Island.

Aye, she preferred anger to sorrow, to pain. Anger burned and gave her strength, and Yvaine squared her shoulders, her muscles tensing in preparation as she stared across the small stretch of grassy land at the darkened forest.

The figure stepped closer, detaching from the shadows around him, and Yvaine saw that it was a man. He was tall and broad, with a rugged face and deep-set eyes, and he carried a large sword in his right hand that reminded Yvaine of the old broadswords her grandfather had kept in the ancient armory. Dressed in a tartan plaid cloak slung over his shoulders and pinned at the front, he approached slowly, with almost graceful movements, his hand tight upon the sword's hilt. Then he stopped, and his gaze bore into her. "Who are ye?" he demanded, his voice hard, as his gaze swept her from head to toe, and a slight frown showed upon his features, as though she had put on her dress backward this morning. Then his eyes fixed hers.

Refusing to be intimidated, Yvaine returned his stare. "Who are ye?" she countered, lifting her chin in haughty challenge. After all, she had grown up with three elder brothers, and she knew how to stand her ground.

The man's lips pulled back in a mirthless grin as he regarded her, no humor in his brown eyes. Then, he advanced on her.

More than the sword even, it was the sudden look in the man's eyes that sent a wave of panic through her. It was predatory and whispered of danger, of violence and savagery, and despite her own rough upbringing, Yvaine realized in that moment that nothing in her life thus far had prepared her for men like him.

Without hesitation, the man lunged for her, his sword hissing through the air. The sound reminded Yvaine of her own arrows, of that soothing hum when they soared toward their target.

Instinct took over then, and Yvaine ducked and rolled, dodging the man's blade, before spinning behind him. Seizing the opportunity, she snatched up the dagger that was strapped to his hip and brandished it in front of her. Only compared to the man's sword, it impressed neither him nor her.

Still, the man roared in rage, his face turning a deep shade of red. "Ye'll pay for this!" he shouted, the promise of retribution clear in his hard gaze. "Come now! I'll enjoy taming ye!"

Yvaine felt a chill run down her spine and knew she was in over her head, with no one to come to her aid. If only she could get back to the cavern and her own time. The thought hit her like a falling tree, and she realized that it had to have been the shimmering pool of water that had sent her here. Had she not lost consciousness upon touching it? Indeed, Yvaine remembered how her head had begun to spin, her thoughts slipping away until blackness had engulfed her.

Now, though, it was too late.

Before, she could have made her way back to the cavern, returned to the ruins and followed the tunnel she had discovered after waking. Only now, that was out of the question. Now, she found herself face-to-face with... an ancient warrior determined to... do what?

Yvaine did not wish to find out, and yet she could not ignore the hulking man advancing on her, his narrowed eyes lit with a need for dominance. Then what ought she to do? Run and hide?

Perhaps not a bad idea.

Yet in the next instant, the man called out to someone in the distance, his face twisted in a malicious grin. "Caelen!"

Yvaine froze at the name, certain her heart stilled in her chest, too shocked to resume its natural activity. "C-Caelen?" she murmured, staring wide-eyed at the threat across from her.

The man turned back to her then, and with a sudden lunge, he grabbed her, twisting the dagger out of her hand.

Yvaine screamed out in surprise, her body too stunned to react as he held her in his iron grip. She fought against him, trying to pull away, but the man only laughed at her feeble attempts.

"Ah! I have ye now!" he crowed triumphantly, and his arms wound around her in a grotesque embrace. "Ye canna escape me! Ye might as well cease yer struggling."

"Let me go!" Yvaine demanded with a grunt, trying desperately to break free from his grip. But no matter how hard she fought, the man only laughed in response.

"I told ye to cease struggling," he reminded her, his hot breath upon her neck as he leaned closer, holding her tighter… until she could no longer draw breath into her lungs.

Swallowing hard, Yvaine raked her mind for a way out of this situation. Bright spots appeared in her vision, and every cell in her body cried out for air.

"Cease struggling!" the man commanded, annoyance in his tone at seeing his orders disobeyed.

Hanging her head, Yvaine forced her limbs to still. She closed her eyes, silently counting every beat of her pulse, until she felt the man's iron grip slacken. Then with a sudden jerk, she thrust her head backward, feeling it connect painfully with his nose.

The man, too, howled in pain, and his arms released her. Instantly, Yvaine spun around and out of reach, drawing air back into her lungs.

"How dare ye?" he growled, once more advancing on her despite the drops of blood running from his nose.

Yvaine shrank back. "Stop!" she commanded, stunned when he pulled to a halt, his gaze widening in surprise. "What do ye want from me?" Yvaine panted, her gaze flickering over her surroundings, searching for a way out. She knew she had no chance of overpowering him physically or even outrunning him given their difference in size and strength. She could try appealing to his better nature, but the menacing look in his eyes promised little success.

"Please," Yvaine pleaded, forcing herself to bow her head so as not to further incite the man's anger. "Ye dunna need to do this." Desperately, she tried hard not to let fear creep into her voice lest it push the man over the edge and further into violence. "Let me go and I'll leave —no one needa get hurt."

The man laughed, but it was a mirthless laugh, one that sent icy shivers down her back. "Say what ye will, lass, but I'll not leave here without ye." His gaze narrowed as he regarded her, seemingly oblivious to the blood that dripped from his nose. "Ye have the look of the MacLeòirs." He frowned. "What is yer name?"

MacLeòirs?

The name echoed through Yvaine's head, and memories of her grandmother telling her of the two feuding clans in the old legends came flooding back. The MacLeòirs and the MacCarmaigs, who had been locked in a long-standing battle over land and resources. Only that had been centuries ago, and Yvaine knew that neither clan remained, their legacy lost.

At least... in her time.

Had she truly traveled to a time where the MacLeòirs and the MacCarmaigs still existed? And which clan did this man belong to?

Yvaine lifted her chin, determined to deny him his answer. "I dunna have to tell ye," she said firmly, though her heart thundered against her chest. Still, she stood her ground, refusing to give up her name or any other information about herself. Who knew what he would do with it?

The man's lips thinned into a tight line as he stared at her for a few moments before finally speaking again. "Ye are right," he conceded with a sigh. "Ye dunna have to tell me yer name." He paused then added with a smirk, "But I'll find out one way or another." With that said, he slowly drew his sword from its scabbard and pointed it menacingly toward Yvaine.

"Run if ye dare," he challenged her with a sneer, his eyes glinting dangerously in the fading light as thunder rolled ever closer. "I'd enjoy nothing more than a good chase."

Yvaine knew that she had no choice but to comply. She slowly backed away from the man, her eyes never leaving his. The sky had darkened, and the wind had picked up, howling through the trees, and whipping her hair around her face. Lightning flashed in the distance and thunder rumbled ominously overhead. The man seemed unaffected by it all; he simply stood there, sword still pointed at Yvaine, waiting for her next move.

Her heart pounded in her chest as she spun around and bolted away from him, desperately trying to outrun the darkness that pursued her. But no matter how fast she ran, it seemed to cling to her like a specter, stalking her as she fled into the depths of the woods. Panic clawed at her throat as she felt its icy breath on the back of her neck, sending shivers down her spine.

Her feet pounded against the earth as she sprinted through the forest, branches and twigs lashing at her face with sharp fury. She could feel her energy ebbing away yet she raced onward, determined to escape with her life. Then, something hard and unforgiving jutted up beneath her foot and before she could react, Yvaine was sent crashing down by a tree root that had seemed to snatch at her ankle. With a startled cry, she plummeted toward the ground, and then a gasp of pain escaped her lips when she hit it hard.

The man was on her in an instant, seizing Yvaine and holding on to her despite her struggles. "Cease!" he growled menacingly, and when she did not comply, he put a knife to her throat. "Now, ye'll tell me yer name."

Yvaine felt the icy steel of his blade, like a cold caress against her neck. Terror surged through her veins as he spun her around, pressing her back hard against the rough bark of a tree. His hand locked onto her shoulder in a cruel grip as his menacing eyes narrowed into hers.

"My name is Yvaine."

As though slapped, the man flinched, his brows furrowing. "Nah, ye canna be." He stared into her face as if the truth were somehow written upon her forehead. Then, his eyes narrowed in suspicion. "Ye lie," he snarled, and yet the tone in his voice suggested that not even he believed his words to be true. "Tell me true. Who are ye?"

But before Yvaine could say another word, a deep command rang out from behind them both: "Unhand her!"

Chapter Nine

A RED-HAIRED LASS

With his cousin's voice echoing in his ears, Caelen raced across the land, the wind whipping at his hair, and the earth shaking beneath his boots. His men followed close behind, thunder upon their heels as though it, too, gave chase. They vanished into the nearby woods, slipping past tall-standing trees, and jumping over fallen ones. In the distance, Caelen glimpsed the colors of Lachlan's green-blue tartan, and he doubled his efforts.

As they drew closer, Caelen felt a chill seize his heart as though danger lingered nearby. Yet he could see his cousin was unharmed.

With his back to Caelen, Lachlan stood leaning over a red-haired woman, a blade to her throat and his right hand grasping her by the shoulder, holding her pushed against a tree.

Indeed, the woman looked fearful as she spoke, whispered words passing between the two. Still, there was defiance in her gaze, and she stood tall, her fiery-red hair whipping around her face.

Caelen drew in a sharp breath as he signaled to his men to stay back, intrigued by the sight before his eyes. He approached slowly, trying to hear what was being said as he moved silently in between the trees, his gaze fixed on them.

And then Lachlan growled at the red-haired woman, and her eyes widened in a way that had Caelen rush forward. "Unhand her!" he ordered in a commander's voice, his heart pounding in his chest…

… and not from the run.

At Caelen's order, Lachlan and the woman, both turned to face him, and the moment, her emerald eyes met his, Caelen was struck by the intensity he saw there.

A strange energy seemed to whir between them, like lightning crackling in the air. It made his skin hum and sent a chill into his bones. "Who are ye?" he asked, stepping closer and nodding to his cousin to release her.

Reluctantly, Lachlan stepped back, removing his hands from her shoulders. "She has the look of a MacLeòir," he remarked with a scowl at the woman. "She says her name is Yvaine."

Thunderstruck, Caelen stared at his cousin and then at the woman. His mind whirred as he took in Lachlan's words. It could not be possible. It simply could not! The MacLeòir's daughter had been long dead, had she not? He studied her features again and noticed that she did indeed bear a resemblance to the clan. "How can this be?" he muttered under his breath. "Ye're dead."

Yet here she stood, a proud and defiant woman, her eyes gleaming with fierce fervor. Still, there was a touch of disbelief in her gaze as she looked back at him, as if she, too, felt unhinged by his presence. "Ye're… Ye're Caelen?" she murmured, swallowing hard. "From the… From the legends?"

Caelen frowned, uncertain what to make of her words and demeanor. What legend was she speaking of? "Aye, I'm Caelen," he nodded slowly, his bearing hesitant as he stepped closer. "What legend d'ye speak of?"

The young woman simply stared at him, her gaze wide and unreadable. Caelen had the feeling that there was something she did not wish to tell him, but his instincts told him to press on. "Are ye the MacLeòir's daughter?" he asked cautiously, trying to read her reaction.

Her enchanting emerald eyes widened as though in shock at his question. Then her gaze softened and understanding descended upon her features. She looked away for a moment, her thoughts clearly occupied, then back up at Caelen. Her lips, though, remained sealed.

Intrigued, Caelen gazed at her. "Ye're Yvaine, are ye not, lass?" He shifted upon his feet, inching closer, his voice dropping to a murmur, the words spoken between them not meant to be heard by others.

"Aye," the young woman replied then with a gentle nod of her head. "Aye, I'm Yvaine." She swallowed, and for a moment, doubt lingered in her gaze as if she were not quite certain in regard to her own identity. Indeed, there was something... foreign, almost otherworldly about her. Her attire was not quite what Caelen would expect a chief's daughter to be wearing—Gwyneth would certainly never dare. The skirt was too short, revealing her booted feet, clearly designed for daring activities unbefitting a proper maiden, and her unruly curls were in wild disarray, dancing around her face as though wishing to carry her away upon the breeze.

"Where have ye been all these years?" Caelen inquired, his gaze searching her face, wondering about the secrets he glimpsed just beyond the surface. "We thought ye dead. The world thought ye dead."

A deep breath rushed from her lungs, and she briefly closed her eyes. "'Tis a long story." A tentative smile teased her lips, one that whispered of a heart overwhelmed by a truth unexpected. "I'm not sure where to begin."

Nodding to his cousin, Caelen waited until Lachlan and his men had retreated, giving them privacy to speak. Then Caelen nodded for her to follow him as he moved a few steps farther away. "I still canna believe it," he murmured, seeking her gaze once more, mesmerized by the vibrant emotions upon her face.

Yvaine sighed, a faraway look in her eyes as she shook her head. "Neither can I," she replied, and Caelen had the distinct impression that she was not speaking to him.

He reached out and touched her arm until her eyes found his once more. "What happened to ye?" Caelen asked cautiously, worried what painful memories might live in her past. "Do ye remember who took ye?" After all, someone had to have. As a wee lassie of only three years, she could not have survived on her own. If she had simply wandered off, someone would eventually have found her. Yet no one ever had, and she had been missing—presumed dead—ever since.

Yvaine's lips parted, and yet words seemed to fail her. Her gaze rose to find his and lingered, as though she hoped his presence might give her the strength she needed to tell her story. Then, though, she shook her head, her shoulders rising and falling in a defeated shrug. "'Tis too difficult to explain. I didna..." She sighed, and to his surprise, tears filled her eyes.

"Are ye hurt?" Caelen asked as his right hand settled upon her shoulder without another thought. Of course, it had only been meant as a sign of comfort.

At his touch, though, Yvaine flinched, retreating a step, her eyes wide as she stared at him. "Ye're Caelen," she repeated, again shaking her head, disbelief clinging to her features. "Ye're truly him, are ye not?"

Confused, Caelen watched her, wishing he understood what made her so fearful, so uncertain. Clearly, something awful had happened to her. He could see pain in those emerald eyes, and loss. "There's no need to fear me, lass," he assured her, surprised by his own words considering that their clans were at war... and had been for the past years. Indeed, his father would want him to seize her without delay and bring her to him at MacCarmaig Castle. Would her family negotiate in order to see her returned to them?

Caelen cringed at these unbidden thoughts, guilt twisting his heart painfully. Enemy or no, this woman was innocent. Whatever had happened to her, she had not caused the animosity between their clans and did not deserve to be taken prisoner, to be used as a bargaining chip. But what if a deal could be made? Could it not prevent further bloodshed?

"I'm not afraid," Yvaine said unexpectedly, her chin rising as she sought his gaze. "I... I needa go." She made to step past him, and Caelen experienced a moment of panic at the thought of watching her walk away, never to cross his path again.

Instinctively, he reached out and held her back, his grip gentle but firm. "I canna let ye go," he said softly, his voice barely more than a whisper. He watched her carefully, searching her gaze for any sign of understanding. "Yer safety is in my hands now," he added, wanting to believe his own words, knowing she would be far safer with her own clan.

Yvaine stared at him, anger flaring up in her eyes as she shook off his grip. "Ye have no right to order me around," she snapped, glaring at him defiantly, strands of her red tresses curling around her face, as though a fire had just been lit within her.

Caelen frowned at her, momentarily taken aback. Then he closed the distance between them in one large stride, his gaze drilling into hers. "Ye have no idea what has happened here since ye disappeared, do ye?"

Yvaine's lips thinned, and for a moment, Caelen was certain she would bow her head. "Aye, I do," she retorted instead, not shrinking away from his hulking presence. Indeed, she lifted her chin another fraction, a clear challenge burning in her eyes. "I ken all about it. The MacCarmaigs and the MacLeòirs have been locked in a bloody feud, each fighting the other, each seeking ways to gain the upper hand, each blaming the other for what's happened." Scoffing, she shook her head. "'Tis as though neither one ever thought of peace, of coming together and making things right. Ye'll simply continue as ye have until all is destroyed."

Caelen stared at her, thunderstruck to hear his own thoughts fall from her lips. Did she truly know what had happened in her absence? More than that, did she truly believe that a peaceful solution could be found?

"If I let ye go," Caelen murmured, afraid to be overheard, his heart pounding in his ears like drums of war, "will ye speak to yer father? Will ye persuade him to seek peace?"

Yvaine blinked, and a frown descended upon her features. "My... My father? Ye..." She swallowed, then dropped her gaze, regret darkening the glowing green of her eyes.

"Aye, yer father," Caelen pressed, reaching out to touch her arm once more.

Though startled, she did not flinch away, her gaze lingering upon his hand for a heartbeat before once more seeking his eyes. "I canna," she murmured, regret weighing upon her voice as well. "I'm sorry. I wish I could... help, but I..." She closed her eyes and bowed her head. Her shoulders sagged, and she sighed heavily, turning away from him as though ashamed.

Caelen frowned, remembering how fiercely she had spoken only moments earlier. And now? "Why not?" he demanded, unable to prevent a tinge of anger from showing in his voice.

"Ye wouldna understand," Yvaine murmured before she made to turn away but paused and looked back at him. "I'm not meant to be here. 'Tis a mistake." She nodded her head vehemently, as though trying to convince herself and not him. "I have to go."

"I canna let ye," Caelen objected, stepping into her path. Again, his pulse thundered in his ears, and a part of him felt appalled. Yet if there was any chance to end this feud, he could not let it slip through his fingers.

Yvaine's brows drew down as she regarded him, and he could see tension coiled tightly throughout her body.

"I ken this isna what ye want," Caelen said quietly, hoping that if he could just make her understand why he was doing this then perhaps some of the bitterness between them would lessen. "But I'm afraid I must insist that ye stay with me until..." He swallowed. "For now."

Her eyes burned fiercely, and for a moment, Caelen feared she would lash out at him. Yet she did not move, her chest heaving with each agitated breath and her hands clenched into fists at her sides.

Exhaling slowly, Caelen shifted closer, his gaze on hers before continuing in a softer tone of voice, "'Tis the only way I can protect ye." Aye, he wanted to protect her, to ensure that she would be safe. That, at least, was the truth.

To his surprise, her features softened, that touch of disbelief once more in her eyes. "Is... Is there a lass in yer life," she murmured, crimson blossoming on her cheeks, "by the name of Yvaine?"

Confused yet again, Caelen frowned, and yet for a heartbeat his breath seemed to falter in his chest. "I had a great-aunt once by the name of Yvaine," he volunteered with a hesitant smile.

A chuckle fell from Yvaine's lips, and her gaze seemed to pierce him.

In that moment, Caelen was suddenly taken aback by her beauty. She seemed to have a light within her that illuminated the darkness of the forest around them. Her eyes were like two emeralds that shone brightly in the gloom, and her skin was so pale that it almost seemed as if she glowed with an inner fire; even the little freckles on her cheeks seemed to sparkle. Her lips were full and inviting, her hair a wild halo of flaming red curls that cascaded down her back. She was fierce and strong, yet so fragile all at once. Caelen felt his heart skip a beat as he stared at her, captivated by this woman who held his gaze without fear or hesitation.

Caelen was so transfixed by Yvaine's beauty that he forgot his surroundings for a moment until she spoke again, breaking the spell between them. "Nay," she said quietly, her gaze lowering slightly as though embarrassed by his scrutiny. "I meant, a lass who holds yer heart."

Caelen's breath caught in his throat. He had no answer to her question, for he had never been able to give his heart away. It was a part of him that he kept hidden from everyone, even himself.

A blush crept up his neck and cheeks, and he quickly turned away from her, not wanting her to see the flush on his skin. "Nay," he said firmly, trying to keep his voice steady despite the sudden wave of emotion that swept over him. "I have no lass like that."

Caelen was about to turn back around when a shout rang out, piercing the stillness of the air. "The MacLeòirs are coming!"

Fergus!

Caelen recognized his old friend's voice instantly and knew how to interpret the anxiety he heard within. His gaze swept past Lachlan and his men, all now drawing their swords, until he spotted Fergus, emerging from in between the trees.

"Prepare!" his friend shouted as he flew toward them, his own sword at the ready. "There's at least twenty of them."

Indeed, with his mind focused, Caelen could now hear warriors crashing through the underbrush as they moved closer and closer to their position, their cries of battle ringing in the air like thunder. The sky seemed to darken above them, and Caelen knew he could not avoid this battle.

Despite a sense of defeat, adrenaline surged through his veins, and he grabbed Yvaine's arm in one swift motion, their eyes meeting for a brief moment, before he pulled her behind him. Then he turned toward his men, barking orders for them to take defensive positions around them. He could sense Yvaine trembling slightly at his side, yet she stood tall despite her fear—a testament to how bravely she faced danger head-on.

Caelen watched as each of his men took up positions around them with practiced ease; some standing ready with bows drawn while others held their swords aloft in anticipation of battle. The tension in the air was palpable as they waited for their enemies to appear from among the trees.

Chapter Ten

SWEPT AWAY

The sun filtered through the branches of the ancient trees of the forest and a warm breeze kissed Yvaine's skin as she ran. Her chest heaved as her feet pounded against the dirt, pushing her onward as quickly as she could. The sounds of battle reached her ears, and the fear of what lay ahead held her captive and urged her on faster.

Running almost blindly through the forest, Yvaine could not help but think of the man she had left behind. Caelen, the hero of legends, who had looked upon her with such intense eyes. She had grown up with his brave deeds, with the whispers of the love that bound him to Yvaine; yet never had she expected to see him in person. The sight of him had transfixed her, and still her heart beat faster every time she thought of him.

Yvaine, her heart whispered, clinging to Caelen's image. *Could it be me? Am I the Yvaine who lived in these legends?* It seemed unfathomable, and yet in an odd way, it made sense, did it not?

Indeed, if what Caelen had said about the disappearance of the MacLeòir's daughter was true, if the pool in the cavern had truly sent her back in time, then, aye, she could be the legendary Yvaine, could she not? It was a thought that made Yvaine's head spin.

The cries of battle echoed to her ears from behind, and Yvaine's heart sank at the thought of Caelen in its midst. What if he was injured? What if he was killed? Would the tales of Caelen and Yvaine never be told? Would they never save their clans?

An icy lump settled in Yvaine's belly. *If I return home, what will then happen here?* Had the pale-haired woman spoken true? Had Yvaine been meant to return now to fulfill her duty to her people? After all, it was Yvaine and Caelen who stood as the origin of Clan MacKinnear. If she left now, what would happen to her family?

Dizziness engulfed Yvaine as her mind boggled under the onslaught of these thoughts, and yet her heart seemed drawn back to Caelen, to the memory of his dark eyes looking into hers. Only she could not stay. She could not help him. She simply could not. She had to return to her own time, and it filled her with an intense sadness, for a part of her wished she could stay and fight alongside him.

Forcing herself to turn away from the sound of clashing blades and battle cries, Yvaine pushed onward, her heart aching fiercely, for every step felt like a betrayal.

I canna stay, Yvaine screamed at herself, afraid to be swayed from her path. *I dunna belong here. I dunna.* And so, she ran, determined to reach the ruins, find the tunnel, and get back to the cavern before it was too late. Tears stung her eyes as she thought of Caelen and the possible fate that awaited him, and it ate away at her.

For the second time that day—as though Fate stood against her—her foot caught on the uneven ground, and she was flung forward. Her head struck a nearby rock, and the force of the blow sent her into a daze. Pain seared her mind, and her vision blurred.

For a few moments, Yvaine simply lay there, the sounds of battle still ringing in her ears. Then she blinked her eyes open and tried to focus her gaze upon the canopy of the trees around her. The various shades of green seemed to move like dancers, twirling this way and that, before vanishing and then reappearing elsewhere. Yvaine's head throbbed, and she could sense a darkness nearby, luring her closer by promising relief from this turmoil.

And Yvaine wanted to give in. Not only were her heart and mind in an uproar, but her body felt weakened as well. Dimly, she recalled that she had not eaten since the day before, her stomach rumbling in protest.

Still, allowing unconsciousness to take her would solve nothing. In fact, it would only make matters worse. Eventually, she would be found either by Caelen's men or... her father's? Again, Yvaine's mind reeled from the thought that she could have another family here somewhere, and she pushed it firmly away.

Gritting her teeth, she pushed herself up, her vision worsening briefly before the world settled back into focus. Then she slowly managed to get to her feet, her balance precarious at best. Before she could attempt even a few steps forward, though, large arms engulfed her from behind, and Yvaine screamed.

"Who do we have here?" a dark, unfamiliar voice asked, its tone slightly mocking. The man—whoever he was—stood tall, his arms muscular as they held Yvaine in a tight grip, his hot breath upon her neck as he spoke.

Yvaine's heart pounded painfully against her rib cage as she tried to break free. But the warrior was too strong. Without even the slightest grunt of effort, he picked her up and slung her over his shoulder, chuckling as Yvaine pummeled his back with her fists, her mind overwhelmed from the suddenness of the attack.

Swiftly, with his senses clearly attuned to his surroundings, the man carried her through the forest, the sounds of battle growing dimmer as he moved. Panic gripped Yvaine's heart as she saw her one chance to return home slip away.

Then the man paused and listened before he gave a call that sounded like the trill of a bird.

Instantly, the sounds of battle changed, and as he continued on quick feet, Yvaine glimpsed other men, all wearing the colors of Clan MacLeòir, appear from between the trees and follow.

Yvaine's captor called out orders to his men as they traveled through the forest, more light filtering in from overhead with each step forward. Soon enough, she could make out the soft lapping of waves upon the shore, the cry of seagulls in stark contrast to the clashing of swords echoing to her ears from behind.

Rushing out of the forest, the men—perhaps twenty in all—headed for a number of boats set upon the pebbled beach. "Ready the boats," Yvaine's captor called before he turned to one of his men, a young lad with hair as red as her own. He looked uncertain, his face pale and his green eyes wide; yet he clutched a dagger in his hands, brandishing it as though he feared an attack.

Yvaine frowned, for something about him struck her as familiar. If only she knew what it was.

"Put that away or ye'll put an eye out," Yvaine's captor growled, yet there was a touch of softness in his tone as he spoke to the lad. "Go and signal the others. We'll leave immediately."

The young lad dashed off, and the warrior set Yvaine down in one of the boats. Again, the world swayed, and the man grabbed her arm to keep her from keeling over. "Ye have a nasty gash on yer head, lass," he remarked with a chuckle as he bound her hands. "How did ye come to be h—?"

His voice broke off as Yvaine lifted her head and looked up into her captor's face. Not unlike Caelen, he stared at her with wide eyes before they swept her features in an almost gentle caress. "It canna be true," he murmured, and his hand moved to touch her face but then stopped a hair's breadth away. "Ye have the look of..." He cleared his throat, and as shouts rang out from the forest, he shook off all thoughts and secured her in the boat. "We'll sort that out later." Then he turned and signaled to his men to push the boats out into the water.

Trembling, Yvaine stared at the man who had carried her here from the forest, for he, too, possessed the same flaming-red hair as the young lad. The same flaming-red hair as she did. Aye, he looked familiar, and a strange sense of belonging swept through Yvaine in that moment. Could that man, could that lad...?

The boat swayed as it left the beach alongside the others. Men came rushing out of the forest, sprinting after the boats as their comrades already on board beckoned them forward. They splashed into the shallows, giving the boats one last push before heaving themselves inside.

Belatedly, Yvaine realized that she knew this beach. Countless times, she had played here as a child with at least one of her brothers there to guard her should her sense for adventure lead her astray.

Yvaine closed her eyes. Oh, it had, had it not? Yet never would she have expected this, and a heavy lump settled in her throat as she contemplated what her family was going through at this moment.

Only two days ago, they had berated her for coming home after sundown. And now? Now, she had been gone for a whole day and would be gone for many more. No doubt, they were beside themselves with worry, and although Yvaine did not doubt that they would come to her aid without a moment's hesitation, she doubted they would find out where she had gone. After all, to her knowledge, no one had ever discovered the secret tunnel that led to the island in the bay.

Only her.

Slumping down in the boat, Yvaine was barely aware of the men who worked to set the sail. Her heart broke at the thought of her family combing MacKinnear Island, frantic with worry, and never finding any answers.

And then movement caught her eye, and a moment later, Caelen and his men poured out of the forest and charged after the MacLeòir men down onto the beach. Yet, they were too late.

The boats were already too far out, and the last of the MacLeòirs was just now pulled from the water. His clothes were dripping wet, but a triumphant smile shone upon his face as he waved cheerfully to the enemy warriors back on the beach.

Yvaine's heart fell as her gaze met Caelen's, his dark gaze overshadowed with something that looked like betrayal. Aye, he had been ready to protect her, and she had left him. Truth be told, as Yvaine looked at the MacLeòir men around her, she would have preferred to stay with Caelen. Odd, because these men were... her kin while he... was not.

If the legends could be believed, Caelen would come to mean much more to her than simple kinship. Indeed, he would steal her heart, and she would win his in return. It was a thought that stole the air from Yvaine's lungs and made her stomach turn all the same.

Only from experience, Yvaine knew that not all stories proved true. Some simply contained a grain of truth that later was spun into a fantastic story to inspire generations to come. Had it not been the same with the legend of the sea serpent? Now, Yvaine knew that there was no snake dwelling in an underwater cave. Yet only the day before she had discovered the grain of truth that had inspired the tale.

As the island disappeared from view, Yvaine sank down into the boat, her mind filled with fear and confusion. What would happen to her now? Where would her life take her? MacKinnear Island—or whatever it was called in this time—was slowly slipping away, and with it, every chance of returning home.

Chapter Eleven

ON THE SHORE

The sun still hid behind dark clouds, the occasional roll of thunder crashing in the distance, as Caelen led his men onward, out of the forest and onto the beach. If not for the cries of anger that echoed from his men's throats, it would have been a tranquil day, lazy seagulls circling overhead, their soft cries mingling with the gentle lapping of the waves.

Ever since he had learned Yvaine's name and understood who she was, Caelen had been hoping for a peaceful solution to this years' long feud with the MacLeòirs. He had hoped to end the long war between the two clans once and for all.

Aye, he ought to have known it had been foolish to have hope.

Hope never survived long in these lands, and disappointment overwhelmed Caelen the instant his feet touched the shore. His eyes darted around, looking for any sign of his adversaries. In the dim light of day, he spotted the MacLeòirs' boats in the distance, sailing away with Yvaine on board.

For a moment, their eyes met, and he thought to see a touch of regret come to her face. Then, however, she was swallowed by the faint mist dancing upon the waves, and Caelen could only glimpse her silhouette as she receded farther away from him. When she eventually vanished into the horizon, his heart clenched painfully.

Aye, today could have ended better.

As his men came to a stop beside him, Caelen muttered, "She's gone." Bitterness grew inside him, and he felt an almost overwhelming urge to drive his sword into the MacLeòir who had stolen her away.

She went willingly, didna she? A voice deep inside whispered, and Caelen's jaw tensed, his teeth gritting together against the harsh truth. *Ye stood ready to protect her and she left ye. She ran.*

Caelen hung his head. "They're her people," he muttered under his breath, reminding himself that Yvaine owed him no loyalty. Indeed, he had been a fool to believe so, after all, they were from rival clans. A war stood between them, and yet—

"What happened?" asked Fergus, tearing Caelen from his thoughts. "Who is the lass?"

Caelen turned to face his men. He could tell from the look on their faces that they were all expecting an answer. "That is Yvaine," he said slowly, seeing the confusion upon their faces quickly replaced by a dawning sense of understanding. "The daughter of the MacLeòir's clan chief."

The men exchanged wide-eyed glances, for they all knew of the lassie's disappearance all those years ago. After all, the MacLeòir clan chief had laid blame at their feet, accusing them of robbing him of his daughter, no matter how vehemently the MacCarmaigs had denied their involvement.

Outspoken as always, Lachlan met Caelen's gaze, his own narrowed in disapproval. "Ye let them steal her away." He glared at Caelen, his accusations clear. "She was within our grasp." His voice rose. "I caught her."

Caelen inhaled a slow breath as he held his cousin's accusing gaze, well aware that his men hung on every word. "Aye, ye did," he admitted with a nod of his head. "And I thank ye for that. Ye did well, Cousin."

At Caelen's words, Lachlan straightened, a pleased smile coming to his face. Still, the hard expression in his eyes remained. "Ye oughtna have talked to her for so long. It gave them the chance to sneak up on us."

Caelen took a step toward his cousin. "Did they sneak up on us? Truly?" He glanced at Fergus, standing an arm's length in front of Caelen's men. "I remember Fergus alerting us to their presence." He lifted his brows in challenge, wondering what his cousin intended by voicing such accusations in front of his men.

Lachlan's body tensed, and his voice took on an even harsher tone. "That doesna change that ye let her slip away."

"I fought to protect us all," Caelen reminded his cousin. "Would ye rather I had stepped aside and let ye fight alone?"

"Ye ought to have tied her up the moment ye saw her."

"Did *ye*?" Caelen challenged. "After all, ye were the one who found her."

A shadow fell over Lachlan's face, fury now burning in his eyes as he glared at Caelen.

Unwilling to let his cousin's disrespect stand, Caelen chuckled, his gaze lingering upon Lachlan's bloodied nose. "Who broke yer nose?" he inquired with a sideways glance at his men. "It didna happen during the fight, for I saw it like this even before the MacLeòirs came upon us."

A muscle in Lachlan's jaw twitched, anger radiating off him in waves. "She caught me by surprise," he gritted out through clenched teeth.

"I see," was all Caelen said, satisfied with his cousin's answer and not willing to embarrass him further. He turned toward his men; yet before he could say a single word, Lachlan addressed him yet again.

"We need to fetch her back," he snarled, his right hand upon the hilt of his sword. "She'll be the means to destroy the MacLeòirs."

Caelen almost flinched at his cousin's words, for although he, too, wished to end this feud, Lachlan had not spoken from a place of peace but of triumph. "Ye wish to use her as a bargaining chip?" Caelen clenched his fists, anger rising inside him.

Lachlan growled. "Dunna be a fool. Ye ken 'tis the only way."

Caelen shook his head. "'Twouldna be right. Would ye speak like this if it were Gwyneth?"

Lachlan advanced, his nose almost touching Caelen's. "Ye're the one who wants to put a stop to this conflict, are ye not?" Something menacing glittered in his dark eyes. "This is yer chance. Dunna waste it." He paused. "Yer father wouldna."

"Aye, he wouldna," Caelen replied calmly despite the blood pounding in his veins. "Only I am not my father." He nodded to Fergus. "Return to the boats. We're headed home."

With a nod of his head, Fergus turned toward the men, and before long, they were trudging back along the shoreline toward the spot where they had landed. It seemed ages had passed since then.

"Are ye a coward?" Lachlan snarled. "Or a fool?" He shook his head. "Yer father will have yer head for this."

Caelen sighed and stepped back. "Aye, he will." He held his cousin's gaze. "Never question me in front of my men again or I will forget that yer my cousin. Is that understood?"

Lachlan's lips thinned, and Caelen saw his cousin's desire to ram his fist into Caelen's stomach flash in his eyes. "Understood," he finally gritted out before whipping around and following the men down the beach.

Caelen exhaled a deep breath before his gaze moved back out to sea. In his mind's eye, he could almost glimpse Yvaine's silhouette in the mist, her head bowed as she had sat in the boat. He had wanted to get to know her, and now he never would. It would be dangerous and foolish to pursue her. It would risk all their lives. It would enrage the feud between their clans even further.

Caelen's heart ached, nonetheless. There had been something in her emerald eyes that had touched him, and the breathless words she had spoken still echoed in his mind. *Ye're Caelen? From the legends?*

Aye, her words had made no sense. Still, Caelen could not shake the feeling that they knew one another... or had known one another in another life.

He chuckled at the thought, for he had never been one to believe in the dealings of Fate. Only today had been a day like no other, and Yvaine was unlike any woman he had ever met. She intrigued him, and he longed to see her again.

If only she were not a MacLeòir!

Chapter Twelve
BROTHERS

The sleek boats cut across the waves and headed for shore, gliding over the iridescent ripples on the water. The midday sunlight caressed the hulls, catching each plank of wood like a kiss against white skin and staining the water blood red. Yvaine watched the shoreline of the mainland, her heart beating fast in anticipation. She squinted at the men in the boat, her heart racing with recognition as she watched the two red-haired men from before. Could it be? Could she have brothers? Were they them? She desperately wanted to know, from the moment she looked into their faces, a ripple of familiarity stirred within her heart.

Living as a daughter of the MacKinnears, Yvaine had always known that there could be another family out there. Or, at least, that there had been once. Often had she contemplated various scenarios of how she had come to be in the middle of nowhere, all alone at only three years of age. Had her family abandoned her? Had they been slain by bandits while *she* had escaped somehow? Yet Yvaine had never unearthed any answers. She had simply appeared out of nowhere one day... and been embraced by the MacKinnears, becoming a daughter of their clan.

The Fey sent ye away many years ago to protect ye. Was that not what the pale-haired woman had said? If only Yvaine knew who she was and if her word could be trusted. Yet everything that had happened since she had found the secret cavern suggested that the impossible had happened. Had she come from a different time? This time? Had the Fey sent her away to see her safe, only to bring her back now to... do what?

Yvaine's head spun, and yet she could not avert her eyes, her gaze drawn to the tall warrior as well as the young lad. Were they truly her brothers by blood? The elder was older than her and would remember the younger sister who had vanished one day. The younger, though, looked barely twelve years of age.

As she stared at them, they became aware of her interest, and while the older eyed her with contemplative suspicion, the younger stared with unabashed interest right back at her.

"Who are ye?" Yvaine asked, her voice raw and her throat sore, her mind still clinging to a deep sense of disbelief. "Can I... Can I have some water?" Bright spots began to dance in her vision, and for a second, she feared she would keel over yet again.

A warm hand upon her arm held her upright, though, and as the fog cleared from her vision, she looked up into the red-haired warrior's stern face. "Here, lass," he said, his rough voice less hard than she would have expected. He held a water bag to her lips and tilted it until she drank greedily.

The red-haired man's gaze bored into her as if he were trying to pierce her very soul. He seemed to be searching for something, and she wondered how much he knew or at least suspected. Did her face stir a sense of familiarity in him as his did for her?

As the cool liquid ran down her parched throat, the man spoke. "Who are ye?" he asked in a gruff voice, though his gaze betrayed a hint of kindness. Yvaine hesitated, for she had no answer to give him other than a feeble shrug of her shoulders. The man frowned but did not press further; instead, he squinted at the shoreline and then back at Yvaine before finally turning away from her with a slight nod of his head.

Yvaine released a shaky breath as she looked around at the two whom she presumed to be her brothers. "Do ye ken who I am?" Yvaine asked hesitantly, fear running through her veins like ice water as she waited anxiously for their response. Her heart leaped as the warrior nodded. The lad, though, seemed uncertain, his gaze seeking his brother's, who nodded to him. Then the lad stepped closer so that his face was level with hers and said softly yet firmly: "Ye are our sister, Yvaine."

Yvaine flinched as though he had slapped her, for the thought was too overwhelming for her to contemplate in earnest. Nay, this had to be a dream. Perhaps she was still at home at MacKinnear Castle, lost in a nightmare.

Unable to hold his gaze, Yvaine looked away, her eyes drawn to the shore of the mainland, looming tall and dark before her—a physical representation of the fear that twisted in her gut. The boats arrived swiftly and silently as if foreshadowing something ominous; the men rushing to disembark like shadows brought to life in the fading light of day.

The red-haired warrior—*my brother!*—lifted Yvaine from where she sat and once more slung her over his shoulder. Then he hopped into the shallows and carried her ashore, setting her down before assisting his men in hiding the boats away in crevices along the shoreline.

Yvaine's heart raced with dread as she tried to make sense of what was happening. Her hands were still tied, and her body felt too exhausted to even attempt an escape. Still, her gaze once more drifted out to sea, and in her mind's eyes, she could see MacKinnear Island. "How will I get back there?" Yvaine murmured as the wind picked up, tossing her hair about and tearing at her skirts as though wishing to carry her away.

Back home.

"Ye're truly Yvaine?"

Swallowing the lump in her throat, Yvaine found the red-haired lad standing before her, his green eyes wide as he stared into her face. "Aye," Yvaine croaked, suddenly saddened that she did not know him, had not seen him grow up. "And ye are?"

The lad cleared his throat, as if preparing himself to announce the arrival of the king. "My name's Rory MacLeòir, second son to the chieftain of Clan MacLeòir."

Yvaine could not help but smile at the lad as he studied her face; there was something so familiar about him. She had heard the tales of Clan MacLeòir countless times, but up until this moment, it had been no more than a name and a tale of days long past. Now, here Rory stood, her brother, and for the first time, Yvaine felt a true connection to this place.

This moment.

Then Rory stepped forward, a small dagger in his hands, and cut the rope that bound her hands. "'Tis an honour to meet ye," he said with a shy smile as he held out his hand to her, his eyes dancing with the same emotion that Yvaine felt in her own heart—the thrill of kinship.

"What are ye doing?"

At the warrior's rough voice, Yvaine flinched, her gaze flying up as he stomped toward them. "He did nothing," she quickly replied, suddenly feeling protective of young Rory and worried of what his elder brother might do. "He simply—"

"He cut ye loose," the red-haired warrior interrupted, turning a hard glare onto his brother. "Do ye not ken how to follow orders, lad? If ye dunna, ye're no good to me."

Instead of cowering before his large brother, Yvaine was surprised to see Rory lift his chin. "She's our sister," he declared, not once averting his eyes. "Ye said so yerself. Is it right to keep her hands bound?"

Although the elder brother's expression remained stern, Yvaine thought to see a touch of amusement flare up in his eyes. "Ye're not wrong," he conceded, placing a hand upon Rory's shoulder. "Yet that is for our father to decide. At present, she's our captive, ye hear?"

Rory frowned, clearly disagreeing with his brother. "I dunna think it right," he insisted, crossing his arms.

"'Tis always wise to be cautious," his brother counseled in such a voice that Yvaine felt reminded of Duncan, who knew how to scowl and growl like no other, and yet he possessed one of the kindest hearts

Yvaine had ever known. "After all, how can ye be certain who she is? Ye were not even born when our sister was lost to us."

"But ye were."

"Aye, I was. But I was only a lad then, barely as old as ye are now. Not even I can be certain."

Rory grinned. "But ye are."

"How would ye ken?"

"If ye were not certain, ye wouldna have told me she was our sister. Ye would have waited and spoken to Father first."

For the first time since he had come upon Yvaine, the red-haired warrior grinned. Then he reached out to tousle his brother's hair. "Ye're a wise one, Rory. Ye'll serve our clan well."

Although he had ignored her thus far, the warrior then turned his hard stare on Yvaine, and she felt it like spiders crawling down her arms and legs. "I'll leave yer hands unbound if ye promise to stay close." His brows rose in warning.

Yvaine nodded. "Aye, I promise." As much as she wished to turn back, she knew she would not make it in her current state. For now, it would be wiser to cooperate, to remember the location of the hidden boats and the way they would ride toward whatever their destination would be. "Will ye tell me yer name?"

The red-haired warrior regarded her intently for a moment, and Yvaine could not help the slight shiver that danced down her back. Indeed, his size and air of command felt intimidating. "I am Logan MacLeòir of Clan MacLeòir, eldest son of the chieftain of Clan MacLeòir," he echoed Rory's words, a touch of mischief suddenly in his blue eyes.

A smile flitted across Yvaine's face, for she recognized the bond between the two brothers. Aye, she shared the same with Duncan, Keir, and Magnus. The thought of them threatened to break her heart all over again, and so she firmly pushed it aside and faced the brother she had never known until today. "'Tis an honor to meet ye," she replied with a teasing arch of her right brow.

Unexpectedly, Logan chuckled, his blue eyes searching her face. "Ye're a handful, are ye not? I always knew ye would be." His voice sobered then, and a shadow fell over his face, one that spoke of pain and loss. "Welcome home, Yvaine. Ye've been gone a long time." Then he spun upon his heel and called to his men.

Thunderstruck, Yvaine stared after him as he rallied his warriors. Horses were led forward, and the men mounted with practiced ease, their faces eager for home. Rory pulled himself into the saddle of a honey-colored mare, murmuring softly as he stroked her neck. Then she saw Logan returning, leading a prancing mare by the reins, her coat as white as the snow-capped mountains. "Do ye think ye can handle her?" he asked with a challenging gleam in his eyes.

Yvaine nodded, deep emotions swelling in her heart as she looked into her brother's eyes. "Aye." She took the reins and made to pull herself into the saddle. Her muscles, though, were not up to the task, and her head began to spin once more.

In the next instant, Logan grasped her by the waist and set her atop the mare. "Here, eat this," he ordered, thrusting a piece of dried meat into her hands. "Ye look as though ye're about to fall flat on yer face." He chuckled then turned to walk away.

"Where are we headed?" Yvaine called out, halting his steps.

His gaze met hers. "Home," was all he said before he swung himself into the saddle of his own steed, a chestnut-colored horse with a spirit not unlike her mare's. He signaled to his men, and a moment later, they were off, following him as he led them away from the sea and into hilly terrain with thick forests on either side of them. The sun was setting in the distance, creating an orange glow behind them that illuminated their way ahead like a beacon in the darkening sky.

For a long time, they rode on in silence, giving Yvaine time to eat the piece of dried meat in peace, her eyes taking in her new surroundings. She tried to memorize every stretch of land, every tree and bush, every boulder and hilly slope, hoping that one day they might lead her back home.

"How are ye?" Logan inquired as he urged his gelding alongside her mare. "Ye look... less pale." Still, his gaze remained upon her, and Yvaine even thought to see a touch of concern.

"Better."

He nodded and made to gallop to the front of their group when Yvaine lifted her hand to stop him. "Ye said we were headed home."

He nodded again, and she swallowed, urging herself to speak. "Where is home? Who awaits us there?" Her hands gripped the saddle tighter.

Logan inhaled a slow breath, his eyes ever watchful. "'Tis not far," he finally said, offering her an encouraging nod before a distant look claimed his eyes. "Mother will be overjoyed to see ye."

Yvaine's heart stilled in her chest. "Mother?" She swallowed hard, unable to imagine the woman who had given her life. The only mother she had ever known was the one she loved with all her heart. What would it be like to come face-to-face with the woman who had birthed her? Would there be a spark of recognition? *Will I be able to love her? Does she still love me?*

"Aye, she'll ken ye for who ye are."

Yvaine tensed at his words, understanding them precisely the way they were meant, as a warning in case she was not who they believed her to be. "And yer father? Will he be overjoyed as well?"

Logan nodded in response. "He'll be glad to see ye returned." Yet there was something in his eyes that made Yvaine feel uneasy. She dared not ask any more questions, and neither did he volunteer answers. Instead, he pushed onward, galloping to the head of their group.

Yvaine was overwhelmed at the prospect of seeing the family she had lost as a wee lassie. Could they ever compare to the family she knew? Yet in truth, Yvaine did not intend to stay long enough to find out. As much as she loved the idea of finding answers to the mystery of her origin when she had no longer expected to find any, she could not imagine living another life than the one she had always known.

Swallowing the lump in her throat, Yvaine focused her attention on the countryside, cataloguing everything she saw and heard as darkness slowly fell over the world. She knew every moment that passed would make it more impossible for her to find her way back.

Yet before the sun had completely set, already casting long shadows across the path before them, they reached the end of the forest and Yvaine saw a looming fortress upon the horizon. Its grand silhouette shone silvery in the dusk light, its ramparts and spires imposing, curling around the walls like protective arms from all sides. Its stone walls appeared in a rosy hue as the sky darkened and the last rays streaked across its surface.

An icy chill gripped Yvaine as she stared at the keep of Clan MacLeòir, wondering what awaited her inside. Would she be welcomed or met with hostility? What was her family like? Would she ever make it back to the cavern and her own time?

Yvaine did not know, and it frightened her.

It was an utterly new sensation.

Chapter Thirteen

A NEW THREAT

The wind rustled around them as Caelen and his men made the long journey back to his father's keep. The early morning sun was just beginning to break through the clouds, and the terrain had changed from the rocky shorelines of the island they had been on to the gentle grassy hills of his home. Caelen had always welcomed the calm that spread through him when he returned to MacCarmaig lands; now, though, there was a sense of apprehension that needled him as they drew closer to the keep. His thoughts continued to linger upon Yvaine and the many questions her unexpected return to the land of the living had stirred up. Indeed, turbulent times lay ahead; Caelen was certain of it.

Lachlan, too, seemed lost in thought, his gaze distant and the expression on his stern face one of contemplation; a fact which only served to increase Caelen's unease. After all, he and his cousin rarely saw eye to eye on things, and Caelen worried what Lachlan might do upon their return.

"Ye look worried," Fergus remarked with a friendly grin as he pulled up alongside Caelen's black gelding. "Is it the lass?"

Caelen threw a furtive glance over his shoulder, reassuring himself that Lachlan was not eavesdropping. "I suppose I am worried," he finally admitted to his childhood friend.

"About the lass?" Fergus's grin stretched a bit wider. "I saw the way ye looked at her."

Caelen tensed, feeling suddenly defensive. "How did I look at her?" he snapped, his tone rough. "Were *ye* not surprised to see her?"

Fergus nodded. "Aye, I was," was all he said; still, the expression upon his face spoke volumes. "What do ye intend to do now?"

Caelen frowned at his friend. "'Tis Lachlan I'm worried about," he clarified, once more glancing over his shoulder at his cousin. "Ye ken as well as I do that he is always out for blood. Ye heard what he said on the island. His thoughts never seem to dwell upon the possibility of peace."

Fergus sighed. "Aye, he's a man born for battle." He paused, running a hand through his dark hair. "What do ye fear he'll do?"

Caelen shrugged, patting his gelding's neck reassuringly as the animal began to toss his head, clearly picking up on his rider's agitation. "I dunna ken."

"And the lass?"

Caelen suppressed a groan at the memory of her sailing away with her kin. Aye, in that moment, he had felt a sense of loss. There had been something about her that called to him. She intrigued him, and not simply because of her sudden reappearance after years of believing her dead. Aye, she was clearly a woman who knew how to keep her secrets close. Still...

"Ye do wanta see her again, do ye not?"

Caelen swallowed hard, for the truth was that he did. "She's a MacLeòir."

Fergus nodded. "Aye, that she is." He grinned at Caelen before dropping back when the keep came in sight, taking his place behind his commander, and Caelen breathed a sigh of relief.

The keep of Clan MacCarmaig stood majestically against the backdrop of the rolling green hills and shining sky. Its dark stone walls glinted in the sunlight and tapered off into towers and turrets. Arrow slits ran along the top, and an imposing arched entrance stood in the center, allowing them into the courtyard.

Dismissing his men, Caelen dismounted from his horse and handed the prancing gelding to a stable boy. Then he made his way inside and headed straight to his father's chambers, Lachlan and Fergus by his side.

While Caelen had always been certain of his friend's support, he could not say the same for his cousin. Lachlan often appeared unsatisfied with his lot in life, begrudging Caelen his position, no doubt wishing he were the clan leader's son and not merely his nephew. Truth be told, there were days when Caelen wished for the same.

"Father," Caelen exclaimed as he strode into his father's large study. An enormous tapestry hung on the back wall showing not only MacCarmaig land but also those of the clans sharing a border with them. In addition, Caelen knew his father possessed a large collection of maps that had been painstakingly collected throughout the years in order to aid in strategic planning.

His father sat behind a heavy wooden desk, its surface covered with parchment and ledgers. His uncle Angus stood by his side, just now pointing to something on a parchment in front of them and murmuring into his brother's ear. As the three young men entered, though, the two elders looked up from their work, his father's deep brown eyes fixing on each of them in turn before finally settling on his son.

"I see ye've returned," his father remarked gruffly, though there was an underlying warmth in the tone of his voice that belied his gruff exterior.

"Aye," Caelen said, gesturing for Lachlan and Fergus to remain quiet for the time being. "Can we speak?"

His father nodded once in acknowledgment before motioning for him to proceed. "I'm glad to see you safe and well. How went your mission?"

Caelen cleared his throat. "As expected. The MacLeòir had already reached the island by the time we arrived. However, we managed to drive them off." Behind him, Caelen sensed Lachlan shifting from one foot onto the other, and he knew that he would not be able to keep Yvaine MacLeòir's reappearance a secret. Indeed, the thought was ludicrous. In the next few days, the news of her mysterious survival would spread far and wide through the Highlands. Why he sought to conceal it, Caelen did not know. Yet he did not wish to speak of her.

Not to his father, at least.

And especially not to his uncle.

Lachlan clearly had no such qualms, for he stepped forward and with a sideways glance at Caelen said, "We encountered a young woman upon the island who had the look of the MacLeòirs."

Caelen inhaled a slow breath as he saw his uncle's jaw drop and his father's shoulders tense. Then Lachlan continued. "She claimed to be Yvaine MacLeòir, the daughter of the MacLeòir clan chief who disappeared years ago."

His father looked thoughtful, his lips thinning. "Ye spoke to her?" His hard gaze moved from Lachlan to Caelen, suspicion in his eyes.

Lachlan nodded. "Aye, I caught her as she tried to flee. I canna say how she came to be on the island. It didna seem she came with the rest of her clan."

Caelen braced himself as his father nodded slowly, and his attention once more settled upon his son. Before he could say anything though, his uncle stepped forward, his lips in a snarl. "If Lachlan caught her, why did ye not bring her?" Indeed, there seemed to be no doubt in his uncle's mind that they had *not* brought Yvaine.

Caelen swallowed, wondering how to explain the situation to his father—and his uncle!—for although he could speak of the MacLeòirs' attack, deep down, there was a part of him that knew he had hesitated in securing her.

"The MacLeòirs attacked," Fergus volunteered as he, too, stepped forward, bringing all three of them back in line. "As we fought, the lass fled and then left with the MacLeòirs."

Caelen stilled at his friend's words as an image drifted back into his mind. Had she truly left with them? Aye, she had run. But had she gone with the MacLeòirs willingly? Caelen could not shake the thought of seeing her hands bound as he had stood upon that beach staring after them.

"Is that true?" his father demanded, pushing to his feet. "Did ye let the lass escape?"

Of course, Caelen ought to have known that his father would find fault with him; after all, his uncle already had. Sometimes Caelen wondered if his father, too, wished Lachlan had been his son instead of merely being his nephew.

Pushing that thought away, Caelen squared his shoulders and met his father's gaze unflinchingly. "My focus was on aiding my men and ensuring they would all return home safe and sound. Aye, the lass took the opportunity to slip away."

For a long moment, his father looked at him, and Caelen wondered if there was doubt in his father's heart. Then he seated himself once more, a heavy sigh drifting from his lips. "Rumors have been swirling for years—some say she drowned, others whisper that the Fey took her." He met Caelen's gaze, the look upon his face suddenly weary and exhausted. "We needa be certain that she is who she claims to be. If she is," he closed his eyes, "Heaven help us."

Frowning, Fergus spoke up. "Why?" he inquired as Lachlan rolled his eyes as though the answer should be obvious. "Even if she is the daughter of the MacLeòir chieftain," Fergus continued undeterred, "why should it matter to us?"

The chief rested his elbows upon his large desk, steepling his fingers as he looked at Fergus. "Aye, the three of ye were only wee lads at the time," he remarked, a faraway look coming to his eyes, as though he longed for easier times. Then he sighed, and his vision cleared. "Before the MacLeòir's daughter vanished, there was a marriage contract between her father and the leader of Clan Morganach." Out of the corner of his eye, Caelen saw his uncle's hands clench and curl into fists as he listened to his brother's words. "'Twas a dark time for us, as we stood alone against two strong allies."

Lachlan nodded, his arms crossed over his chest as he moved to stand beside the chief's desk, beside his father. "Yet when the lass disappeared, yer father," he met Caelen's gaze, "was able to set up a new contract for his own daughter. Thus, Clan Morganach became our ally instead."

"I am aware, Lachlan." Caelen felt his insides tense. "Do ye truly think that if the lass is indeed who she says she is, her father will seek to renew that contract?" Of course, he had known of the contract between Clans MacLeòir and Morganach. Only it had not crossed his mind that the MacLeòirs would seek to renew it.

While his uncle's face turned red with fury, his father looked pale as he pushed to his feet, then walked around his desk and came to stand beside Lachlan. "Aye, I fear he will." He looked at his nephew, who nodded in silent agreement. "We must ken for certain if this woman is indeed the daughter of the MacLeòir; it would mean a great disadvantage for our clan."

Caelen nodded. "I'll set out at first light."

"Take Lachlan with ye," his uncle commanded, looking from his nephew to his son. "Find out the truth. If MacLeòir claims her as his…" He broke off, shaking his head.

"I'll see ye tomorrow at dawn," Lachlan said by way of farewell as they left the chieftain's study, his brows drawn, and his lips pressed into a thin line. "Be ready." Then he walked away.

Fergus chuckled. "He isna one to smile a whole lot, is he?"

Caelen could not help the chuckle that dropped from his lips.

"Do ye wish for me to come along?" Fergus asked, his expression sobering.

"Aye, I'd appreciate it."

Just as the two of them rounded a corner, they came upon Gwyneth, standing in a doorway, her eyes wide and curiosity sparking in them. "Is it true?" she asked, rushing toward them.

Caelen frowned. "Is what true?"

Gwyneth glanced over her shoulder, as though she feared to be overheard. "The MacLeòir lass," she murmured, her pale blue eyes seeking his. "Did the Fey return her?"

As Caelen heaved a deep sigh, Fergus chuckled. "Do ye truly believe that the Fey took her?"

Gwyneth regarded him shrewdly. "Why would I not? Where else could she have been? After all, she vanished as a wee lassie. She couldna have simply walked away, could she?" Her brows rose markedly, and Caelen wondered at the forward attitude his timid little sister often showed whenever she spoke to Fergus.

"We canna be certain," Caelen replied before Fergus could say something that would rile Gwyneth. "However, we shall ride out tomorrow to find out more. The truth, if possible."

Clasping her hands together, Gwyneth sighed. "I wonder what they're like," she murmured, an enchanted expression upon her features.

"Will ye do me a favor?" Caelen asked, gently grasping her hand to draw her mind back to him. When she nodded, he continued, "Will ye watch over Father in my stead? He feels rather agitated by the news."

Gwyneth cocked her head, confusion alight in her gaze.

Caelen inhaled a slow breath, afraid of what his next words might do to his sister. Would they give her false hope? Or rather cause her worry? "He fears the MacLeòir will renew the original marriage contract with Clan Morganach," Caelen said, "and see his returned daughter married to the chief."

Gwyneth stared at him, and Caelen knew precisely what she was thinking. "Could that... truly happen?" she asked breathlessly, a touch of hope shining in her eyes; yet it was overshadowed by guilt.

Caelen's heart ached for her, wishing she could be happy without being bound in obligation. "I dunna ken." He squeezed her hand. "But I will find out," he promised her, feeling torn between wishing for the best for his clan and seeing the sister he loved happy. Part of him hoped that Gwyneth would not need to marry the Morganach clan chief while another part of him felt uneasy at the thought of Yvaine marrying the man instead.

If only he knew what to do.

Chapter Fourteen

COME HOME

The sun shone brilliantly as Yvaine and the MacLeòir men approached the old keep, a massive stone structure that chased a chill down her back. What would she find inside? Yvaine wondered as Logan led her through the gates, with Rory trailing close behind.

The moment the heavy iron portcullis clanged shut behind them, Yvaine felt trapped.

As they pulled to a halt in the courtyard, Logan helped her off her horse, his strong arms steadying her as she descended. The hint of a smile teased his lips, and Yvaine felt a sudden bond to the brother she had never known. Yet he reminded her so much of the brothers she had grown up with. "Ye look as though ye're about to faint, lass," he remarked dryly, yet the smile remained.

Leading Yvaine inside the keep, Logan guided her through the grand entry hall. Torches burned brightly on either side of them, lighting their way as they passed beneath a large archway into a long hallway lined with doors. They passed by servants and guards, all bowing their heads in courtesy to the chief's sons.

As they walked, Rory pointed out various features of the keep, providing an interesting history about its builders and occupants over the centuries.

Yvaine smiled at him, taken by his eagerness despite the way Logan occasionally rolled his eyes at his younger brother. "How do ye ken all this?"

His young eyes lit up with awe. "There are more books in the library than I'll ever be able to read," he breathed with a wistful sigh, reminding Yvaine of her brother Magnus. "I wonder about all the stories I dunna yet ken."

Yvaine chuckled, and the sound echoed along the hallway, easing the tension that lingered in her limbs at the prospect of meeting her father. *My father!* It was unfathomable, and although two days had passed since her unexpected… journey, she still experienced moments of sheer disbelief.

Finally arriving at their destination—the great hall—Yvaine paused, taken by its grandeur. Tapestries adorned the walls while flags hung from the rafters above them. Servants bustled around carrying trays filled with food and drinks in preparation for tonight's supper.

Yvaine marveled at how similar this place was to where she had grown up. It was a different keep with different people, and yet something about it felt reassuringly familiar.

Tables stretched out into the vast space, and along the walls stood suits of armor and weapons that glinted in the light streaming through the windows. At the far end of the room was a great chair, its high back carved with intricate designs. Seated in the chair was Douglas MacLeòir, the chief of the MacLeòir clan—her father!—one hand resting on the carved armrests. His face was unreadable, with a stern jawline and deep-set eyes that seemed to look beyond them. He wore the traditional clothes of his clan, enhancing his proud stature, with an air of power that commanded respect.

Logan stepped forward, bowing his head. "Father," he said. "We have returned."

The chief nodded. "Welcome back, my sons," he said. "Did ye encounter the MacCarmaigs on the island?" His gaze swept over Yvaine, where she stood half-hidden behind Logan's large shoulder.

Still, it caused a shiver to snake down her back, for the chief's eyes narrowed in contemplation.

"We did," Logan said, a hint of anger in his voice. "The MacCarmaigs arrived not long after. They knew what we had planned. No doubt they have spies nearby... or even amongst us." His brows rose meaningfully, and the chief nodded, a question in his gaze.

Logan cleared his throat. "Father," he said. "We have something to show ye." He stepped aside, motioning for Yvaine to come forward.

The chief's gaze now shifted fully to Yvaine, and she felt a sudden wave of unease pass through her. She had never seen such penetrating eyes before, and for a moment, she felt as if he could see into her very soul.

"She claims her name is Yvaine," Logan remarked with a sideways glance at her. "We found her on the island."

The chief continued to stare at her, his expression inscrutable, and Yvaine could feel her heart pounding in her chest as he regarded her.

As silence hung over the great hall, Rory stepped forward, eagerness in his expression. "She is Yvaine, Father" he stated, not a single doubt in his voice. "Our sister."

At these words, the chief rose to his feet. He was an imposing figure, tall and broad, with the hard face of a warrior. He walked slowly toward Yvaine, his gaze never leaving her face, and as he stopped just a few steps away from her, Yvaine was overcome by the intensity of his stare. "Is this true?" he asked, his voice low and husky.

Yvaine swallowed hard, wracking her mind for what to say. Indeed, for the greater part of their ride from the coast, Yvaine had contemplated what to say, how much to say. Yet here, in this moment, she still felt uncertain. A part of her wanted everything out in the open. Never had her family been one to keep secrets—although Yvaine had kept the occasional one. Though she had always felt awful for doing so.

Still, if she confided in these strangers, told them everything, what would they do? Would they believe her? Would they think her mad? Or worse, a witch? Would they lock her up? Aye, as much as Yvaine wished to speak truthfully, she did not dare.

"I... I dunna ken," she finally stammered, wondering what life she could have had had she grown up here. Would she love this man now standing across from her?

The chief regarded her for a moment longer and then stepped away, returning to his chair. "We shall find out soon enough." He snapped his fingers and two servants appeared from the shadows. "Ye will look after her," the chief commanded, gesturing to Yvaine. "If she is indeed my daughter, then I want her safe and protected at all times."

The servants bowed and stepped toward Yvaine, one of them taking her arm in a gentle but firm grip.

Frowning, Yvaine jerked her arm free. "Am I a prisoner?" she demanded, lifting her chin and glaring at the man who was her father.

His gaze narrowed as he regarded her, the expression in his eyes clearly suggesting that he had not expected such defiance. "If ye are who ye say ye are, then ye are family and we will treat ye as such. However, deceit lurks everywhere, and I willna risk the safety of my people on yer word alone."

Gritting her teeth, Yvaine nodded, not unfamiliar with the responsibilities of a clan chief. Her father—her true father!—had often found it difficult to balance everyone's needs in his decisions for their clan.

Acquiescing, Yvaine glanced back at the chief who was speaking with Logan and Rory in hushed tones. He caught her gaze for a moment before turning away again, and Yvaine felt a sudden pang of sadness at being left alone with these strangers. Logan and Rory, in particular, had come to feel... familiar, reminding her of the family who no doubt awaited her return most anxiously. *Oh, no, dunna think of them now!* she commanded herself silently.

As they continued down the long hallway, passing by servants who bowed their heads in respect as she passed by them, Yvaine focused her attention on the subtle changes in her surroundings. The walls were decorated with ornate tapestries that depicted scenes of battles and victories, and the floor was covered in a thick carpeting which muffled their steps as they walked.

Finally, at the end of the hallway, they reached a large wooden door with intricate carvings along its edges. One of the servants opened it, revealing a grand chamber on the other side.

Yvaine stepped inside and looked around curiously. The room was filled with luxurious furniture and various trinkets that spoke of wealth and power. A fire blazed in one corner while a four-poster bed stood in another. A large window overlooked the courtyard outside, giving Yvaine an unobstructed view of her surroundings.

The servant gestured for Yvaine to take a seat on one of the chairs while he motioned for his companion to lock the door from outside. With one last glance at Yvaine, both men bowed their heads before leaving her alone in that room—locked away until further notice.

Yvaine sighed as she paced around nervously, not sure what to do next as she contemplated her fate. If she remained locked away like this, there would be no way for her to find her way back home. But if she revealed too much about herself and who she truly was... she could incur the wrath of these strangers who were now her captors.

With a frustrated growl, Yvaine moved toward the window and looked out over the darkening world. All around her were tall stone walls that seemed to stretch up forever into the sky—it was clear that this keep was well-fortified against any kind of attack or intrusion from outside forces.

She watched as servants scurried around below in their duties while guards patrolled along the walls above them—everyone seemed extremely vigilant in their roles here at this castle, which only made Yvaine feel more uneasy about staying here any longer than necessary.

Just as she was about to turn away from the window, she heard a voice from outside in the hallway. It was a woman's voice and it sounded oddly familiar, demanding that the guards unlock the door. Yvaine stepped back and watched in surprise as the door opened and a woman stepped inside, her eyes wide as she took in Yvaine's presence.

Yvaine was taken aback by how familiar the woman looked—she had long auburn hair and green eyes, her features almost mirroring Yvaine's own.

The woman stepped closer, staring at Yvaine in disbelief before finally whispering, "'Tis true. Ye've returned." Then she suddenly rushed forward and embraced Yvaine tightly, wrapping her in her arms. Tears streamed down her cheeks as she murmured words of relief and joy. "Ye've returned, my wee lassie. Ye've returned home."

Yvaine stood in her mother's arms—for that was who this woman had to be!—feeling a flood of emotions wash over her. She had been searching for her family for so long, never knowing who they had been or what had happened to them, and now here she was.

Her birth mother's embrace was warm and comforting, and Yvaine's arms closed around her in return. Her throat closed up, and as much as she tried, she could not prevent herself from breaking down and weeping openly, every fiber of her overwrought with the upheaval of the past few days.

Together, they sank down onto the rug, wrapped in each other's embrace, and cried out the pain of the past years. Eventually, her mother moved back to look at Yvaine with a puzzled expression on her face. "What happened? Where have ye been all these years?" Tears stood in her eyes, and her voice hitched with every sob drawn from her throat.

Yvaine hesitated before shaking her head slowly, pretending not to remember. After all, she could not tell the truth. What would her mother think if she spoke of traveling through time? "I-I dunna ken," she stammered softly, unsure of what else to say, afraid to say too much. Still, a part of her almost desperately wanted for her mother to know her.

Her mother's voice wavered with emotion as she said, "It all happened so long ago. We were ambushed on our way to visit another clan and ye... ye were taken from us. We searched everywhere for any sign of ye, but it proved hopeless."

Yvaine felt a lump form in her throat, and she squeezed her mother's hands tightly as the older woman continued, "But now, here, ye are! After all these years, we've found ye again! Ye're home now, Yvaine, and we love ye."

Yvaine held back a sob and managed a small smile. Her family had not abandoned her! Growing up, that possibility had always been in the back of her head, and it had weighed heavily on her heart. "Ye never knew what happened to me?" she asked, nevertheless, disappointed that a puzzle to her past still eluded her.

Her mother shook her head sadly. "Nay, we didna ken," she said, squeezing Yvaine's hand tightly. "We searched for ye everywhere—near and far—but ye were gone without a trace." She paused for a moment before continuing. “I’m sorry that we could never find ye.” Her voice broke. “We thought ye dead or...”

“Taken by the Fey,” Yvaine finished, brushing tears from her cheeks, a small chuckle escaping her lips.

“Aye,” her mother replied with a smile as she brushed a curl of Yvaine’s flame-colored tresses from her forehead. “Aye, I liked that thought. I always pictured ye among the Fey, safe and sound and happy.”

The two embraced again tightly before Yvaine finally pulled away with a small smile on her face, glad that after all this time she had finally received some answers. Yet her body still trembled as she pushed to her feet and began pacing around the room, her mind spinning. She could feel her mother’s eyes watching her intently as she tried to wrap her head around everything that was happening. Finally, after several minutes of silence, Yvaine turned toward her mother and asked softly, “What... What is yer name?” Only moments before meeting her father, she had turned to Logan to inquire after his name. Yet she knew not her mothers.

“Elsie,” her mother smiled at her warmly, tears still misting her eyes. “My name is Elsie MacLeòir.”

Yvaine nodded, uncertain how to reply. So, instead she asked, “What will happen now?”

Her mother stood up and enveloped Yvaine in another tight hug. “Of course, ye’ll stay with us! Dunna worry, lass. Ye’ll be safe here.” She smiled warmly at Yvaine before adding softly,” We’ve been waiting for this day for so long... we would never let ye go again.”

Yvaine felt fresh tears well up in her eyes, and yet her heart clenched in fear.

Chapter Fifteen

LYING IN WAIT

The three men were crouched low in the darkness of the woods, their eyes ever watchful of the looming castle in the distance. They kept their weapons close by, and their faces were shadowed by the hoods of their cloaks, making them appear to be part of the surrounding trees and shrubs.

Even in the dark of night, Caelen could make out the massive walls of stone that surrounded the fortress, and he could see the faint light coming from the windows within, hinting at life. They had been staking out the keep for the past two days, yet there had been no sign of Yvaine. Caelen felt a twinge of fear that he suppressed each time his mind wandered to what might have happened. The MacLeòir warriors had taken her away, that he knew. But where was she? Were they holding her now? Or had she been welcomed back as a daughter of the clan?

Over the course of the next few days, these thoughts continued to torture Caelen, constantly testing his loyalty, urging him to choose between what was best for his clan and... what he had felt in that moment on the Fey Isle. He remembered Yvaine fondly, her green eyes flashing with defiance and courage, her sharp tongue as well as the flames of her streaming hair. Oh, he had been impressed by the sight of her, for she had struck him as a woman of the ancient legends. A woman compelling warriors into battle, forging the fate of the land and winning the hearts of her people. Aye, there was something about her. Something that—

"There!" Lachlan exclaimed in a hushed voice before his right arm flew out and he pointed toward the castle. "The gate's opening."

Unfortunately, the only ones to set foot outside the safety of the castle walls were a group of shepherds, heading out to tend to their flock of sheep that they kept in the nearby fields. Caelen watched as the farmers worked, some tending to their animals while others were out harvesting the crops. He could also make out a few MacLeòir men, riding out for a hunt with their hounds by their side.

The seconds of Caelen's life seemed to stretch endlessly, his minutes ticking by like hours as he awaited a sign from the keep. The wind whipped down upon him fiercely as if determined to mock him, bending grass in its wake in homage. Just when it seemed that nothing else would happen, Caelen spotted a messenger galloping out from the keep in a flurry of hoofbeats and dust. His heart hammered in anticipation as he wondered who was sending this message and why it had to be done so urgently. Could his father's suspicions about the Morganach be true?

Caelen longed to be able to jump onto a horse and gallop off in pursuit. Yet answers would not be his, he knew. After all, the fastest he could walk would never get him to his mount in time, and so he felt powerless once again, unable to take any action for himself; yet he still had orders to obey.

Casting a furtive glance at his comrades, receiving their silent nods of agreement, Caelen led them through the darkening forest and toward the looming castle, glittering red in the setting sun. Fearful whispers clung to the air like mist, they carefully skirted around any potential disturbances that could make their presence known to the watchmen or worse, the hunting party that had yet to return. Their hearts pounding against their chest, every step was taken with utmost caution in hopes of reaching their destination undetected.

As they approached the castle walls, Caelen could make out the silhouettes of the guards posted atop them. He looked around for any sign of Yvaine, but, of course, there was none to be found.

Deep down, he hoped that she had been welcomed back into her clan and silently wished her well, praying that she would be safe. Yet the thought alone felt like a betrayal, and Caelen bowed his head in shame.

Not long after, though, a thundering of hooves echoed through the night air, followed by a cacophony of barking dogs, which drew his attention and shoved aside unwelcome thoughts. It was then that he saw the hunting party returning from their venture with a large deer slung over one horse's back. As they drew closer to the castle gates, Caelen saw that each man looked exhausted from their journey yet proud and content with what they had accomplished—another successful hunt for the MacLeòir clan.

Caelen heard the gates clang shut behind them, and a crushing silence filled the air.

"So, what d'ye reckon we ought to be doing next?" Fergus asked him with a sideways glance at Lachlan. "We could be sitting out here for weeks and not catch a glimpse of the lass."

Lachlan nodded. "We oughta grab someone," he remarked in a sour tone, as though he had put this suggestion to them long ago and they had refused.

"Grab someone?" Caelen echoed his cousin's words. "And who? Do ye see anyone wandering around here? Or do ye propose we go after the hunting party?"

Lachlan scoffed. "We'll wait until tomorrow." He retreated quietly, turning back in the direction of their camp.

"What do ye think?" Caelen asked Fergus as they followed yet kept their distance, his gaze sweeping over the castle outlines, gliding from window to window. Where was she?

Fergus cast him a contrite look. "He isna wrong." He elbowed Caelen affectionately in the side. "Of course, that doesna make him right." He chuckled, and Caelen felt the strain of the day fall away.

A grin stretched across Caelen's face. "What would *ye* do then?" His brows rose mockingly. "Grab someone?"

Fergus laughed. "Perhaps. Yet I wouldna worry about that now. There's always time for that tomorrow."

Together, they returned to their makeshift camp and prepared a cold meal with what little food they had. As darkness fell, they all settled down for the night and drifted off into uneasy sleep, clinging to the hope of better luck in the days to come.

Chapter Sixteen

ANOTHER LIFE

Yvaine slowly stirred from her slumber, a dream just out of reach as she opened her eyes to the bright morning light. Her heart sank as she realized that she was not in MacKinnear Castle, the place that was her home, but instead in the unfamiliar halls of MacLeòir Castle among a family that was hers by birth, yet still felt so foreign. Tears pricked her eyes as her heart ached for the people and places that were now lost to her, and a furious growl tore from her throat as she shoved the blanket aside. "Dunna be a coward," she admonished herself, for the last few days had felt far from real. "Ye're not one to cower. So, get up and meet the day."

And with that, Yvaine decided to explore the castle more thoroughly and finally meet its people. She ventured through the winding corridors, peering into each room she passed as she went. Everywhere she turned, there were people of all ages bustling about, their conversations echoing off the stone walls.

As Yvaine continued her exploration, children began to gather around her curiously. "Who are ye?" asked one of the little girls with braids, a shy smile upon her lips. "Are ye the lost daughter of our chief?"

Stunned speechless, Yvaine stared at the children. Indeed, it felt odd to have a new identity here. Granted, on MacKinnear Island, she had also been the daughter of the chief, and yet this here now felt so very different.

"Aye," Yvaine eventually managed to say, her voice a bit of a raspy croak, still, a smile stole onto her face as the little girl beamed up at her.

"Have ye returned to us?" the girl inquired as more children gathered around, all wide-eyed and listening. "Or will ye leave again? Were ye truly with the Fey? What are they like? Are they kind? Or...?" She broke off as a shiver seemed to grip her, but she shook it off quickly and launched into another volley of questions.

Yvaine laughed, and it was then that she realized just how much her return had been prayed for by these people who were her birth family, the clan that would have been hers. She did her best to answer the children's questions before quickly excusing herself, afraid she might say something unwise.

Eventually, Yvaine found herself in the great hall filled with people breaking their fast while talking loudly amongst themselves. The scent of freshly baked bread tickled her nose, and the atmosphere felt warm and inviting. Absentmindedly, Yvaine ran her hand over the cool stone wall beside her as she lifted her head and spied long banners hung from the ceiling, each bearing the MacLeòir crest. Aye, this place felt familiar, and it made her heart ache. "Dunna dwell upon that now," Yvaine reminded herself sternly as she snatched up a piece of warm bread and then rushed from the hall, not paying any attention to the people who watched her with ill-concealed interest. "Ye needa find a way back home."

Quick steps carried her down the corridor and then out into the courtyard. The sun shone brightly, and the air was crisp and fresh. Taking a deep breath, Yvaine closed her eyes, allowing the warmth of the sun to wash over her.

Then, though, she heard a voice calling out from behind her: "Yvaine!"

Startled, her eyes flew open, and she spun around to find a familiar boy standing there, a wide grin on his face. His green eyes sparkled in the morning sun, and his flaming hair hung in disheveled curls over his forehead. His kilt was slightly too large for him as it almost pooled around his feet, yet he seemed to wear it proudly all the same.

"Rory!" Yvaine gasped, surprised by the joy that surged through her at the sight of him. All her life, she had been the youngest of four siblings, and now she had a little brother. It was a strange feeling.

Walking up to her, Rory gestured to the piece of bread in her hand. "Do ye not want to eat in the great hall?" He looked at her quizzically.

Yvaine shrugged. "I dunna ken anyone in there. So, I thought..." She shrugged again, torn between this odd sense of familiarity and foreignness.

"Do ye want me to show ye around?" Rory offered, stepping back, and gesturing proudly toward the castle walls surrounding them. "There's much to see. Do ye remember any of it?"

Yvaine shook her head. "I was too little when I..." She sighed. Had this truly happened? Was this truly her life? Indeed, it sounded like a story told on a stormy night.

"Welcome home," Rory said with a grand flourish of his arm before taking Yvaine by the hand and leading her around the courtyard, telling her stories of Clan MacLeòir as they went.

He pointed out each building of importance while explaining its purpose within their clan: there was the blacksmith's shop where their cousin Roland worked; there was the great hall where their family would hold feasts for special occasions and where they stopped to snatch another piece of fresh bread; there were the servants' quarters, the kitchen, the storerooms; and, of course, several bedchambers and solars where the chief's family lived, along with many other buildings that made up this ancient castle.

As they walked along, Rory eagerly shared tales about battles fought by their ancestors against rival clans centuries ago. He spun tale after tale of the MacLeòirs' heroic deeds and exploits, and Yvaine listened with rapt attention. Slowly, the people who were her blood started to feel real again, their lives tangible, and Yvaine marveled at the warmth that spread through her chest as Rory eagerly talked of their family's history and lore.

Eventually, they found themselves in a large chamber, its walls draped with tapestries that depicted battles and hunting scenes. Two large broadswords hung above the enormous fireplace, their long blades glinting in the faint light coming in from the windows.

"Aye, these be the weapons of our forefathers," Rory said proudly, his voice filled with admiration as he pointed to each one in turn. "This was our grandfather's claymore and that was our great-grandfather's battle axe." He pointed to a large and formidable axe adorning the other end of the room. The blade shone with a metallic finish that glinted in the light from the fireplace, and its handle was wrapped with leather of a deep red color.

Rory then grabbed a bow and quiver from the corner and turned to Yvaine with a mischievous glint in his eye. "And this is my favorite weapon!" he said with a grin.

Yvaine grinned back at him and replied, "Mine too!"

Rory's eyes widened in surprise before he exclaimed excitedly, "Do ye want to go out and practice sometime? I could show ye how it works."

Yvaine beamed at him. "Aye! I would love to!" Indeed, some of her fondest memories were of shared outings with her brothers, and Yvaine felt a lump settle in her throat at the memory, chasing away the joy of the moment.

"Here ye are."

Logan stood in the doorway, his broad frame filling the entire entrance. He had dressed in a sturdy leather tunic that was cinched at the waist with a thick belt. His fiery-red hair was pulled back in a ponytail, and the bow and quiver over his shoulder made him look like a warrior from another era. *This era!* Yvaine reminded herself with a disbelieving shake of her head. His face wore an expression of patience and determination, and his voice carried throughout the room like a low rumble of thunder.

"I'll see ye at supper," Rory said, looking at her with wide-eyes, a touch of a question in his tone, as though he was not quite certain she would be here when he returned.

Yvaine smiled at him. "Aye, at supper." She met Logan's gaze as Rory hastened toward him, and her eldest brother nodded to her, a kind expression in his eyes.

"Let's go, Rory," Logan said as he ruffled the boy's hair affectionately.

Yvaine watched them walk away, her heart heavy with emotion as she thought of all the years she had been away from them. *If I leave soon, I'll never ken them... not the way I ken Duncan, Keir, and Magnus.* She sighed and turned toward the large fireplace, warming her hands from the sudden chill that chased across her skin. Despite every other emotion Yvaine had encountered since discovering the cavern and the small pool of water within, this sense of feeling torn never quite seemed to leave her.

"Ah, there ye are!" her mother exclaimed with relief as she pulled to a halt in the doorway. "I was beginning to worry! Where have ye been?"

Yvaine smiled at the familiar sound of concern in her mother's voice, for it instantly reminded her of the woman who had raised her, the woman who, for all intents and purposes, *was* her mother. Again, there was that feeling of being pulled in two different directions. "Exploring," Yvaine replied truthfully, gesturing to the weapons adorning the walls of the chamber behind her. "Rory showed me around. This is a wonderful room." She gazed fondly at the crossed swords above the fireplace.

For a brief moment, her mother looked surprised before a tentative smile spread across her face. "Oh? How... interesting! I'm certain soon ye'll feel right back at home." She sighed. "As though ye'd never left."

Yvaine nodded, not knowing what else to do or say. If only she could leave, simply walk out the main gate. "I'd like to go for a walk outside the castle," she remarked, her heart sinking when her mother's expression showed concern. "To discover everything anew."

Her mother nodded, understanding lighting up her eyes, and she placed a hand upon Yvaine's shoulder. "Perhaps Logan can take ye for a ride some time."

"Can we not go together?"

"Alone?" Her mother looked aghast. Then she shook her head. "Nay, lass, it wouldna be safe." She wrapped an arm around Yvaine's shoulders and tugged her along. "Come. I've got something to show ye." Eagerness clung to her voice, and Yvaine wondered what awaited her next.

As they walked through the hallway, Yvaine could feel her mother's excitement building. "What is it?" she asked, curiosity piquing her interest.

Her mother smiled and said, "Ye shall see." They arrived in front of the door to Yvaine's chamber, and her mother opened it with a flourish.

Inside, several gowns had been laid neatly across her bed, and as Yvaine stepped over the threshold, her gaze swept over each one, the delicate fabrics of silk and velvet, intricate embroidery which had been delicately sewn onto each piece, all vibrant colors, all... unfit for Yvaine's favorite pastimes.

Contrite, Yvaine turned to her mother. "What are these for? They're not for me, are they?" she asked against hope. "I have no use for them, after all. A simple linen dress will—"

"Nonsense!" her mother exclaimed, waving away Yvaine's concern, mistakenly thinking her objection had been fueled by modesty. "Ye're the chief's daughter, and ye deserve to dress like a lady."

Never in her life had Yvaine wanted to be a lady. Quite frankly, for her taste, she had spent far too much time indoors these past few days since arriving at MacLeòir Castle. There were no stains upon her dress or rips along its hem. Her sleeves were intact, and her hair was not littered with leaves and petals, pine needles and clumps of dirt. Yvaine did not feel like herself at all; it was as though her journey had stripped her of her identity and forced a new one on her.

One she did not want.

"I'd rather not, Mother," Yvaine said softly. She stepped away from the gowns and moved toward the window, her gaze sweeping over the rolling hills and lush forests beyond. "I dunna want to dress like a lady. I wanta be free. I wanta spend my time outdoors. To go hunting and tracking. To explore the forest and the glens." She cast her mother an apologetic smile. "I'm sorry to disappoint ye, but 'tis who I am."

Her mother stared at her, aghast yet again. Clearly, the thought of a woman wishing for such a life was inconceivable to her. "The life ye lived between... then," she swallowed, "and now, what was it like?"

Yvaine smiled sadly as she remembered all her adventures in the wilds of MacKinnear Island. She had learned so much about nature, about herself, and about life in general, and the thought of living a life of finery and propriety was daunting. It felt wrong, like taking steps backward on a journey that ought to carry her to the horizon. Yet how was she to explain this to her birth mother?

"I canna quite say," Yvaine replied as honestly as she could. "'Twas a wonderful place that allowed me to discover who I am and what I'm capable of." She swallowed as tears collected in her mother's eyes. "'Tis a place I wish I could return to."

With her lips pressed into a tight line, her mother struggled to hold back the tears that gathered. Her jaw trembled, and she wrapped her arms around herself.

"I'm sorry," Yvaine whispered, feeling awful for doing this to her birth mother. After all, she, too, had been innocent in the events that had torn them apart. "I dunna mean to hurt ye, but... I was happy. There were people who cared about me, loved me, and... I loved them as well."

In that moment, Yvaine could not help but wonder who she would have been had she grown up here.

In this time.

With this family.

"I'm glad," came her mother's choked voice, a sad smile playing over her lips. "I'm glad ye were happy, that ye were not alone." A sob tore from her throat. "I missed ye so."

Yvaine wished she could reciprocate, but it would be a lie. Although she had always wished to know the family she had lost, she had never felt love for the parents she could not remember. Now, though, her heart ached for the family who had given her a home, a true home, with love and laughter, stories told around a warm fire and...

An image of Caelen MacCarmaig unexpectedly drifted into Yvaine's mind, of the MacCarmaig chief's son, the MacLeòir's sworn enemy. *Where are ye?* she wondered, remembering the few moments they had spent together on MacKinnear Island. *Are we truly the two who live in the legend of Clan MacKinnear? Are we truly destined to... fall in love?*

Yvaine did not know; yet the thought sent a tempting shiver down her spine.

Chapter Seventeen
LINE IN THE SAND

For four days, the castle remained silent and still. Then, though, a dull creaking sound drifted to the men's ears as the heavy stone blocks began to move. The large iron gates slowly opened, revealing two men—one with blazing hair and an imposing stature, the other tall but sinewy and still a lad. From a handful of hostile encounters over the years, Caelen knew the warrior to be Logan MacLeòir and assumed the lad to be Rory MacLeòir, sons to the chief of Clan MacLeòir.

Together, the brothers rode out from the keep, the elder with his long red hair pulled back into a queue while the younger's wild red curls bounced around his face. As they approached a nearby clearing, its edges lined with tall evergreen trees, Logan dismounted from his horse and drew an arrow from his quiver. His brother followed suit, readying himself for what appeared to Caelen as a lesson in archery.

Quietly, Caelen motioned for his companions to follow, and the three of them made their way cautiously closer to the clearing. As they got nearer, Caelen could hear Logan's voice, strong and confident, as he instructed Rory on how to use his bow properly. Caelen held his breath as he and his companions crept forward until they were just at the edge of the clearing. Peering through the tall grass growing at the foot of the evergreens, Caelen watched as Logan shot arrow after arrow into a target made of straw while Rory tried to imitate his brother's movements. It was clear that there was a bond between them; a bond that had been forged from years of love and loyalty.

Caelen felt an overwhelming sense of regret as he glanced at his cousin. Once, they had been as close as brothers; however, in recent years, something had changed. These days, everything Lachlan did and said appeared antagonistic, as though they were opponents and only one could come out the victor in this game. Where had his cousin's sense of family loyalty gone?

Cowering low to the ground, the three men watched Logan instruct Rory in the art of archery, his demeanor marked by patience despite the occasional scowl that came to his face when Rory's arrow missed its mark. "Take yer time," Logan murmured softly as Rory pulled back the arrow, one eye squinted at the target. "Feel the breeze and calm yer breathing."

Caelen felt his own breathing slow, his heart beating in unison with the soft rise and fall of the lad's shoulders. Then Rory released the arrow, his eyes closing briefly the moment he sent it flying. It soared through the air with a soft hum and struck the target near its outer edge.

"Aye!" Rory shouted, spinning around to find Logan.

"Well done!" Logan exclaimed, beaming at him as he delivered a congratulatory pat on the back. "But dunna forget that ye still have much to learn before ye can call yerself a true warrior."

Lachlan scoffed quietly and muttered, "He's foolish to give this scrawny runt any attention."

Caelen disagreed, for he saw something different; what he saw was a young man determined to make something of himself despite the odds stacked against him. "Quiet," he murmured back, wanting nothing more than to silence his cousin in that moment.

"We ought to have invited Yvaine," Rory said a moment later, his gaze sweeping over the finely carved bow in his hands.

Caelen's heart leapt at the mention of her name, and he stilled, straining to listen.

Logan chuckled. "Women dunna use weapons," he reminded his

younger brother. "They rather care for shiny trinkets to pin up their hair."

With his forehead in a frown, Rory shook his head. "Not Yvaine," he insisted, certainty in his voice. "She told me so herself."

Logan paused, regarding his brother curiously. "What did she tell ye?"

Rory looked down at his bow again. "I asked her if we could... do something together... sometime." A shy smile teased the corners of his lips, and Caelen realized that, at least, Rory already cared a great deal for his newly returned sister. "She said she likes to shoot with bow and arrow. 'Tis her favorite weapon." His smile stretched to encompass his entire face. "Like mine."

Logan's frown deepened. "She said that?"

"She told me so herself," Rory confirmed, his head bobbing up and down eagerly.

Beside Caelen, Lachlan snorted in disbelief. "The lad is mad. Women dunna shoot with bow and arrow," he declared firmly. "Or wield swords. Or—"

"Quiet!" Caelen hissed once more, surprised what little control Lachlan suddenly seemed to have over these outbursts.

Lachlan turned to glare at Caelen. "There's three of us and only one of them." Again, he cast a scornful look at Rory. "We should take them now."

Fergus frowned. "Ye canna be serious. We canna simply capture the heir to Clan MacLeòir."

"And why not?" Lachlan challenged. "It might even the odds, ensure that no contract will be renewed between them and Clan Morganach."

"Perhaps," Caelen admitted, appalled to find himself tempted by the thought of preventing a union between Yvaine and Malcolm Morganach. "But we didna come here to start a war."

Lachlan laughed at that. "'Tis unavoidable," he murmured, casting a careful glance at the two brothers in the clearing. "We must take them now while they are alone."

Caelen shook his head firmly. "Father instructed us to gain information, nothing more."

"Ye ken as well as I do that our fathers would approve," Lachlan challenged, a sneer upon his face as he looked at Caelen.

Aye, Caelen could not deny his cousin's reasoning. Still, there were lines he would not cross, and abducting a child was one of them.

"I willna start a war this day," Caelen insisted, averting his gaze so he would not see his cousin's hateful glare.

And so, the three of them watched as Logan and Rory continued their practice for another hour until finally the two brothers remounted their horses and cantered back toward the keep. The afternoon sun painted a pattern of shadows on the meadow, and a flock of small birds chirped in a nearby tree, fluttering from branch to branch.

Quietly, Caelen, Lachlan and Fergus followed the MacLeòir brothers as they made their way north to the keep, careful to keep out of sight. When the castle came into view, the three men slowed their pace, once again seeking cover in the undergrowth. From there, they watched the two brothers approach the main gate, their bows slung over their shoulders. Logan called something to the guard on duty, and a moment later, the heavy portcullis was raised, allowing Logan and Rory inside.

Caelen stilled, his heart beating fiercely in his chest, when he caught a glimpse of red hair. He squinted his eyes and held his breath as he saw Yvaine standing in the courtyard, slow steps carrying her toward her returning brothers. Words were exchanged, and even from a distance, Caelen thought to see both brothers smile at her.

"There," Lachlan growled beside him. "'Tis confirmed. The lass is with the MacLeòirs, and she doesna look like a prisoner to me." He raised his brows in question.

Fergus nodded. "Aye, 'tis truly her. If she were a liar, they wouldna allow her to roam the castle freely."

Caelen agreed, and yet relief to see their mission accomplished was not the most dominant emotion to sweep through his heart in that moment. Indeed, his mind focused on another aspect, one speaking to Yvaine's safety and well-being. And she was safe, was she not?

After all, she clearly had been accepted back into her clan as one of their own. Yet joy faded quickly as Caelen felt a growing sense of dread. What would happen now? Would his father's fears truly come to pass? Would this development set Gwyneth free and at the same time doom their clan? Would Yvaine soon be married to Malcolm Morganach?

Caelen knew he ought not care what became of Yvaine. She was not his concern after all. Still, he could not deny—even if only to himself—that he wished to see her again. She had intrigued him, and more than ever before, he wished their two clans were not locked in a deadly feud.

Now, though, it was time to return home and report what they had learned to his father. Caelen sighed heavily as they turned away from the keep and toward home. In the back of his mind, he knew that even if he wished otherwise, this was far from the end of this conflict. In fact, it seemed to grow worse with each passing day. If only he could think of a solution.

Chapter Eighteen
A COLD MAN

Ever since arriving at MacLeòir Castle, Yvaine had barely seen her father. While her mother and Rory openly showed their joy in having her back among them, Yvaine's father had barely said a word to her. Even Logan, as reserved as he was sometimes, had made it clear that he welcomed her presence. And now, she was being called to her father's study. Why? Yvaine could not shake the feeling that something was wrong, that her father wanted something from her... something she would not want to give.

Taking a deep breath, Yvaine knocked on the door.

A moment later, it eased open with a soft creak, and she saw Logan appear in its gap. He nodded to her to step inside, and as she did so, she saw a touch of unease flit across his face. Still, he said nothing; merely stood by the door with his strong arms crossed over his large chest, like a guard ensuring no one would enter... or leave.

In the light of the late afternoon sun, Yvaine saw her birth father seated at his desk, reading a scroll. He did not look up as she approached, and she wondered if he even knew she was here. His graying hair made him seem frail for a moment; yet his shoulders appeared broader than Yvaine remembered from the few times she had laid eyes on him.

After another moment of silence, her father finally looked up, and a hint of a smile touched his lips. Still, to Yvaine, it seemed weighted by something... something on his mind. "Yvaine, my daughter, come closer," he said in a kindly voice, gesturing for her to take a seat in front of him.

Eyeing her father, Yvaine crossed the room and sat down. She felt his gaze sweep over her and saw a slight frown tug on his brows as he beheld her simple linen dress. As much as her mother had tried to persuade her, Yvaine had stood her ground. It was something she knew how to do for her parents—her true parents!—had taught her not to bow her head, to stand tall and proud, and doing so made Yvaine feel closer to them despite the distance so suddenly forced between them.

"Are ye well, Child?" Her father asked, scratching his chin. "Yer mother assured me of yer health; yet I wanted to be certain of it."

Confused, Yvaine nodded, trying her best to ignore the chill that crawled down her back. Aye, her father wanted something. But what could it be? "I'm well. Thank ye for asking." She held his gaze, resting herself comfortably in her chair. "And ye? How are ye, Father?"

That seemed to surprise him, for he stilled, his brows drawing down again, and he looked at her with something akin to displeasure in his steely gaze. "I'm well," he finally said but volunteered no further information. Clearly, he was not interested in getting to know her. What did he want then? Why had he summoned her?

Placing his palms flat upon the surface of his desk, her father looked at her for a long moment. Then, rather abruptly, he asked, "What happened the day ye disappeared?"

Ah! There it is, Yvaine thought as a sudden cold gripped her heart. Indeed, her father's gaze narrowed with interest; perhaps she had flinched, and he had seen. Whatever the reason suspicion glinted in his eyes.

"I was only a wee bairn at the time," Yvaine said reasonably, reminding herself that, at least, in this matter she spoke the truth. "I dunna recall what happened." She willed a chuckle from her lips. "Or do ye recall what ye did when ye were a wee lad?" Indeed, it was hard to imagine.

A touch of anger curled her father's lips; clearly, he was not a man who knew how to laugh. "Ye might have been a wee lass then," he said calmly, his voice low and hard. "But ye are not now." His gaze seemed to drill into her as he leaned forward. "How did ye come to be on the Fey Isle? Where have ye been these past years? Surely, ye remember something." And with that, he once again settled himself in his chair, an expectant expression upon his face.

In that moment, as Yvaine saw herself faced with her birth father's cold demeanor, his only concern to unearth the truth that lay hidden in her memory, she thought of her true father, Aiden MacKinnear.

On occasion, his voice thundered with the power of a storm; yet he never feared to speak in gentle tones, showing respect and fairness above all. Yvaine pictured his smile, full of warmth and kindness with a touch of childish mischief, and it gave her the strength to meet her birth father's challenge head-on. After all, no matter who they thought she had once been, today she was Yvaine MacKinnear, daughter to the chieftain and chieftainess of Clan MacKinnear, fierce and bold and daring.

Lifting her chin, Yvaine held her father's gaze. "I remember a great many things," she said softly, aware how her father leaned closer, eager to hear. Even Logan seemed to be inching away from the door and toward her. "Yet they are mine, and I shall not share them with ye." She raised her brows in challenge.

As expected, her father's head turned a dark shade of red. "What insolence is this?" he roared, pushing to his feet, his hands braced upon the tabletop as he leaned forward, his cold gaze drilling into her. "Ye're my daughter, and ye will show me respect!"

Yvaine scoffed and rose to her feet as well, squaring her shoulders and standing at her full height—which was not much but the best she could do. "And ye are my father. Do ye not also owe me respect? Why would ye question me as ye would a prisoner? Or is that what I am to ye?"

Again, her father's face changed color. Only now, it turned pale, an aghast look upon his face as though she had just now risen from the ground in front of him. "What sort of woman are ye?" he demanded with a shake of his head. "I'm yer father and yer chief, and ye willna speak to me like that. Do ye hear?"

Yvaine inhaled a slow breath, a slight tremble seizing her limbs as she spoke the next words. “Then I shall leave,” she said without preamble. “Clearly, my presence here upsets ye; truthfully, it upsets me as well. I willna remain where I am not wanted, where I am treated with such disrespect.” She took a step backward. “I bid ye farewell, Father.” And with that, Yvaine spun around, her heart hammering in her chest as she marched toward the door and her brother. He still stood with his arms crossed, his eyes wide and his jaw set as he looked from his father to her.

“Halt!” her father cried from behind, and she heard him round the desk, angry steps carrying him closer. “Dunna dare take another step!”

Reluctantly, Yvaine turned to face her father, her pulse thundering in her veins as outrage filled her heart. “Ye canna tell me what to do,” she shot back, cherishing yet another moment of utter shock dancing across his features. Indeed, this would be amusing if Yvaine did not—deep down—fear the man’s anger… and what he might do!

“I can and I will,” her father snarled, approaching with menacing steps. “I am yer father, and ye will heed my command.”

Yvaine cursed silently when she realized that her father stood at least a head taller than she did. “Yer command?” she scoffed, then she shook her head. “Is this how ye speak to yer kin?” She glanced at her brother, whose expression urged her to be cautious. Yet Yvaine was beyond that now. “If ye are so displeased with me, then let me go. Why keep me here?” Indeed, she longed to know the answer to that question.

Her father glared at her. “Ye are my daughter,” he said in a chillingly calm voice. “Ye will do as I say. A week from today, ye will be presented at the feast held in yer honor so that all ken that the MacLeòirs always reclaim what was taken from them… no matter how long it might take.” His jaw was set in grim determination. “Ye will do as ye’re told.” He took another step closer and looked down at her with cold eyes. “Ye’ll be the dutiful daughter or… ye’ll regret it. I’ll make certain of that.”

Yvaine swallowed hard, every cell in her body urging her to fire back with equal fervor. Yet her mind cautioned her, reminding her that she was alone among strangers, that she had not a single ally standing at her side.

"Father," Logan spoke up, "kinder words might be more persuasive. As ye said, she is yer daughter, a MacLeòir." His blue eyes met hers for a split second, and Yvaine wondered if Logan would ever choose her side against their father. She rather doubted it; yet she appreciated his support.

One glance at her father told Yvaine that Logan's efforts were in vain. "Dunna forget yer place," he snarled, his face dark with fury. "Ensure she doesna leave the castle," he instructed his son, once more returning to his seat. "The feast in her honor will take place soon. 'Tis yer duty to ensure she attends. Am I understood?"

Sighing, Logan nodded. "Aye, Father." Then he stepped toward Yvaine and took her by the arm, his grip surprisingly gentle. "Come with me," he murmured under his breath, and Yvaine acquiesced.

Once the door to their father's study had closed behind them and they stood outside in the dimly lit hallway, Yvaine spun to face her brother. "What does he want with me?" Her eyes narrowed as she saw Logan cringe. "Ye ken, do ye not?"

For a moment, her brother said not a word, his expression thoughtful. Then he grasped her shoulders, his blue eyes meeting her green ones. "Listen, Yvaine, and listen well. I dunna ken how ye lived these past few years and if ye insist on keeping yer secrets, I'll not force ye to share them. However, ye're a fool if ye think defying our father, our chief, will aid ye in any way." He exhaled a deep breath. "Ye're more shrewd than that. I can see it in yer eyes. Dunna antagonize him, for he will make ye regret it."

At her wits' end, Yvaine closed her eyes, feeling overwhelmed by the ways of the world she had never anticipated. More than anything, she felt alone, and she had never felt alone. Always had there been people to help her, to support her, to fight for her. "What does he want with me?" she whispered before resting her forehead against her brother's wide chest. "Will ye not tell me?"

Logan's heart beat fiercely in his chest, its sound almost deafening to Yvaine's ears. "I canna. First and foremost, I serve my chief," he murmured into her hair, the words spoken like those of a vow, something repeated over and over until it pulsed in one's blood.

Yvaine chuckled and looked up into her brother's eyes. "I thought first and foremost we served our clan." At least, her father—her true father—had always said so. "Our people."

Logan raised a brow. "Is there a difference?"

"Aye," Yvaine confirmed then stepped back. "Ye truly willna tell me?"

Logan looked conflicted, and it endeared him to Yvaine. Still, the expression upon his face made it clear that he would always stand with their father.

"Then I'll find out on my own."

Chapter Nineteen

INNOCENT

Caelen and his companions arrived back at the castle late in the evening. The sun had long since set and the stars were beginning to twinkle in the night sky. Without wasting a moment, Caelen headed to his father's study, Lachlan and Fergus at his side. If only he had better news.

Entering his father's chamber, Caelen spotted him leaning over yet another map, every corner of the room filled with shelves and stacked books, with the occasional tapestry or painting adorning the walls. Various maps and charts were spread across the desk, and a large telescope sat in the corner. As always, Angus stood at his brother's side.

The MacCarmaig chief looked up as Caelen entered, and he could not hide the look of worry in his eyes. "Well?" he asked, glancing at his brother. "What news have ye brought? Have ye seen her?"

Caelen steeled himself for what was to come. Then he nodded solemnly. "Aye, Father," he said. "We saw her." Taking a deep breath, he recounted all that they had learned of Yvaine's whereabouts and her acceptance into Clan MacLeòir. He could see the worry in his father's eyes as the truth sank in, and he knew that this would only be the beginning of their troubles. His uncle, too, looked thoughtful; yet his gaze reminded Caelen of Lachlan's, his heart always riled toward thoughts of war.

A strangled groan rose from the chief's throat, and he ran a hand through his graying hair before curling it into a fist and bringing it down upon the table in front of him. "I feared as much," he snarled, starting to pace around the room in thought.

Caelen exchanged a worried look with Fergus while Lachlan seemed rather pleased despite the stoic expression upon his face. *Does he truly wish for war?* Caelen wondered, wishing he understood his cousin's motivation.

Abruptly, the chief stopped, turning toward Caelen with a stern look on his face. "Ye must understand," he growled, his lips trembling with agitation, "that this doesna bode well for our clan or for Gwyneth's future." He stepped closer to Caelen and looked him directly in the eye. "I ken ye dislike the thought of war, but ye must remember that yer duty first and foremost is to our clan," he said firmly, and Caelen frowned at the doubt he saw in his father's eyes. Could it be that he questioned Caelen's loyalty?

Inhaling deeply, Caelen nodded in agreement. "Aye, Father."

The chief searched his gaze for a long moment before nodding. "We must think of a way to protect ourselves, our people," he muttered gravely, crossing his arms over his chest, his lips pressing into a hard line.

Caelen felt a chill racing down his back even though he had known what was to come. "Aye, we do, Father. What do ye suggest?"

With his arms crossed, the chief paced the length of his study, his gaze alternately determined and marked by uncertainty. Then he pulled to a halt and looked at his brother, something almost helpless in his gaze. He inhaled a deep breath, as though in need of courage, and Caelen thought to see something unspoken pass between the brothers.

Then Angus stepped forward, his gaze fixed upon Caelen. "Ye must find a way to get close to the lass, to get her alone," he murmured quietly as though not wishing to be overheard. "Ye must find a way to kill her and, thus, end the new negotiations."

Caelen stood stunned.

Of course, he had expected something drastic, something desperate, but never this. In comparison, even his cousin's suggestion of abducting the MacLeòir brothers was more favorable.

"I agree," Lachlan chimed in, his shoulders squared, and his chin raised, not a hint of doubt in his demeanor. "'Tis time we act." He cast Caelen a meaningful glance.

His uncle's words seemed to echo in his ears as Caelen stared at him and his cousin in shock, feeling betrayed and angry. He gritted his teeth, struggling to keep his emotions in check. Aye, objectively speaking, it would be best for their clan if Yvaine disappeared again; yet he could not help but feel disgusted by the thought of killing an innocent person simply for political gain.

Only he could not betray his father, either. And although his uncle had spoken the words, they had been his father's. Caelen could see it in the chief's gaze.

"That is madness," Fergus threw in, briefly meeting Caelen's gaze with a desperate one of his own before stepping toward Lachlan. "Ye canna mean to murder the lass. She hasna done anything to ye."

Lachlan fixed Fergus with a hard stare. "She's a MacLeòir; why should she be of any concern to us?" His brows drew together, suspicion darkening his gaze. "Where does yer loyalty lie?"

Caelen had had enough, and he turned to face his cousin. "Dunna dare question our loyalty simply because we dunna hold with murder. Fergus is right; the lass is innocent." He exhaled slowly, looking from Lachlan to his father. "Is this who we are? Are we not honorable men, sworn to defend the weak? The innocent?"

"We're sworn to defend our clan," Lachlan scoffed, moving to stand beside his father. "Our chief is right; sometimes hard choices have to be made for the greater good."

Caelen shook his head, disbelief invading every cell in his body. "Ye canna mean that."

"I'm afraid we have no choice," his father replied, his chin still lifted in determination despite the touch of regret that rested in his old eyes. "If ye canna do it, then I will bestow the task upon yer cousin. Lachlan can—"

"No!" Caelen exclaimed, struggling to ignore an image of Lachlan's knife upon Yvaine's throat. "I'll do it! I am yer son, and 'tis my right."

Nodding to Fergus, Caelen strode from the room, his thoughts in an uproar, and his heart clenching painfully in his chest because for the first time in his life, Caelen found himself wondering who had caused Yvaine's disappearance as a wee lassie all those years ago? Who had gone after her... perhaps to nullify the contract between Clan MacLeòir and Clan Morganach?

"What will ye do now?" Fergus asked in a hush, his quick strides struggling to keep up with Caelen as he charged down the darkened corridor. "Ye dunna truly plan on killing the lass, do ye?"

Caelen drew to an abrupt halt and stared at his friend. "Nay." The word fell easily from his lips, for despite all the confusion that raged in his heart these days, that, at least, was simple. Nay, he would not hurt Yvaine. He would find another way. What that way was Caelen could not even begin to contemplate; yet he knew he could not take her life... nor could he allow his cousin to do so.

Chapter Twenty
ON THE HUNT

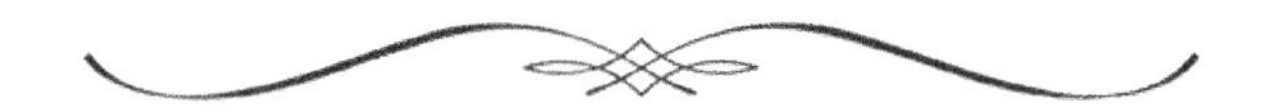

Yvaine sighed heavily, her frustration mounting as she found every path leading outside the castle barred. Doors and gates were locked, and her father had instructed the guards by the main gate not to allow her to pass. Unfortunately, they, too, proved loyal to their chief, for no amount of flattery or threats could sway them.

"I wish to go outside," Yvaine whined as she came upon her mother just outside the kitchen. "There's never been a day in my life when I didna go out." Aye, she was acting like a spoiled bairn, but she simply could not help herself. Her skin felt like it was crawling with spiders, and her limbs twitched from lack of movement.

Clearly distracted, her mother looked at her for a moment, then she hurried down the corridor, calling over her shoulder, "Then go out into the gardens. The flowers are in bloom." She smiled at Yvaine as she caught up to her. "'Tis beautiful there."

Yvaine rolled her eyes. "'Tis not the same. There are walls there as well. I want..." She exhaled a deep breath. "I hate... walls."

Her mother frowned at her then shook her head as though moving on to the next subject. "Have ye given any more thoughts to the gowns I showed ye? Ye'd look so beautiful in the green one. Will ye not consider wearing it to the feast? 'Twould make yer father so happy."

Yvaine doubted that very much, for her father did not strike her as a man who even knew the meaning of happiness. "Why is it so important to him that I wear a *gown*?" she asked her mother with a frown, wondering if a deeper meaning lay beneath her mother's insistence. Yvaine had never minded wearing dresses, so long as they were loose-fitting and the skirt was wide enough so as not to hinder her movements. These *gowns*, however, looked like ancient torture devices, tight and stiff and terribly uncomfortable. Yvaine could barely draw a deep breath into her lungs.

Brushing a hand over Yvaine's unruly mane, her mother smiled at her. "He simply wants people to admire ye, to see all ye are and all ye could be."

Yvaine's frown deepened. "All I could be?"

For a brief moment, Yvaine thought to see a flicker of concern in her mother's eyes; yet it was gone before she could be certain. "Aye, ye're a beautiful young lass, and yer father is proud to present ye to his people." She smiled at Yvaine. "Our people." Then she hurried off down the corridor, mumbling something under her breath that sounded like a list of things to do before the feast.

With a heavy sigh, Yvaine stepped out into the walled-in garden, cherishing the few rays of sunshine that touched her face as she walked from one corner to another, feeling like a trapped animal. With her mother far too preoccupied with the upcoming feast to pay Yvaine any heed, there was very little Yvaine could do to spend her days, not considering *appropriate* pastimes for a young lady such as embroidery, painting or music, of course. However, Yvaine had never been like other lasses her age; she had an adventurous spirit that could not be tamed—at least, according to her true parents. And thus far, no one had ever dared try. While her family—the MacKinnears!—had often shown concern at her more daring exploits, they had never forbidden her from choosing her own path. Indeed, to have someone tell her what she could and could not do was something utterly foreign to Yvaine...

... and she did not care for it.

With an almost desperate need, Yvaine yearned to explore the world outside these walls, to perhaps even find her way back to the coast.

Back home.

With a heavy heart, she strode from the garden. "No one's ever accomplished anything by sitting around and lamenting what was," she chided herself, her grandmother's voice echoing through her head, before quick steps carried her across the great hall and toward the large front doors. "Have ye seen Logan?" she asked one of the servants hurrying by.

"Out in the stables," the young man replied with a respectful nod.

"Perfect," Yvaine exclaimed and rushed past the man without another glance. As she crossed the courtyard, she briefly lifted her face to the sky, praying that her brother would not deny her. If he was riding out, why should he not take her along?

Entering the stables, Yvaine breathed in the familiar scent of hay and horses. Sunlight filtered through the cracks in the walls, hung with saddles and bridles, and bales of hay sat in the corner, dust wafting off them in a golden cloud that filled the air with an earthy smell.

Yvaine's gaze was greeted by a vast array of deep brown stalls, their occupants snorting and shuffling around. The air was alive with the horses' whinnies and nickers, and the crunching of hoof on straw, mingling with the occasional grunt and low muttered curses of stable hands tending to their work.

"Logan," Yvaine called out, her voice soft yet strong as she proceeded down the center aisle. "Are ye here?"

"Yvaine!" came Rory's voice in answer a moment before he poked his head out of a stall at the far back. "Do ye want to come riding with us?"

A large smile seized Yvaine's features, and she felt her heart sigh in relief. "Aye, I'd love that," she replied, hurrying over, before her gaze fell on Logan.

With a bit of a chiding look at his little brother, he stepped out into the aisle. "What brings ye here, Yvaine? I thought ye were occupied with mother's plans, trying on gowns and..." His voice broke off, and he shrugged.

Yvaine glared at him. "I hate trying on gowns. I've never done so in my life, and I dunna intend to start now." She looked down at the simple dress she was wearing. "This'll do just fine. Thank ye."

"Ye look beautiful," Rory agreed with a grin before he looked up at Logan. "Can she come?"

Indecision rested upon Logan's face; yet Yvaine thought to see his hard gaze softening as he looked at Rory.

"Please," Yvaine said quickly, hoping to appeal to his brotherly side. "I'm tired of being cooped up inside. Please, let me come. I want to see the surrounding area, perhaps... something will bring forth a memory of my childhood days." Indeed, every once in a while, something felt familiar: the way the sun glinted off the parapet walls, the soft swaying of the banners in the great hall, the flowery scent of her mother's hair.

Yet no tangible memory had emerged thus far; and considering the age Yvaine had vanished, she did not expect one to.

Logan eyed her carefully, clearly hesitant, as if weighing the consequences of her request. "Only if ye promise to do precisely as I say."

Yvaine clapped her hands together in joy. "Aye, I promise. Let's go." She surged toward the nearest stall, grateful for her brother's indulgence. "Which one's mine?"

Logan chuckled, and Yvaine thought the sound became her often stoic-looking brother. "Ye never do anything halfway, do ye?"

Yvaine shook her head and exchanged a grin with Rory, who seemed to be bouncing on the spot, his red curls swaying with the movement.

Soon, the trio was mounted on their horses, Logan in the lead. The horses' hooves clopped steadily against the dirt path as the wind rustled through the trees. The pleasant scent of flowers and herbal plants brought a smile to Yvaine's lips as she took in her new surroundings.

Seated atop the same mare she had ridden from the coast, Yvaine felt a sense of freedom as they made their way out into the forest. The warm sun upon her skin felt wonderful, and her heart sighed as her gaze swept over the vibrant greens of the forest, standing in stark contrast to the brilliant blue sky.

Together, they headed far into the forest, no words falling from their lips as they each savored the peace and solace that only nature could bring. The farther they rode, the more Yvaine could feel herself settling into her own skin once more, and she breathed deeply, cherishing the moment, wishing it did not have to end.

"Ready for some hunting?" Logan asked young Rory in a soft murmur, his gaze questioning.

Rory nodded eagerly, his hand reaching out to touch the bow secured upon his saddle. "Aye," he breathed then turned to look back at Yvaine. "We needa be very quiet so as not to spook the deer."

Hiding a grin, Yvaine nodded. "Thank ye for telling me. I'll do my best." Above Rory's head, she met Logan's gaze, a twinkle of amusement in his blue eyes. *Could we have been as close as I am with Duncan, Keir, and Magnus?* Yvaine wondered in that moment. *Had I never... left, who would we be to one another?*

Hanging back, Yvaine watched as Logan patiently reminded Rory how to track, what to look for, and how to interpret what he saw. The bond between the brothers touched Yvaine, and her heart ached. What would she not give to have Duncan, Keir, and Magnus here with her right now!

Shaking off her melancholy thoughts, Yvaine followed the brothers deeper into the forest until they reached the edge of a clearing and dismounted. As if on cue, a great stag silently moved out of the thicket on its other side, and Logan instantly froze in his tracks. He raised his hand silently for Rory and Yvaine to be still as well—they were in luck!

Yvaine's heart thundered in her chest with the familiar rush of the hunt, and she watched Rory's eyes widen in amazement at the sight of such a grand animal before them. Slowly and quietly, he reached for his bow with trembling hands. Logan quickly stepped in front of him though, raising his hand again—this time with two fingers held up instead of one—signifying caution.

As the two brothers crouched low, moving into a better position, Yvaine glimpsed Logan's bow and arrows still secured to his horse's saddle. Her fingers itched to reach for them, to feel the smooth wood against her skin. It felt as though ages had passed since her last hunt, and without conscious thought, Yvaine moved closer, her steps soundless in the high grass.

With Logan's attention focused on Rory, Yvaine withdrew an arrow from her brother's quiver and set it into his bow, holding both gently, the bowstring still slack.

With bated breath, Yvaine watched as Logan kneeled down beside Rory and began whispering instructions in his ear: how to nock an arrow correctly; how to pull it back evenly; where to aim; when to breathe; when to hold his breath... Every word was spoken in hushed tones so as not to alert the stag of their presence or disturb its natural surroundings.

Logan's voice echoed through Yvaine's head, though, bringing back memories of her own beginnings. Countless times her father had taken her out into the woods, always patient to explain, always full of praise for her efforts even if they brought failure instead of success.

Eventually Logan nodded in approval as Rory positioned himself perfectly alongside him with an arrow drawn back. One more deep breath, and then Rory released it.

Even before the arrow dug into the ground with an echoing thud in front of the stag, Yvaine knew it would not find its mark and her body moved without conscious thought.

In a blur of lightning-fast reflexes, she pulled her own arrow back and then let it loose. The bowstring snapped with a resounding *twang* and the arrow shot forward like a streak of fire, sinking deep into the stag's chest with a loud thud!

For the moment of a heartbeat, silence fell over the clearing as they all seemed to be holding their breaths. Then the stag dropped to the ground, and Logan whirled around to stare at Yvaine, his eyes wide, every instinct alert, as though he found himself rather unexpectedly confronted by an enemy.

Rory's scream of delight pierced the stillness of the forest. "Yvaine!" he cried, jumping up to run toward her. "Ye did it! Ye got him!" He threw his arms around her in a crushing hug, and Yvaine felt a wave of warmth wash over her. She smiled, grateful for the recognition.

Logan's gaze never left Yvaine's face as she basked in Rory's praise. His expression was unreadable, but there was something in his eyes that made her shiver—admiration? Respect? Suspicion? She could not be sure, but whatever it was, it made her feel strangely alive and powerful at the same time. She felt a deep sense of accomplishment course through her veins, for she had managed to bring down this magnificent creature with nothing more than skill and determination. Even if Logan still eyed her suspiciously, deep down inside, she knew that he respected her for her skill.

After loading the stag onto Logan's horse, Rory eagerly climbed back into the saddle. "Father will be surprised to hear that ye shot the stag," he prattled on cheerfully. "He'll never believe it. I think..." Oblivious to his brother's apprehensive gaze, Rory chattered on.

"Ye disapprove," Yvaine remarked as Logan stepped up to her, his gaze marked by displeasure. "Ye, too, believe women shouldna hunt."

For a moment, Logan said not a word. Then he moved closer, leaning down to her. "Ye are a most unusual lass," he murmured, his voice possessing an almost icy calm. "I suggest ye watch yerself. Unusual lasses have a hard time staying alive."

Yvaine's initial instinct was to laugh; yet the expression in her brother's eyes made the urge die in her chest. "What... do ye mean by that? Is that a threat?"

Logan swallowed. "Not from me." He turned to step away, but Yvaine reached out an arm and held him back.

"Are ye speaking of Father?" she demanded. "Aye, he clearly disapproves of me. I'm aware of that; how can I not be?" She cast a furtive glance at Rory, who still seemed deeply preoccupied with his run-on monologue. "If that is the case though, why does he insist I stay? If I'm nothing but a nuisance, why does he not let me go?"

Logan's lips pressed into a tight line, the expression in his gaze torn. "I am not at liberty to speak of matters of the clan," he murmured in a hushed voice. "Yet I warn ye that ye're not simply Yvaine. Ye're the only daughter of the chief of Clan MacLeòir." His brows rose meaningfully before he strode away, nodding to his brother to lead the way. Then he gathered up his horse's reins and followed suit.

With her heart thundering in her chest, Yvaine stared after them, momentarily too stunned to move. What could Logan mean by that? That she was not simply Yvaine?

"Yvaine!" Logan called over his shoulder. "Dunna make me come get ye." Again, a warning rested in his gaze as he looked back at her.

Swallowing hard, Yvaine pulled herself into the saddle, only now realizing that she had allowed an opportunity to slip away without even thinking of seizing it.

Chapter Twenty-One
AN IMPOSSIBLE FEAT

Leaving Lachlan behind, Caelen and Fergus returned to MacLeòir land. Rolling hills and deep valleys stretched out for miles, the orange sky burnishing everything in a soft, warm glow. The cool air provided a refreshing relief from the scorching heat of the day and seemed to whisper secrets into the night.

As they made their way up the hill, Caelen could see the looming presence of the keep in the distance. It towered above the land, its massive walls stretching out to the left and right, guard towers standing at regular intervals along the walls. In the center, the keep was topped with an even larger tower, built to protect the inhabitants from invaders. The keep was an imposing sight, a grand reminder of the strength and power of Clan MacLeòir.

Caelen and Fergus slowed their mounts and stopped at the lip of the hill, overlooking the keep below. Upon the walls, people moved around in a flurry of activity, some carrying torches, others carrying baskets or crates, most likely preparing for the night. Still, something struck Caelen as odd.

"We should stop here." He dismounted, allowing his gelding to graze after their long ride, and sat down upon the grassy slope. Fergus did the same, and soon, the two friends sat side by side. "What am I to do?" Caelen murmured, speaking not as a commander but as a man with doubts.

Fergus heaved a deep sigh. "I dunna ken. Yer orders are clear, and yet..."

"And yet," Caelen echoed, running his hands through his hair as he stared at the distant keep. "She's somewhere in there, not knowing that we..." He gritted his teeth hanging his head. "I canna take her life."

"I ken," Fergus murmured in comfort, placing a hand on Caelen's shoulder. "And I'm glad that ye canna. It doesna make ye a lesser man that the thought of taking an innocent life plagues ye."

Caelen scoffed. "Lachlan would disagree."

"Dunna compare yerself to him," Fergus counseled, sympathy in his voice. "The man lost his soul somewhere and doesna even have the sense to go looking for it."

Lifting his head, Caelen met his friend's gaze. "What then? What is the alternative to taking her life? For if I dunna, my father will find out eventually, and then he'll send Lachlan."

"And he'll not fail in the task," Fergus finished with a resigned sigh. "I suppose there'd be no sense in telling yer father that there simply wasna an opportunity?" A bit of a sheepish expression rested upon his features.

Caelen shook his head. "Nah."

"Then what do we do?"

Rubbing his temples, Caelen returned his gaze to the distant keep, the faint light in its windows flickering warmly as people settled down for the night. "The only way to protect her is to ensure there truly is no way to take her life," Caelen murmured then turned to look at his friend. "I'll warn her."

"What?" Fergus exclaimed, his eyes going wide. "Ye'll warn her? How?" He shook his head. "Even if ye could, who says she'll believe ye?"

"'Tis a risk I needa take," Caelen replied, suddenly not a doubt in his mind. In fact, the thought of meeting Yvaine again, of standing face-to-face, sent a rather inexplicable thrill through his body. "If she knows of the danger, her father can ensure she is kept safe, that not even an arrow of Lachlan's will have a chance of finding its target."

"And how do ye intend to warn her?" Fergus asked, a mocking tone to his voice. "I dunna see her walking the forest at night or riding in the meadow without anyone accompanying her." He grasped Caelen's arm. "See reason, my friend. After what happened, her father willna allow her to roam free. He'll keep a close eye on her." He shook his head firmly. "There's no way."

Caelen knew his friend's words to be sound; after all, it was reason that fueled his determination. Still, he could not give up now and simply allow events to run their course. He would never forgive himself if he did.

"There's no way," Fergus repeated, a hint of suspicion in his eyes before Caelen had even spoken.

"I'll sneak into the keep."

Fergus flinched. "Ye're mad! Ye canna truly— Nay! Ye canna!" He grasped Caelen by the shoulders. "They'll kill ye."

"Only if they find me," Caelen replied with a chuckle, surprised by his own calm. "If I can get in and out undec—"

"And how do ye hope to accomplish that?" Fergus interrupted, pointing a finger at the dark keep. "Do ye not see how heavily guarded the main gate is? Or do ye believe a fairy will swoop down and aid ye?"

Caelen rolled his eyes at his friend. "I dunna ken yet, but I shall find a way." And with that, he rose to his feet and busied himself setting up their camp.

As though the Fey had truly chosen to intervene on his behalf, an opportunity presented itself only two days later.

A cacophony of sound rang through the air, growing more and more intense as the sun rose higher in the sky. Caelen squinted into the distance, his eyes widening as he watched villagers pour in from all directions, and he summoned Fergus with a twitch of his head.

"Where do ye suppose they're headed?" his friend inquired, his gaze sweeping the countryside. "Are they only passing by or...?"

Caelen grinned at his friend. "They're headed to the keep," he replied eagerly, relieved that they had shed the colors of their clan before their departure from MacCarmaig land and dressed in simple woodsmen attire. "Come. We'll find out what brought them here."

Although Fergus clearly disliked Caelen's plan, he did not object, and so, leaving their horses behind, they headed down the hill toward the path and the small caravan of people snaking along it. Pretending to be traveling merchants, they snuck into the crowd headed for the keep.

As they moved along, Caelen greeted an old man to his right, his step slow, but a glint of determination in his gaze. "Pardon my ignorance, for we are not from these parts." He nodded down the long line of people. "But where is everyone headed?" Indeed, the hum of conversation around them grew louder with each step they took, and Caelen and Fergus could make out snippets of the excited chatter here and there.

"Did the Fey truly take her, Momma?" a little girl asked excitedly. "To bring her back now?"

"I told ye 'twas the MacCarmaigs who took her," a man growled, his gaze angry as he spoke to the one walking beside him. "But ye canna subdue a MacLeòir, ye see. The lass bided her time and escaped. I always knew she would."

Caelen tensed at these words, knowing that he and Fergus would be done for it their identities were discovered.

"The MacLeòir chieftain is holding a feast in his daughter's honor," the old man replied to Caelen's questions. "To celebrate her return."

Caelen thanked the man and returned to Fergus's side. His gaze swept the villagers, all gathering to celebrate with the MacLeòirs and show their support for their beloved laird's daughter, certain the lass's return was a good omen. Instantly, Caelen knew this could be his chance to warn Yvaine without being detected by her father or any of his warriors.

"We should leave," Fergus murmured, leaning closer, tension marking his features. "Ye canna truly mean to enter the keep." He grasped Caelen's arm, his gaze imploring.

Caelen exhaled a slow breath, casting a quick smile at an elderly woman frowning at them. "Quiet," he hissed under his breath, struggling to remain calm himself. "Or we'll be discovered."

"We will be discovered if we enter the keep," Fergus warned, his eyes darting ahead, following the caravan of people snaking closer to the main gate.

"Not among all these villagers," Caelen objected with hope in his heart. He grasped Fergus's arm and urged him forward. "Come, let's enter with the crowd."

Caelen's gaze swept over the looming walls and towering battlements as they approached, for they seemed to cast an ominous shadow over the day, and their sight sent a cold chill down Caelen's back. Still, there was no turning back now.

As they neared the main gate, Caelen struggled not to stare at the guards, who kept a watchful eye on the arriving villagers. He could not help but wonder if he and his best friend would make it out alive.

Yet at least on their way in, no one stopped them, their feet crossing into the courtyard without trouble. Caelen could hardly believe it. Fergus, too, looked filled with disbelief... and concern, of course.

The courtyard was crowded with people of all shapes and sizes. Villagers wearing rough wool cloaks stood alongside fierce-looking clansmen in their tartan kilts. Fergus shuffled nervously, scanning the crowd as Caelen's gaze raced across the melee. Apart from that one glimpse, he had not seen Yvaine since they had parted that day on the island, and the thought of seeing her again filled him with unexpected excitement.

As they made their way toward the great hall, Caelen began to make out the decorations that had been draped over the walls and ceiling. Vibrant colors of gold and silver adorned the walls, and elaborate tapestries depicting battles and feasts hung from the high beams. Large tables had been set in the middle of the hall, laden with food and drink.

Keeping their heads down and avoiding eye contact, they worked their way to the back of the chamber, hoping to avoid being noticed as they searched for Yvaine. "Even if we're to find her in this crowd, how can ye be certain she willna raise the alarm the moment she sees ye?" Fergus muttered under his breath, tension giving his voice a rough edge.

Caelen had to admit that that was, indeed, a possibility. "I'll have to get her alone... somehow."

Fergus frowned at him before his gaze swept the assembled crowd, a doubtful expression coming to his eyes.

Caelen shrugged; he did not have a plan. Yet he knew he had to try. He could not allow her to be killed without even attempting to save her life.

A voice, loud and booming, spoke up in that moment, and instantly, the hall fell silent.

Caelen and Fergus spun around to see the MacLeòir chief standing at the head of the hall, flanked by his wife as well as his two sons, Logan and Rory. Yvaine, though, was still nowhere to be seen.

The chief raised his hands and began to speak. "My people, I greet ye this day with love in my heart. For many years we have been a proud clan, but never have we been so blessed as we are now." He paused for a moment before continuing. "Today, I am pleased to announce that our beloved daughter Yvaine has returned to us after being taken by the Fey for protection! This is a sign of their favor and one day soon, we shall reclaim the sacred island as our own!"

The crowd erupted in cheers and applause while Caelen fought to remain calm. Fergus, too, appeared tense, for they both knew the next words the MacLeòir chief would speak.

"Our enemies sought to destroy us by robbing our clan of its future," the chief continued. "Many years ago, they attacked my wife and daughter, intending to use them in their wicked plans." Anger rumbled in his voice; yet the expression in his eyes was one of calm calculation, reminding Caelen never to underestimate Clan MacLeòir's chief. "Yet the Fey intervened!"

The villagers cheered loudly in response, the expression upon their faces one of awe and admiration.

"The Fey spirited my daughter away to keep her safe from our enemies, and they've sent her back now to ensure our clan's rightful path. This day marks a new beginning," he said, his voice booming, echoing off the walls. "A beginning where we will reclaim our rightful place in this world. We are determined to take back that which was taken from us from those who would seek to oppress us! We are determined to make it our own!"

Caelen shivered at the chief's words, for they all but confirmed what his father feared: that the MacLeòir chief would seek to renew marriage negotiations with Clan Morganach.

"'Tis my honor to welcome all of ye here today, for this feast marks our reunion with our lost daughter." He gestured around him grandly as if inviting them all into his home. "Let us eat together, and celebrate this joyous occasion! We may not yet have reclaimed that which is rightfully ours, but tonight let us raise our glasses high in recognition of what will come." With a sweeping movement of his arm, the MacLeòir chief turned toward an arched entranceway, and the crowd gasped as their eyes fell on the beautiful creature standing there.

Caelen's heart, too, stumbled in his chest, and he stared at her as though he had never seen a lass.

Dressed in an elegant gown of pale blue silk that shimmered in the candlelight from the chandeliers above, Yvaine gracefully moved into the great hall and toward her family, her flaming hair swept up into an intricate braid adorned with delicate flowers. She looked breathtaking, and murmurs echoed around the large chamber as the villagers gazed at her.

Yet Caelen's gaze narrowed as he watched her, suddenly becoming aware of the tightness in her jaw, the way she held her hands clenched, the simmering anger in her green eyes... as she glared at her father.

Aye, the lass was furious. Why? He could not say; still, perhaps it could be to Caelen's advantage. Perhaps she would not give him away once he made his presence known to her.

Chapter Twenty-Two
THE MACLEÒIR'S DAUGHTER

Yvaine gritted her teeth as she marched into the great hall, her spine ramrod straight. Every eye in the room seemed to turn to her, their gazes weighted with awe and whispers of judgment. She felt the heat of their stares as if they were a tangible thing, pressing on her skin, demanding an answer. Yvaine forced herself to keep her chin up even though her stomach churned with a mixture of fear and anger.

Never had she encountered a situation like this before. Never had she been so humiliated and threatened.

A few days ago, Yvaine had returned to the keep with her brothers after their outing in the woods. It had been a wonderful day, and she had been elated despite Logan's words of warning, *Unusual lasses have a hard time staying alive*. Aye, now, she knew she had been foolish not to take him more seriously. Yet Yvaine had never known disrespect in her life, and deep down, her heart did not believe that it could ever befall her.

Only then, her father had learned it had been her arrow that had brought down the stag and not Rory's, and he had been furious.

Bless his somewhat reserved heart, Logan had tried to intervene on her behalf, reminding their father that Yvaine had grown up far from her home and was not familiar with their customs.

Her father, however, had been unrelenting. "All the more reason for her to learn," he had snarled and then sent everyone from his study.

Everyone but her.

"Hear me, Daughter," he had snarled into her face, his blue eyes hard and unforgiving. "I willna say this again, so ye better listen carefully." Raising his chin, he had squared his shoulders, drawing himself up to his full height as he had looked down on her. "I am chief of this clan, and ye are to obey my word. 'Tis the way of the world, and if ye try to fight me on that, I will break ye."

Fear had snaked down Yvaine's spine as a deeply forlorn emotion had taken root in her heart. *Ye're alone*, a voice had whispered deep inside. *Alone among strangers. No one will come to yer aid, so ye must be careful. Bowing yer head to save yer life isna the same as surrendering. Bide yer time, do as ye must, and wait for an opportunity to slip away.*

And so, Yvaine had held her tongue, fighting the urge to let it loose with a flood of words that would no doubt see her locked away until the end of her days.

A glimmer of triumph had come to her father's cold eyes when she had remained quiet, her lips quivering with the need to lash out. "Ye do as I say without question, or I'll see to it that ye'll never set foot outside these walls again. Is that understood?"

"Aye, Father," Yvaine had gritted out through clenched teeth, reminding herself again and again that her father was in the stronger position, that any words she spoke would be met with scorn and derision... and retribution.

And so, Yvaine had bowed her head and returned to her chambers, spending the next few days quietly seething with anger, her mind racing to find a solution. *Patience*, the voice had whispered relentlessly, urging her to listen to her mother's instructions on etiquette, to put on the gown that had been chosen for her for the feast, and to make her way to the great hall and allow her father to present her to his people like a prize.

Now, here she stood among her newly discovered family, trembling with anger and yet fearful of her father's wrath. Unwilling to look at him, Yvaine swept her gaze over the assembled crowd, her heart loathing the sight of all the beaming faces around her, when one face suddenly made her breath catch in her throat.

Caelen?

Blinking, Yvaine shook her head, certain she had simply imagined him. After all, the MacCarmaigs and the MacLeòirs were locked in a deadly feud. There was no earthly reason for Caelen to be here. He would not be foolish enough to endanger his life like that. Yet, truth be told, she did not know him. Although she had listened to the legend of Yvaine and Caelen countless times, that did not mean she knew the man of flesh and blood.

The man alive today.

As her vision cleared, Caelen's face had vanished, the man she was looking at was just another with dark hair and blue eyes. A wistful smile tugged on Yvaine's lips. *Ye feel helpless for the first time in yer life. No wonder ye imagine a dashing hero to come to yer aid.*

Her father's booming voice echoed through the hall like drums of war. "Let the feast begin!"

Yvaine took her place at the table with her family but could not keep from stealing glances at the crowd as they began to eat and drink. People nodded in her direction, some of them even smiling, clearly happy that she was here and safe. She felt a swell of pride in her chest despite everything that had happened. If only she were a guest and not a prisoner.

The feast continued late into the night, with musicians playing lively tunes and people laughing and talking around her. All the while, Yvaine kept searching the crowd for Caelen's face, unable to help herself. Of course, he was not here; yet her heart knew no reason and continued to hope. Eventually, Yvaine rose from her seat, her senses spinning, and her mind in need of peace and quiet.

Yet before she could take a single step, her father's hand clasped her arm like an iron vice.

Yvaine gasped, her fingers reaching for her father's, seeking to pry them loose... but with no success.

"Where are ye going?" he demanded in a quiet hiss, a warning in his hard gaze as his eyes found hers.

"I only wish for... some fresh air," Yvaine replied breathlessly, hoping her anger did not spark in her eyes. "I feel faint, and I... I dunna wish to embarrass ye."

For a moment, her father held her gaze. Then he nodded. "Dunna stay away too long," he warned before releasing her.

Yvaine nodded and then walked through the crowd, her gaze fixed on a side door. Still, people called out to her and welcomed her back, their eyes shining with awe and admiration. She could feel their respect washing over her like a warm wave of acceptance, reminding her of home.

Of MacKinnear Island.

And her family.

Her true family.

With quick steps, Yvaine left the joyful crowd behind, drawn down a long corridor away from the great hall where music still filled the air along with laughter and conversation. The corridor felt like an escape from reality, and her mind instantly drifted back to the life she had lost, wishing she could return.

Eventually, Yvaine came upon a door at the end of the corridor, which opened up into the walled-in garden, now full of night blossoms. As soon as she stepped outside into the cool night air, she let out a sigh of relief. Yet her feet carried her onward, down a small cobblestone path in between dark shadows of bushes and trees. The breeze stirred her hair, and Yvaine wished she could simply pull out all the pins and ribbons. Yet her father would no doubt punish her for it. Perhaps it would be wise to gain his trust, to prove herself loyal and... obedient, and once he believed her his to command, she would steal away.

A little way down the path, Yvaine spotted an old stone bench tucked away in a secluded corner of the castle garden, and her steps quickened.

Grateful for finally finding a moment's peace and quiet away from prying eyes and ears, Yvaine plopped down onto the bench with a contented sigh. Here in this forgotten corner of the castle grounds surrounded by tall trees rustling in the night breeze and fireflies flitting through shadows cast by moonlight streaming through branches above, she finally felt at least a flicker of her true self again.

But just as she was about to settle in and relax, a sound drifted to her ears, and she froze, her body tensing up as her gaze darted around the garden. Was it only the wind rustling through the branches? Or something else?

Yvaine's heart raced as she rose to her feet, her eyes frantically scanning the shadows looming nearby. The silence was deafening, making her acutely aware of every rustle and scrape in the trees and bushes.

Yet nothing stirred. Nothing came toward her. No one intruded upon her solitude.

Just as Yvaine was about to lower her guard, strong arms seized her from behind, crushing the air out of her lungs. Fear squeezed her heart, and she parted her lips to scream... yet a calloused hand clamped over her mouth, suffocating her cries for help. She tried to kick and bite against her assailant, but it was no use.

"Hush, lass. I mean ye no harm."

Yvaine froze at the words, recognizing the voice immediately although she had only heard it once before. Yet in her mind's eye, she saw an image of Caelen with his unruly dark hair and piercing blue eyes. Had she truly seen him earlier today? Was he here? Now?

Even though Caelen was her clan's enemy, Yvaine felt her fear subside, her pounding heart easing into a gentler rhythm. And despite the hand still clamped over her mouth, she gave a short nod, indicating that she would not scream.

Slowly, the man released her and stepped back so Yvaine could turn around to face him.

Aye, it was Caelen, and Yvaine felt her heart quickening once again... yet not with fear.

Feeling unhinged, she stared into his eyes, overcome with something she could not name. His gaze shone fiercely in the moonlight, and the air between them crackled with tension and a dangerous energy hung thickly around them like an invisible shroud.

Yvaine stared at him wide-eyed, suddenly uncertain if she was awake. "Ye're here," she murmured, flinching at the hushed whisper of her own voice. "How can ye...?" To Yvaine's shame, tears stung her eyes, and she bit her lower lip.

Over the past few weeks, Yvaine had done her utmost to focus her thoughts, to be rational about her situation, to plan and strategize, to accept what she could not change and snatch up whatever small advantage might come her way. She had suppressed her emotions as well as she could, one in particular.

Fear.

Never had Yvaine known true fear, the sort of fear that paralyzed the heart, which made one feel utterly and completely alone with not even a sliver of hope left to carry one to the next day.

She knew it now, though.

Alone among strangers, Yvaine had walked through each and every day with fear's tight grip upon her heart. Aye, there had been a few good moments with her mother and brothers; yet they had always been overshadowed by that nagging fear of what the next moment might bring. After all, her father had made it unmistakably clear that he did not care for her happiness, for what she wanted.

"Are ye all right, lass?" Caelen murmured, jarring her from her thoughts. His dark eyes held kindness as they swept her face, his forehead furrowed in concern. "Yvaine?" He shifted upon his feet, his tall stature a looming shadow as he leaned closer, and then he reached out a hand as though longing to touch her face.

Yvaine tensed, suddenly overcome by the realization that Caelen—Caelen MacCarmaig!—was standing right here in front of her. Caelen MacCarmaig from the legends of old with eyes the color of a deep sky, and hair as dark as night. The sight of him sent her pulse racing. His powerful frame, toned and tall, exuded strength, and yet shrouded in darkness, a certain air of mystery surrounded him. Always had he been her hero—he and Yvaine both—and now...

Withdrawing his hand, Caelen cleared his throat. "I'm sorry," he murmured, misinterpreting her flinch. "I meant what I said. I mean ye no harm. Ye have my word." He sought her gaze, and the right corner of his mouth twitched with a hint of amusement. "Although I can understand if ye dunna believe me... given that our clans have been enemies these past—"

Without thought, Yvaine flung herself into his arms. It was an impulse she could not deny, and she clung to him, needing his comfort after feeling so afraid and alone for so long, wanting nothing more than to remain in his embrace forever.

Caelen tensed at first, clearly taken aback by the gesture, then he gently encircled her with his arms, strong and powerful, promising safety. "What's wrong, lass?" he asked softly against her hair. "Are ye in danger?"

Yvaine shook her head, pulling back enough to look at him. Her heart swelled with emotion as she lifted her chin to meet his gaze, and she could not help the small smile that tugged at the corners of her mouth. "I never thought I'd see ye again," she said quietly, tears now spilling down her cheeks. She dropped her gaze to his broad chest, feeling embarrassed and foolish for having acted on impulse like that.

Caelen exhaled slowly, and she felt his strong arms tighten on her ever so slightly before he nodded. "Aye," he murmured gruffly. "Our last meeting didna go well." His expression softened as he looked away from her, shame written all over his face. "Forgive me for threatening to abduct ye." He paused before looking back at her, a faint smile on his lips this time. Then he tentatively reached out and brushed a tear from her cheek with the pad of his thumb.

The touch was gentle, and yet it felt like a lightning-strike that hummed through Yvaine's limbs, stealing her breath and quickening her heart yet again. She swallowed, struggling with the urge to throw herself into his arms once more, and exhaled a deep breath. "Ye're forgiven," she whispered then, still wondering if this was a dream after all.

Caelen nodded, and his gaze held hers for a long moment, something unreadable hidden there. Then he exhaled a deep breath and stepped back. "I came to warn ye, lass. I—"

Realization slammed into Yvaine like a falling tree, and her eyes flew open wide as she jerked back, staring up into Caelen's face. "What are ye doing here?" she demanded, her voice quivering as she glanced around the dark garden, shadows looming everywhere, shadows that could easily conceal someone. "Have ye gone mad? If my father finds ye here, he'll have ye killed." Yvaine's stomach twisted and turned at the thought of Caelen coming to harm, and she pushed away from him. "Ye needa go! Now!"

Yet, he did not.

Instead, Caelen once more closed the distance between them, his hands grasping her arms as he pulled her closer, the expression upon his face intent, his eyes wide with... fear? Yet not for the reasons she had just named but rather... for her. "I canna. Not yet. Ye needa listen to me, lass, for yer life depends on it."

Shocked witless, Yvaine stared into Caelen's eyes, overcome by the need to sink into his arms and have him hold her. *Are we truly the star-crossed lovers of the old legends?*

It seemed impossible.

It felt real, though.

Chapter Twenty-Three

DEFIANCE

The feel of Yvaine in his arms briefly robbed Caelen of every last conscious thought, and for a moment, he lost himself in those wide green eyes of hers, glowing like stars in the moonlight. Her warm breath teased his skin, and as she licked her lips, his gaze strayed to her mouth and he felt his hands tighten upon her arms, drawing her closer.

"My life depends on it? Whatever do ye mean?"

Blinking, Caelen lifted his gaze and met her eyes, reminding himself why he had come tonight, why he had risked his life and sneaked into Clan MacLeòir's keep. "Aye, I'm afraid 'tis true." He swallowed hard. "Yer unexpected return has stirred the hornets' nest." He released his hold on her and stepped back, willing his thoughts to focus. Indeed, the closer he stood to her, the more unfocused his mind became. It was truly odd!

"Do ye speak of my father?" Yvaine inquired, fear slowly leaving her eyes, replaced by a burning fury. "Do ye ken what it is? He willna tell me; yet I ken that—"

"Nay," Caelen interrupted, casting a furtive glance past Yvaine's shoulder, praying that no one would come upon them. "The danger I speak of comes from my clan." He swallowed hard as her eyes narrowed in confusion. "My father ordered me… to take yer life."

Her eyes flew open wide, and she retreated a step. Her right hand flew to her waist, as though reaching for something, yet whatever she had sought was not there and she cursed under her breath. "Is that why ye're here?" she snapped, her eyes searching their darkened surroundings as she continued to back away.

"Nay, 'tis not," Caelen tried to reassure her. "I said I meant ye no harm. I swore it, and I would never break a word given." He held her gaze, his hands lifted in appeasement. His breath came fast, and his heart hammered almost painfully in his chest as he waited to see if she would run from him or stay and listen.

Yvaine eyed him cautiously, both her hands clenched into fists and lifted before her as though she meant to strike him. "Then why did ye come here tonight?" she demanded without lowering her guard. "Why come and… and warn me?"

Caelen sighed, relieved that she still stood before him. "I will never lay a hand on ye," he vowed, his voice low. "I hope that ye can believe that; yet if I fail, my father will send another." At the thought of his cousin, his jaw clenched.

"Why does he want me dead?" Yvaine's voice quivered as she spoke, yet her gaze remained hard. "What have I ever done to him? I dunna even ken him."

"Ye returned," Caelen said simply before he turned and walked a few paces down the cobblestone path toward a lone stone bench. "Allegiances were forged in yer absence," he glanced back at her, offering an apologetic shrug, "and yer return now threatens to upend our world."

Yvaine swallowed, and Caelen was relieved to see her lower her fists. "I ken that my father is planning something," she growled, and her gaze fell to her gown, its soft blue fabric shimmering in the moonlight. "He insisted I wear this tonight." She lifted her chin and met Caelen's eyes, her lips trembling with anger. "He made it clear that he had plans for me, for *his* daughter, yet he willna tell me what they are." She took a step toward him. "Do ye ken?"

Caelen nodded. "I believe so."

"Then tell me." A few quick steps carried her over, and Caelen was surprised when she grasped his arm and pulled him down onto the stone bench beside her. "I dunna understand any of what is happening, and everyone—including my mother and Logan—speak in riddles, offering no more than vague warnings." She shook her head in annoyance before her gaze fixed upon his. "Tell me."

Caelen swallowed. "As far as I ken, ye were betrothed to the heir of Clan Morganach upon birth."

At that revelation, Yvaine's gaze narrowed, and fury sparked in her eyes once more.

"Yet when ye vanished," Caelen continued, "everything changed. Yer father no longer had a daughter to marry to the Morganach's son, and so a new contract was agreed upon." Caelen exhaled a slow breath, his thoughts straying to Gwyneth. "Between the Morganach's son and my sister."

Yvaine's eyes closed as understanding dawned upon her face. "And now that I've returned..."

Caelen nodded. "Aye, my father believes that yer father is once again in negotiations with the new chief of Clan Morganach and that they'll return to the original agreement."

Staring into the night, Yvaine breathed in softly, her gaze distant. "He wishes to see me wed," she murmured before her voice grew hard, "without even telling me." Fury pushed her onto her feet, and she spun around, something fierce in her gaze as she looked at Caelen. "I willna wed anyone." She shook her head defiantly.

Caelen frowned, taken aback by the outrage in her eyes, by the courage in her words. Some of her flame-colored curls had come loose and seemed to tug upon her, lured by the night's breeze, as though wishing to carry her away. Unbidden, his thoughts strayed to the whispers he had heard all his life: that the Fey had carried Yvaine away in order to protect her. Was that true? Here, in this moment, Caelen could almost believe it.

"Yer father willna ask," he murmured softly as he rose from the bench and took a careful step toward her. "Surely, ye ken that yer father," he sighed and added, "as well as my own willna ask anyone's opinion. They will do what they deem right." He bowed his head. "I tried to reason with my father, believe ye me," he sought her gaze, "yet he didna listen. He made it unmistakably clear that I am to…" He swallowed, unable to say the words.

To his surprise, Yvaine's gaze softened. "And yet ye will not?" she asked, her feet now moving her in the other direction—toward him. "Ye came here to warn me. 'Tis what ye said, isna it?"

Caelen nodded, that odd sensation flowing through him once more, that sensation that made him wish to draw closer still. "Aye."

Yvaine shrugged. "How do ye expect I protect myself?" She shook her head, her lips curled into a snarl. "I am nothing but a puppet here. I dunna even have power over my own life, where I go, what I do, how I…" Again, her gaze drifted lower and swept over her gown. "How I dress." Her eyes met his, and Caelen felt a strange stirring in his chest, as though he were called upon to do more than simply utter a warning.

Caelen swallowed hard. "If yer father knows there is danger to ye, he will keep ye safe. It'll be in his own interest to ensure yer well-being."

Yvaine scoffed. "By locking me away, ye mean." Her lips thinned, and she shook her head in defiance. "Nah, I willna agree to that." A deep breath shuddered past her lips before a new sense of determination lit up her eyes. Then she surged toward him and grasped his hands. "Help me escape."

Caelen stared at her, certain he had misunderstood, and his hands grasped hers in return, feeling her warmth and the fierce pulse of her life. "Ye canna mean that," he gasped, staring down into her face, knowing without a doubt that she did.

Yvaine heaved a deep sigh. "I dunna belong here," she whispered, as tears filled her eyes. "I might have been born to this family but…" She pressed her lips together, struggling to banish the glistening shimmer in her eyes. "I will never call this place home. My home… is far from here, back on MacK—" She broke off, as though she had been about to say something she never meant to share with him. "Back on the island just off the coast." Her hands tightened upon his, and Caelen felt his head begin to spin. "Can ye help me? I needa get home."

Overwhelmed by this unexpected turn of events, Caelen stared at her.

"Please," Yvaine begged, the expression upon her face full of longing and heartbreakingly vulnerable. "Please help me."

Caelen closed his eyes, desperately trying to organize his thoughts. Indeed, his father would see it as a betrayal if he aided their enemy in any way. Yet he was already betraying his father, was he not? And if he assisted Yvaine in returning home, then she would no longer be a threat... and Gwyneth's betrothal would remain intact. Was there no way to protect Yvaine and Gwyneth as well?

"Someone's coming," came a low voice from the door through which they had entered the garden. "We needa leave."

Yvaine flinched and spun toward it, her hands slipping from Caelen's grasp. "Who is that?" Again, her right hand flew to her waist, and again, she cursed under her breath, which made Caelen wonder if she usually carried a dagger upon her belt. Yet what sort of woman would carry a weapon?

"He's a friend," Caelen rushed to assure Yvaine as he waved Fergus over. "He willna give us away. Ye can trust him."

As Fergus stepped out of the shadows, Yvaine eyed him curiously, the expression in her eyes suggesting that she was not quite certain what to believe. "Who is coming?" she asked then.

Fergus shrugged, looking over his shoulder. "I dunna ken who, but someone is." He shot Caelen a meaningful look. "We needa go."

Caelen nodded, his mind still spinning with what to do. "I'll help ye," he said in the next instant, surprising not only Yvaine but also himself. Yet when her face lit up, a smile of deepest relief gracing her features, Caelen felt all doubt melt away. Aye, a creature like her ought to be free. Perhaps the Fey would smile upon him if he aided one of their own. And strange as it was, Yvaine did seem as though she came from a different world.

"Ye will?" she breathed then flinched when the sound of thundering footsteps reached their ears. "Ye needa go!" She grasped his hand and pulled him deeper into the shadows of the garden.

Fergus followed. "This is not the way out," he protested with a growl, yet fear laced his voice.

"Stay here," Yvaine urged them. "I'll draw them away so ye can slip out."

She spun to hurry down the path, but Caelen grasped her arm, pulling her back. "Comply with yer father's wishes, prove yer loyalty, make him believe that ye've... come to yer senses and will obey his every word." At the glower in Yvaine's eyes, Caelen chuckled. "Find a way to leave the castle. I'll be nearby watching." He held her gaze, his heart pounding in his chest. "I'll find ye."

For a heartbeat, they both seemed to stop breathing, their eyes locked, until Fergus cleared his throat. "We needa go."

Caelen nodded and reluctantly released his hold on Yvaine. "I'll see ye soon," he murmured, and she nodded, her eyes wide and her teeth toying with her lower lip. "Be careful." Then he turned toward his friend, and together, they melted into the shadows of the garden while Yvaine hurried back toward the door.

Creaking hinges told them that it opened, and then voices drifted to their ears, dark and chiding. Every instinct told Caelen to rush to Yvaine's aid, and his limbs began to tremble as he forced them to remain still.

Yet no one approached, and after a while, silence once more fell over the garden, the only sound that of the breeze whistling through the tree branches as well as the hoot of an owl beyond the walls in the forest.

Beside him, Fergus breathed a sigh of relief, a bit of a chuckle falling from his lips as he clasped a hand on Caelen's shoulder. "I ken the lass was trouble." He grinned. "And ye're no better."

Smiling, Caelen hung his head, knowing his friend's words to be true. Aye, something had changed in the span of the last few moments; he could not deny that. Neither could he deny that something deep inside him was suddenly impatient, eager to see Yvaine again.

Chapter Twenty-Four

A NEW PLAN

"I canna shake the feeling that there's something on yer mind," Logan grumbled as they walked back the long corridor toward the great hall. The entire keep was afire with torchlight, a cheerful reminder of the warmth that filled the ancient stone walls this night, delighted voices and music echoing along its corridors. "Ye look..." He frowned at her, his gaze watchful... and suspicious.

Yvaine shrugged, casting her brother an unconcerned smile. "I dunna ken what ye speak of. I told ye I simply needed a wee bit of fresh air." She heaved a deep breath, willing a look of exhaustion upon her face despite the energy that hummed in her limbs since meeting Caelen—*Caelen!*—in the garden. "'Tis been a long night, and I felt a bit unsteady upon my feet." She paused and met Logan's quizzical gaze. "I doubt Father would have approved if I'd fainted in front of his guests. Or what should I have done?" Yvaine asked, remembering Caelen's urgings to act like a lady, to gain her father's trust. Of course, it would not be easy. Yvaine, though, had never turned away from a challenge.

Logan eyed her with a frown upon his face as though he was not quite certain whether to believe her. "Ye oughtna have gone alone," he finally said, though, his voice did not ring with reprimand and there was a touch of amusement in his eyes.

Yvaine nodded, doing her best to appear honestly appreciative of her brother's counsel. "I'll keep that in mind." They arrived at the great hall, and Yvaine paused in the doorway, her gaze instinctively seeking out her father. He was seated at the head of the table, looking more imposing than ever surrounded by his guests. Her heart beat a bit faster as she walked forward, Logan just behind her.

Yvaine bowed before her father and spoke in a voice that was calm yet steady. "Father," she addressed him, grateful for the noise echoing through the hall that kept her words between them, "I apologize for my earlier behavior. I didna wish to embarrass ye. Yet I ken now that I oughtna have left without an escort. Logan already counseled me on proper behavior."

Though a touch of disbelief remained in her father's gaze, he nodded in acceptance of her apology.

Yvaine sighed, offering him a weak smile. "I am tired from this long day and would like to retire to my chamber if ye will permit it."

Her father's face softened slightly as he looked upon her with a mixture of relief and pride. "Of course, my dear," he said kindly, the expression upon his face one of triumph; after all, he did not truly see her as a threat to his plans. Well, she would prove him wrong.

Eventually.

For now, she needed to bide her time, though.

Yvaine smiled gratefully before taking her leave of her father and Logan as well, relieved that everything had worked out so well. She felt lighter now that she had an ally, now that she had begun to gain her father's trust, now that a plan guided her next steps, now that there was hope.

As she returned to her chamber, Yvaine moved to the window and looked out, hoping that Caelen and his friend had managed to leave the keep without being seen. She wondered where he was sleeping that night, still overwhelmed by the fact that he had come to warn her.

Thoughts of him flooded her mind and she could not deny that seeing him again tonight had stirred something inside of her. And she wondered if it was truly their destiny to fall in love... and do all the things Yvaine and Caelen had done together in the legends her parents and Mrs. Murray had often told her before bed. Aye, Yvaine had grown up with these legends, never suspecting that she had once lived them.

Or would eventually...

Yvaine shook her head, her mind overwhelmed by these thoughts of the past and the future and the way they connected. Whether they were the Yvaine and Caelen from the old stories, whether they were meant to fall in love, Yvaine could not deny that Caelen—*this Caelen!*—meant something to her, that she felt something when he was near, when he looked at her and...

A deep breath left her lips as she reminded herself that it would be a long road ahead before she could earn back her father's trust, before she might find a way out of the keep...

... and see Caelen again.

Yvaine paused, a frown coming to her face. "Before I can go home," she murmured, surprised that she had momentarily forgotten about her reason for seeking to gain her father's approval.

With a sigh, Yvaine turned away from the window and slowly prepared for bed, the echo of the feast down in the great hall drifting to her ears. She could only hope that with patience she would find her way back home.

The next few weeks passed in relative peace, and yet they were the hardest Yvaine had ever known. Every day, she struggled to act like a lady, as her father expected, but still her thoughts stirred restlessly. She was far from the image of proper womanhood he desired, and she knew it would take time before he would learn to trust her. Her loose tongue often curled to retort with equal measure, and she had a hard time keeping that spark of defiance out of her gaze. She was not permitted to run but rather walk in an agonizingly slow pace. Weapons, of course, did not belong in a woman's hand, and so her beloved bow and arrows were replaced with needle and thread.

Yvaine wanted to scream as she spent her days, sitting with her mother and other esteemed women of the clan, chatting about feasts and gowns and embroidery. She felt her mind growing dull and restless, longing for something more than the life of a lady.

But knowing that she must obey if she wanted to gain her father's trust, Yvaine kept quiet, listening in silence as the women discussed their day-to-day lives. She dreamt of the open fields beyond the keep's walls, where she could run free with the wind in her hair, of galloping horses and archery practice and all manner of adventures...

And yet, here she was—stuck inside these walls—with nothing but daydreams to keep her company.

Still, despite this drudgery, there were moments in which Yvaine's spirit rose tentatively and she managed to find a wee bit of joy in the simple things that surrounded her: the laughter of children playing in the garden, a song sung by a young lass near the hearth in the great hall, or even an old tale told by a woman who reminded Yvaine of Mrs. Murray.

Slowly but surely, Yvaine began to understand what it truly meant to be a lady, not only in the way one behaved or dressed but also in terms of loyalty and responsibility. After a long while, she finally saw how her mother put her family first and led them with kindness and strength, never wavering from her duty despite all odds. Yvaine admired that greatly and knew that if she wanted to go home again someday, she had to learn to do the same.

Thoughts of Caelen still filled her mind during these days—days that seemed to pass oh-so-slowly—yet Yvaine kept them silent behind pursed lips as she continued on with life at the keep. She looked forward every day to nightfall when she would retire alone to her chamber and allow herself some peace amidst all this chaos; here was where memories of Caelen grew ever stronger as if he were only a whisper away from joining her once more. Was he still outside the keep somewhere, waiting for her? Or had he given up by now? After all, weeks had passed since he had sneaked into the keep during the feast. He would not wait endlessly, would he?

Thoughts of Caelen also conjured thoughts of home, of the family Yvaine had lost so abruptly. Despite her adventurous spirit, there had rarely been a day when they had not shared meals together. She remembered sitting with her mother and grandmother by the fire, sharing stories and laughing until their sides ached. She remembered riding out with Keir and Duncan, exploring the many villages scattered upon MacKinnear Island. She remembered spending days locked in the library with her father and Magnus, researching one thing or another in order to learn from the past, from the experience of others, to help their clan.

Tears often wet Yvaine's pillow in the dawn hours when her heart felt heavy and her spirit sank so low she almost lost hope of ever returning home, of ever finding herself embraced by her loving parents once more. Yet each day when the sun rose, so did Yvaine's determination to make it through this trial, to prove her worth and her strength and find a way back.

"Patience," Yvaine whispered to herself as she descended the stairs toward the great hall, another day of drudgery looming ahead of her. "Patience."

Chapter Twenty-Five
UNDER PRESSURE

The mist had just begun to settle, casting a pall of gray over the countryside. Caelen and Fergus watched in silence as the keep of the MacLeòir clan gradually came into view, the last rays of the sun setting behind it. They had been camping out here for the past few weeks, ever since the feast, and as the days had passed, the weight upon their shoulders had grown. Caelen did not doubt that his father awaited news eagerly, news of Yvaine's death, news Caelen could never bring. How long before his father grew impatient? How long before he would send someone? Lachlan, most likely.

Squinting his eyes, Caelen swept his gaze over the keep, wishing he could catch a glimpse of Yvaine's flaming red hair. Of course, they were too far away to make out any details, let alone recognize someone. Yet every day, the sight of the keep's imposing walls reminded Caelen of the circumstances that had brought him here.

"Aye," Fergus said after a few moments as they stood upon the small slope, their eyes directed into the distance. "It takes time."

Caelen nodded, knowing that Yvaine would not have it easy to prove herself the dutiful daughter, to gain her father's trust to such a degree that she might find a way to slip from the keep.

As though echoing his thoughts, Fergus remarked, "I dunna think the lass has ever bowed her head in her life." He chuckled, and Caelen could feel his friend's gaze shift to him. "I dunna even think she kens how."

Caelen could not help the grin that came to his face. "Aye, 'twill be a challenge for her."

"D'ye truly think she'll master it?" Fergus inquired with a frown, casting another doubtful glance at the keep in the distance. "We could be waiting here until we're old men."

Caelen nodded, the grin upon his face shifting into a deep smile as he remembered the fierce expression in Yvaine's eyes that night. "Aye, she'll manage. The lass has never backed away from a challenge."

"How would ye ken?" Fergus pressed, humor in his voice despite the way he rested his hands upon his sides. "Ye've met the lass a grand total of two times." His brows rose challengingly.

Caelen shrugged. "I canna say. 'Tis simply the way she..." He shrugged again, recalling that spark in her eyes when she had found herself alone in the garden with him. Indeed, she was fierce and brave and—if he was not at all mistaken—knew how to fight, how to defend herself. Had she not given Lachlan a bloody nose that first day upon the Fey Isle? The thought made Caelen smile yet again.

A chuckle, though, drew his attention back to his friend, and he glanced at Fergus, noting the mischievous glint in his eye. "What?" he asked warily.

"Ye ken what?" Fergus teased. "Ye've been smitten since the moment ye saw her."

Caelen shook his head in exasperation, but he could not help the small smile that tugged at the corners of his mouth. "Smitten? Hardly."

Fergus scoffed and waved his hand dismissively. "Oh, aye. I saw how ye looked at her during the feast... and in the garden."

"I was simply being... observant."

"Observant?" Fergus repeated, a smirk playing over his lips and doubt ringing in his voice. "Is that what we're calling it now?" He chuckled. "Nay, I think 'twas more than that."

Caelen frowned and shook his head. "She's a wild spirit, that one," he said, and a sudden longing to look upon her awakened in his chest, catching him off guard and making him grit his teeth as he struggled to regain control.

"Aye," Fergus agreed, admiration in his voice. "She's unlike any lass I've ever met before."

"I rather like that about her," Caelen admitted, looking back at the keep and not at his friend.

Fergus was quiet for a few moments and then cleared his throat. "Ye ken, if Yvaine were to disappear again, if she were to find her way back home—wherever that is!—Gwyneth would have to marry the Morganach chief."

Caelen glanced over at his friend, noting the serious expression on his face. "'Tis true."

Fergus nodded, but he said nothing more. Caelen looked at him for a moment, noting the worry in his eyes. "Do ye care for Gwyneth?" he asked bluntly, not surprised when his friend flinched at his question.

"Nay," Fergus replied quickly, his eyes widened in surprise, and he quickly shook his head. "Nay. I simply… wish to see her happy."

Caelen studied his friend for a long moment, doubt in his heart about the truthfulness of his friend's words. Still, for now, he decided not to press him. After all, to find oneself strangely taken with a lass was not something easily admitted to. "Aye," he said softly. "We both do."

They sat in silence for a few moments, both lost in their own thoughts. Caelen wished there were some way to protect both Yvaine and Gwyneth from marriage to the Morganach chief, yet that seemed impossible. With a sigh, he stood and stretched his back. "We should be getting back," he said.

Fergus nodded and stood, and they both began to make their way back to camp. As they walked, Caelen prayed that Yvaine was well and had not given up hope. Yet he rather doubted it, for the lass did not strike him as someone who ever gave up.

As the two men stepped back into their makeshift camp, they were surprised to find Lachlan standing tall and imposing there, his steel-hard gaze focused on the keep half-hidden by the trees surrounding them. Caelen felt a chill come over him, certain that he already knew why his cousin had been sent here in the first place. He stepped forward and cleared his throat, causing Lachlan to turn and look at them.

"What brings ye here?" Caelen asked cautiously, dreading the answer he would get.

Lachlan shrugged, his gaze meeting Caelen's. "Ye two have been gone a long time," he said gruffly, and yet there was a touch of satisfaction in his gaze. "Yer father expected to hear from ye long before now." His eyes moved to Fergus and then once more glanced at the keep in the distance. "What news of yer mission?"

Caelen frowned at his cousin, taken aback by how much Lachlan seemed to enjoy this moment, seeing it as a moment of failure for Caelen and a moment of triumph for himself. "What message does my father send?"

Lachlan sighed, then he stepped closer, his gaze still unwavering. "He wishes to ken what's keeping ye. How hard can it be to kill a lass?" His right brow drew upward into a daring arch, his voice hard and unforgiving as he spoke, and Caelen felt a chill run down his spine at the implication of his words.

Fergus stepped forward then, a determined expression on his face as he spoke, "There simply hasna been an opportunity yet. We've tried our best to get to her, but she hasna left the keep since we arrived." He looked back at Caelen then shrugged. "What do ye expect us to do? Storm the keep?" He grinned. "Would ye?"

Lachlan's gaze shifted from Caelen to Fergus before settling back onto Caelen again. He studied him for a few moments before finally speaking. "I find that hard to believe," he said slowly with a slight shake of his head as if doubting their words entirely. "It has been too long," he muttered under his breath before turning away from them and looking back toward the keep once more. "Well then," he said finally after a few moments of silence, "I suppose it now falls to me to save our clan."

Caelen swallowed hard, then he stepped toward his cousin, his jaw clenched and his gaze hard. "Did my father give ye permission to do that?" he challenged, uncertain what he would do if it were, indeed, so. "Or are ye simply to report back?"

Lachlan's gaze narrowed, and a muscle in his jaw twitched furiously as he glared at Caelen. "He will soon enough," he hissed, his lips twisted into a snarl. "Ye're too weak, Cousin," he murmured, leaning closer. "The lass bewitched ye; I knew it the moment I saw ye looking at her."

Caelen grinned at his cousin, determined to hide his unease with the situation, certain Lachlan would use it against him. "Believe what ye will, Cousin, but I have done what I can to protect our clan," he said slowly, his gaze still locked on Lachlan's. "Go home and tell him what ye will. I'll deal with Yvaine before ye return."

Lachlan's gaze briefly shifted to Fergus before settling back onto Caelen, and his expression hardened as a warning came to his eyes. "If that be yer wish," he said slowly, his voice laced with thinly veiled anger as he spoke, "I shall do so… but mark my words, if I find out that ye've failed in yer task, I shall come back here and make certain 'tis done." With that, he turned on his heel and walked away, soon swallowed up by the darkening forest.

Both men watched him go until he was out of sight. Then Fergus turned to Caelen, an anxious expression upon his face. "What do we do now?"

Caelen sighed heavily then shook his head in frustration. "We have to find a way to get Yvaine out of there soon or our hands will be tied." He looked at Fergus, hoping for some kind of assurance that they could truly accomplish this feat.

Fergus nodded slowly in agreement; though, he did not look convinced. "Any ideas how we are to do that?"

Caelen shook his head then raked a hand through his hair in frustration. "We needa hope that she'll make it out on her own soon. We only managed to find a way inside because of the feast, because of all those people arriving and the gates being wide open. Now, though," he gestured toward the keep, hidden behind the trees, "there will be no chance."

Fergus nodded in resignation.

Staring into the darkening forest, Caelen felt certain Lachlan would find a way into the castle if they failed. His cousin could be ruthless at times and crossed lines that Caelen would never even consider crossing. He sighed heavily then glanced around the area one last time before turning to Fergus with a determined expression on his face. "Perhaps we oughta try... tomorrow."

Fergus stared at him, frowning. "Try what? Sneak into the keep?" He shook his head. "Ye canna be serious, Caelen. We canna—"

Caelen swung around. "What else can we do? If we do nothing, Lachlan will—" He broke off, his teeth gritted against this awful feeling that all hope was already lost.

Chapter Twenty-Six

BROTHER & SISTER

Whenever free of her parents' watchful eyes, Yvaine followed Rory around the castle, for it seemed that her little brother knew more than anyone else about the MacLeòirs' history. In many ways, his inquisitive mind reminded her of Magnus back home with his nose stuck in a book day in and out, and the thought made her smile. Also, she found his company comforting, for only Rory understood her desire to explore MacLeòir castle. In everyone else's eyes, she was to be a proper lady, and it would not do for her to be caught wandering the halls and cloisters of the castle unescorted.

And so, Rory escorted her.

Together, the two of them roamed the halls, marveling at its ancient walls and feeling the weight of its tumultuous past. Rory knew every secret passageway and staircase, and he was eager to show her the inner workings of the castle. As they walked, Rory regaled her with stories of the MacLeòirs' past battles and heroic deeds done by their ancestors many generations ago.

"Ye ken, Yvaine," he said, his face full of excitement. "In one of the castle sieges, a MacLeòir warrior escaped the keep through a secret tunnel to get help from our allies. He was brave enough to make the journey and the help he brought back turned the tide of battle." His eyes glowed with wonder as his fingers trailed almost affectionately over the rough stone walls.

Yvaine, too, was captivated by the story, yet for quite different reasons. "A secret tunnel, ye say? Do ye believe it still exists?" she asked her brother as they strolled down a deserted corridor near the old dungeons. Her heart beat wildly in her chest, for the thought of running through said tunnel and finding herself emerge on its other side—free!—made her limbs tremble. If only she could find it and use it to escape as the MacLeòir warrior had done so long ago.

Rory looked up at her, his little forehead furrowing as he seemed to stare at something far away. "I suppose 'tis possible," he murmured, his mind clearly darting back and forth between various passages he had read about the siege.

"Do ye ken where it is?" Yvaine asked breathlessly. "Or at least suspect?"

Rory's eyes found hers, and she saw excitement brighten them even in the dim corridor. "I canna be certain," he murmured almost reverently, "but perhaps we can try to discover it."

Such eagerness stood on his face that Yvaine hugged him impulsively, delighted with the honest joy and compassion he showed her every day. "That is a wonderful idea," she exclaimed before lowering her voice, reminding herself that no one else must know. "Where do ye suppose we should start to look?"

Rory put a thoughtful finger to his chin. "Somewhere down below, of course. I was thinking that—" He broke off and when his gaze met hers, Yvaine saw something other than excitement there. "Why do ye wish to know?"

Yvaine swallowed, unable and unwilling to lie to Rory. "Ye ken that Father wishes for me to be a lady," she began tentatively, trying her best to explain, to make him understand. She looked down at her fancy skirts, lifting the fabric slightly and then meeting Rory's eyes with a huff of exhaustion. "I canna be a lady, not every moment of every day. Ye understand, do ye not?"

Rory nodded, the touch of suspicion that had come to his eyes before slowly waning, replaced by compassion and understanding. "Father and Logan always want me to train outside with the other boys. They want for me to become a warrior." He shrugged sheepishly, his gaze dropping to the tips of his shoes. "I like shooting with bow and arrow just fine," he peeked up at her, "but I dunna wish to wield a sword. 'Tis heavy and its blade is sharp, and I'm afraid..." He closed his eyes and shook his head.

"I understand," Yvaine whispered softly, placing a hand upon his shoulder. When he looked up at her, hope shining in his eyes, she smiled at him. "We can live part of our lives for our family, but we can never completely deny who we are, can we?"

Rory sighed, and the corners of his mouth strained upward.

"I wish to be outside again," Yvaine confided in her little brother, for the first time in weeks speaking the words out loud.

As much as she had been focused on gaining her father's trust, on being allowed to go where she pleased, nothing had truly brought her closer to leaving these walls. Guards were posted everywhere, and Yvaine had no doubt that they would stop her or at the very least inform her father the instant she walked through the gate. How was she supposed to leave these walls behind and meet Caelen? If, indeed, he was still waiting for her? After all, weeks had passed since the night of the feast. "I wish to feel the wind in my hair and run through the tall grass. I wish to hear the trilling of birds and chirping of crickets." She smiled at Rory and saw that he understood. "Yet I fear 'tis something Father doesna understand."

Rory nodded, his slender shoulders slumped. "He doesna like it when I spend too much time in the library. He doesna like it when I dunna show up for training. He often yells at me, saying I will never be a man if I dunna learn how to fight."

Yvaine grasped her little brother's hand, tugging him closer and meeting his gaze. "Father is wrong," she said determinedly, needing Rory to hear her. "Where I grew up, people were not told what to do or who to be. Everyone needs to find that out for themselves. Everyone deserves the freedom to choose and not to be judged for their choices by others."

Rory stared at her wide-eyed. "Where ye with the Fey?" he whispered awestruck. "Is it a magical place? What was it like there?"

Yvaine stilled, having forgotten the rumors that circulated around her. Indeed, after that first day when her father had pushed her for answers, no one had ever quite addressed her again. Sometimes, Yvaine had heard people whispering, casting curious glances in her direction. Sometimes, her mother would look at her in a way as though she wished to ask; yet she never had. And so, as long as Yvaine complied with her father's wishes, he did not seem overly interested in discovering her past. He seemed far more concerned with the future. Was he truly arranging a match for her with the chief of Clan Morganach?

Yvaine pushed these thoughts aside, for they served no purpose. If necessary, she could consider them later.

Squeezing Rory's hand, Yvaine sighed. "I canna quite tell ye where I was for 'tis a secret," she told him, glancing over her shoulder as though making certain that no one was overhearing what passed between them.

Rory's eyes shimmered with wonder. "Did the Fey make ye promise?"

Yvaine nodded. "Aye, they did, for the truth is something people willna understand." That, at least, was not a lie. "All I can tell ye is that the place... where I was," she sighed wistfully, unable to help herself, "was wonderful. I was loved and respected, free to be who I was." Indeed, not until now did Yvaine realize how wonderful her life had been, for although her parents had been constantly worried, advising her, urging her to be more careful, they had never once forbidden her from making her own choices.

That had been priceless.

"I'll try to help ye find the tunnel," Rory whispered conspiratorially, a spark of adventure lighting up his eyes. "However, I think we must do so in secret, for if Father finds out, he shall forbid us."

Yvaine nodded, hope pulsing in her veins. "I think that is wise," she replied approvingly. "Where do ye suppose we should start?"

"The lower corridors," Rory replied with a soft, thoughtful expression upon his young face, "near the dungeons. I've often thought that there are walls that... dunna make much sense." He blinked, shaking his head as though the memory was unclear.

Yvaine smiled at him encouragingly. "Well, then let's go. Lead the way."

Together, they hastened down the corridor; yet before they had taken more than a few steps, a loud voice echoed to their ears, followed by thundering footsteps. "Yvaine," Logan called, his large strides carrying him closer. "Mother is searching for ye. She says ye are to meet her in her quarters."

Yvaine barely managed to hold back the sigh of disappointment that wanted to slip from her lips. "Can it not wait?" she asked in an even voice, trying her best to hide the excitement that bubbled in her veins. "We went over proper etiquette only this morning."

Logan shrugged, his gaze slightly narrowed as he looked from her to Rory, as though, somehow, he knew that they were hiding something from him. "I dunna ken. All she said was that ye are to come to her now." Then he turned to look at Rory, and for a moment, Yvaine thought to see something almost apologetic in her brother's gaze. "And Father insists I give ye a swordfight lesson. Meet me in the courtyard after ye've retrieved yer equipment." He nodded to Rory before turning on his heel and walking back the way he had come.

For a few heartbeats, brother and sister remained standing in the hallway, the only sound those soft groans of disappointment that would not be denied. "Logan often has awful timing," Yvaine snapped, gritting her teeth against the anger that swept through her at being prevented from searching out the tunnel this very instant. She looked down at Rory, seeing his face equally crestfallen. "Has he always been like this?"

Rory nodded; yet the hint of a smile teased his lips. "But he understands," he murmured then. "Or he tries to. He isna as harsh as Father and often lets me go early." Rory grinned up at her. "Shall we meet here again after supper?"

Yvaine nodded eagerly.

Then they both parted ways, determined to hold on to the prospect of an adventure, of something that they both truly longed to do instead of this daily repetition of forced training. Indeed, Yvaine barely paid attention to her mother's urgings that afternoon, for her thoughts always strayed back to the possibility of such a tunnel. Did it still exist? Or had its walls perhaps crumbled centuries ago? Indeed, that thought was damning; yet Yvaine knew she could not give up.

Oddly enough, though, holding onto this secret made it easier for Yvaine to try and do her best to win her parents' favor. She dressed herself in her finest gowns and conducted herself with the utmost decorum, smiling meekly and bowing her head when her father spoke, always ready to accept his guidance and respect his wishes. Why that was, Yvaine could not say; however, she felt her heart beat with more strength these days, with more determination, eagerly awaiting every free moment that granted her the chance to meet Rory and continue on their hunt.

And so, longing to explore the castle and seek out the hidden tunnel, Yvaine bided her time until her parents were busy, and then she and Rory began their search. They explored the castle's nooks and crannies, giving each room a thorough examination; yet luck did not seem to be on their side. Not even the old dungeons with the walls that seemed to make no sense revealed anything to them—no secret passages, no hidden doors, nothing that could lead them to the tunnel they were seeking.

Day after day, they searched the castle, and although their spirits soon sank, Yvaine refused to give up. After all, this was her only hope. If they did not find the tunnel, she doubted she would ever discover another way out of this castle. And then what? A forced marriage to a man she had never even met?

At the thought of being married to the Morganach clan chief, an image of Caelen instantly took shape in Yvaine's mind, and her heart twisted at the thought of never seeing him again. It was truly odd, for she hardly knew him. More than anything, she knew the legends told about him. But the man? They had only ever spoken upon two occasions, and yet Yvaine could not forget the future that was to be theirs if they were truly the people she had grown up hearing about.

Still, her thoughts ran in circles, her emotions unclear and utterly confused, so that she preferred to occupy herself with something more tangible, focusing her mind on searching the castle instead of her heart. And so, it happened when Yvaine and Rory no longer quite expected to find anything.

Once again, they stood down below in the dungeons, at the end of the corridor that seemed to lead nowhere. Yvaine had already spent hours sweeping her hands over every rock, every crevice, every little something that ultimately proved to be nothing.

Until her eyes spied something in the half-dark.

It was barely noticeable, hidden as it was in the darkest corner of the corridor, yet there it was—a tiny crack in the wall that seemed to be beckoning them closer. She saw Rory's eyes widen when he realized what they were looking at. "Do ye think this could be it?" her little brother asked, his voice barely audible for he spoke with his hands clamped over his mouth.

Yvaine simply stared at the crack, suddenly overcome with emotion. She embraced Rory in a tight hug, her limbs trembling with excitement. "We found it," she whispered, hope sending her heart into a gallop. *This has to be it! Please!*

Rory nodded eagerly, and then he quickly began examining the crack more closely. He ran his hands along it and tapped on it lightly here and there until he found what seemed to be a loose stone—when he pushed on it gently, the entire wall moved!

Like a door, it swung inward, and the two of them stared in awe as it revealed an ancient-looking tunnel beyond.

"How can it move like that?" Rory gasped as he inched forward, his hands running over the smooth stones of the door. "How is this possible?"

Yvaine shrugged and followed her little brother into the dark tunnel. "We'll need torches to light our way," she remarked, gazing into the blackness that met her eyes. "I hope it didna cave in anywhere."

"Aha!" Rory exclaimed with a hint of triumph. "Do ye see this?" He waved Yvaine over as he stood at the edge of the door. "'Tis not simply a stone wall. A stone wall couldna have moved like that. See here?" He stepped aside to allow Yvaine a better view. "There's a wooden structure back here, and the stones are set on top of it. Look! There are the hinges."

Still overwhelmed, Yvaine swept her gaze over this ingenious construction, for the hinges could not be seen from the inside of the dungeon. Once pushed back into place, the stones would seem like a wall… as they had for many centuries. Indeed, Yvaine and her brother had been fortunate to find it, and she wondered if no one before had ever felt the urge to do so. Or had they? In truth, she could not know if not countless ancestors before her had stumbled upon this wall, had used it for some reason or another, and had kept the secret, none-theless.

Reaching for the torch they had brought down with them, the torch they had set upon the holding in the wall, Yvaine stepped forward and looked over her shoulder at her brother. "Shall we?" A wide smile spread across her face.

Rory stepped toward her, eagerness in his eyes. Then, however, he paused, his body stilling as he listened. "I believe 'tis almost supper time," he said then, casting a wistful look down the dark tunnel. "Per-haps we should wait until tomorrow. Father will no doubt send someone searching for us soon."

Yvaine heaved a deep breath, knowing that her brother was right. If she truly meant to get away, she needed to leave the very moment when people did not expect her elsewhere, when her father would not be looking for her. Otherwise, her escape might end quickly, returning her to the castle and possibly robbing her of this only means of escape.

"Tomorrow then," Yvaine murmured, stepping back out into the corridor before she watched Rory pull the wall back into place, as though the tunnel did not exist. "Tomorrow."

Chapter Twenty-Seven

THE TUNNEL

All day, Caelen and Fergus walked the grounds surrounding MacLeòir Castle, inspecting every gate and tower from a distance—or as close as they dared, searching for a way in that was not so well guarded. Yet, they found none, and their hearts sank. "'Tis hopeless," Fergus muttered as they retraced their steps, heading back in the direction of their camp.

Caelen exhaled a deep sigh, discouraged to see his hopes dashed. Only the feast had provided a chance inside these walls, and without it, every gate stood heavily guarded.

Yet as they rounded a small copse of trees, Caelen tripped over something in the ground. He stopped, squinting in the darkening light. "What is that?"

"Probably a tree root."

Caelen kneeled down and touched his fingers to something that lay in shadow. "It feels smooth," he remarked, brushing away dirt and pine needles. "'Tis... 'tis a rock."

Fergus scoffed. "Dunna act as though ye've never seen a rock before. Come. Let us get going."

"Nay, ye dunna understand," Caelen replied as his pulse sped up.

Inching closer, he brushed aside ferns and tall grass. "It feels like a brick, its edges worked by tools."

Tearing into the overshadowed thicket of brambles and ivy, Caelen gasped when he spotted a small stone structure, hidden away under layers of green, as though the forest did its utmost to keep its existence a secret.

"What do ye think it is?" Fergus asked, scratching his chin. "It doesna look tall enough to have been a dwelling. Look, how low the roof is."

Caelen grinned at his friend. "It looks like a secret passage if ye ask me." His hands trembled with excitement. "Perhaps 'tis a way into the keep."

Fergus shook his head. "Why would the MacLeòirs leave an entrance into their keep unguarded?" He frowned at Caelen. "Nay, that would be foolish, and as low an opinion as I might have of them, I have to admit that they are not fools."

Caelen stared at the small structure, the stones covered in moss, some even out of place, half-crumbled or broken. "Perhaps they dunna ken of it," he said with a grin. "It looks old. Who ken how long 'tis been here?" He strode forward. "Come. Let's have a look."

Half-rotten boards had been nailed in place, covering the entrance; yet they proved no obstacle. The two friends pried them loose with their swords then ripped them away and peered into the darkness beyond. Stone steps descended into the ground, leading to unknown depths below.

Caelen felt the urge to surge forward but reminded himself to be cautious. "Well, we might as well find out where it leads." He stepped inside and reached for a torch sitting in a holder as though waiting for them. "Hold this," he said and thrust the torch into Fergus's hands before reaching for flint and rock to light it. "We'd better do it in here where 'tis shielded. I dunna want the guards upon the walls to see the light."

Fergus nodded, holding the torch as Caelen lit it. Still, the expression upon his face spoke of reluctance.

Caelen, though, knew there was no turning back. If he did not find out where this tunnel led, he would lie awake all night wondering about it. "Come on."

Fergus hesitated but then followed Caelen, allowing his friend to take the lead. The air smelled musty and damp, and their footsteps echoed in the darkness, their hands upon the hilts of their swords, ready to defend themselves should the need arise. The tunnel was narrow, though, and they had to walk slightly crouched-over. The flickering torchlight barely lit their way, and Caelen's heart pounded against his chest as he thought of what could be waiting for them around the corner—hope as well as danger. Yet they kept going, determined to discover the mystery of this passage.

As they trudged through the tunnel, the darkness was thick and palpable, and it felt as though hours had passed before their eyes finally began to adjust. Few words were spoken between the two friends, their eyes fixed up ahead until eventually, they spied a sliver of dim light glowing at the end of the tunnel; yet it was so faint that Caelen wondered if it was truly there or if hope made him see it.

However, as they drew closer, a heavy wooden barricade blocked their way. It stretched out from floor to ceiling, coated in thick planks of dark, aged wood, its surface worn with time, bearing subtle etchings that hinted at stories untold, and the faint light that spilled through its cracks only served to enhance its imposing presence.

Caelen and Fergus pushed against it, their muscles straining as they poured all their might into every shove, but it would not budge. They tried every maneuver they could think of, even resorting to using makeshift tools from rocks and sticks that littered the ground around them, but nothing worked. Sweat beaded on their furrowed brows as they panted in exhaustion.

Just as they were about to give up and turn around in defeat, a metallic groan suddenly echoed through the chamber as the wall—seemingly solid moments before—slowly began to swing open.

Caelen's eyes widened as he and his friend scrambled out of its path, their torch dropping to the ground and their blades clanging against each other as they readied themselves for whatever might come next.

What came next was a single beam of light cutting through the darkness, and Caelen could not believe his eyes when he saw that the person standing there, illuminated by the torch in her hand, was Yvaine.

She was stunningly still, her fierce gaze mirroring the stars in the sky. Her navy velvet cloak floated around her like a dance, hugging her close and sheltering her from the world, its hood relaxed to show her delicate features. She breathed slowly and deeply as she looked into his eyes, her own widening as recognition flared. "Caelen?" she gasped, her mouth suddenly agape. "Is it truly ye? What are ye doing here?"

Momentarily stunned, Caelen stared at her, his heart pounding in his chest. "I... I came for ye," he said simply.

Yvaine shook her head as joy misted her eyes. "How did ye find this tunnel?" Her eyes darted to the side in alarm as Fergus stepped forward; yet when she recognized him, the expression upon her face relaxed. "My... My brother told me of this tunnel, and we've been searching for it ever since." She looked away from him then, guilt suddenly overshadowing her gaze before she quickly brushed it aside.

Caelen wondered what lingered upon her mind, and he stepped forward, casting a quick glance past her before meeting her eyes. "Yer brother? Logan?" Was it possible that the fierce warrior of Clan MacLeòir was nearby?

A wistful smile came to Yvaine's face. "Nay, Rory. He spoke to me of the stories of the MacLeòir and mentioned a tale about a warrior who—"

"I hate to interrupt," Fergus threw in, his gaze moving back and forth between Caelen and Yvaine. "However, I think it wise we leave now and discuss everything else later."

Caelen nodded then reached out and touched Yvaine's hand gently, giving it a reassuring squeeze before he spoke again. "Yer brother doesna ken ye're here, does he?"

Guilt once more flared in her gaze before she shook her head. "I'm betraying him by leaving," she murmured, her jaw clenched. "I never thought I'd feel guilty. From the first moment I came here, I only dreamed of finding my way back." She sought Caelen's gaze, and he felt it deep in his heart. "I care for him. He's my brother. My little brother." A surprised chuckle escaped her lips. "I have never had a little brother. I only ever was the little sister."

Caelen frowned, confused by her words, wishing she would explain. Indeed, to this day, he did not know where she had been all these years. Of course, they had not had much chance to speak, and at the time, something else had been more prominent upon his mind. Perhaps, though, soon, he would receive some answers.

Yvaine blinked, and her green eyes settled upon his. "I canna believe ye're here," she exclaimed as Fergus took the torch from her hand. "I was so afraid ye had left... without me." She shook her head, a spark of fury lighting up her eyes. "I'm sorry it took me so long to find this. I tried everything, but all the gates were too well guarded. I couldna risk it. If my father had become suspicious..."

Caelen nodded. "I understand. We found ourselves equally frustrated. Yet now—"

"Again, I must insist we leave now!" Fergus said more urgently, moving a few steps down the dark tunnel and taking the light with him as he walked.

"He's right," Yvaine exclaimed, her hand still resting in Caelen's. "We needa go now before my absence is discovered."

Caelen nodded. "Help me push this back into place." He chuckled as they leaned their shoulders against the wooden beams. "If only we had known it opened to the outside. We only tried to push." Slowly, the wall swung closed again, the soft creaking of the hinges echoing along the tunnel.

Yvaine smiled at him, and it was a smile that Caelen knew he would never forget. He took a step closer to her as if drawn by an invisible force, and in that moment, he could not help but feel that fate had brought them together once again and that perhaps, just perhaps, there was a reason for it.

Chapter Twenty-Eight

ESCAPE

Yvaine kept her gaze fixed upon the torchlight up ahead as she walked beside Caelen through the narrow tunnel, every emotion that pulsed beneath her skin strangely heightened and overwhelming. Indeed, everything had happened so fast that she had not had time to make her peace with this decision. Guilt still lived within her for betraying her little brother. What would he think when he woke up in the morning to find her gone? Would his thoughts immediately stray to the tunnel? Undoubtedly, he would feel betrayed —and rightly so!—and relay what they had done these past few days to their parents. Her parents, of course, would then come after her; her father, in particular. Aye, he would be furious, and if he were to catch up to her, he would make her pay.

Yet at the same time, Yvaine knew that this was her best chance for success. She had retired that evening as she always did, wishing her family a good night and retreating to her own chamber. She had waited there long enough for the castle to fall silent before she had tiptoed back out into the corridor. Then she had silently picked her way down to the dungeons, her heart hammering in her chest, every inch of her alert, afraid that she might be discovered. Yet everything had gone well.

And then Caelen had stood there.

Deep in her heart, Yvaine had not truly believed to ever see him again. After all, they hardly knew one another. What on earth could prompt him to be this patient, to wait for this long, to risk discovery? Aye, the old legend said that Caelen and Yvaine shared a great love; yet the two people they were today had barely spoken more than two words to one another. How could they share love? Indeed, it was ludicrous.

Yet whenever Yvaine dared look up into Caelen's face and felt his piercing blue gaze seeking hers, she could not deny that... there was something there—whatever that something was! She could not put a name to it, certain she had never experienced anything like it before. He seemed to call to her, his presence like a beacon drawing her closer.

Indeed, it was truly odd.

As Yvaine followed Caelen and Fergus, she abruptly felt all her nerve endings begin to tingle and then grow cold with a sudden realization. Her feet drew to a halt, and she reached out and grasped Caelen's arm. "Where exactly will we come out?"

Caelen stopped and turned around in the darkness, his face illuminated by the torch in Fergus's hand. "Not far from the castle," he said, and in the dimming light, Yvaine thought to see a touch of concern upon his features.

"Did ye ken this tunnel was here all along?" Yvaine squinted her eyes, wishing she could see his face better. "Does yer father ken?"

Taking a step toward her, Caelen shook his head. "I had no idea 'twas here. We stumbled upon it by sheer happenstance." He paused, tension in his voice now. "Why?"

With each step that Fergus continued onward, the darkness around them seemed to swallow them up a bit more. She heard Fergus's footsteps farther down the tunnel, the flicker of his torch the only light in the dark.

"I need ye to promise me something," Yvaine said quietly. "Dunna tell yer clan, yer father, about this tunnel. I dunna want my family in danger."

Caelen heaved a deep breath, and Yvaine understood that he

wished more than anything to deny the implication of her words. Yet he did not; instead, he nodded solemnly, the subtle movement barely visible in the dark. "I promise," he said, his voice heavy with regret and laced with a touch of anger. "I wish there was a way for all this fighting to end."

Yvaine sighed, remembering the stories her father and her grandmother had told her when she was a child about the ancient feud between the two clans, about the many raids and battles that had driven them so far apart that eventually peace had been inconceivable. Yet according to legend, it had been Caelen and Yvaine who had brought peace, not to the clans they had been born to but to their people. Was that what was to happen? Yvaine wondered, reminding herself that if she were to return home now... there would be no Yvaine to do the things of legends. Or was she mistaken? Was there another woman by that name, a woman who would soon reveal herself and conquer Caelen's heart?

Part of Yvaine felt relief at the thought, to have this burden lifted off her shoulders. Another part, though, rebelled at the thought of Caelen's heart belonging to anyone else but her. *'Tis foolish*, Yvaine thought. *I have no claim on him. There's nothing between us. Why do I care?*

Ignoring the drum-like beat of her heart, Yvaine nodded and moved on, following the path of light ahead of her. "I do as well," she whispered to the man walking quietly beside her. "Perhaps one day... someone... will come to change all that is."

As Yvaine lifted her gaze tentatively to glance at Caelen, her foot caught on a loose stone, and she stumbled forward. Before she could fall, though, Caelen leaped to catch her, his hands warm upon her arms as he steadied her. Yvaine's pulse raced, for she barely knew this man, yet legend said he would be her great love and she would be his. Truly, it was enough to addle her mind, for she could not remember ever having felt like this.

So weak.

So indecisive.

So uncertain.

So unhinged by his mere presence.

In the dark tunnel they seemed to drift closer, like two magnets inevitably drawn to one another. And then she felt his hand upon her cheek, his touch gentle but electric, sending sparks through her body like lightning in a summer storm. She looked up into his eyes and saw a spark of something there that made all of her fear and doubt melt away in an instant.

As though they had never been.

And then darkness fell over them like a blanket, obscuring Caelen's face from view so that all of Yvaine's senses were reduced to a single one: touch.

Suddenly, she was intensely aware of how close they stood, of how their hearts beat in tandem with each other. She gasped as Caelen pulled her closer, the feel of his warm breath on her skin sending shivers down her spine. It was almost too much for Yvaine to process. All this time she had been running from the truth, afraid to confront the possibility of what they could mean to one another.

What they were meant to mean to one another. Was it truly Fate?

Then a sudden wave of bravery swept over Yvaine, and she reached up to cup his cheek in her hand, feeling his soft stubble beneath her fingertips. Caelen leaned into her touch, and Yvaine felt herself melting into him.

Everything else around them seemed to disappear as they drifted closer to each other in the dark tunnel. Yvaine could feel Caelen's warm breath against her lips, sensed him so close that if she were to lift her head by a mere fraction—

"What's the hold-up?" Fergus called from somewhere up ahead. "Quickly! We mustna linger."

As though slapped, Yvaine and Caelen surged apart, their breaths coming fast. She could hear him pant, the sound echoing with something overwhelming and altogether unexpected. *Aye, I feel the same,* Yvaine thought to herself, struggling to calm her thundering heartbeat.

"We needa go," Caelen murmured in the dark, his voice reverberating with deep emotions kept at bay. "Come."

Yvaine paused, for she could all but sense him hold out his hand to her. Of course, she was tempted, more than that even. She could feel something stirring deep inside of her, and yet she feared to see it awaken. And so, instead of taking his hand, Yvaine stepped back from Caelen, increasing the distance between them. "I'm all right," she murmured and then turned down the tunnel.

Aye, whatever it was that had nearly awoken within her, whatever it was that had almost happened between them, it had left its mark—a warmth that filled every cell of her body like liquid fire—and she knew that if something were to happen between them ever again...

Gritting her teeth against a sudden wave of longing, Yvaine quickened her steps and hurried after Fergus, overwhelmed by her emotions for Caelen.

Both caught up with him soon enough, and then stepped out of the tunnel into a night sky filled with stars. Fergus quickly extinguished the torch so they would not be seen from the keep, and Yvaine welcomed the continued darkness. It gave her time to compose herself, the cool night air soothing against her flushed cheeks. She took a deep breath, and the warmth inside of her slowly receded.

Yvaine glanced at Caelen in the dark, but he seemed lost in thought and did not notice her gaze. She wondered if he could feel it, too—the same warmth that had stirred within both of them back in the tunnel —and yet neither one of them spoke a word about it as they breathed in the night air.

Silence lingered, and Yvaine looked up at the stars, feeling something akin to awe as she took in their beauty—a beauty that seemed infinitely more powerful out here than it ever had within the castle walls.

"We mustna linger," Caelen said quietly beside her, his voice low and tinged with an emotion Yvaine could not quite decipher. "Our camp isna far." She glanced sideways at him, searching his face for answers before turning away again.

"Let's go," she murmured softly, her gaze still fixed on the stars above as they walked away, leaving behind the keep and all those within.

Farewell, Rory, Yvaine thought fervently, hoping that on some level her brother knew that she had never meant to betray him, that she had even come to care for him deeply in the short time they had known one another. If possible, Yvaine would have loved to bring him back home. Yet some things were simply not to be, she thought, casting another glance at Caelen.

Chapter Twenty-Nine

A KINK IN THE PLAN

As Caelen, Fergus, and Yvaine made their way back to the men's makeshift camp, none of them spoke a word. The air was thick with tension as their footsteps echoed softly in the night, their thoughts lingering upon what would happen should the MacLeòirs discover Yvaine's absence before they managed to put enough distance between them and the keep.

Caelen's thoughts, though, circled around something else entirely, for he still found himself taken aback by what had almost happened between him and Yvaine in the tunnel.

In the dark.

His breath shuddered past his lips as he remembered vividly how he had held her in his arms after she had tripped. Aye, he remembered the spark of electricity that had passed through them, and he felt heat rush to his face, to every inch of him, filling him with an almost desperate need to restore the closeness that had found them so unexpectedly. Swallowing hard, Caelen looked away, trying his best to contain his emotions, for they would not serve him now. Indeed, it was paramount that he keep his wits about him. Neither one of them could know what would happen next, how much of a head start they would have. Things could go wrong at any moment.

Finally, it was Fergus who broke the silence. "What are we going to do now?" he asked, looking back at the keep in the distance.

Yvaine did not look at Caelen, her expression a bit flustered as well. Instead, she focused her gaze on her feet. "I needa go home," she said softly.

Fergus frowned, looking confused. "Home?" Again, he glanced up at the keep, still too close for comfort.

Yvaine nodded.

"The keep?" Fergus asked to clarify. "The one ye just escaped from?" He arched an eyebrow.

A small smile came to her lips as she shook her head. "Nay, the island." Her gaze darted to Caelen, and he felt it like a punch to the chest. "Where... Where ye found me."

Fergus still did not seem convinced, his forehead furrowed. "As far as I ken, no one lives there." He chuckled. "Some say the Fey live there, but—" He broke off, casting a curious glance at Yvaine. "Ye dunna mean to say that..."

Yvaine did not respond but simply walked onward at a steady pace.

Caelen exchanged a confused look with Fergus, and then he stepped forward, asking the question that had been on his mind ever since they had met. "Do ye truly live... with the Fey?"

Yvaine avoided his gaze.

"'Tis what people have been whispering about ever since ye disappeared as a child," Caelen added before reaching out and grasping her arm, pulling her back to face him. The moment he touched her, he felt that sizzling spark again, felt it grow and reach out to him. He knew he ought to release her immediately—for both their sakes—yet he could not. His hand remained upon her arm, and he exhaled a slow breath when she finally lifted her chin and met his eyes.

"I canna give ye the answer ye seek," Yvaine finally said, a touch of anger in her voice as though she wished she could. "All I can say is that I needa return home." She swallowed, lifting her chin another fraction. "Back to the island." She held his gaze, searching, clearly uncertain. "Will ye take me?"

Without even a single conscious thought, Caelen knew that he could not deny her request, that there was, in all likelihood, very little in this world he would ever deny her. Indeed, there was not a moment of hesitation in him. Still, he shared a look with Fergus, and they silently acknowledged that they would escort her.

"Aye, I'll take ye," he murmured, and without his doing, his hand on her arm tightened, urging her closer. He sensed Fergus turning away and busying himself with packing up their belongings as he looked down into Yvaine's eyes. "Even if ye dunna wish to tell me where ye've been or where ye're going, at least tell me if ye remember." He searched her gaze. "Some say the Fey hide themselves by taking people's memories, by making them forget what was."

Yvaine's gaze darted to his hand upon her arm, and yet Caelen did not see even a touch of resistance or a wish to be released. It seemed a mere acknowledgment of what had been between them, of what might still be between them. "I do remember," she finally breathed, her voice no more than a whisper, drifting away upon the soothing night air. "I remember everything. I remember the life that was mine and the woman I was, the woman I am meant to be. I remember my home and my family, and I simply wish to return."

Caelen stared at her, still unable to make sense of her words. After all, the island was deserted, no one lived there. Yet if it was truly the Fey she spoke of, Caelen could not imagine what home and family looked like to her. Were they people perhaps, simply hidden from their eyes? Their homes there as solid as any brickwall but unfathomable to people like Caelen?

"I shall return ye then," Caelen promised her, "if that is yer wish." He could not deny that he was curious, and yet, deep down, Caelen knew that if she returned to the island, he would never see her again, for it would swallow her up as completely as it had all those years ago.

"Aye, 'tis my wish." She smiled at him before reaching out a tentative hand, once more cupping his cheek. The spark that zapped through them both in that moment had their eyes fly open and their breaths catch in their throats. They stared at one another, and Caelen wondered what he would do once she was gone.

"Do ye feel this, too?" Yvaine murmured, her gaze searching his face. There was a touch of shyness in her eyes, and yet she did not drop her gaze, curiosity lingering there.

"This?" Caelen asked, a teasing tone in his voice as his fingers curled more tightly around her arm, tugging her closer.

Yvaine gasped, yet the smile upon her face never waned. "Aye, this." As he tugged on her arm, she came, cutting the distance between them in half. "I already felt it in the tunnel and in the garden the night of the feast." Her green eyes held his, waiting, asking.

Caelen nodded. "I felt it that day we first met on the island," he murmured, and his hand slid from her arm and onto her back while his other reached to touch her face. "Did ye?"

Her teeth teased her lower lip as she nodded. "Aye, I did. What do ye suppose it means?" For a moment, she closed her eyes and leaned into his touch. "It feels…" Her green eyes opened, and Caelen felt his heart skip a beat. "It feels…"

Caelen nodded, knowing precisely what she meant. "Aye, it does."

Fergus cleared his throat rather loudly. "What route to the coast do ye suppose we should take?"

Gritting his teeth, Caelen closed his eyes, silently cursing his friend for interrupting this moment. Yet, of course, his rational mind argued that Fergus was not wrong. Indeed, there was no time for this…

Whatever this was.

Yvaine chuckled. "He has awful timing, doesna he?" she whispered, her breath teasing his lips before she took a step back and slipped away, robbing him of something he had never known he longed for. "Yet he is not wrong." She glanced toward the keep, and her expression hardened. Gone was the lightness and emotion Caelen had seen in her face a moment ago. "We only have a few hours before they'll know I'm gone." She met Caelen's eyes. "We needa leave."

Heaving a deep sigh, Caelen nodded, struggling to remind himself of what was important. To keep Yvaine safe, they had to leave now and travel as far as they could during the night before the MacLeòirs awoke in the morning and found her gone.

Yet as Caelen turned toward the belongings Fergus had already packed, their horses ready to set off at a moment's notice, a strange sound echoed to his ears. It drifted closer from somewhere in the woods around them. Caelen could not even say what it was; yet he knew in his bones that it spoke of the presence of another.

Slowly, he shifted his gaze to Fergus, seeing that his friend had heard it as well, for his gaze looked suddenly alert. "We are not alone," he whispered, turning to look at Yvaine.

Although she was a woman and not a warrior, not familiar with the ways of stealth and all that came with growing up amidst a blood feud, Caelen knew that she understood. Either she had heard the sound as well or could tell from the expressions upon their faces that something was wrong. Her eyes were slightly narrowed and watchful, her muscles tense, ready to react at a moment's notice. Indeed, if it were not impossible, Caelen would have mistaken her for a trained warrior. Aye, had she not broken his cousin's nose the day they had met? Had Rory not spoken of her fondness for archery?

In a way, a small eternity had passed since that day, and yet Caelen still knew so very little about her. Secrets surrounded her like mist on a cloudy day, with the sun barely peeking through tiny gaps here and there, its rays shrouded and weak.

A twig snapped a moment before Lachlan stepped out of the shadowed forest, armed warriors at his sides. "I ken ye were a traitor," he snarled, his voice dripping with disdain. "I ken ye couldna do it." His lips curved upward into a dark smile. "That is why I'm here, to ensure that our clan triumphs."

Caelen's heart stilled in his chest as fear gripped him, for he knew precisely why Lachlan had come—perhaps even with his father's blessing.

His cousin was here to kill Yvaine, and Caelen knew he would not hesitate.

Chapter Thirty

RUN

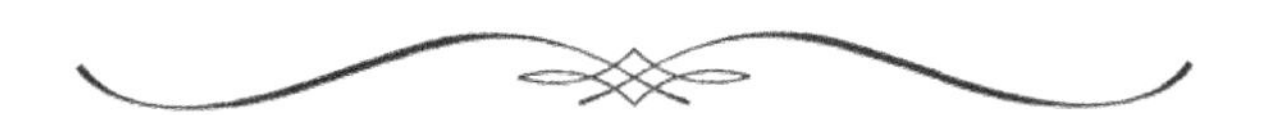

Yvaine stood motionless, her heart pounding in her chest, as the man stepped out of the dark forest, warriors on either side of him. His presence was threatening, his face a cold, expressionless mask, and Yvaine knew that she had seen him before. Aye, on the island the day after she had arrived in this... time. Even now, even after everything that had happened thus far, a part of Yvaine still had trouble believing that all this was real.

"I ken ye were a traitor," the man snarled, his gaze cold and calculating as he studied first Caelen and then her. "I ken ye couldna do it." His nose crinkled in disdain, and an icy smile came to his lips. "That is why I'm here, to ensure that our clan triumphs."

Despite the warmth of the evening, ice-cold shivers slithered down Yvaine's back, for the intent in the man's eyes was unmistakable. She remembered how Caelen had confessed that his own father, chief of Clan MacCarmaig, had ordered his only son to take her life in order to ensure that his own daughter would marry the leader of Clan Morganach.

Yet Caelen had gone against his father's orders; this man clearly would not. What now? Would Caelen still stand with her, or would he remain loyal to his clan?

Shifting her attention from the man across the clearing, fierce-looking warriors standing on each side of him, Yvaine sought Caelen's gaze, for she needed to know if she was alone in this.

Only he did not look at her, his body rigid, his hands curled into fists and every muscle tight as a bowstring as he glared at the new arrival. "Lachlan," he spat, his voice a low growl, laced with barely-contained anger. "There is no need to interfere. Do ye truly seek glory that desperately that ye would go against my father's—?"

"I have yer father's blessing," Lachlan retorted, a satisfied smile curling up the corners of his mouth. "I told him of what I had observed during my last visit, of how ye had yet failed to show any progress in yer mission." He moved forward, stepping into the clearing, his right hand on the hilt of his sword. "Quite naturally, he was concerned."

Yvaine watched as Caelen drew in a slow breath, her own heart hammering wildly in her chest. "As ye can see," Caelen replied in an equally icy voice, "we *have* made progress." He glanced toward Yvaine but did not meet her eyes before he moved forward as well, slow and measured steps carrying him closer toward the man called Lachlan.

"Aye, I see she's here." The man's gaze lingered upon Yvaine in a way that once more made her want to reach for her dagger. "Yet I canna help but doubt yer intentions, Cousin." He cast her an almost sickeningly sweet smile. "For one, she is still breathing, and for another, she doesna seem like a prisoner." He arced up an eyebrow in question.

Cousin? Yvaine wondered, squinting her eyes. Aye, there was a certain resemblance between the two men. Yet despite their familial connection, they appeared to stand on opposite sides in this matter; and Yvaine was grateful for it. Yet would it matter? After all, they were greatly outnumbered.

"Ye have no say in how I fulfill my father's orders," Caelen replied in a calm tone, his demeanor self-assured despite the slight tremble Yvaine saw in his clenched hands. Indeed, any other observer might have mistaken it for anger or fury even; yet for some reason, Yvaine knew beyond a shadow of a doubt that Caelen was a man torn. Of course, he felt loyalty toward his clan, and yet something had placed him firmly at her side.

Lachlan scoffed. "There is only the one way." He signaled his men to stay back then moved farther into the clearing. "Let me assist ye then," he remarked in a detached voice as though speaking of the weather, and drew his sword, the blade glittering in the starlight.

Yvaine felt a wave of fear wash over her, and she fought the urge to flee, her right hand flying to her waist out of habit for the second time that night. Yet her dagger was still gone, and she cursed her own foolishness, wondering what good lady-like behavior did for her when she could not even protect herself in the face of danger.

Then Caelen and Fergus stepped into Lachlan's path, putting themselves between her and the man who intended to take her life. Their faces were determined as they drew their swords, ready to protect her against their own clan.

Yvaine felt a sudden swell of emotion in her chest at the sight of them, their jaws set, willing to risk their lives, betray their own clan, for her—a woman they barely knew.

"Ye're a fool," Lachlan spat, his voice razor-edged and threatening. "Will ye truly throw away yer life for this woman?" He shook his head, disbelief in his gaze; yet Yvaine saw no compassion for his cousin in his eyes but rather ill-concealed satisfaction, as though Lachlan had always hoped that one day this would happen.

Yvaine glanced at Caelen, who looked tense, torn about what to do. No doubt he wondered if there was anything he could say to change his cousin's mind, hope making him hesitant. Yvaine could not imagine what it would feel like to stand at such a crossroad: to remain loyal to the people one loved or to stay true to one's own beliefs.

"Say what ye will," Caelen told his cousin, his grip tightening upon his sword, "but I willna allow ye to interfere."

Lachlan heaved a deep breath, curiosity in his gaze as he looked from his cousin to Yvaine. "I have no intention of interfering so long as ye stay true to yer word." He lowered his sword slowly until the tip brushed against the grass upon the clearing. "Go," he said in a commanding voice. "I'll wait while ye kill her."

Yvaine stepped forward, her heart pounding as she met Lachlan's gaze, wondering if he could be reasoned with. Yvaine rather doubted it; however, she had to try. Only she had never been one good with words. If only Magnus were here. "Please," she said softly, her voice barely a whisper in the night air, a sign of surrender that left a sour taste upon her tongue. "Ye dunna have to do this. Surely, we can reach an agreement, some sort of understanding that will benefit both of us." She paused, her gaze steady and unwavering as she continued. "I understand yer loyalty to yer clan, and I respect it; but surely ye must see that there is no need for violence here? We can find a way to settle this without bloodshed."

Lachlan's expression remained stoic as he glared at her, his stance tense and wary. "What kind of agreement are ye proposing?"

Yvaine took a deep breath, feeling Caelen's gaze upon her. "We both want something: I want my freedom and ye want safety for yer people," she began slowly, speaking carefully so as not to offend him further or invoke his anger. "Yer chief ordered my death," she swallowed, the word feeling heavy upon her tongue, "to ensure that his daughter will be the Morganach's bride. Is that not so?"

Lachlan's lips thinned, and Yvaine could see that he was displeased to hear what Caelen had shared with her. "Indeed," he replied in a voice as hard as steel. "So, ye see, there is no compromise to be found."

Lifting her hands, Yvaine took a step forward, surprised to see Caelen tense, a muscle in his jaw tightening. "Aye, there is, for I have neither the intention nor the desire to marry the leader of Clan Morganach. All I want is to go home." Despite his hostility, Yvaine held his gaze. "I shall leave these shores never to return. Ye have my word that ye will never lay eyes on me again. This can be ended without bloodshed. If ye let me go, yer clan's future will be secure."

Lachlan's gaze was still hard, but Yvaine could sense the slightest hint of hesitation in his eyes; at least for a split second, it seemed he was considering her words before making any decisions. "I suppose if I had any reason to trust ye, a compromise could be found," Lachlan finally said, the expression upon his face suggesting that there were no words on this earth to sway him. "Yet I dunna. Ye're a stranger, the daughter of my enemy, and I canna place my clan's future in yer hands." He held her gaze, slowly shaking his head, and for a moment, Yvaine thought to see a touch of regret in his dark eyes. Then he looked to Caelen. "Well, who will do it then? Ye... or me?"

Yvaine bowed her head, a deep sense of failure sweeping through her. She wanted to release Caelen from whatever vow he had taken to protect her; yet before she could speak, he suddenly stood at her side, his gaze still fixed upon his cousin. "Go home, Lachlan. I willna allow ye to lay a hand on her."

Lachlan sighed, his broad shoulders rising and falling with a deep breath. "If ye stand with our enemies, I canna guarantee yer safety. Choose wisely."

Caelen nodded. "I am," he murmured, lifting his sword, his gaze meeting Fergus's as they stood side-by-side. The other man looked a bit uncertain yet equally determined.

"Do ye have a dagger?" Yvaine asked from behind them, hating this feeling of helplessness, standing by and contributing nothing while others placed themselves in danger, and for her no less. "Anything? Anything sharp and pointy?"

Caelen turned to look at her over his shoulder, and she was surprised to see a smile twitch his lips. "Run," he whispered then, his voice barely audible as his lips formed the words. His gaze drilled into hers, and for a moment, Yvaine thought she could feel it like a touch of skin on skin. "Run to the tunnel. We shall keep them back."

Yvaine stared at Caelen, her ears ringing with disbelief. "Nay, ye canna mean that. I—"

Caelen's jaw hardened, and an icy quality came to his gaze. "Run!" he snarled before turning back around to face his cousin.

Despite the reluctance in every fiber of her being, Yvaine felt her feet move, felt them spin her around and carry her away from the clearing. As she ran, sounds of battle drifted to her ears, metal clashing on metal, cries of pain and defiance echoing in the night air. She risked a glance over her shoulder and saw Caelen and Fergus still facing off against Lachlan and his men; their swords slashing through the darkness with deadly precision as they fought to protect her. Guilt filled Yvaine as she watched them, knowing that it was because of her they were now risking their lives—but no matter how much she wanted to turn back and fight by their side, she could not deny Caelen's command: *Run!*

Yvaine picked up speed until she was sprinting full-tilt toward the tunnel, dark shapes of trees and bushes flying past her. Her pulse pounded in her ears, almost blocking out all other sounds. She tripped over a tree root or perhaps a large rock—in the dark she could not tell—and fell to her knees, scraping her hands upon the rough ground. Yet a moment later, she was racing forward once again, momentarily confused where she was going, where the tunnel entrance was, her heart still urging her to go back. It was a battle deep within, and Yvaine did not know which side she wanted to win.

Finally, she stumbled to a halt, her chest heaving with exertion. She looked around, squinting into the darkness, desperately searching for the tunnel entrance. Everything looked different in the night; shadows seemed to move and shift shape as if alive, mocking her confusion. Yvaine's heart sank as she realized that she had no idea where she was or how to get back. Tears of frustration pricked her eyes, and she blinked them away angrily; there was no time for tears now! Taking a deep breath to calm herself down, Yvaine slowly began to walk in what she hoped was the right direction.

She moved cautiously through the darkness, her eyes darting from side to side as she searched for any sign of the tunnel entrance. Every now and then, she thought she heard a faint sound coming from somewhere nearby—perhaps it was Caelen and Fergus… or rather Lachlan and his men? She wanted so badly to go back and help them but knew that would be foolish; instead, Yvaine kept walking forward until finally, after what felt like an eternity of searching in the dark, something caught her eye.

Stepping around a group of trees, she spotted the well-hidden tunnel entrance just ahead, overgrown by moss and brambles and ivy, as though the world itself sought to hide it.

She was almost there, almost safe! And still, relief and regret warred within Yvaine, her feet pounding fast in her ears. Then, just as she was about to enter the tunnel, arms suddenly grasped her from behind and a hand clamped over her mouth. Fear shot through Yvaine's veins like ice water, and she screamed—only for the sound to be muffled by a hand against her lips. She tried to break free, but the grip only tightened, hot breath teasing the skin below her ear as whoever held her whispered words that were lost in the chaos of her struggles.

And then it hit her.

In an instant, recognition flooded through her senses—Caelen's scent of pine needles and leather filled her nose; his strong arms held her tight; his voice whispered soothingly into her ear: "'Tis me."

Yvaine exhaled in relief as realization dawned on her that it was not Lachlan who had grabbed her but Caelen instead. She relaxed into his arms as he pulled her closer and spun her around, so they were facing each other, her back against a tree trunk. "How can ye be here?" she gasped. "What of Fergus?" She glanced behind Caelen, but his friend was nowhere to be seen.

"He's well," Caelen murmured softly, still holding onto Yvaine with one arm around her waist while the other gripped his sword. "He's leading them away to give us a moment. We've done it many times, ever since we were children." He sighed then shook his head as though pushing that thought away. "Ye have to go, but first..."

The distant sounds of men rushing through the underbrush seemed to fade away as their eyes met and held; Yvaine felt like time had stopped and all that existed in that moment was only the two of them. Even in the darkness of night, she could see how deep blue Caelen's eyes were—like the dark sky above them filled with stars twinkling brightly at nightfall. "First?" she whispered breathlessly.

Caelen leaned in closer, his gaze never leaving hers, and Yvaine felt her heart pounding against her ribcage. His lips were so close to hers, she could feel the warmth of his breath on her face. And then, without warning, Caelen was suddenly kissing her—not with the gentle tenderness she had somehow expected but with a desperate passion.

Her heart seemed to pause, as though holding its breath, and she felt the warmth emanating from his body, the passion simmering in both their veins. It was a desperate kiss—one that marked a farewell—

but at the same time it felt like an eternity, like they were saying goodbye to something that had been between them all along but never spoken of until now.

For a few moments, Yvaine allowed herself to get lost in it, then reality hit her once again and she pulled away from him, tears brimming in her eyes. Still, for another heartbeat, neither of them moved.

"Go," Caelen said softly, breaking the silence. "Go. 'Tis the only place where ye're safe."

"But—"

"Nay." His lips thinned, and his gaze hardened. "Another time, Yvaine. I wish I could see ye safely home, but not now. If ye stay, he will find ye and..." Caelen did not finish the thought, his lips pressed into a tight line, fear and anger in his gaze.

"What of ye?" Yvaine asked, still breathless, still clinging to Caelen as though her next breath depended upon his presence. "If yer father learns—"

"Dunna worry," Caelen said softly, brushing a tear away from Yvaine's cheek with his thumb. "I'll be fine, and... I will be back." He gave her one last lingering look before turning around and disappearing into the night.

Yvaine watched him leave until he faded out of sight; her heart still hammering in her chest. Had this truly just happened? Aye, her lips still tingled from his kiss.

"Caelen," Yvaine whispered into the night, suddenly terrified, knowing that she had taken a large step away from ever returning home; not because she was now forced to return to the keep but because... her heart no longer beat steadily in her chest.

Chapter Thirty-One
THE ENEMY'S DAUGHTER

Crouched low, Caelen crept through the shadowed forest, his heart thudding against his chest. He had heard the menacing cries of Lachlan and his men a few moments earlier, and he dared not linger, suddenly worrying if Fergus was well. Yet he knew his friend to be capable, certain that nothing had befallen him. Indeed, he was grateful that Fergus had taken such a chance to allow Caelen a moment of farewell with Yvaine.

He had not meant to kiss her. It had been a rash decision, but one he had found himself unable to resist; their last moment together marked by an eternity of passion and longing that lingered even now in his heart.

A part of him still wanted to go back, keep her by his side; yet it was impossible. Even if Lachlan did not find them, Caelen's father—and his uncle as well, perhaps even more so—would be furious when he discovered what had happened tonight.

And he would find out. Lachlan would make certain of that.

Nay, for now it was best that they part ways until the time came when they could see each other again. Still, Caelen felt as though he had broken his word to her. Had he not promised to see her safely home? Of course, he could not have known that his cousin was lying in wait, fiercely determined to end Yvaine's life. Caelen had not had a choice, and Yvaine's safety was far more important than him keeping his word.

Even now, Caelen remembered the way she had spoken to Lachlan in the clearing. He remembered the words she had said, speaking of her home, of returning to it and of never posing a threat to their clan again. Her words had been meant as reassurance, and yet in that moment, every inch of Caelen had tensed in anguish. Indeed, the thought of never seeing her again pained him, tormented him, and so a part of him was relieved that she was now headed back to the keep because it kept her here...

... near him.

Only one day, he would have to fulfill his vow. He would have to take her to the island and watch her walk away to whatever home she had come from.

Lost in his thoughts, Caelen stumbled over a fallen branch, wincing as his foot caught its jutting edge. Biting his tongue, he scanned the darkness, his breath caught in his throat as he waited to see if he was being followed, if someone would come upon him at any moment, certain that the noise would carry and alert Lachlan to his presence.

Fortunately, the only sound that met his ears was the distant hooting of an owl, and Caelen exhaled in relief, quickly continuing onward. After all, there was no time to lose.

Just ahead, Caelen spotted the dark figure of his friend waiting for him, half-hidden behind a large thicket of brambles. Caelen would have walked right by him had they not come upon this very place earlier in the day. "Are ye all right?"

Stepping out into the dim starlight, Fergus nodded. "They might still be chasing their tails," he said with a grim smile, and Caelen saw a faint trickle of blood run down his friend's temple. Aye, despite his words, Fergus's face was lined with worry. "What are we to do now?"

Caelen swept his gaze over his friend, wanting to be certain that he had sustained no other wounds. "We return home."

Fergus paused, a look of disbelief coming to his face. "Surely, ye dunna mean that." He stared at Caelen, clearly still doubting his senses. "If we return now, yer father will throw us in the dungeon. Ye heard what Lachlan said. This," he swept out an arm toward the clearing and everything that had happened there, "canna be kept quiet."

Caelen nodded. "That I ken. I assure ye." He stepped forward and placed a hand upon his friend's shoulder. "Yet we canna run away. Lachlan would use it against us, twist it into an admission of guilt." He sighed, holding his friend's gaze. "Nay, we must return and face my father, explain what happened and provide reasons for our decision."

"Reasons?" Fergus shook his head. "I doubt we can provide reasons that would satisfy yer father."

Caelen shrugged, gesturing for his friend to move on, and together, they headed back toward their packed belongings. "Perhaps not," he admitted in a low voice. "However, we didna act against our clan. What we did was done in its best interest."

Fergus chuckled, eyeing Caelen curiously. "So, ye believe that stealing a kiss from our enemy's daughter is in our clan's best interest?"

Caelen felt as though he blushed to the roots of his hair. "Ye truly have a way with words, my friend," he remarked with a dry chuckle. "Nay, what I meant was that Yvaine's intention to leave," he struggled to keep his voice light, "is in our clan's best interest. There is no need to kill her if she canna marry the Morganach chief." That, at least, was truly good news!

At their campsite, Caelen and Fergus quickly gathered their few belongings and then whistled for their horses. Their soft bird calls echoed across the clearing, easily mingling with the rhythmic sounds of night. Soon after, Caelen heard the soft sound of hooves upon the forest floor, and then their two steeds materialized in the night. "We must be quick," Caelen said as he pulled himself onto his gelding's back. "The sooner we reach the keep, the more time we will have to explain everything to my father without Lachlan interfering."

Fergus nodded, his hands clenched upon the reins. "Well, lead the way."

Silently, they found their way through the densely growing forest until they reached the road that led up to the MacLeòirs' keep. There, they allowed their steeds free rein, spurring them on and galloping away, their horses' hooves pounding against the dirt road.

Caelen glanced back at the looming shape of the keep, half-hidden in darkness. A few lights shimmered here and there, torches left burning overnight to light the walls or perhaps a candle, lit late in the night when sleep proved elusive. A deep feeling of sorrow spread through Caelen's chest as he thought of Yvaine, left behind at the castle among family she did not consider her own. Indeed, Caelen had never before considered what it might feel like to return to people who were of one's blood, but people one did not remember. She had been a child when she had disappeared, only a few years old. Try as he might, Caelen could not remember that time of his own life, those first few years when his mother had still been alive. He barely remembered her, and he wondered if it was the same for Yvaine. Perhaps she truly felt as though she was trapped with strangers, longing to be reunited with those she loved. Only who could that be?

The Fey?

The thought seemed as ludicrous as it had before; still, there had to be some sort of explanation. Yvaine could not have survived as a small child on her own, and when she spoke of those she cared for, there was substance there. Her words were not those of a feeble mind, prone to imaginings. Nay, she had been loved wherever she had been. Yet the question remained, by whom?

None of these thoughts would aid him now, though, and Caelen forced himself to focus on what lay ahead. Only if he kept his wits about him would he be able to return someday and hopefully keep his word to Yvaine. Now, though, he needed to ride hard and reach the keep before Lachlan and his men.

With a last look back, Caelen and Fergus rode off into the night, their horses galloping faster and faster as they raced toward MacCarmaig lands and home.

Chapter Thirty-Two

WITH BOWED HEAD

Yvaine crept through the secret tunnel, her heart heavy with sorrow. She had left the keep earlier that day, fleeing in the night without any of her kin knowing of her departure. Now, she was returning in the same manner, burdened by the weight of her choices and the consequences that were sure to follow. Aye, if she were caught, she would be punished severely, and she would lose every bit of trust her father had bestowed on her these past few weeks. Trust that had been hard to come by. If she were caught, would there then ever be another chance for her to get away from the keep, to flee and return home? Most likely, her father would truly lock her up, enraged by her disobedience.

The tunnel was dark, damp, and cold, and Yvaine shivered as she crept along, her boots echoing in the darkness. After what felt like an eternity, she finally reached the end of the tunnel—at least she supposed she did. They had not left a burning torch behind, and so there was no light. Still the ground beneath her feet felt different; so, did the air she drew into her lungs. Reaching out her hands, Yvaine found the wall that blocked her path, the wall that had earlier this night swung open to guide her to freedom. She pulled it back open, her heart heavy, now that she was willingly returning to her prison. Yet there was no choice, was there? Indeed, Caelen was right; if Lachlan found her, he would most certainly kill her. He had made that unmistakably clear.

Careful to close the secret door behind her, to leave behind no trace of her having been here, of this wall not being a sturdy wall like all the others, Yvaine turned away from it, wishing this night had ended differently.

Fortunately, the keep was silent as she moved through the shadows, her steps light and quick. She made her way to her chamber as swiftly as she could, her heart pounding in her chest. More than once, a shadow made her heart still in her chest, her mind certain that she had now been discovered. Yet it always proved to be nothing. No one came upon her, and the only footsteps that ever drifted to her ears echoed away into the distance. Still, when Yvaine finally reached the door to her chamber, she was out of breath, her heart exhausted. Stepping across the threshold, she closed the door behind herself, and with a deep breath, sank down onto the floor, resting her head against its smooth wood.

The very moment the threat of discovery vanished, Yvaine's mind drifted back to one particular moment earlier this night. "Caelen," she whispered into the stillness of her chamber, her lips once again tingling from his kiss. She still could not quite believe that it had happened. It had, though, had it not? Caelen had kissed her. The hero of the old legends had kissed her!

Resting her forehead upon her bent knees, Yvaine exhaled a deep breath, allowing her mind to drift backward upon those memories, reliving them as though they were happening again. It had been unexpected, and yet wonderful. It had felt right, overwhelmingly right; and in that moment, Yvaine had known that she belonged at his side as much as he belonged at hers. Was she a fool to think so? After all, they were barely more than strangers. Yet he had not hesitated to risk his life for her tonight.

"'Tis only a story," Yvaine whispered as she lifted her gaze, and her eyes found the starry night outside her window. "Caelen and Yvaine lived hundreds of years ago. 'Tis no more than a legend that has no bearing upon my own life." Aye, not long ago these words would have sounded reasonable in every way. Yet the world had turned upon its head, changing everything that was and would be. "Am I truly Yvaine? Caelen's Yvaine?"

And if she was, could she then leave? Even if her heart were not on the line, would it not be selfish of her to leave this time without fulfilling... her destiny? Was there some sort of grand plan or was everything truly just coincidence? Yvaine wished she knew. She wanted some sort of certainty, something to guide her in the days to come. What ought she to focus her mind on? On returning home... or on returning to Caelen?

Eventually, exhaustion closed Yvaine's eyes, and yet her sleep was not undisturbed but overshadowed by fear and uncertainty, which remained with her even as the bright morning sun climbed the sky outside her window. Always had Yvaine been someone to rise early and do it with a light heart. Today, though, all her limbs felt heavy, and more than anything, she wished she could simply turn around and pull the blanket over her head. Yet life continued on, and so must hers.

Dressed in one of the gowns her mother had provided her for everyday life, Yvaine left her chamber, suddenly hungry after last night's chase and excitement and... heartbreak. She walked down the long corridor, offering a kind word or smile to the occasional servant she encountered; yet when she came close to the stairs, voices echoed to her ears from down below. Her feet pulled to an immediate halt, keeping her hidden, as she strained to listen.

"Can ye be certain who it was?" Every muscle in Yvaine's body tensed when she recognized her father's voice. "Which clan they belonged to?"

"Unfortunately, we canna," came Logan's reply, his voice low. "No one truly saw them. All we heard was the clash of swords and some indistinct shouting. We found tracks of a scuffle, of men chasing one another outside our walls." He paused, and Yvaine held her breath as she listened. "It appears they left... whoever they were."

A displeased growl rose from her father's throat. "Of course, I wish we knew for certain who they were." He chuckled then, a dark sound echoing off the walls. "Perhaps we'll be fortunate, and 'twas the MacCarmaigs fighting amongst themselves. No doubt, they feel ill at ease now that my daughter has returned." He laughed, and Yvaine felt a coldness in her stomach as she heard it.

"Nonetheless," her father continued, "I want ye to keep a watchful eye on the situation. 'Tis always advantageous to ken what yer enemy is planning. If they are aware of the changed circumstances, they might be desperate enough to try something... rash."

Logan made a noncommittal sound in his throat, and although Yvaine could not see his face, she thought that her brother was rather displeased. If only she knew why. Did he dislike their father's order? Or was he upset about the scuffle that had happened last night as well as its implications?

"What of Yvaine?" Logan asked unexpectedly, and Yvaine flinched, clamping a hand over her mouth to stifle the gasp that left her lips. "Have ye already spoken to her?"

Silence followed, and Yvaine could imagine her father's exasperated expression.

"She deserves to know," Logan pressed, his tone respectful and yet imploring. "After all, this affects her the most."

"When everything is settled, I shall inform her," their father replied, a disapproving tone in his voice.

"Why not tell her now?"

Their father scoffed. "Ye ken how headstrong she is. I have no doubt she will refuse to bow her head."

"All the more reason to tell her now and give her time to make her peace with this union. Do ye not think, Father?"

A heavy sigh drifted from their father's lips. "Perhaps ye're right."

"If ye wish I could speak to her," Logan suggested, a touch of unease in his voice.

Again, a moment of silence lingered, heavy and almost suffocating. "If ye wish," their father finally said, his voice hard and unforgiving. "Yet make it unmistakably clear that she is to comply, do ye understand? She is my daughter, and she will do as I say."

No words left Logan's lips, and Yvaine imagined him nodding his head in agreement. Then she heard footsteps drifting away as her father and brother parted ways.

Union? Yvaine thought, remembering what Caelen had told her about the marriage contract that had once existed between her father and the Morganach chief. Was it true what Caelen's father feared? That her father had truly reentered negotiations with Clan Morganach? Was this what they had just spoken about? Seeing her, Yvaine, married to its current chief?

Yvaine felt a chill of fear run through her body at the thought. Of course, she knew that even in her own time marriages were often arranged, unions entered into for reasons other than love. Yet upon MacKinnear Island, among her clan, it was not common practice. Long ago, her people had made a choice to live differently, to change the rules and decide for themselves. Not until stepping into that small pool of water in the hidden cavern had Yvaine ever imagined a life like this. She had never contemplated one, and why would she have? To be here now, trapped, not free to make her own choices was almost unbearable. Yvaine struggled with it every day, and yet there was this part of her that still felt as though she were asleep... and all she had to do was wake up.

"I willna be forced into marriage," Yvaine murmured under her breath, her hands balling into fists; yet she was far from home and the understanding counsel of her parents. Here, in this place, her birth father would not be swayed by her anger or her refusal. No, he would find a way to force her hand.

In that moment, in particular, Yvaine's heart yearned to once more head down to the dungeons and slip out through the secret tunnel. Yet if she were to do so, what then? As far as she knew, Caelen and Fergus —if they had survived as she hoped they had—were on their way back to MacCarmaig land, hoping to appease Caelen's father. And without them, even if she were to find her way back to the coast, it would take too long. Her absence would be noted, and her father would send out Logan and his men, ordering them to return her to the keep. Nay, she would not get far.

With her mind in turmoil, Yvaine slowly made her way downstairs to the great hall, voices echoing in her ears that she barely heard. People were chatting and eating, discussing matters for the coming day as Yvaine walked among them, forcing herself to act the part, to maintain the mask she had worked on so hard these past few weeks. Aye, she did not yet have a plan on how to escape, but she swore that she would. And she knew it would be all the more easier if her father did not look at her with suspicion in his eyes. "Patience," Yvaine murmured to herself again as she crossed the great hall and moved to her family's table, offering her father a kind smile. "Good morning, Father. I hope ye slept well."

A pleased smile touched his features, and he nodded for her to sit. "I did indeed," he remarked, exchanging a meaningful look with Logan, who in turn eyed her with a rather quizzical expression upon his face. "It promises to be a beautiful day, doesna it?"

Yvaine smiled at him and nodded. "Indeed, it does."

Patience.

Chapter Thirty-Three

DISGRACE

Caelen and Fergus rode their horses home with weary steps and heavy hearts, Caelen's thoughts circling around what had happened and what might happen next. Was there any way he could convince his father to spare Yvaine's life? Or would all his words be in vain? After all, had he not already tried and failed?

Again and again, Caelen pictured the moment in his mind, him and Fergus standing before his father, revealing that they had failed in their mission to end Yvaine's life. Of course, his father would be furious and disappointed, undoubtedly inclined to trust Lachlan with his next orders. His uncle would press for it. Only Caelen could not allow that to happen.

Even though, Yvaine was safely back with her family—at least, he hoped she was—there might still be a chance that Lachlan would find his way to her. After all, Caelen doubted that Yvaine would remain safely behind clan walls for the rest of her life. Nay, she had made it unmistakably clear that she intended to return home, and if she did not hear from him, Caelen, if he did not go back soon to take her home himself as he had promised, she would go on her own.

Caelen did not doubt that for a moment. She was not the kind of woman to sit back and wait. She possessed a fierce spirit and more courage than he had ever glimpsed in a lass. Aye, she would use the secret tunnel to leave the MacLeòir keep and then it would be all too easy for Lachlan to get his hands on her. Nay, Caelen could not allow that to happen. No matter his father's decision today, somehow, he needed to find a way to see her safe. If only he knew how.

After what seemed like ages, the two riders arrived on MacCarmaig land and made their way to the keep and the clan chief's chamber. As they entered, Caelen once more spotted his father standing behind his large desk, countless rolls of parchment and maps littering its surface. "Father," Caelen called, striding into the chamber, Fergus only a step behind him. "We needa speak."

Straightening, his father regarded them with a mixture of exasperation and disapproval, as though he could already tell the news they would bring. "Is the lass dead?" he demanded without even a word of greeting, glancing at his brother, who rose from where he sat studying a map, his expression far from pleased, his forehead in an eternal frown.

Having expected no differently, Caelen remained calm, linking his arms behind his back as he held his father's gaze. "Nay, she isna," he replied calmly, holding back words of explanation despite the rapidly hammering pulse in his neck.

His father's gaze thinned, and yet Caelen detected a hint of surprise in his eyes. Indeed, it seemed his father had never truly believed that Caelen would see this task accomplished the way he intended him to do. It was a sobering realization, and yet Caelen reminded himself that he did not wish to be the kind of man his father wanted to see in him. Some lines were not meant to be crossed, and he refused to feel guilty for sparing the life of an innocent.

"Why not?" his father demanded after the silence between them stretched into something deeply uncomfortable.

"Because there is no need," Caelen replied, still holding his father's gaze, not wishing to convey even a touch of uncertainty. "We camped out near the MacLeòirs' keep for weeks, watching and observing. As ye well ken, Father, their walls are impenetrable, and so we knew we had to wait for an opportunity that would see the chief's daughter leave the safety of the keep."

His father nodded, a thoughtful expression on his face. Caelen's uncle, though, regarded him with suspicion, the expression upon his face reminding Caelen of his cousin.

"A few nights past, such an opportunity presented itself," Caelen continued on undeterred, his hands tensing behind his back as he fought to maintain the calm he needed to project. "We came upon her outside the castle walls."

His father leaned forward, eyes fixed upon Caelen's face. "And then? Can ye truly tell me that an arrow could not have seen her dead?" His brows rose in challenge.

"Nay, Father." Caelen swallowed hard then lifted his chin another fraction. "I chose not to end her life." Behind him, he sensed Fergus shift uneasily from one foot onto the other.

"Ye chose?" his uncle suddenly boomed, red darkening his cheeks as he straightened, his narrowed gaze fixed upon Caelen. "Do ye mean to say that ye disobeyed yer father's orders out of yer own free will?"

Caelen stepped forward, not afraid to speak his mind, knowing it to be the right thing. He lifted his chin and looked from his uncle to his father. "Father, I told ye before that I disagreed with yer choice, and so when an alternative presented itself, I—"

"My choice?" his father snapped, and his uncle nodded in agreement. "'Twas an order! I gave ye an order, and ye disobeyed me."

"The reason ye wish to see her dead," Caelen hastened to explain, "is so she canna wed the Morganach chief, isna that so?"

His father exhaled a deep breath then gave a quick nod.

Waiting for the tension in the chamber to ease, Caelen stepped toward his father, seeking his gaze. "I spoke to Yvaine," he said quietly, seeing his father's eyes widen slightly in response. "She didna return to these shores willingly. She didna come to upend our alliance. In fact, she seeks to return home, unwilling to be a pawn in her father's strategic negotiations."

Caelen's uncle frowned as he stepped forward. "Return home?" He shook his head, uncomprehending. "She *is* home; that is the problem."

"Nay, she isna, for she considers the Fey Isles her home."

Caelen's father recoiled in surprise at hearing this whereas his uncle laughed in disbelief. "How is that possible?" the chief breathed, his eyes narrowed as he stared into Caelen's face. "No one lives there. 'Tis an island of the Fey alone."

Caelen sighed, wishing he knew more, wishing he understood what Yvaine truly meant by *home*. "Whether ye believe it or not, Father, the Fey Isles are the place where she dwelled all these years, safe from her family and her father's intentions."

A touch of awe lingered in his father's gaze, and Caelen saw that he wished to ask questions, clearly intrigued by his enemy's daughter and the mystery that surrounded her. Yet he could not because his brother spoke for him. "What she says doesna matter. She is alive, and she is the MacLeòir chief's daughter; thus, she poses a threat to us."

Caelen sighed, wariness lingering on his bones as he shifted his gaze to his uncle. "She gave me her word, Uncle. She has no intention of entering the union intended by her father. If we can only assure that she returns home safely, we will have won without bloodshed."

His uncle looked disbelieving. "Do ye trust the word o' a woman? She'll do as her father commands. Why should ye believe her?"

Caelen did not hesitate. "Because I have no doubt she is sincere in her wish to return home. If we can help her, we will be helping ourselves." Caelen paused, his gaze returning to his father's. "How would ye feel if the MacLeòirs sought to take Gwyneth's life in order to prevent an alliance?"

Caelen watched as his father paused, a flicker of pain and anguish passing through his eyes before he sighed heavily and bowed his head.

Just then, though, the door burst open, and Lachlan strode in, followed by a group of men. He stopped abruptly when his eyes fell on his chief, and he bowed low, his breath coming fast, his features tight with anger. "My laird," he said, bowing his head respectfully, his gaze briefly shifting to his father.

Caelen groaned, cursing his cousin's timing. If only he had had a few more seconds to plead his case, perhaps everything would have turned out all right. Now, though, he could already see doubt clouding his father's gaze like a dense fog.

Nodding to Lachlan in acknowledgment, Caelen's father straightened then rounded the table to stand in front of them. "What have ye to say?" he asked his nephew, meeting Lachlan's eyes.

The sneer upon Lachlan's face told Caelen that all hope was truly lost. "I have come to report that Caelen refused to kill Yvaine and even fought us to ensure her escape."

Lachlan met Caelen's gaze then, a look of mock disappointment upon his face. "It pains me to say so, but it appears as if yer son isna loyal to ye Chief," he said, his voice laced with accusation. "He sides with our enemies."

The room was deathly quiet as everyone stared at Caelen in disbelief. His father's expression had hardened, and his uncle's eyes were stormy with emotion.

Caelen remained stoic in his expression despite the icy lump settling in his throat. He had known this would be a difficult moment to explain away, and he wished it had never come to that. A heavy sigh lifted his shoulders, for he had simply wanted to do what was right and fair and just for Yvaine as well as for his clan without any bloodshed or harm being done. Yet now he found himself in a very precarious situation indeed.

"Is this true?" his father demanded of him, his voice low and dangerous.

Caelen nodded slowly, refusing to look away or back down, his gaze as steady as his father's. "Aye, 'tis true," he replied quietly. "I let her go because I believed 'twas the right thing to do for all of us."

His father's expression darkened further, and he shook his head in disbelief. "The right thing would have been to kill her and spare our clan from any more suffering," he spat out angrily before turning to his nephew. "Lachlan—"

"Do ye never tire of it, Father?" Caelen interrupted, stepping in between his father and Lachlan. "Ye've been fighting this war all yer life." He sighed deeply, ignoring the glare his uncle cast his way. "As have I. From the day I was born, ye taught me that the MacLeòirs were our enemies, and I've hated them on yer behalf ever since." He held his father's gaze then shrugged. "Is it worth it? Why do ye insist on clinging to this hatred? Can we not at least try... to find another way?"

In the back of Caelen's mind, memories stirred of when he had been a lad, barely able to understand the difficulties his father faced every day. He remembered joy and laughter and kindness. He remembered having once been close to his father, and he could not rightly say when that had changed or why. Had his father once been hopeful of ending this feud peacefully? Had he once hoped to find a different solution that did not include bloodshed as Caelen did now?

Indeed, he remembered traces of resignation coming to his father's face over the years, as though with time the burden had become too much to bear. Had life hardened him? Made him unyielding? *If I dunna step carefully*, Caelen wondered in that moment, *will I one day be like him as well? Will I order a life to be taken without even a second thought?*

"There is no other way, Son," his father hissed, his expression hard. "Believe me. This is the way 'tis, the way 'tis always been. I understand that ye're young and dunna yet have the experience to teach ye the consequences of offering a hand in friendship. Yet that is no excuse for what ye have done."

Caelen felt his heart sink as his father stepped toward him, his gaze hard and his lips curled in hatred.

"Ye've disobeyed my orders," his father hissed quietly. "Ye've disobeyed *me*." He shook his head from side to side, his gaze never leaving Caelen's. "I can no longer trust ye."

Those few words felt like a punch to the stomach to Caelen. As often as he had disagreed with his father over the years, he had never before lost his respect or his trust, and the feeling was crippling.

Looking past his son, the chief spoke to Lachlan. "Ye will go after the MacLeòir lass, and ye will kill her the first chance ye get. Is that understood?"

Although having expected it, Caelen gasped in shock at his father's decree but knew better than to argue with him now. All he could do was stand by helplessly as Lachlan bowed again, nodded to his father and then left with his warriors to carry out the chief's orders.

The moment the door closed behind them, Caelen's father turned to face him, staring at him with a disappointed expression that cut deeper than any sword ever could have. "Ye have failed me, Son," he said simply, the anger gone from his eyes, replaced by fatigue. He sighed deeply, and his lips thinned, and his voice was like a growl as he spoke, his gaze shifting between Caelen and Fergus. "Ye've both failed me, failed our clan." He shook his head at them. "I canna let this go unpunished."

Caelen's heart sank, for he knew what was coming, but could do nothing to stop it. His father bellowed, "Guards! Take them to the dungeons until I decide what to do with them!" He then turned to Caelen with a cold look in his eyes. "Rethink yer position," he snarled quietly. "For I will show ye no mercy if ye continue on this path."

Though clearly surprised, the guards dragged them away, their faces grim.

"Mind ye, I didna fancy being right," Fergus murmured, as they were being pushed down the corridor, a dark chuckle rumbling in his throat.

Caelen met his friend's gaze. "I'm sorry for this. I didna—"

"Stop yammering and think of a way out of this," Fergus interrupted as they stumbled down the stairs, the damp air of the dungeons below slowly enveloping them. "I'd rather not die down here."

Caelen nodded, his jaw set. "I'll think of something."

He hoped he would.

Chapter Thirty-Four
TO BE WED

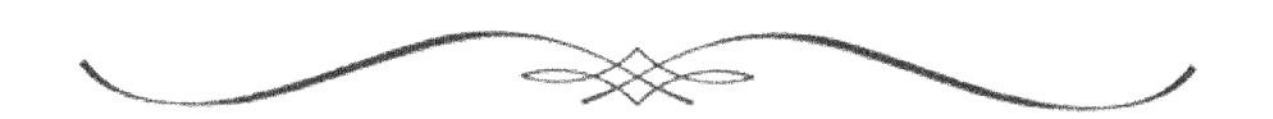

Logan and Yvaine rode quickly out of the castle keep, their horses' hooves pounding the hard earth with a thunderous tempo. Glancing back at the castle, Yvaine wondered why her brother suddenly wished to speak to her alone, for clearly that was what was on his mind this morning, his expression grim and his lips sealed as they rode on side by side.

"What's this about, Brother?" Yvaine asked, savoring the fresh air as well as the breeze that tugged upon her curls. Despite the tension that lingered, simply being outside the castle walls felt invigorating. "Why did ye not want Rory to accompany us?"

Logan cleared his throat and cast a sideways glance at her. Indeed, he hardly seemed able to meet her eyes; he acted quite unlike the fierce older brother, who had never shown any degree of fear or uncertainty in Yvaine's presence. "I needa speak with ye," he finally replied, his voice gruff, as though he wished he could simply drop the subject.

Frowning at her brother, Yvaine wondered what had happened. After all, she had not been allowed out of the castle in weeks. Her father had all but locked her away ever since she had brought down that stag with her brother's bow and arrow, hoping if he forced her into more ladylike pursuits, she would eventually become the model daughter he hoped to see in her.

Yvaine knew there was no hope of that ever happening; yet at least, for now, it was safer for her to allow him to believe so.

Annoyed with her brother's taciturn way, Yvaine kicked her horse's flanks, urging her mare into a gallop. "Verra well, if ye insist to be like that." She grinned at him over her shoulder and then charged down the field.

The breeze whipped through Yvaine's hair, and a feeling of freedom coursed through her veins. She was happy to be out of the keep for the first time in weeks, unwilling to allow Logan to spoil this unexpected moment of fun.

The sound of thundering hoof beats drew closer, and Yvaine looked over her shoulder to see her brother charging after her, his red hair gleaming in the sun. His face still bore a grim expression, and yet Yvaine thought to see something almost resembling joy sparking in his eyes. As serious as he often seemed, deep down, Logan was a man who enjoyed adventure.

Their horses surged forward, galloping across the field, their manes and tails streaming in the wind as if they too were caught up in the excitement of the moment. Yvaine laughed as she urged her mare on, enjoying the wild ride.

Finally, they slowed to a canter as they entered a small wooded area, its trees reaching up toward the sky like outstretched arms. A few birds sang sweetly from high up in the branches, and Yvaine breathed in deeply the scent of pine needles and fresh earth.

Pulling alongside her, Logan slowed his horse to a trot, a wide smile upon his face and mirth gleaming in his eyes. "That was quite a ride" he said with a laugh.

Yvaine grinned back at him and nodded in agreement, feeling lighter than she had in weeks. They rode on like that for some time until Logan pulled his horse to a stop. He dismounted before offering to help Yvaine down from hers.

"There's no need," she said, waving him away. "I can do it myself." In one fluid motion, Yvaine swung her legs to the side and jumped to the ground.

Logan eyed her with interest. "Ye're an unusual woman," he remarked as he had before, weeks ago. Then, he had spoken with warning; now, his voice rang with acceptance. "May I?" he asked, offering her his arm. "Or will ye slap it away?"

Yvaine chuckled. "Dunna worry. I bark but I dunna bite... often." Logan laughed as she accepted his arm, and together, they walked toward the edge of the trees.

"We have much to discuss," Logan remarked then, his gaze trained upon the MacLeòir keep in the distance.

"Do we?" She looked up at him, seeing a muscle twitch in his jaw. "Whatever it is, ye're clearly bothered by it. Tell me then." Despite her brave words, Yvaine felt a shiver snake down her back. Could this be about the match her father sought to arrange for her? The match to the Morganach chief?

Logan sighed then turned and met her eyes. "Father wishes for you to be wed." Though discomfort lingered in his gaze, he did not avert his eyes.

Yvaine sighed, trying her utmost to ignore that icy shiver crawling across her skin. "To the Morganach chief," she said with a nod of affirmation.

Surprise marked Logan's face, and his eyes slightly narrowed as he squinted at her. "How do ye ken?"

Yvaine rather liked that she had caught him off guard, that he had not even suspected she knew. "I have my ways," she told him with a brief chuckle, wanting the kindness she saw in his eyes instead of the hard determination that rang in his voice.

A small smile flitted across Logan's face. "I see," he murmured, his gaze watchful as it searched her face. "And?"

"And what?" Yvaine retorted, knowing precisely what it was he wanted to know.

"Are ye amenable?" He cleared his throat, a touch of discomfort once more in his gaze.

Yvaine scoffed. "Of course, I am not amenable," she snapped, annoyed by his question. "How can ye ask me that? Are ye truly suggesting I marry him?"

Logan frowned. "'Tis a good union," he pointed out matter-offactly. "'Twill result in a beneficial alliance for our clan. Why would I not advice ye to accept him?"

Yvaine heaved a deep sigh because for a brief moment she had forgotten that she was not at home, on MacKinnear Island. Here, things were different. Here, nothing mattered more than strengthening one's clan's standing by gaining alliances. "I willna marry," Yvaine stated, her eyes holding her brother's. "Ye can save yer breath, Brother. I willna marry a stranger. I willna marry a man Father chooses for me simply because he's the chief of another clan." Slowly, she shook her head. "I have done everything within my power to do as he wishes; yet this is something I simply canna agree to."

Deep down, Yvaine knew that she was making a mistake. At the very least, she ought to play along until another opportunity might arise for her to slip away unseen. Yet somehow, there was a part of her that needed to speak truthfully in this moment not because she wanted to make a stand, but simply because Logan was her brother and... she had come to care for him, to respect him even. He was a good man, and if it were not for their father, Yvaine felt certain he would understand.

Logan closed his eyes and shook his head. "Father willna accept that," he murmured, looking back at her. "Ye ken he will be furious."

Yvaine nodded. "Aye, I do." Sighing deeply, she leaned her head against her brother's shoulder, ignoring the way he cleared his throat uncomfortably, clearly surprised by this gesture of affection.

"Why this need for an alliance?" Yvaine murmured as the birds chirped around them and the wind rustled through the leaves. "What happened? How did this feud even start?" She looked up at her brother.

Logan shrugged. "'Tis simply always been a part of life," he murmured, his gaze distant as though he were no longer aware of her presence. "We dunna like the MacCarmaigs, and MacCarmaigs dunna like us."

Yvaine scoffed. "This is not about liking someone or not," she pointed out. "Ye're at war with one another. Surely, ye must ken why."

She grasped Logan's arm until he met her eyes. "Do ye honestly tell me ye dunna ken?"

Logan's lips thinned. "I've asked Father many times," he admitted, anger in his gaze, regret as well as helplessness. Then he hung his head. "Aye, ye're right. I dunna ken."

Yvaine sighed.

"'Tis been this way for many years," Logan continued, his voice heavy with sadness. "The two clans have been at odds since before either of us were born. There have been skirmishes, stealing cattle, interference in treaties, destruction of crops, 'tis never ending." He shook his head.

"Have there ever been any attempts at peace?" Yvaine asked softly, her heart heavy to hear the story of her clan laid out like this. "Has anyone ever tried to bridge the gap between the two clans? To find a way for them to live peacefully side by side?"

Logan shook his head sadly. "Nay," he said quietly. "Not that I know of." He looked into Yvaine's eyes. "I'm sorry."

Yvaine nodded and squeezed her brother's arm reassuringly before stepping away from him and looking out over the landscape once more. She was silent for a long moment as she processed all that had been said, then she finally spoke again: "We must do something," she said firmly, turning back to look at Logan with determination in her eyes. "We canna let this feud continue on forever; it has gone on too long already. We must find a way to bring peace—no matter what it takes."

Logan looked at Yvaine for a long moment before finally speaking. "Ye seem verra dedicated to this cause," he said, his voice filled with admiration. He placed one of his large hands upon her shoulder, giving it an affectionate squeeze. "I am glad to have ye back home."

Yvaine averted her gaze, touched by his words and yet filled with guilt over her own desire to return home to her true family.

Clearly, the expression upon her face had not escaped Logan, for he remarked in a soft tone, "Ye're not, though, are ye?"

Yvaine stepped back, and Logan's hand slid from her shoulder. Turning away, she walked a few steps then stopped, her gaze lifting to the far horizon.

"Where were ye?" Logan asked gently from behind her, the soft sound of his footfalls announcing his approach. "What happened to ye while ye were away?"

Yvaine sighed heavily before turning back to look him in the eyes. "There are some things I canna share," she said quietly, her voice thick with emotion. "But I… I canna stay. This isna my place, my…" She broke off before she could say something unwise. After all, Logan would not understand, how could he?

Regret and sadness gathered in Logan's eyes, and for the first time, Yvaine thought of him as a brother. Not simply the brother who shared her blood, but the brother who knew her and cared about her. "Ye ken Father willna let ye go," he murmured softly, his voice once again ringing with warning.

Yvaine nodded. "I ken." She searched his gaze. "Will ye help me?"

Closing his eyes, Logan hung his head. "Ye ask the impossible," he muttered, anger mingling with frustration as he spoke. "Yer return," he lifted his gaze to meet hers, "has been a blessing to our clan. How can I—?"

"Because of the union Father intends to force on me, is that not so?" Yvaine retorted, crossing her arms over her chest. "This is all I am to ye, a bargaining chip." She took a step back, aware that her words were unfair, that not unlike herself Logan, too, was trapped in this life, his choices not his own.

Running a frustrated hand through his fiery red hair—so much like her own—Logan stared at her. "What is it ye wish for me to do, Yvaine? Even though ye've been gone so many years, ye ken by now the precarious situation we find ourselves in. Without a union with Clan Morganach, we are weakened. How can I weigh yer happiness against the safety of all of our people?" He shook his head sadly. "I'm sorry. I canna."

Heaving a deep sigh, Yvaine nodded; after all, she did understand, for her thoughts drifted back to the legends she had been told ever since she could remember.

In a time of need and a time of war, Yvaine and Caelen had found one another and while their love had not ended the feud, it had saved both their clans. Together, they had begun again and found a new home on the Fey Isles just off the coast.

Am I selfish for wanting to return home? Yvaine thought for the hundredth time, her heart torn in two. *How can I when it would condemn two clans to continued warfare?* Perhaps she ought to stay after all, at least for a while, at least until the legend came true, at least until...

Nay, she could not wait, for if she did, she would lose her heart to Caelen. Despite the many gaps in the stories of old, that much was clear. Now even more than before, Yvaine knew it to be true. She knew what she had felt every time their paths had crossed. She knew what she had felt that night Caelen had kissed her, when he had risked his life for her, when he had promised to return. Aye, if she stayed, if she did not leave now, soon, she might not want to anymore. And what then? Would she never see her family again? Her parents and her brothers? Her home?

Tears gathered in Yvaine's eyes, and a deep sorrow swept through her heart, making her ache and long for the tight embrace of someone who loved her. If only her mother were here. Or her grandmother. They would know what to say. They would know how to lift her spirits and soothe her heart.

Bowing her head to hide her tears, Yvaine was about to turn away when Logan was suddenly there, his arms enveloping her tightly. He rested his chin on the top of her head, a deep sigh leaving his lungs, one that spoke of the same hopelessness Yvaine felt in that moment. "I'll speak to Father," he murmured as Yvaine wrapped her arms around his middle, hugging him back.

"Thank ye," Yvaine whispered despite knowing that nothing he did would change anything. Still, it felt good to have someone close who cared.

Chapter Thirty-Five

A BRAVE HEART

The air in the dungeon was oppressive and stale, and Caelen was beginning to feel the weight of it pressing down on him. He had been in this cell for two days now, ever since his father had him and Fergus brought down here the day of their return. He had expected his father to act quickly to punish him, but instead, he seemed content to let them stew in their own frustrations.

Beside him, Fergus paced anxiously, his heavy footsteps echoing through the damp dungeon, clanging off the walls with a dull thud. They had gone over and over the possibilities of escape, but none of them seemed viable, each one flawed in some way.

"What do ye think will happen to us?" Fergus asked as his hands clenched and unclenched as if seeking something tangible to hold onto for comfort.

Caelen shook his head. "I dunna ken. My father is taking his time, and I'm sure 'tis because he wants to break us, to teach us a lesson." He sighed deeply, certain his uncle had had a say in the matter as well. Once, Caelen had been certain that his father would never harm him, yet things had changed lately. He had seen the fear in his father's eyes as well as a frightening rage as though after all these years he had gotten lost in his hatred for the MacLeòirs and now knew no greater achievement than to strike out against them... even if it meant harming his own son.

Fergus stopped pacing and leaned against the wall. "What do ye think will happen to Yvaine if we canna escape?"

Oh, Caelen had thought about Yvaine at great length. Whenever his thoughts had not been on any means of escape these past two days, they had lingered upon the redhaired lass. "If we fail, she will be forced to marry the chief of Clan Morganach." Despair filled Caelen's heart at the thought, and yet a part of him wondered if Yvaine might not find a way around her father's wishes after all. Indeed, the lass was fierce and headstrong and resourceful. Caelen smiled as he remembered the steely flash of her green eyes. Aye, she was a brave one, and there was no saying what she might do.

Silence fell over their cell as they both contemplated the future that awaited them, each one lost in thought as the day wore on, moments ticking by. The guard sat down the corridor, his feet propped up and his eyes closed, loud snores echoing off the dungeon walls. Caelen and Fergus both knew the man and had done their utmost to sway him into letting them go; however, the guard had remained loyal to his chief—another hope dashed.

At sundown—at least, Caelen supposed it was sundown—they heard footsteps echoing down to them and then saw another guard descend the steps, a mug in his hand. His expression was grim, and he yawned widely, scratching his chin. Approaching the sleeping guard, he called out then kicked the man's feet off the stool, making him jump up. "Ye can go," he growled with a nod toward the stairs. "I'll take over."

The other guard rubbed his eyes and then hurried away.

Caelen sighed, leaning back against the wall beside Fergus. "Perhaps I oughta ask to speak to my father," he remarked, growing impatient with this immobility, this waiting with no end in sight. "Now, that Lachlan is gone, perhaps he will listen."

Fergus shrugged. "Perhaps." He paused and looked at Caelen. "By now, Lachlan's probably already back on MacLeòir land." His gaze was overshadowed by concern.

"Aye." Caelen ran a hand through his hair, then he pushed off the wall and resumed Fergus's pacing, frustration clawing at him. "As long as she remains behind castle walls, she should be safe." He looked up at Fergus, wanting nothing more than for his friend to confirm his reasoning.

Dutifully, Fergus nodded. "Fortunately, Lachlan doesna know about the secret tunnel."

Indeed, Caelen was grateful for that; however, he could not help but worry that his cousin might accidentally stumble upon it. And then what? No, they could not wait. Somehow, they had to find a way out of here.

Caelen looked up and toward the guard. The man moved up and down the corridor, his steps slowly becoming uneven, his boots scraping across the stone floor as though he no longer possessed the power to lift his feet. "Are ye well?" Caelen asked the man, stepping up to the bars in the door and looking out.

To Caelen's surprise, the man began to sway and stumble, his gaze narrowed as he stared down at the mug in his hand. "What…?" He blinked his eyes rapidly a few times before they closed and remained so. His knees gave out then, and the man collapsed on the ground, his mug shattering on impact, coating the stone floor in a brown liquid.

"What's happened?" Fergus inquired a moment before he stepped up to stand beside Caelen, peering out between the bars and into the corridor. "Did he fall ill?"

Staring at the guard, Caelen frowned before his gaze drifted to the shattered mug. "No, it almost seems as if…" He broke off the moment another sound drifted to his ears: soft footfalls echoing down the stairs.

Stunned beyond belief, Caelen stared at Gwyneth as she appeared at the foot of the stairs. Her eyes were wide as she stared at the guard lying motionless in front of her. For a moment, she did not move; then, however, quick steps carried her forward, determination shining in her eyes. She kneeled down by the guard's side and quickly unlatched the key from his belt, her nose slightly scrunched as though she smelled something foul. Then she was back on her feet and walked quickly toward their cell, her hands clutching the key so tightly that her knuckles had turned white.

"Gwyneth?" Caelen gasped, thinking himself lost in a dream. Up until now, he had been utterly certain that his timid little sister would never even have dreamed of daring something like this. Yet no matter how often he blinked his eyes, she still stood before him, her small frame silhouetted against the torchlight. "What are ye doing?"

Despite the trembling in her hands, Gwyneth gave him a rather exasperated look. "Getting ye out of here." She fumbled with the key then thrust it into the lock. A moment later, the door sprang open, allowing them out into the corridor. "Quickly. We dunna have much time," she said, her eyes wide with fear before she looked over her shoulder toward the stairs, clearly afraid that they might be discovered at any moment.

Glancing at his friend, Caelen saw an equally shocked expression upon Fergus's face as he stared at Gwyneth. Yet there was something else in his friend's eyes as well, something Caelen had seen upon occasion, something Fergus usually knew how to hide.

Still taken aback, Caelen grasped his sister's hands, his eyes seeking hers. "What about ye?" he demanded in a gruff tone, angrier with himself than her, worried what she was risking for them. "What if Father learns that 'twas ye who freed us?" Indeed, the thought brought him physical pain. "Come with us." His hands tightened upon his sister's, his gaze imploring.

Gwyneth shook her head. "I canna go against Father's wishes," she said, tears collecting in her eyes.

"Yet ye are here," Caelen pointed out.

A helpless chuckle fell from Gwyneth's lips. "I canna bear the thought of ye down here." Her hands tightened on his. "I couldna simply stand by." Her gaze held his for a long moment before her eyes darted sideways, and Caelen knew that they lingered upon Fergus for a heartbeat or two.

"Ye're braver than I thought, little sister," Caelen told her with a smile, wondering if she knew what she was doing, if she knew the consequences that awaited her should he be able to keep his word to Yvaine.

Shyly, Gwyneth averted her eyes, a faint blush coloring her cheeks. "Ye needa go now. I shall help ye as much as I can and distract the guards at the gate. Please, be careful." She hugged him tightly, her arms almost squeezing the air from his lungs. "Please, be safe. Whatever ye do, be safe." A moment later, she surged out of his arms, grasped his hand and tugged him toward the stairs. "Hurry! We mustna linger."

Fergus looked grim as they followed Gwyneth up the stairs, and Caelen wondered what thoughts were currently going through his friend's head. Indeed, his gaze was fixed upon Gwyneth while her gaze darted to him time and time again, yet never dared linger.

"Let me go ahead," Caelen murmured as they neared the stop of the stairs. He grasped Gwyneth's arm, halting her steps, and then he moved past her.

Fortunately, the corridor lay deserted, but the faint murmur of voices drifted to their ears from somewhere nearby.

"We must be quick," Gwyneth whispered from behind him, her gaze searching the shadows for any sign of danger.

Caelen nodded and then spotted a corner where their weapons had been stored. He retrieved them quickly, relieved to feel the familiar weight of his sword once more. As he turned to hand Fergus his own blade, Caelen stilled when he saw his friend pull Gwyneth into his arms. For a heartbeat, Gwyneth looked startled, yet the moment Fergus's lips claimed hers, she melted into his embrace.

Stunned, Caelen simply stood there; then his friend released Gwyneth and stepped away from her, saying something in a low voice that Caelen could not quite make out. Yet whatever it was seemed to have been enough for Gwyneth nodded slowly before turning away from him, her blush deepening.

Without another word, they hurried onward. Fortunately, the courtyard lay equally deserted—with its shrubs and trees, it was a far cry from their cold stone prison cell below ground. Caelen spotted no additional guards, only the sentries up upon the wall. Clearly, his father did not expect them to escape, and thus, they reached the gate without incident.

The guards there were not especially alert, as most were involved in conversations amongst themselves or playing games of chance with no hint that something was amiss in their midst.

"Wait here," Gwyneth murmured and then before Caelen could

stop her, she approached the guards, her steps sure and graceful. A smile lit up her features as she began chatting about the weather and the latest gossip from court, voicing her admiration for the guards' diligence to their duty. The men smiled, their chests puffing out with self-importance, when Gwyneth's eyes suddenly rolled backward, and she slumped to the ground.

Caelen froze while Fergus made to rush to Gwyneth's side. In the last instant, though, Caelen managed to hold him back, shaking his head. "She's only pretending," he whispered. "Let them tend to her."

Sure enough, the guards quickly rushed to Gwyneth's side, their expressions filled with worry as they tried to revive her.

Caelen watched in amazement as Gwyneth stirred and then sat up, her gaze still unfocused. The guards hovered around her, asking if she was all right while Gwyneth thanked them for their help and apologized for causing them such a fright.

The men were clearly relieved by her recovery and offered to escort her back inside the keep. Gwyneth politely accepted their offer and soon she was walking away from them, the guards steadying her, watchful at her sides.

"'Tis our chance," Caelen murmured, tugging on Fergus's arm. Over his shoulder, he saw Gwyneth give them both one last, longing look before she disappeared back into the darkness of the castle.

For a moment, Caelen and Fergus simply stood there in stunned silence. Then, with a renewed sense of purpose, they made their way out into the night.

Chapter Thirty-Six

WHERE WE BELONG

Yvaine waited outside the door to her father's chamber, feeling her heart beat faster in her chest. Why on earth had he summoned her? This did not bode well. Yvaine was certain of it, fearing that whatever her father wished to share with her related to his efforts of forming a union with Clan Morganach. As she stepped inside, the look of determination on his face was one that Yvaine knew well; yet what truly sent a shiver of unease down her back was that hint of a smile that lingered upon his face. It spoke of success, of triumph as though he had just returned victorious from battle, acting modest about his heroic deeds.

Yvaine felt her heart sink as she heard her father's voice from the other side of the chamber. "Come closer." He gestured for her to approach, regarding her with a stern expression; yet that hint of a smile remained. Aye, it was deeply unsettling.

The chamber was sparsely decorated. A simple wooden table and chairs, a few sturdy chests, and a large hearth. Her father stood in the center of the room, and Yvaine could feel the weight of his gaze upon her.

"Daughter, I have something to discuss with ye," he stated in his booming voice, waving her forward.

Yvaine stood tall, determined not to show her dismay. Truth be told, she had expected something like this after Logan had informed her of their father's intention to see her wed. She had known that sooner or later—probably sooner—she would find herself in this situation, facing her father about a matter that would never see them in agreement.

"Aye, Father, what is it?" she inquired in a calm voice despite the nervous tingles that chased across her skin.

Her father cleared his throat and paced the room. Then he stopped and looked at her, his gaze hard and unrelenting, making it perfectly clear that whatever he wished to share with her was not a request but an order instead. "I have all but secured a match for ye," he said finally, and that hint of a smile upon his face stretched wider, becoming more pleased with every moment that passed. "'Tis the chief of Clan Morganach, a powerful and wealthy clan." He sighed as though a long battle lay behind him and he had finally come out the victor. "A union between the two of ye was agreed upon years ago. Then, however, ye disappeared." He spoke as though it had been her fault, as though he blamed her for the audacity to have thwarted his plans at only three years old.

Yvaine wrung her hands, struggling to maintain her composure.

"Those were dark times for our clan," her father continued, his gaze strangely distant, as though for once his thoughts did not dwell upon himself. "Of course, the MacCarmaigs seized the opportunity instantly." He scoffed, a dark sound drawn from his throat. "Within months, their chief had arranged for his own daughter to wed the Morganach heir instead of ye." He shook his head, his lips pressed together tightly. "Aye, those were dark times." He blinked, and his gaze found Yvaine's once more. "Only now ye have returned, and 'tis perfect timing no less. The new chief of Clan Morganach was to wed the MacCarmaig lass in only a few months' time; however, they are not married yet." Rubbing his hands, he chuckled, clearly delighted, clearly pleased with what Fate had offered him this time around. "Of course, I wasted no time in renewing negotiations with the Morganach."

Yvaine's stomach twisted and her heart pounded in her chest. She was certain that her hatred and outrage were plain on her face; yet she remained calm and composed and her father gave no indication that he suspected her inner turmoil.

"Negotiations are still ongoing," he continued undeterred. "However, I have no doubt that ye shall be wed soon." He clapped his hands together and for the first time fully met her gaze. "Is this not joyous news?"

Despite his words, threats rested in his gaze, and Yvaine knew well that there was only one answer that would satisfy her father, one answer that would keep her safe... at least for now. And thus, she respectfully inclined her head, forcing a submissive expression upon her face and said, "Aye, they are. 'Tis an honor, Father. Thank ye."

Her father nodded graciously, and Yvaine breathed a sigh of relief that he remained oblivious to her inner thoughts. "I expect ye to fulfill yer duty to the clan and make the Morganach chief a good wife." He gave her a stern expression, no doubt remembering the many occasions since her return when Yvaine had spoken out against him, forcefully rejecting his orders, his opinions, his demands.

More than anything, Yvaine wished to speak out, wished to answer that challenge the only way she knew how. Yet if she did so, he might lock her up right away to ensure her compliance in this matter. Nay, she needed to remain free to go where and when she pleased. There was no telling how soon—if at all—Caelen might return. And if he did, she needed to be ready, she could not be locked in her chamber, a guard posted outside her door.

And so, Yvaine held her tongue, and it was the hardest thing she had ever done. She inclined her head as before, a sign of submission, as her mind raced.

Of course, she had to get away from the keep, away from her father's plans for her. Yet at present, Yvaine did not quite know how to go about it. Aye, she knew a way out of the castle, but what then? Alone and on foot, she would not get far, and then she would have wasted her only chance.

Taking a deep breath, Yvaine stepped out of her father's chamber, her mind already turning to a possible escape plan. As she made her way down the stairs, across the courtyard and toward the old dungeons, she thought of Caelen, hoping that he was well and that he would keep his word. Even though Caelen had proved himself to be a man of his word, Yvaine knew that there were other reasons—reasons outside of his control—that might prevent him from keeping his promise to her. After all, Caelen and Fergus had been gone for at least a fortnight, and Yvaine worried what might have happened to them upon returning to their home keep. Had Caelen's cousin Lachlan been able to sway the MacCarmaig chief in his favor? Was it possible that Caelen and his friend were now locked up somewhere, traitors to their own clan?

"Have faith," Yvaine murmured under her breath, reminding herself that no good ever came from worrying. The best she could do was to prepare for Caelen's return, knowing that when he did, he would no doubt approach the keep through the secret tunnel. After all, it was the only way in for him.

As Yvaine made her way down to the dungeon, though, she heard a noise behind her, like someone shuffling his feet. With her heart thundering in her chest, she spun around, only to spot Rory, standing in the shadows, a deeply disappointed look on his young face.

Yvaine hung her head. She had been so focused on pleasing her father that she had all but forgotten about the tender bond that had formed between her and Rory. Together, they had discovered the secret tunnel down in the dungeons. Together, they had made plans to explore it further. However, the night Yvaine had almost escaped with Caelen, she had known that she could not allow Rory down there. She could not allow him to discover what had almost happened and what she was planning. And so, she had lied to him when he had found her the next day, excited to go on this adventure.

"Rory, ye gave me a fright," she exclaimed, her voice trembling. "I didna see ye there."

Rory stepped forward, his expression serious. "What are ye doing here, Yvaine?" he asked, the sound of betrayal etched into his voice. "Ye said we couldna explore the tunnel. Ye said 'twould be too dangerous, that if anyone ever found out, 'twould be a weakness, a danger to our clan." He stared at her, his usually so cheerful eyes narrowed, and shook his head. "Then why are ye here now?" His frown deepened. "Did ye lie to me?"

Yvaine's lips parted and her mouth dropped open, her heart crying out in that moment, her mind urging her to reassure him. Yet if she lied to him now...

Heaving a deep sigh, Yvaine sat down on one of the stone steps leading down into the dungeon. She looked up at Rory and patted the spot beside her. "Come. Sit with me." She scooted to the edge to make room for him.

"Ye seemed so busy lately," Rory murmured as he sat down beside her, pulling up his legs and wrapping his arms around them. He barely glanced at her, and yet Yvaine could see that he was hurt. "I thought we wanted to do things together."

"I ken," Yvaine replied, sadness weighing upon her shoulders. "I'm sorry. 'Tis simply that..." She groped for words, trying to think of some way to explain without lying.

"Ye dunna remember us, do ye?" Rory asked unexpectedly, his eyes looking directly at her. "I dunna mean me, of course. I wasna born when ye disappeared, but..." He trailed off but the look in his eyes explained precisely what he wished to say.

"I dunna," Yvaine admitted, suddenly feeling far more at ease than she would have expected. "I have come to care about ye, though." She cast him a small smile. "Ye in particular, Rory. 'Tis the truth. Believe me."

He nodded, an answering smile gracing his features. "I do ken." His gaze searched hers, asking.

Yvaine sighed. "I canna tell ye everything, but what is important is that I was happy where I was. I had people there who loved me, who I thought of as family, whom I still think of as family today." She gently took Rory's hand. "I miss them, and I wish to return to them. Can ye understand that?"

Rory nodded, his eyes overshadowed by sadness and a rather grown-up notion of knowing that despite one's own wishes some things could not be prevented. "I knew ye would never wed the Morganach chief."

Yvaine stared at her little brother. "How do ye ken about that? Father only just told me moments ago."

Rory grinned at her. "I ken how to listen at doors," he remarked not at all sheepishly.

Yvaine laughed, delighted with Rory's honesty and his sneakiness as well. "I dunna believe it." She paused and held his gaze. "But I must admit I'm proud of ye."

Rory chuckled. "Dunna pretend ye didna ken before Father told ye," he said, once more searching her gaze. "Ye knew, did ye not? How?"

"Perhaps I, too, ken how to listen at doors." She tousled Rory's hair then sighed. "Logan told me about Father's intentions. Yet... he also said he wouldna be able to help me." She sighed, not wishing for Rory to feel torn. "I do understand why he canna. He is loyal to our father and our people, and that is good. Still, I canna remain here, and I hope that ye can understand that."

After a long heavy sigh, Rory nodded. "I will miss ye. When are ye leaving?"

Yvaine shrugged. "I dunna ken yet. If I simply walk out on foot, Father will no doubt catch up to me rather quickly. I need a plan, and I... dunna have one yet."

Rory eyed her curiously. "There's something ye're not telling me, is there?" he frowned, and for a moment, his gaze became distant. "Is it that man? The one I saw ye with down in the gardens the night of the feast?"

Stunned, Yvaine stared at her brother. "Ye saw us? How? Where were ye?"

"I was up in my chamber, and I saw shadows move down below. Then I heard voices. I knew 'twas ye, but I wasna certain who ye were speaking to." He held her gaze, questioning. "He's not of our clan, is he?"

Yvaine shook her head.

"Can ye trust him?"

To her own surprise, Yvaine nodded without a moment of hesitation.

"Is he waiting for ye out there?" Rory inquired, nodding toward the dungeons and the secret tunnel that lay hidden there.

"Not right now," Yvaine admitted with a deep sigh. "But I hope he will come for me. Only I dunna ken when... or if at all."

Rory squeezed her hand. "Dunna worry. He will come." He smiled at her in that deeply endearing way of his. "If ye truly trust him, then he must be a good man."

Yvaine gave him a hug. "Thank ye," she whispered, feeling lighter than she had in a long time. "For understanding. For everything. Rory, ye're wonderful, and I shall miss ye dearly."

Rory nodded, and the two of them rose from the stone steps and stood in silence for a few moments. Then he stepped back and gave her a lopsided smile. "Go on then," he said. "Do what ye were going to do, and I shall keep watch."

Yvaine hugged him once again, wishing in that moment that she could simply take Rory home with her. Of course, the thought was ludicrous, and she quickly shoved it away as she hurried down the stairs and into the dungeon.

Chapter Thirty-Seven
THROUGH THE TUNNEL

Caelen and Fergus made their way through the outskirts of a nearby village, their steps kicking up the dust beneath their feet. The air was heavy with the cloying scent of baked earth and the oppressive heat of a late summer's day. Caelen felt sweat dripping down his back beneath his shirt, and he wiped his arm across his forehead.

"Where do ye think he is?" Fergus asked, snapping Caelen from his thoughts.

"Lachlan?" Caelen replied, his voice heavy with concern. "I dunna ken. No doubt he is at the MacLeòir keep already; yet I pray that he hasna found some other way to snatch Yvaine from the safe grasp of her family."

Fergus nodded, his lips pressed into a thin line. Neither of them spoke as they continued on their way, the only sound the song of the birds in the trees and the occasional whinny from a horse in the distance.

The sun was setting, casting an orange hue over the village they spotted at the foot of a small hill. "We need horses," Fergus remarked, glancing at Caelen. "Yet with no coin..."

Caelen grinned at his friend, lifting a small purse that hung on a string around his neck. "Gwyneth gave me this as we left. 'Tis not much, but it'll do."

Fergus smiled, his gaze distant, and Caelen guessed his friend was reliving the farewell kiss he had shared with Gwyneth. "Aye, she's a fine woman," he murmured, then he cleared his throat, abruptly realizing that Caelen was grinning at him. "What?" he demanded, a touch of red coming to his cheeks.

Caelen laughed then shook his head. "Have ye ever told her how ye feel?"

Fergus shook his head, his gaze fixed upon the tips of his dusty boots.

"That kiss might have given ye away, though," he teased, wanting for once not to worry. It had been a long time since they had laughed.

Fergus grinned at him, running a hand through his sweat-soaked hair, an expression of utter discomfort upon his face. "Aye, I suppose she kens now."

Caelen elbowed his friend playfully. "She cares for ye as well. Ye ken that, do ye not?"

Fergus stared at him, a slow breath leaving his lungs. "I... hoped."

"Why did ye never say anything?"

Fergus shrugged, the joyous expression vanishing from his face. "She has been betrothed since the day she was born," he remarked dryly then looked up at Caelen. "What would've been the point?" he looked back over his shoulder, as though he could glimpse Gwyneth in the distance. "It would've hurt her. She feels bound to do her duty. Nothing and no one will ever convince her to go against yer father's wishes."

Sighing heavily, Caelen nodded. He grasped his friend's shoulder, giving it a comforting squeeze. "I'm sorry, my friend. Ye deserve better. Ye both do."

There was nothing more to be said, and so the two of them simply continued on, their eyes now fixed upon the village at the bottom of the hill. They passed by small shacks and cottages, the smell of woodsmoke in the air, and then approached a larger homestead with horses grazing nearby.

Caelen and Fergus exchanged a look then walked over to the owner of the property. He was an older man with white hair and a kind face, and he listened as they explained their situation.

"Aye, I have two fine horses that might suit ye." The old man gestured for them to follow him into the barn.

As they entered, Caelen saw two horses that immediately caught his eye—a chestnut mare with a white star on her forehead and a dappled gray gelding with white socks. They were both strong animals with gentle eyes, healthy and up for a hard ride.

After paying the old man, Fergus and Caelen mounted their horses and galloped out of the village. The sun was setting, and the sky was turning purple. They rode in silence for some time, the only sound being the clop of their horses' hooves against the rocky terrain.

Caelen was deep in thought, contemplating what they would do once they reached MacLeòir land. In the end, it all depended on whether Lachlan had already found the entrance to the secret tunnel. If he had, would he truly sneak inside to find Yvaine? Or would he rather return to Caelen's father and share this news with him? Indeed, knowledge of such a tunnel would surely turn the tide in their feud, giving the MacCarmaigs the upper hand should they ever decide to attack.

Still, before Caelen could settle on a course of action, he needed to know where Lachlan was and what his intentions were. If there was no danger of his cousin discovering the secret entrance, Caelen himself could seek it out and try to find Yvaine. *Am I truly thinking of entering an enemy castle? Again?* He wondered. *If I'm caught...*

Caelen pushed these thoughts firmly away.

Three days after their departure from MacCarmaig land, the sun was making its descent when they finally spotted the MacLeòir keep in the distance.

The rolling hills ahead of them were dotted with patches of wildflowers, and the sky above streaked with fading touches of pink and orange. Caelen and Fergus paused for a moment, their eyes sweeping over the landscape.

"We should split up and search the surrounding area," Caelen said. "Ye take the west, and I'll take the east. But be careful. Dunna confront Lachlan. He mustna see ye or all will be lost."

Fergus nodded, and without another word, they parted ways.

Caelen rode on in silence, his mind alert and his eyes watchful. He combed the area carefully and was about to turn back when he spotted a campfire in the distance. Pulling his horse to a halt, he dismounted and tied the animal to a tree, carefully hiding it from sight. Then he crouched low, peering through the shadows as he tried to make out the figures around the fire.

As he crept closer, he heard voices, low and gravelly, speaking in hushed tones, and he froze when he recognized his cousin's. "Any suggestions?" Lachlan barked, his voice hard and full of frustration.

Hearing it, Caelen felt a thrill of satisfaction and a wave of relief. At least, he thought, his cousin had not yet found the secret tunnel. If so, he surely would not sound so surly.

Hidden in the shadows, Caelen listened as his cousin and his men continued to discuss strategies. Yet what he heard posed no threat to Yvaine, and so he silently crept away from the camp and regrouped with Fergus, relieved to find that his friend had not come across any of Lachlan's men. They retrieved their horses and then made their way to the secret tunnel, both of them wary of being caught.

Once inside the tunnel, the darkness enveloped them, and Caelen felt his heart pounding in his chest. "Do we have a plan?" came Fergus's concerned voice in the dark. "More precisely a plan that doesna involve capture?" His tense chuckle echoed off the walls around them.

"I ken 'tis not a good idea to enter the keep, Fergus," Caelen said, his voice a mere whisper in the darkness. "But I gave her my word, and I canna go back on it. I must find a way to get her safely back to the Fey Isle." In his mind, Caelen added, *Even if I never see her again, she will at least be alive and well.*

Fergus was silent for a moment. Then he chuckled, the sound clearly meant to break the tension. "So, what ye're saying is that there is no plan," he remarked dryly. "We are to go in there and then...?"

Caelen sighed, wishing he could see his friend's face. Yet lighting a torch might have alerted others to their presence, others who were potentially waiting for them at the tunnel's end. Indeed, they should probably not be discussing anything right now, for Caelen could hear the echo of their voices drifting onward, racing ahead to whoever might be there to hear it. "I'm not asking ye to accompany me," he whispered, his voice barely audible as he placed a hand upon his friend's shoulder, pulling them both to a halt. "This is something that I must do, and I would never dream of endangering ye, my friend. As soon as we reach the end of the tunnel, ye stay behind while I go on. Ye can—"

"Out of the question!" Fergus snapped, and Caelen could sense him shaking his head vehemently. "Where ye go, I go."

Caelen smiled, touched by his friend's loyalty. "I need ye to be the lookout, to make certain that Lachlan and his men dunna find this entrance, to keep this exit clear for when I return with Yvaine." *Hopefully*, Caelen added silently.

After a long moment of silence, of indecision, Fergus finally gave his assent, and with no more words passed between them, they continued onward. With their hands outstretched, they followed the tunnel, their eyes squinted, trying to see despite the dark. Yet here, below ground, there was not even a sliver of light from anywhere, and when the end of the tunnel finally came, it came abruptly with no warning.

"Ouch!" Fergus exclaimed the very moment Caelen's right boot tip bumped against the wooden construction that he knew could swing outward and allow them in.

"This is where we part ways," Caelen muttered in hushed tones, his fingers running over the smooth wood, seeking to grab hold of something that would allow him to pull upon the heavy door.

"Are ye certain?" Doubt swung in Fergus's voice, and apprehension as well. "If we go together—"

"No," Caelen interrupted, turning toward his friend. "If anything goes wrong, ye must decide what to do."

"And what would that be?" Fergus inquired with a touch of incredulity. "The moment I share this secret with yer father or Lachlan even, they will attack MacLeòir Castle. Ye ken that. Is that what ye want?"

Caelen closed his eyes, overwhelmed by the heavy burden that had been placed upon their shoulders. "Of course not. I canna tell ye what to do, for I dunna ken what the situation will be. Yet I think it prudent that ye remain out here, aware of what's going on, able to do... something if need be."

A dark chuckle fell from Fergus's lips. "I hope ye dunna expect miracles from me."

After a quick embrace, Caelen pulled upon the heavy door and felt it swing toward him. He turned his head toward where he assumed his friend was standing in the dark, praying that they would see each other again soon. Then he turned away and stepped out of the tunnel and into the MacLeòir dungeon, pulling the wall closed behind him.

Chapter Thirty-Eight

A SHADOW

Alone and exhausted, Yvaine sat in her chamber, a storm of thoughts and emotions raging in her mind and heart. She could no longer bear the waiting, the not knowing of what would come, of what would happen. She felt completely adrift like a piece of wood, bobbing upon the waves, pulled this way and that, powerless to choose its direction.

Months had passed since Yvaine had stumbled into the cavern that had sent her back in time, and now she was stuck in a world she disliked with every fiber of her being. Far away from the only place she had ever known, the only place that had ever felt like home. And what of her family? Her parents and her brothers? Her grandmother?

Closing her eyes, Yvaine sank onto the edge of her bed. Most days, she tried not to think of them, pushing all thoughts of what she had lost far away, knowing they would cripple her. What was her family doing at this moment? No doubt they were frantic with worry. Months had passed and Yvaine doubted they had any clue where she had gone or what had happened to her. She had simply vanished without a trace after all. Did they think her dead? Did they think she had left voluntarily, abandoned them, gone without a word?

It pained Yvaine to think that they might feel betrayed, hurt, believing her so callous, so unfeeling that she would do this to them. If only there were some way for her to explain. Even if she could not return, at least they would know that she wanted to, that she was doing everything within our power to find her way back.

To find her way home.

Burying her face in her hands, Yvaine gritted her teeth, willing back the tears that threatened. Aye, tears had never served anyone, had never solved anything. Nay, she needed to keep her wits about her. She needed to keep trying, doing all she could. Yet here in this moment, Yvaine felt weak and disheartened, and she simply wished that she had heeded her parents' counsel and not gone out on her own that day. After all, they had never meant to take away her choices or her freedom; they had simply been concerned.

And with good reason, it turned out.

However, lately, there was yet another thought Yvaine could not seem to banish from her mind whenever she dwelt upon what had happened and what might have happened.

The truth was, had she heeded her parents' advice, Yvaine would never have crossed paths with Caelen. They would never have met—of course not! And then what? Would the legend of Yvaine and Caelen have been erased from history? Or would another woman have taken her place?

Yvaine could not deny that the thought made her furious, stirring her blood and sending a fierce sense of possessiveness through her veins.

Aye, the mere thought of Caelen caused her heart to beat faster in her chest even though she had known him only for a few short months, spent no more than a few hours in his presence. Still, it felt like she had known him all her life, her heart free of doubt and her mind unable to sway her to caution. Even though he was from a rival clan, her enemy for all intents and purposes, his strong presence, his kind eyes, and the way he treated her with such gentleness and respect, all these things made her feel warm and safe.

And then there was their kiss.

Yvaine felt her cheeks burn with the memory of the passionate kiss they had shared, electricity coursing through her veins at the mere thought of it. Her breath quickened, and every cell of her body seemed to yearn for Caelen's touch. No one had ever made her feel so alive before, made her feel so deeply engulfed in bliss; and now, the thought that this moment could never be repeated left a stone in her throat. How could she possibly leave this place—this time!—when it had brought her to the one man who had ever stirred her heart? If she left, she would never see him again, for they would be separated by an insurmountable barrier of time, centuries standing in their path.

If?

"Am I a fool to be thinking thus?" Yvaine whispered into the eerie silence that lingered upon the castle tonight. Was she perhaps reading more into these few shared moments than there truly had been? Of course, a kiss could simply be a kiss, free of any emotional entanglements. Perhaps Caelen had simply been caught up in the moment when he had pulled her into his arms that night. Perhaps his thoughts did not linger upon her the way hers dwelled on him.

Outside Yvaine's window the night was dark and still, whispering of many more such nights to come with her stuck in this chamber, unable to go anywhere, unable to choose her own path. She tried to push these thoughts away, for they were crippling and made her feel powerless. Yet it was hard, and her mind kept returning to Caelen for comfort.

A sudden noise outside her door made Yvaine flinch, and she spun around, staring at the smooth oak wood, her heart pounding in her chest. Who could be outside her door at this time of night? Or had she simply imagined the sound of heavy footsteps upon stone floor?

Cautiously, Yvaine rose from the edge of the bed and moved toward the door, her heart racing, threatening to jump out of her chest. Despite her father's callous manner and unwelcome intentions with regards to her future, Yvaine had never felt physically threatened at MacLeòir Castle. After all, these people were her family. Why then were they sneaking around outside her door in the middle of the night? Who else could it be?

Clutching the handle, Yvaine took a deep breath, steeling herself for whatever or whoever was on the other side. Then, she slowly opened the door.

Peeking through the gap between door and wall, Yvaine could not glimpse anything beyond a shadowed darkness, distant torchlight flickering like ghosts across the walls. No one was there, and the sound had disappeared. Had she truly imagined it?

An icy chill chased down her spine, and Yvaine glanced up and down the hallway, still expecting to see a figure lurking in the shadows.

Yet all remained quiet.

And then, as if out of nowhere, a voice whispered her name.

Yvaine gasped, her eyes widening with fright and her heart almost tripping over itself in its haste to flee. Instinct urged her to call out for help when a figure suddenly materialized out of the shadows.

Caelen.

His clothes were disheveled and dirt-stained, his hair unkempt, and his dark eyes were filled with intensity and emotion as he stared at her out of the shadows.

Disbelief flooded Yvaine, and her pulse quickened. "What are ye doing here?" she breathed, her voice quivering. "Are ye mad? If my father finds ye, he will have ye killed!" As he stepped forward, she grasped his arm and pulled him across the threshold into her chamber, swiftly closing the door on his heels.

Still afraid to trust her eyes, Yvaine sagged back against the door, staring up at the man who had materialized out of thin air. "I canna believe ye're here."

His breath came fast as Caelen moved toward her, his gaze never leaving hers. No doubt the thrill of invading his enemy's keep had sent his pulse into a run, yet there was something else shimmering in his gaze, something else in the way his chest rose and fell with each breath. His muscles were taut as if preparing for a fight, a struggle within him that...

Yvaine swallowed, heat sizzling across her skin as her heart beat furiously in her chest. Despite her better judgement, she felt herself drawn to Caelen like one of the moths attracted to a flame on a moonless night.

Caelen stopped just before her, so close they were almost touching. His eyes bore into hers as if searching for an answer that only she could provide—an answer that he needed desperately but did not know how to ask for.

Then, without warning or explanation, Caelen reached out and took her face in both hands. His touch was light and gentle yet fiercely protective as he carefully searched her expression for clues—clues to something unknown even to himself.

A wave of emotion welled up inside Yvaine at the connection between them—a connection she had never experienced before but one that seemed strangely familiar, nonetheless. She wanted nothing more than to surrender herself completely to this moment and discover where it would lead them.

As though reading her thoughts, Caelen leaned in closer, his gaze filled with an intensity that both scared and excited Yvaine. She felt as if she were standing on the edge of something unknown and magical—a feeling that was both frightening and exhilarating.

Slowly, Caelen lowered his head until their lips were almost touching. A wave of electricity surged through Yvaine, making her heart race and her skin tingle with anticipation. It was as if all the secrets of the universe were about to be revealed to her in this single moment.

And then he kissed her.

Yvaine felt a wave of emotion surge through her as Caelen's lips met hers in an all-consuming embrace. It was gentle yet passionate, tender yet urgent—a kiss that spoke of endless possibilities and unexplored paths.

Caelen's hands moved from her face to wrap around her body as he pulled her closer against him. His kiss deepened as they both surrendered to the wave of emotion that was surging between them—an emotion so intense it was almost tangible.

Slowly, Yvaine's lips parted, allowing Caelen to explore the depths of her mouth with his tongue, deepening the kiss even further and coaxing forth a low moan from deep within her throat.

The sound seemed to trigger something inside Caelen, and he suddenly pulled away, their breathing heavy and ragged as they both gazed into each other's eyes in confusion and wonderment.

It was then that Yvaine finally understood what this moment meant: for better or worse, their destinies were now intertwined, and she could no longer deny or ignore it. Aye, she was the Yvaine from the legends of old, Caelen's love, their bond something that could never be taken away or forgotten.

A bond that threatened to trap her here...

... in this place...

... in this time.

Chapter Thirty-Nine

TEMPTATION

Caelen stared at Yvaine, his mouth slightly agape and his breath coming fast. Not for a second had he expected to...

He breathed in deeply to calm his thundering heart, reminding himself that he had come here tonight to keep the promise he had made her. Instead, the moment his gaze had fallen upon her, all thoughts had scattered. His heart, his emotions had taken over immediately, pushing him forward, pushing him closer.

Closer to her.

Temptation had tugged upon him, making him want and yearn, making him forget everything beyond the wildly beating pulse in his veins.

And then he had kissed her, and it had been everything and more. He had lost himself in that moment, and the feel of her: her lips beneath his, her fingers curled into his hair, her heart beating as fast as his own. Aye, she had felt it as well, had she not? This all-consuming sense of having found the one person one belonged to despite all the odds stacked against them.

Caelen's heart was still racing in his chest as he looked upon Yvaine, his eyes taking in the changes in her since he had last seen her. Her almond-shaped eyes were wide and filled with surprise, her pale face still flushed with the heat of their passionate kiss. She looked as if her world was spinning out of control, and she struggled to find her footing.

Caelen felt precisely the same way.

Clearly overwhelmed, Yvaine looked down for a moment, her dark lashes fluttering against her smooth cheeks. When she looked back up, her expression was of one deep in thought, her gaze piercing straight through him.

Caelen cleared his throat uncomfortably and looked away. "I apologize," he said gruffly, suddenly uncertain if he had overstepped. "I oughtna have kissed ye." *Again*, he added in his mind. "I was... I was simply relieved to find ye unharmed."

Yvaine swallowed hard and nodded silently, her gaze still darting away as though something tugged upon her mind. Then, though, she gave herself a shake, pushing away whatever thoughts drew her attention; her eyes were overshadowed with sadness, nonetheless. "What happened?" she asked quietly.

Caelen's heart felt heavy with the weight of his next words. "Fergus and I raced home to my father." He sighed and shook his head, touched by the gentle compassion he saw in her gaze, as though she already knew what he would say. "I tried to explain, and for a moment, it looked as though my father would listen. Then, though, Lachlan arrived..." Again, he shook his head, seeing in her eyes that the expression upon his face left no doubt as to what had happened. "My father had Fergus and me locked away in the dungeon. I'm sorry it took me so long to return."

Yvaine's eyes widened, and she moved toward him, her hands reaching out to him in an offer of comfort. "He locked ye in the dungeon?" Her mouth opened in outrage, and yet she found no words to express her shock. "What is it with fathers these days?" she spat, throwing up her hands instead of placing them upon his chest as Caelen had hoped she might. "Do they truly not care for us? Do we mean nothing to them?" Her lips thinned, and she shook her head, exasperated.

Caelen sighed. "These are difficult times. Our fathers have known nothing but war for so long." He shrugged. "Sometimes I fear they no longer even know the meaning of peace. I wish..." He broke off, shaking his head. After all, there was no point. The world was what it was, and there was no changing it. As much as he wanted to believe the opposite, he had tried, and he had failed.

Yvaine nodded, a soft smile upon her face, full of wistfulness and longing. "Aye, I wish it to." Again, her gaze sought his, and he saw an apology there. "I'm sorry for what happened. I ken 'tis my fault that ye—"

Without thinking, Caelen bridged the distance between them, his hand cupping her cheek.

Her eyes widened in surprise, and he felt a shuddering breath leave her lips. Still, she did not pull away, did not flinch or avert her eyes. Nay, for a moment, Caelen even thought she leaned into his touch... just a little.

"Ye have no reason to blame yerself, for I chose my own path. We can only ever do what we deem right, and I simply couldna obey my father's orders." He exhaled slowly, mesmerized to be standing so close, to feel her soft pulse beneath his hand. "I couldna..."

Again, that swirl of temptation engulfed him, and his gaze dropped to her lips. He could see that she was aware of the direction of his thoughts, and to his surprise, she tilted her chin a little higher in silent invitation.

Caelen moved closer—just one small step —and leaned in until he could feel the warmth radiating from her body against his own... until he could almost taste the sweet temptation on her lips...

And then, suddenly, he found himself in heaven. Her lips felt like a feather on his, tender and fervent as she closed the gap between them. He ran his hands over her waistline, embracing her intensely, as their lips moved in perfect harmony. It was as if they had been made for each other, and Caelen felt an overwhelming sense of peace wash over him.

He wrapped his arms around her tightly, not wanting this moment to ever end. He wanted to stay here forever, with Yvaine in his arms and nothing else between them.

Yet they could not.

When they finally pulled apart, Caelen felt his heart pounding wildly in his chest and saw the heat of a blush on Yvaine's cheeks. "We needa stop doing that," Yvaine murmured with a chuckle, and Caelen was relieved not to see the distance from before return.

Caelen took a step back, needing a bit of space to clear his thoughts.

"My father informed me of the match he seeks for me," she told him abruptly, her eyes suddenly hard. "He's determined to get what he wants." There was something stubborn in her gaze, a fire that burned fierce and strong.

Caelen felt mesmerized, and yet his insides tensed at the thought of Yvaine's union to the Morganach chief. "What will ye do?"

"I willna marry him," Yvaine said, her voice firm and determined, steel in her green eyes. "I willna."

Caelen exhaled a deep breath, only now realizing that he had been holding it, and a slow smile spread across his face. "Then I shall help ye in any way I can."

Yvaine looked at him curiously, a tentative smile upon her lips. "Thank ye," she whispered then, that inquisitive look still in her eyes. "Why do ye help me?" she suddenly asked, taking a step toward him. "Why do ye take these risks? I'm no one to ye. In fact, I'm yer enemy, and yet ye disobey yer father... in order to protect me." A frown drew down her brows as she held his gaze. "Why?"

Caelen swallowed hard, uncertain how to reply. After all, he had asked himself that very question many times. Of course, it was true that she did not deserve to die for political reasons, that she was an innocent whom he ought to protect. And yet, deep down, Caelen knew that that was not the reason that had sent him to her side this night.

Aye, she was right. She was no one to him or, at least, she ought to be no one to him. As little as he knew her, Caelen could not deny the bond he felt between them. Whenever she drew near, whenever he laid eyes on her, he felt a spark in the air, something tugging him closer, something urging him to take her hand and stand by her side. It was overwhelming and deeply unsettling, and yet it was irresistible. It did not even feel like a choice to Caelen. Somehow, this was where he was meant to be, what he was meant to do. Of that, at least, he was certain.

Yet the thought of sharing this with her tightened his stomach, and so Caelen merely shrugged and said, "We all deserve the freedom to choose our own path, and I believe that ye should be able to make yer own choices without being forced by anyone." Indeed, it was a gallant thought, and although it was the truth, it did feel like a lie in that moment.

Because it was not the whole truth.

Because... there was one far more compelling.

For a moment, Caelen thought to see tears shimmering in Yvaine's eyes, the expression on her face suddenly torn, as though she did not quite know what it was that she wanted. Then she swallowed, and the expression vanished, changing to one of determination. "Thank ye," she said again, a soft smile upon her lips. "Is there any way ye can help me return to the island? I've contemplated using the tunnel countless times. Yet without any means of transportation, I ken that my father will catch up to me long before I can reach the coast."

Caelen nodded. "Fergus is waiting down in the tunnel, and we have horses nearby." He thought of Lachlan, wondering where his cousin was and if he had drawn any closer to the entrance of the tunnel.

"What is it?" Yvaine inquired, a slight frown creasing her forehead. "Ye look suddenly worried?"

Caelen sighed. "After I failed to..." He held her gaze and saw that she understood. "My father ordered Lachlan to take over. He is here, near the castle with his men." He stepped closer, his gaze seeking hers, holding on, needing her to understand. "There is a risk in leaving the castle now."

Yvaine nodded, a deep sigh leaving her lips. "There is a risk in staying," she replied, that steely expression once more coming to her eyes. "I canna stay. I've already stayed for far too long." Her gaze fell from his, and for a moment, Caelen dared believe that the thought of bidding him farewell pained her as much as it pained him.

Then, though, Yvaine straightened once more, and the expression was gone, as though it had never been. "We should leave now." She stepped away from him and toward the door. "The night is still young, and if we are careful, we might be able to get far enough away before anyone realizes that I'm gone."

Caelen nodded then took Yvaine's hand, his heart briefly pausing in his chest as he felt her warm skin against his own. He pulled her toward the door, opening it merely a crack to peer out into the darkened corridor. Nothing stirred, and his ears caught no sounds that spoke of danger, of the potential of discovery.

With bated breath, he led the way out of Yvaine's chamber, one arm holding her behind him, shielding her from anything they might encounter. Adrenaline surged through his veins, and his chest swelled with a rush of emotions—fear and excitement competing for dominance. Step by step, Caelen guided them onward, along the corridor and then down the stairs, his mind alert and his eyes searching every corner, every shadow.

Behind him, he could hear Yvaine's shallow breathing. He felt her hand holding his tightly, her presence so all-consuming that it threatened to distract him from his surroundings. They tiptoed down the stairs, on the lookout for any guards that may be roaming the castle at night. And just when they thought that no one was nearby, the sound of hurried footsteps suddenly drifted to their ears.

For a moment, they both froze, his eyes finding hers, his hand now clutching Yvaine's.

"This way," Yvaine whispered, tugging him after her. Within only a few steps, they reached a small alcove, a heavy curtain shielding it from the corridor. Without a moment of hesitation, Yvaine slipped inside, pulling him along. Complete darkness engulfed them as they stood in the small space, her arms around his middle, her head upon his chest as he held her in his embrace. Both their hearts beat fast, thundering, hammering against their ribs as though they wished to break free and join together.

The footsteps drew closer and closer, and Caelen felt his arms upon Yvaine tighten. She looked up at him in the dark, and although he could not see her face, could not read the expression in her eyes, he was tempted to dip his head and steal yet another kiss, wondering if this might be their last chance, if at any moment now they would be discovered.

Then, though, the footsteps faded away.

Whoever had drawn closer had turned down a different corridor and was now hastening in the opposite direction. For another moment, they remained hidden in the alcove, their breaths slowly calming as they closed their eyes, allowing themselves a moment of rest and respite.

"That was close," Yvaine whispered, and Caelen once more took her hand before peeking out from behind the curtain.

Again, everything looked deserted, and so they quickly hastened to the end of the corridor and then made their way outside. Almost pressed to the wall, they crossed the courtyard of the castle, doing their utmost to remain out of sight, to melt into the shadows. Above them, star lights lit the dark, and a faint breeze blew in from the east.

His eyes remained fixed upon the entrance to the dungeons as Caelen moved onward, his hand holding on tightly to Yvaine's. His heart still thundered in his chest, and yet he could already feel the first sparks of relief shooting through his body with their destination so close. There was only a small stretch to the dungeons that remained, and so they swiftly stepped out of the concealing darkness of the night's shadows and hurried onward.

In the next instant, a voice called out, "Halt!"

Caelen froze in his steps, his eyes widening as he turned around. A guard stood at the entrance to the castle courtyard, his torch illuminating the area around him. Caelen could feel Yvaine tensing up beside him, her grip on his hand tightening as she also froze in place.

The guard's eyes widened when he saw them, and he immediately started running toward them. "Intruders in the castle!"

Almost instantly, the sound of more footsteps echoed through the air, coming from behind them, and Caelen knew that they were done for.

Without another word, he pulled Yvaine with him and started running toward the entrance to the dungeons as fast as their feet could carry them, hoping against hope that they would make it in time before anyone else did.

Chapter Forty

IN THE GREAT HALL

Yvaine and Caelen flew across the moonlit courtyard, their feet barely touching the cold, hard stone beneath them. Yvaine's hair streamed wildly behind her as she ran, her pale dress flapping around her in a mad dance of desperation. Caelen was only a step ahead of her, his hand still clinging to hers, his strides long and powerful as he raced toward the dungeon, his face set with grim determination.

The castle guards who had spotted them only a moment ago were already in pursuit, their swords drawn and ready. Yvaine's heart raced as she heard their boots echoing behind them like claps of thunder. She glanced up at Caelen and found his gaze locked on the dungeon doors, so close and yet so far away.

Yet as if by some miracle, their strides ate up the ground before their pursuers could reach them. Caelen grabbed the heavy wooden doors, swinging them open with an audible creak.

There was no time to pause.

Yvaine and Caelen charged inside, their eyes snapping to the spiral staircase in the eastern corner that would lead them down to the cells... and the tunnel that promised freedom.

Only before they could take more than two steps, more guards charged in from a side door, their path now blocked by gleaming swords. Yvaine's hopes plummeted. Surrounded by a circle of guards, their faces hard and unyielding, she knew there was no way out.

Caelen stepped forward, his voice echoing through the chamber as he addressed the guards. "I surrender," he said simply and released her hand as he lifted his in defeat. "Take me to yer chief, and I shall confess that I entered his keep tonight with the intention of stealing his daughter."

Thunderstruck, Yvaine stared at Caelen, certain that she had to have misunderstood him. Yet the grim set to his jaw proved her hearing had been far from impaired. "What are ye doing?" she hissed quietly. "Ye canna—"

Caelen turned his back to her and faced the guards. "I acted alone, and I will accept the consequences of my actions. No one else aided me, nor do they bear any responsibility for what I have done."

The guards frowned slightly at his words, clearly surprised, though their swords still remained drawn. "Verra well," the lead guard replied gruffly. "Ye shall come with us so that our chief may decide yer fate." He gestured for Caelen to come forward before instructing another guard to fetch the chief to the great hall. Then he turned his gaze to Yvaine. "He will want to see ye as well," he paused, and Yvaine thought to see a hint of doubt spark in his eyes, "and hear yer side of the story."

Yvaine swallowed hard and nodded, not daring to speak. She glanced at Caelen, her eyes wide with fear. Fear for him, she realized, knowing that her father would not show leniency. She tried to catch Caelen's gaze, yet he refused to look at her, his eyes fixed ahead, his face almost stoic in the silvery light from the moon.

Together, the two of them were led out of the dungeon and along a hallway illuminated by tall torches before they reached the great hall of the castle. Yvaine's gaze drifted to the flags of Clan MacLeòir hanging proudly upon the walls, a crackling fire in the hearth casting shadows over the vaulted chamber. And there, at its end stood Yvaine's father, his stern gaze a reminder of what Yvaine knew to be true: that this day would not end well.

Aye, his face was like thunder, his gaze piercing, and he glared at Yvaine and Caelen as the guards brought them before him, only a mere flicker of incomprehension in his eyes. "Explain yerselves," he boomed, his deep voice reverberating off the walls.

Yvaine opened her mouth, but before she could speak, Caelen stepped forward, his gaze still firmly fixed ahead and away from her. "My laird," he said in a strong, clear voice as though he knew not the meaning of fear and foreboding. "I entered yer keep tonight, intent on stealing yer daughter away. I threatened her life in order to gain her compliance, and I shall accept any punishment ye seek to place upon me."

Although she had known what he would say, Yvaine still felt stunned, her body immobile, her mind frozen. Why on earth was Caelen so determined to sacrifice himself for her? Did he not know that her father would execute him? Surely, he had to. Yet he acted as though taking the blame for this was no more severe than admitting to having stolen a horse from the stables.

Even if there were no bad blood between their two clans, no chieftain would allow such an atrocity go unpunished. If Caelen truly managed to convince her father that he had entered their keep on his own behest, seeking to steal the chief's daughter for his own gain, he would most definitely not be leaving here alive.

Yvaine was certain of it.

Although she had only met her birth father a mere few months ago, those months had taught her that he always did as he pleased with no consideration for anyone's wishes but his own. And now, he had his enemy's son in his hands.

Yvaine paused, wondering in that moment if her father had recognized Caelen. Was it possible that he did not know? Hope swelled in Yvaine's chest…

… and then died a quick death when her father's booming laughter echoed through the hall. "Ye seek to prevent our union with Clan Morganach," he snarled, his eyes sparkling with triumph as he stared at Caelen. "That is why yer father sent ye, isna it?"

Standing tall in the soldiers' tight grip that flanked him, Caelen returned her father's icy stare, no words leaving his lips now.

Yvaine's father was silent for a moment, studying first Caelen before his gaze moved to her. Yvaine felt it like an icy shower of rain on a hot day, stinging her skin and chilling her soul. She could see without a doubt that her father did not believe Caelen's story, that he suspected something, his gaze slightly narrowed as he stepped toward Yvaine, his voice dropping to a whisper. "What happened here tonight?"

Yvaine pressed her lips into a tight line as a war raged within her. More than anything, she wished to spit into her father's face and tell him the truth, admit that she had taken the first opportunity to flee his presence, that she was not loyal, not to a man like him. Yet what good would that do?

This very moment, Caelen was risking his life to protect hers, and if she now spoke against him, his sacrifice would be in vain. Because there was not a single doubt in Yvaine's mind, that her father would execute Caelen no matter what she said. Yet if she could convince her father of Caelen's story, then perhaps she could find some way to free him. If she were locked up as well, all hope would be truly lost.

"He speaks the truth, Father," Yvaine replied, each word feeling like ash in her mouth, and her hands balled into fists as she fought down the urge to withdraw them. "He found me in my chamber tonight and held a knife to my throat." She swallowed hard, then she bowed her head, thinking that perhaps she ought to show some sign of fear, of terror, of being shaken by this experience.

With her gaze averted, Yvaine could no longer see her father's face, could no longer read his expression, and for a long, seemingly endless moment, he said nothing.

Then he stepped back, and Yvaine raised her chin, her balled up fists trembling as she waited for her father's verdict. "Verra well," he said to Yvaine's surprise, and yet every instinct told her not to believe him. If he acted as though he did, he surely had his reasons, and she would be wise to try and unearth them.

"Take him to the dungeon and lock him away," her father ordered, nodding to his guards, "until I decide what to do with him." His gaze never left Caelen as he was led away, his face still as stoic as before, not betraying a shred of emotion.

Yvaine, too, could not avert her eyes, could not even blink, her gaze fixed upon Caelen as he was being led from the great hall. And then, the moment before he disappeared, their eyes met for a heartbeat and Yvaine almost sagged to the ground, sobs threatening to tear from her throat.

Yet she held on, her fingernails digging into her palms she clenched her fists so tightly, fighting to remain in control and meet her father's gaze as he turned back to look at her. "I ken ye're lying," he murmured in a soft yet icy voice, his words only meant for her. "I ken he didna threaten ye, that ye went with him willingly."

Yvaine stared into her father's face, wondering what he hoped to gain by speaking to her thus. Why had he not admitted so before? "What makes ye think so, Father?" Yvaine asked in her most feeble voice, blinking her eyes as though to discourage tears. "Have I not done my utmost to prove my loyalty to ye these past few weeks?"

Her father heaved a deep sigh, a knowing smile tugging upon his lips. "Ye have certainly tried. It must've been hard for ye to hold yer tongue." He chuckled darkly. "Ye must think me a fool," he hissed then, leaning in closer, "if ye truly believe I didna see through yer charade. From the first moment we met, I knew the kind of woman ye are. After all, that day ye made it unmistakably clear."

Yvaine gritted her teeth against a wave of fury, of rage that shot through her in that moment. Indeed, she had fought hard to gain her father's trust, only to learn now that it had all been in vain, that he had never believed her. "What is it that ye want?" she demanded, lifting her chin and dropping her mask.

Her father smiled, and it almost seemed to be a smile of approval that she would finally reveal her true self to him again. "Ye ken verra well what I want," he said slowly, his gaze sweeping over her features, wishing to catch every subtle reaction. "I've never hidden that from ye." His brows rose challengingly.

For a moment, Yvaine felt a cloud of confusion descend before it was suddenly ripped away and everything became crystal clear. "Ye want me to agree to marry the Morganach chief."

Her father nodded in confirmation. "Ye have a quick wit, lass. I'll give ye that." He exhaled a slow breath, still watching her. "Malcolm Morganach has made it clear that he willna wed a lass who is unwilling. Therefore, I need ye to be *willing*. Do ye understand?"

Yvaine nodded, cursing the shivers that made her limbs tremble as she found herself backed into a corner.

Her father scoffed. "He's not like his father, who understood the importance of an alliance, who never hesitated to do what needed to be done." He shook his head, his eyes rolling in annoyance. "Yet we need the Morganachs. They're fierce fighters, and they're great in number."

Yvaine gritted her teeth. "What is it that ye're saying, *Father?*" she spat the last word, giving it as much disdain and contempt as she could.

Yet her father merely grinned, clearly amused. "If ye wish for me to release the MacCarmaig lad, ye needa agree to this union to the Morganach chief." He stepped closer, his gaze hard and drilling into hers. "Ye needa be convincing and gain his favor, and once the wedding has taken place, ye have my word that I shall release the MacCarmaig lad."

Inevitability settled in Yvaine's heart, robbing her of every bit of hope to sway her father, to find some way to see Caelen safely from this keep without tying herself to a man she had never even met.

"Ye have one day to think about this," her father murmured, a warning in his gaze. "Tomorrow at sundown, I wish to hear yer answer, and believe me when I say that only yer consent can set the lad free. If ye try anything, it'll cost him his life."

"How can I trust ye?" Yvaine hissed, welcoming the anger that surged through her, preferring it to the fear that held her in its grip. "How can I be certain that ye will release him once I'm wed?" Glaring at her father, she shook her head. "Nay, if ye truly want this union, then ye needa set him free before."

Her father regarded her carefully, and for a brief moment, Yvaine thought to see a spark of pride light up his eyes, as though part of him admired her. "Well, it seems we both have something to think about then." He stepped back then nodded to the remaining guards. "Take her to her chamber and lock her in. I want two guards posted outside her door at all times." Again, he met Yvaine's gaze. "I ken how resourceful ye can be, but believe me, I will not take any chances. Ye either agree or ye dunna. There will be no other option."

Two large guards took up either side of Yvaine, their broad shoulders and stern features dwarfing her as they took hold of her arms. Their footsteps were heavy as they marched her out of the great hall, her own light and soundless in comparison. Her body felt taut with fear and anticipation, and her heart almost stilled in her chest as she spotted Logan standing in a shadowed corner, his blue eyes holding hers with a tight expression upon his face. Aye, Yvaine saw concern there as well as regret, and yet she knew he would not intervene on her behalf. He had made that unmistakably clear. His loyalty lay with their father and always would.

Once locked in her chamber, Yvaine sank onto the bed in despair, feeling completely helpless and alone. She had no idea what she was going to do, or how she was going to get out of this mess. All she knew for certain was that if she did not agree to marry a complete stranger by sundown tomorrow then Caelen would pay the price for it with his life.

Chapter Forty-One

BACK IN THE DUNGEON

Caelen stumbled to a stop, his mind racing and his heart pounding as anger surged through his veins. How could he have let this happen? They had been so close to making their escape. And now?

Now, he stood in the doorway of a small, dank dungeon, barely lit by the faint glimmers of the two torches that flickered in their sconces and painted the walls with moving shadows. In one of the cells, a single figure stood, his eyes wide with shock and his hands gripping tightly to the bars in the cell door.

Fergus.

Caelen's blood ran cold. What was Fergus doing here? How had he been caught? Or had he come in to try to save them?

There was no time, though, to seek answers to his questions, for the guards that had brought Caelen down suddenly seized his arms and pushed him along the corridor toward the cell. The door was unlocked, and Fergus stood back as it swung open. Then with a flurry of angry shouts, the guards shoved Caelen inside, then shut and locked the door behind him before climbing the spiral staircase to the upper floor of the dungeon.

Caelen stumbled forward, his gaze fixed upon his friend, his mind still slow to comprehend how all this had happened. How had everything gone so very wrong? And yet there was a part of Caelen that was not in the least surprised; after all, it had been a great risk to enter the keep alone. Aye, he ought to have known this would happen... and perhaps a part of him had.

Fergus watched him, his face a mix of resignation and grim humor. "I'm afraid to say I had hoped not to be seeing ye anytime soon." He stepped forward, clasping his hands upon Caelen's shoulder, his gaze narrowing in concern. "Are ye all right?"

Leaning back against the cold stone wall, Caelen ran a hand through his disheveled hair. Then he nodded. "Aye, I'm all right. Ye?"

Fergus nodded. "Couldna be better aside from the part where we are probably going to be executed soon." His right brow rose in question.

Caelen heaved a deep sigh, momentarily too overwhelmed to reply as the burden upon his shoulders grew heavier with each breath he took. Not only had he failed Yvaine, delivering her back into her father's keep and making the man once more suspicious of her. Now, he was also responsible for his friend sharing his fate. After all, had Fergus not argued that it would be too dangerous to enter the keep. Aye, it would seem his friend had been right.

"I'm sorry," Caelen said quietly, meeting his friend's gaze only with great reluctance. "All this is my fault." He shook his head in resignation. "They discovered us only a stone's throw from the dungeon, yet they caught up with us before we could make it to the tunnel."

With an equally heavy sigh, Fergus leaned against the wall side by side with Caelen, briefly bumping his shoulder in a gesture of comfort. "Aye, I heard the commotion, and I couldna simply stand back and wait. I opened the doorway and—"

"Did ye leave it open?" Caelen inquired, his mind suddenly churning. "Do they ken about the tunnel?" He dropped his voice as he spoke the last word. His gaze drifted to the barred window in the door, and he hoped that no one had overheard.

"Nay." Fergus shook his head, his expression unreadable as he glanced around the dungeon, his brows knitted in thought. "Yet what good will that do us?" He looked back at Caelen. "Any ideas?"

Caelen shook his head, still deep in thought. "Not yet," he murmured before lifting his head and squaring his shoulders. "Somehow, we'll find a way out of here." He glanced back at the locked door. "All we need is a key." Indeed, all they needed was a key to unlock the cell door and the tunnel would lead them to freedom. Yet what of Yvaine?

Fergus chuckled. "Truly? All we need is a key?" He shook his head grinning. "That hadna occurred to me."

"I ken 'twill not be easy," Caelen replied, struggling to ignore that sinking feeling in the pit of his stomach. "Yet perhaps there is a way." He exhaled a slow breath. "We canna give up now. We simply canna."

"I wasna suggesting we should," Fergus replied before his gaze sobered. "Where is Yvaine?"

Just then, the sound of footsteps echoed from the stairs, and Caelen and Fergus exchanged a glance before turning to see who it was. As the steps drew closer, both men braced themselves for what might come. Had the MacLeòir chief decided what to do with them so quickly? Were they to be executed this very night?

A cold chill ran down Caelen's back, and he gritted his teeth, reminding himself not to cower under the chief's gaze. If he had to die tonight, he would do it well. If only he could do it without regret.

Finally, a figure appeared in the gloom, and Caelen was surprised that it was no guard that came to the cell but the MacLeòir's clan chief himself.

The man's face was a stony mask as he stepped forward and came to stand just outside the cell door, his gaze locking with Caelen's. "So, it seems ye ken my daughter," he remarked, his voice a low rumble. Still, Caelen thought to hear a question ring in the man's tone.

Swallowing hard, Caelen held the chief's gaze, praying that Yvaine was safe, wishing he could trust that as her father, the chief would never harm her. Yet as of late, Caelen had learned that a parent's love for their child could be easily outdone by what they feared. "Where is she?" he asked, his voice tight.

The chief's lips curled into a small smile. "Why, it seems that ye care for her," he murmured, and his gaze narrowed into hard slits. "Clearly, ye lied to me before... as did she."

Caelen wanted to strangle the man, his skin crawling with a sense of dread, of fear. "What did ye do to her?"

The MacLeòir chief chuckled. "That is none of yer concern." He stepped closer to the iron bars, his gaze drilling into Caelen's and his lips twitching into a snarl. "How do ye ken her? Was it ye and yer kind that stole her away all these years ago?" Then something flickered in his gaze, and he shook his head. "Nay, if it had been ye and she had escaped ye after all these years, ye wouldna seek to protect her now. Why then?"

Although Caelen knew it to be unwise, he could not seem to hold his tongue. "I'm certain ye would like to know," he replied in a rather suggestive tone. "Yet I'm afraid I canna tell ye. All I can say is that ye wouldna like the answer."

Rage flashed in the chief's eyes, clearly struggling to remain in control. "Did ye bed her?" he growled, and for a second, Caelen thought to see a touch of fear spark in his eyes. "Tell me!"

Again, Caelen could not hold back, could not hide the smirk that came to his face. Yet deep inside, despair spread into every fiber, surging through his body, for he suddenly understood the spark of fear he had seen in the chief's eyes.

Aye, the man feared that Caelen had bedded his daughter because undoubtedly the Morganach clan chief wished for an untouched bride. Otherwise, he would most certainly withdraw his marriage proposal.

"Aye, I did," Caelen replied with a smug smile, his thoughts racing. Was this a way to protect Yvaine from this union?

The chief's face darkened, and he clenched his jaw so tightly that a vein began to pulse in his neck. He stepped forward and slammed his fist against the stone wall. The sharp sound echoed through the dungeon, and Caelen could hear the man's knuckles crack as they connected with the cold surface. His temper had finally snapped, and for a moment, it seemed that he had forgotten all reason.

Then suddenly, the man stilled, taking a deep breath to calm himself and block out the pain before he turned back toward Caelen with a menacing look in his eye. "Ye will regret this," he said in a low, menacing voice. "If ye speak true, yer blood will soon stain these walls." With another hateful glare, he spun around and stormed off, his footsteps thundering along the corridor.

For a long moment, silence held the cell in a tight grip. Then Fergus stepped toward Caelen, his eyes troubled as he shook his head, incomprehension marking his features. "Are ye mad? Ye heard the man. He will kill ye for this. Even if it were true, ye oughtna have said so. Ye oughta have lied." He squinted his eyes, as though it would help him understand. "Why? Why are ye so ready to throw yer life away? I ken ye care for the lass, but ye barely know her."

Caelen stared at his friend, then he shrugged his shoulders, completely at a loss. "I dunna ken," he murmured, thinking of that odd sensation that always fell over him whenever he thought of Yvaine, whenever she drew near. He could not explain it. He could not even attempt to try; yet he knew it to be true.

She was his to protect, to keep safe. At all costs. No matter what.

She was his.

Chapter Forty-Two

A CHOICE

The morning sun had just begun to crest the horizon, bringing with it a gentle warmth, and yet Yvaine had never felt so cold in her life as she lay awake in her chamber. Her eyes stared straight ahead, her mind numb with the rumblings of the previous night. Endlessly, she had contemplated her options, every scenario she dared to think of. Yet it seemed there was no way out; at least not for all of them.

Especially not for Caelen.

After all, what could she do? She was only one person with no allies to call her own. No one would dare stand with her and oppose her father. Never in her life had Yvaine felt this alone, this hopeless, her heart constricting painfully at the thought of Caelen being executed for trying to help her. If this were truly to happen, she knew she would never recover from it.

Her thoughts were soon interrupted when her mother's agitated voice echoed to her ears, ordering the guards outside Yvaine's chamber to allow her to pass. A moment later, the door burst open, and her mother entered with an expression of deepest concern. "Yvaine, lass, do please tell me what made yer father so angry with ye last night," her mother asked in a quiet but stern voice.

A bit taken aback by her mother's sudden entrance, Yvaine sat up and quickly gathered her thoughts to answer. "'Tis a long story, Mother." She slid off the bed and experienced a moment of unsteadiness as the world began to sway around her. Aye, perhaps she ought to have slept yet with her heart so burdened she doubted anyone could have.

Surging forward, her mother grasped her by the arms and eased her back down onto the bed, her eyes wide with concern, her features softening "Are ye unwell?"

Yvaine shook her head. "Nay, I'm only tired. Please, Mother, ye must help me. Father locked Caelen in the dungeons and plans to have him executed unless I agree to marry the Morganach chief."

Her mother's face paled, and for a brief moment, Yvaine feared she would faint. Then she swallowed, her lips moving as though she were searching for words. "Caelen?" she whispered, pinching her eyes shut for a moment before shaking her head. "Ye're not speaking of the MacCarmaig lad, are ye? What does he have to do with anything?"

Words quickly rolled off Yvaine's tongue, unable to pace herself, to allow her mother time to understand everything she was hearing. Clearly, she knew nothing of what had transpired the night before, every bit of news unknown to her.

Yvaine's mother sighed and then turned her gaze toward the window, as if she were watching the sun break over the horizon. "Ye oughtna have done as ye did, Child," she murmured before once more turning to look at Yvaine. "Yer father is a proud man, and he doesna take kindly to his daughter misbehaving."

Angry, Yvaine jumped from the bed, and this time she did not sway. "I am not simply misbehaving, Mother. I have good reasons for acting like this. Ye canna truly mean to tell me that ye would rather stand by and risk an innocent man being executed instead of having an unpleasant conversation with Father?" She searched her mother's gaze, and yet even as she did so, Yvaine knew that there was no bravery, no courage left in her mother. Had there been once?

Her mother's lips thinned. "The lad is far from innocent," she snapped, crossing her arms over her chest in a rather childish yet defiant gesture. "He's a MacCarmaig, son to our greatest enemy." Her brows drew down in anger, and yet sadness lingered in her eyes, pain even. "How do ye even know him? Aye, I understand yer father's anger, for I dunna like what I'm hearing, either."

A frustrated growl tore from Yvaine's throat. "Arg, what is wrong with ye? How can ye not care?" She stared at her mother. "I spoke to Logan, and he told me he doesna even ken why the feud began in the first place. Ye've all been enemies for so many years now, and ye dunna even ken why." She stepped closer, holding her mother's gaze, daring her to give her the same answer. "Do ye?"

Instantly, her mother's gaze fell from hers, and Yvaine realized that at least her mother knew what had started the feud. Yet the defiant expression upon her face, mixed with shame and regret, said equally loud and clear that she was not ready to share this information.

Yvaine heaved a deep breath, struggling to calm her temper. "Can ye please find out how he is? He tried to help me, and now he's locked in the dungeon. He deserves better, far better." Closing her eyes, she sank back down onto her bed. "'Tis all my fault. I asked him to help me, and he agreed." Lifting her gaze, Yvaine looked at her mother. "Please."

Despite the compassion in her mother's eyes, she shook her head. "I'm sorry, lass. I truly dunna ken what befell the lad, and I wouldna dream of interfering in yer father's affairs."

Yvaine's heart sank. She had so desperately hoped that her mother could shed some light on the matter, but it seemed that fear stood in her path. Indeed, Yvaine had long since realized that the MacLeòirs did not look at their chief the way the MacKinnears regarded Yvaine's true father. There was fear, and there was respect, and she understood now what the difference was, could feel it deep in her heart.

Before Yvaine had time to truly process her emotions, however, the chamber door burst open once more, and her father strode into the room. His face was stern, and he snapped at her mother to leave.

Without a moment of hesitation, her mother complied, her eyes wide with fear as she hurried away without a word or look back at her daughter.

Yvaine watched her mother leave and knew that Heather MacKinnear, the woman who had raised her and been her mother all her life, would never have bowed her head like this. Of course, Aiden MacKinnear would never have dreamed of speaking to his wife in such a manner. Aye, Yvaine had stumbled into a foreign world, and strangely enough, the oddest thing was not even the hundreds of years that separated them.

Steeling herself for what was to come, Yvaine turned her gaze to her father, her heart still heavy with thoughts of Caelen.

Fury blazed in her father's eyes, and yet it was not the sort of fury that overtook one in an unexpected moment. Nay, it was the sort of fury that still lingered long after something had started into life. What had happened the night before that Yvaine had no knowledge of? She wondered, regarding her father curiously. Yet whatever it was, it clearly was nothing good.

"What is yer answer?" he snarled, his jaw tense as he stared at her.

Yvaine frowned. "What happened?" She took a step toward him, her eyes narrowing. "Ye were not this angry last night."

The glare in her father's eyes intensified, and he exhaled a slow breath as though seeking to calm himself. Indeed, his right hand was bandaged, spots of red here and there revealing blood had been spilled. But how?

"Yer answer," he snarled yet again.

Yvaine shook her head. "Ye first."

Again, something flashed in his eyes: outrage at her audacity but also pride at her strength. He regarded her for a long moment then stepped toward her. "Did ye allow that MacCarmaig scoundrel to bed ye?"

Not having expected that, Yvaine almost stumbled backward, completely taken aback by his accusation. "What?" she gasped, wondering if she might have misunderstood.

Her father's face twisted in a scowl. "He claims that he bedded ye and that ye allowed it," he spat, cringing at the pain when his injured hand clenched into a fist. "Tell me true!"

Yvaine could not fathom why Caelen had made such a claim. After all, it had clearly enraged her father, something that would certainly not serve him. At the same time, Yvaine doubted that Caelen had spoken without thought. He had to have had some sort of reason for saying what he had, and so she knew she could not contradict him.

"'Tis none of yer concern," she finally said to her father, lifting her chin another fraction as she held his gaze unflinchingly.

The urge to strike her flickered across her father's face, and yet he held himself in control. "What is yer answer?" he demanded in a tight voice. "Am I to send word to the Morganach chief or arrange for an execution?"

Tears shot to Yvaine's eyes, and she fought to blink them away, not wishing to give her father the satisfaction of seeing her beaten. Yet she could not allow Caelen's life to end like this. "I... agree." Speaking those two words broke something deep inside of Yvaine, and for a moment, she was certain her knees would buckle.

Yet they did not.

Her father exhaled a breath of relief, the anger in his eyes slowly receding. "Verra well." Then he paused, though, and leaned in closer, his gaze holding hers. "I warn ye, lass. Should ye try anything untoward, the MacCarmaig lad shall pay with his life. Do ye understand?"

Pressing her lips into a tight line, Yvaine nodded. "Aye, I understand. Ye've made that unmistakably clear." Indeed, he had.

Despite arguments and squabbles, Yvaine had never before seen the harsh side of the world. She had never met truly awful people, selfish and without compassion. She had grown up in a place where respect for one another came as easily as the sun rose every morning. It was not something people thought about much because it was simply there. It was a part of life, and Yvaine had always taken it for granted. Now, though, she knew better.

If only she could go back and do things differently.

Yet then she would never have met Caelen.

That, though, would probably have been for the better.

Chapter Forty-Three

A RESOURCEFUL LAD

The walls of MacLeòir Castle were thick, and the morning light had yet to reach down into the depths of its dank dungeons. The only sound that stirred in the darkness was the faint scuffle of two pairs of feet, colliding against the cold stone floor as Caelen and Fergus rose after a sleepless night. They had been locked down here for hours, and Caelen was becoming increasingly worried for Yvaine, and what the day may yet bring.

His heart tensed at the sound of someone coming down the stairs, and he grabbed Fergus's arm and both men moved to the door, flanking it. Caelen wondered how many guards there were and if they could manage to overtake them all. In truth, he rather doubted it. Yet it was the only plan they had been able to conjure.

Staring into each other's eyes, Caelen and Fergus held their breaths, waiting for the figure to emerge from the shadows.

At first, Caelen thought it was a guard, his large form slowly descending the stairs. Then, though, he realized the footsteps were too light and quiet, not like those of the guards. He met Fergus's gaze and placed a finger on his lips as he strained his ears to distinguish the treads.

Peering out through the iron bars, Caelen stilled when he saw a slender, red-haired lad emerge from the darkness and step into the low torchlight.

"Who is it?" Fergus murmured from the other side, his view obstructed.

Caelen frowned. "'Tis Rory," he whispered when the lad's eyes met his. That, he would not have expected. What on earth was the lad doing down here? Caelen could have believed the chief sending his eldest son, Logan. But not Rory.

"I heard that ye were here," the lad said, his voice laced with anger as he stepped closer to Caelen's cell. "I heard that ye tried to steal my sister away."

Caelen let his forehead fall against the iron bars as he looked at the lad, wondering what to say, not wishing to make things worse for Yvaine.

"Is it true?" Rory asked then, cocking his head slightly as he regarded Caelen. "Did ye try to steal her away?"

Caelen swallowed, shaken by the wide-open look in the lad's eyes. "I never meant her any harm," he finally said, wondering if the lad knew more than he let on.

As though on cue, Rory said, "She asked ye to come, did she not? She asked for yer help." A deep sigh left the lad's lips as Caelen stared at him, stunned. "She said she couldna remember us, that she didna feel at home here, that she wished to return to her true home." Sadness came to his wide eyes, and yet there was a deep sense of compassion and selflessness upon his features.

"Aye," Caelen answered, "she asked me for help, and I came here last night to see her home." He shrugged helplessly. "I'm sorry I couldna."

"Ye came through the tunnel, did ye not?" Rory inquired, a rather shrewd expression in his green eyes now.

Caelen nodded, surprised how much the lad knew, wondering if he had been told or if he was simply one of those people who found out things by keeping their eyes and ears open. "Aye, we came through the tunnel." He paused, exchanging a glance with Fergus, then asked, "Is Yvaine safe?"

Rory sighed deeply. "Safer than ye." He clearly had meant to say it lightly, and yet the humor in his voice never quite manifested. "Father demands she marry the Morganach chief in order to spare yer life."

Caelen felt a boulder of guilt and regret hit him square in the chest, and an anguished groan slipped from his lips. He had meant to help Yvaine, not make things worse for her. "We canna allow that to happen," he murmured, casting a glance at Fergus, who merely shrugged, hopelessness etched into his eyes.

"There's nothing we can do," Rory piped up, the same anguish in his tone that Caelen felt constricting his own chest. "Father has her locked in her chamber and under guard. No one can get to her." He heaved a deep sigh and reached inside his pocket and pulled out an iron key. "But I can help ye."

Caelen gasped. "Is that—?"

Rory nodded, fingering the key absentmindedly for a moment. Then he looked up again. "I can set ye free, and ye can get out of here through the tunnel."

Caelen stared at the young lad. "Why would ye do that?" he asked, wondering if it was wise to do so. What if Rory changed his mind?

Rory shrugged. "Ye're a good man. I can tell. Ye dunna deserve to die for trying to help my sister, and she doesna deserve the burden of yer death upon her head." He stepped forward then and inserted the key into the lock. As he turned it, a loud metallic clack echoed through the damp dungeon, and for a moment, Caelen feared that all hope was lost, that within moments a myriad of guards would be down upon them.

Yet all remained quiet and deserted.

Slowly, Caelen pushed open the door, and he and Fergus stepped out into the corridor. "Thank ye, Rory," he said to the lad as Fergus quietly moved up ahead toward the secret entrance to the tunnel. "Is there any way ye can get word to her? Can ye tell her that we've escaped so she willna agree to this union?"

Rory shrugged. "I dunna ken. Even if I can, I dunna think 'twill do her any good. Father is more determined than ever to make this union happen, and he will find some way to force Yvaine's compliance." He hung his head. "She's right. She should never have come back."

Caelen nodded sadly, placing his hand upon Rory's shoulder. "She's fortunate to call ye brother. Ye're loyal and kind and brave." He squeezed Rory's shoulder. "Thank ye."

Rory nodded. "I wish I could help her as well."

Caelen understood the sentiment well, for every cell in his body urged him not to leave Yvaine behind. Yet it would be foolish to try to get to her. He would most certainly be caught, once again unable to help her, his capture a tool her father could use to force for compliance. But would she comply?

In that moment, Caelen could not help but wonder if Yvaine would truly agree to marry the Morganach chief in order to save his life. Aye, it would be a great gesture, one that warmed Caelen's heart, one that made him wonder what lived in hers. He remembered well the way she had clung to him, had responded to his kiss; but did that mean there was love for him in her heart?

"If ye can," Caelen said to Rory, grasping the lad's shoulders, "tell her I will be back. Somehow, we shall find a way to see her back home. I promise."

Tears misted Rory's eyes and he nodded. "Go now. Before the guard realizes I've sent him on a fool's errand. He shall not be gone much longer."

Caelen nodded, casting Rory a grateful smile before hurrying down the corridor after Fergus. Together, they pushed open the secret door that led out into the tunnel, carefully closing it behind themselves before making their escape. Who knew, one day they might need it again.

Chapter Forty-Four

BETROTHED

Yvaine heard the drums in the distance, beckoning her to the great hall. Yet her feet would not move. Instead, she stood at her window and gazed out at the land, her gaze finding the small group of riders approaching the keep only a day after she had agreed to her father's demands. Aye, he had clearly anticipated her acquiescence or it would have taken longer for her *betrothed* and his warriors to arrive. Her gaze swept over the riders, one of whom, Yvaine knew, was Malcolm Morganach, the leader of Clan Morganach, and her heart grew heavy. Although she had made her decision, some wild, untamed part of her still urged her to reconsider, reminding her that she could not bow her head like this.

She simply could not.

"I ken," Yvaine whispered in answer as the cool morning breeze teased her skin. "Yet what of Caelen?"

Only too easily could she imagine him down in the dungeons in a cold, dark, damp cell. Yet if she opposed her father, Yvaine knew Caelen would not remain in that cell for long. Nay, in that case, a worse fate awaited him.

"I have no choice," she murmured to the wind, wishing it could carry her away, wishing it could carry them both away. Never before had Yvaine felt this helpless, robbed of all her strength, all her options. Indeed, her parents—her true parents!—had taught her never to give up, always to find the silver lining and make her way onward undeterred, no matter what.

Yet what was her way now? Were there options she simply could not see? If so, they truly lay hidden from her.

Squinting her eyes, Yvaine watched the riders charge through the gate and then pull to a halt in the courtyard. From this distance, she could not make out their faces, yet the man leading the group, the man she presumed to be Malcolm Morganach, stood tall, his hair as dark as Caelen's. Would she truly have to marry him? Of course, an agreement to marry was not yet a sealed marriage contract, was it? Perhaps later, an opportunity would present itself for Yvaine to escape this fate.

Perhaps.

Or perhaps not.

Before she stepped away from the window, Yvaine's gaze drifted from the tall clan leader to the corner of the castle where the dungeon was located, and in her mind's eye, she saw Caelen in shackles, his jaw set in grim determination. Aye, he had tried everything within his power to protect her, he had even risked his own life—*was* risking his own life—and yet all had come to naught.

With great apprehension in her heart and flanked by two guards, Yvaine made her way down the winding corridors of the keep until she arrived at the great wooden door that led into the hall. Taking a deep breath, she pushed it open and stepped inside, knowing that every moment of hesitation would only see her nerves more aflutter. And she refused to cower, to show fear and give her father and her future husband the satisfaction of seeing her this unhinged.

Nay, she would hold her head high and meet his eyes without a flicker of fear in them.

As always, the large hall stood imposing, full of shadows and secrets. Her eyes wandered around the room, taking in the flags hung from the walls, the tapestries that shimmered in the sunlight, and the life-sized paintings of the MacLeòir clan chiefs. For a moment, Yvaine held her breath, remembering how she had been overwhelmed by the sheer grandeur of it all the first time she had set foot in it.

Now, though, it was a place of regret, a place that held only awful memories of her father talking down to her, commanding her life and those of others as well. No sparkling feast could ever erase this, could ever bring back the grandeur of this hall.

At the far end of it, Yvaine spotted her father, the proud and powerful chief of Clan MacLeòir, standing next to a tall, dark-haired man. For a moment, Yvaine could almost imagine this man to be Caelen, a kind expression upon his face and something deeply meaningful in his gaze. Yet as she stepped closer, every muscle in her body taught as a bowstring, Yvaine finally caught a glimpse of the man's face.

Indeed, it was not Caelen, for this man looked not simply stern and distant, his expression guarded beyond all else, but he bore the scars of a man touched by fire. Aye, the right side of his face looked almost raw, the flesh mangled there, and Yvaine could only too easily imagine the pain and suffering he had gone through. Still, despite his scars, it was easy to see that he did not yet count as many years as a father, and yet Yvaine knew without a doubt that this man was one of power and prestige. He was dressed in fine clothes that spoke to his position, and he wore a broadsword at his side, his hand upon its hilt.

When Yvaine reached her father's side, he gestured for her to step forward, and she reluctantly complied, feeling Chief Morganach's stern eyes burning into her. His gaze was hard and unyielding, as though he, too, already disapproved of her. Had her father perhaps shared any of her *misconducts* with him?

Yvaine doubted it. After all, her father sought this alliance more than anything. He would do nothing that would see it fail.

"So, this is yer daughter," Chief Morganach remarked, his voice low and commanding as he regarded her.

"Aye," Yvaine's father replied with a smile that spoke of pride and admiration, yet Yvaine recognized the man she had come to know with a single glance into his eyes. "My only daughter."

Chief Morganach said nothing for a moment. Instead, he looked her up and down, taking in her form and appearance with a scrutinizing gaze.

Yvaine felt her cheeks heat up in embarrassment despite her efforts to the contrary. Still, she refused to bow her head, her gaze fixed upon his as he crossed his arms over his large chest, the expression in his eyes almost punishing as though he wished to send her fleeing from his presence. Yet Yvaine did not yield but instead notched her chin a bit higher. Of course, it was foolish of her to do so. After all, just like her father, she needed this man to accept her as his bride. For if he did not, it would be Caelen's death sentence.

To Yvaine's surprise, Chief Morganach nodded his head in acceptance. "She'll make a fine wife," he remarked in that dark, hoarse voice of his. "I am satisfied." His gaze held hers, and Yvaine felt a shiver crawl down her back at the sudden fire she saw in his eyes—yet he extinguished it quickly.

Yvaine's heart sank at his words despite her relief over seeing her bargain with her father fulfilled. Caelen would soon be a free man again and leave this castle alive. That was all that mattered. Everything else she would deal with later. After all, there was always a way, and no matter how much it lay hidden from her, she would find it.

As Chief Morganach and her father continued to exchange words about their upcoming wedding, Yvaine turned away, unable to listen. Her thoughts inevitably drifted to Caelen once again, every fiber of her being still surprised at how quickly he had captured her heart. Never would she have expected this, and yet now there was no point in denying it any longer, was there? Aye, she cared for him. She cared for him deeply, and the thought of never seeing him again broke her heart. Even now, she could still feel the warmth of his embrace and the fire in his kiss, and she longed to be with him. Yet such a thing was impossible, for she was now expected to marry Malcolm Morganach and fulfill her duty to her clan. How had this happened?

Only a few months ago, Yvaine had led a carefree life, her days her own, her heart soaring with thoughts of adventure. Now, the burden of duty rested upon her shoulders with its crushing weight. More than that, her heart ached day in and out, wishing and dreaming and hoping with no chance of ever seeing its desires fulfilled. How had this happened?

Chief Morganach's approach startled Yvaine out of her thoughts, and she turned to him, her chin rising without conscious thought.

His dark eyes met hers as he stepped closer. "In three days' time," he murmured, leaning in so only she would hear, "yer father will bring ye to Castle Morganach." He exhaled slowly, audibly, his gaze holding hers in an odd way as though he were searching for something. "Then ye shall be mine."

Yvaine stared at him, her heart beating wildly in her chest. Still, she could not shake the feeling as though... he were testing her, trying to provoke a reaction out of her. Yet as much as she wished to comply, she did not dare, her thoughts drawn back to Caelen, to his fate.

And so, instead of giving her tongue free rein, Yvaine bowed her head in acquiescence. "Aye, Chief Morganach." She inhaled a slow breath, praying for strength, for control, before lifting her eyes once more.

The expression upon the chief's face was one of disappointment for the first time that day. What was it that he wanted from her?

Yet he said no more, and with a last look into her eyes, he took his leave, large strides carrying him from the hall, his footsteps thunderous upon the stone floor.

Remaining behind, Yvaine waited until her future husband had gone and the door had closed behind him. Then she found her voice and immediately turned to her father, determination surging through her veins. "Ye must release Caelen from the dungeon now," she demanded in a hard voice that rang with authority. "Our bargain was that if the chief accepted me, ye would let him go."

Her father, though, seemed in no rush. For a moment, he even appeared not to have heard her, a sickeningly satisfied smile upon his lips. Then he turned to face her and slowly shook his head. "Nay," he said firmly, his gaze hard and unyielding, sending a stab of hopelessness through Yvaine. "Ye must marry Malcolm Morganach first. Only then will I release the MacCarmaig lad."

Yvaine balled her hands into fists, her anger boiling over. She wanted to scream and rail against her father, but she knew it would do no good, for she was in no position to bargain. She had already made up her mind, and she would not change it now. No matter the cost, she would not let Caelen rot in the dungeon or have him executed for coming to her aid.

Nay, her heart broke at the mere thought of it. Even if he were an innocent, a stranger she barely knew, she could not allow it to happen. Yet this was Caelen! As little as they knew one another, Yvaine had felt a strong bond to him from the first. A part of her had even come to believe that perhaps they truly were the two lovers of legends old, the Caelen and Yvaine she had grown up hearing about, their story an inspiration she had carried with her all her life.

Yet if they were, could their story end like this? It seemed impossible. There had to be some way, and perhaps there was. Yvaine simply had to find it. If only she knew where to look. Perhaps there was something she did not consider, something she did not see that was right in front of her eyes. Yet in this moment, Yvaine could not imagine what it could be. All she saw were these two options: let Caelen die or save him and bind herself in marriage to Malcolm Morganach.

Defeated, Yvaine hung her head, wondering what would have happened had she never stepped into the cavern to begin with. Would none of this have happened? Or was there truly a different Yvaine yet to come? So many questions and so few answers.

What would tomorrow bring?

THE END

Of course, this is not the end. It is merely the beginning. Follow the legend of Yvaine and Caelen and find out how the MacKinnears came to live upon the Fey Isles. Get your copy of By the Grey Light of Morning now!

Read on or a sneak-peek!

By the Grey Light of Morning

BOOK 2

Chapter One

MacKinnear Island, Scotland 1401 (or a variation thereof)

As Yvaine stepped out of MacLeòir Castle and into the courtyard, the morning sky was painted in brilliant saffron and pink hues, reaching out to the world in a glorious sunrise. Yvaine's heart, though, felt heavy as her gaze flew over the carriage prepared for them. Warriors, their escort to Castle Morganach, were mounted atop their horses surrounding the carriage.

Her brothers Logan and Rory, too, were seated on their mounts, both their faces grim. Not even young Rory with his easy laugh managed a smile, and yet Yvaine could not shake the feeling that there was something on his mind. His green eyes met hers, and the expression there was almost imploring.

A few paces ahead of her, Yvaine saw her mother walk upon her father's arm as he escorted her to the waiting carriage. Only there was nothing gallant in the gesture. Indeed, her father's gaze was hard, and as they reached the carriage, his hand clamped down upon her mother's, causing a gasp to fly from her lips. "Not a word," he hissed, leaning in close, his eyes commanding.

Swallowing hard, Yvaine's mother nodded, her own eyes downcast in obedience and fear, and Yvaine's heart twisted in outrage. If only she could... say something, put her father in his place, demand he treat them with respect.

All of them.

Including her.

Yet it was not to be. Yvaine knew so, and yet her mind constantly ran away toward this hopeful place that reminded her of the life she had had before.

Before she had stumbled into the past.

Still, in a strange way this was her home. After all, she had been born in this time, to this family. She had been only three years of age when circumstances had guided her to a secret island just off the coast. Yvaine could not remember those days. She could not remember how she had found her way there; yet she had to have. Somehow, she had to have found her way to the island, found the cavern there and stumbled into the glistening pool of water in its midst.

Somehow, she had traveled to the future and found her family, her true family. People who had loved her all her life. People who respected her and encouraged her. People who had never stood in her way, only ever concerned with her well-being, her happiness. Aye, it had been a wonderful life, and only now that Yvaine had been jerked back into her old life—so markedly different from the way she had grown up—did she realize how fortunate she had been.

Aiden MacKinnear, the man who had become her father, would never have dared decide her future for her. He would never have contemplated the thought of arranging a union, much less one against her wishes. Heather MacKinnear, the woman who had been mother to Yvaine for as long as she could remember, had always been a proud and strong woman, her eyes only ever downcast in moments of deep sadness... or moments of mischief. There had been such joy and merriment in Yvaine's family that its absence now weighed heavily upon her heart. Every once in a while, she shared a smile or a laugh with Rory, yet beyond that, there was no happiness here.

As Yvaine watched her birth mother seat herself in the carriage, her gaze collided with her father's. He watched her carefully, as his gaze slightly narrowed. "Mind yer manners," he warned in a chilling voice, his hand now clasped hard around her upper arm, holding her in place. "Ye will do as is expected of ye." His brows rose meaningfully as his eyes drilled into hers. "That is if ye still want the MacCarmaig lad to see the next sunrise." A dark chuckle rumbled in his throat, and Yvaine stared into her father's face, aghast at the lack of emotion she saw there. Did he truly not care? Could he end another's life just like that without a moment of hesitation? Without even a touch of regret?

Finally seated in the carriage across from her mother, Yvaine watched from the window as they pulled out of the courtyard, leaving MacLeòir Castle behind. Slowly, their small family party surrounded by an imposing group of warriors made their way along a path winding northward toward Castle Morganach.

Yvaine's mother sat with her hands folded stoically in her lap, her face set in an expression of calm reserve. Not a word left her lips, and Yvaine could not shake the feeling that her mother did not dare meet her eyes.

"What does Father not wish for me to ken?" Yvaine asked in a quiet voice, not wanting to be overheard by the riders flanking the carriage.

As if slapped, her mother's head snapped up, her eyes wide as she stared at her daughter.

Yvaine heaved a deep sigh. "Tell me."

Swallowing hard, her mother shook her head, a forced smile curling the corners of her lips. "There is nothing, Child. Where would ye get such an idea?" Again, her mother's gaze returned to her folded hands, now clenched in her lap.

"Mother, ye're an awful liar," Yvaine exclaimed with an exasperated sigh. "Tell me. Please." She leaned forward, bracing her elbows upon her legs. "Does it have anything to do with Caelen? Is he all right? Did Father—?" Yvaine swallowed hard, unable to finish the question, unable to even contemplate that her father might have already broken his word... and done something irreversible to Caelen.

Her mother remained silent for a few moments, yet there was guilt etched into her eyes.

Seeing it, Yvaine's heart sank, suddenly weighted down by pain and sorrow. "Please, Mother," she begged as tears shot to her eyes. "Tell me what Father has done."

Finally lifting her head, her mother reached out her hands and grasped Yvaine's, regret in her eyes and a soothing smile upon her lips. "He hasna done anything. I assure ye, Child, nothing has happened to the lad. He is well... as far as I ken," she added like an afterthought, and her gaze instantly fell from Yvaine's.

Desperate hope surged through Yvaine, and she clasped her mother's hands more tightly. "Yet there is something ye're not telling me. 'Tis written all over yer face. Tell me true."

Her mother shook her head. "Ye're right," she finally admitted, chancing a glance up at Yvaine. "But I assure ye, 'tis not what ye think. Yer father hasna broken the word he has given ye."

Yvaine gathered strength from the way her mother's eyes looked into hers, for once not wavering but steady. She exhaled a deep breath then leaned back in the upholstered seat and closed her eyes for a precious moment.

All night, she had lain awake, thinking of Caelen, wishing she could sneak down to the dungeons and, at least, speak to him. He had come to help her flee her father's grasp, promised to take her back across the sea to the island and the cavern with that shimmering pool of water that she hoped possessed the power to send her back to the place she called home. And now? Now, Caelen was locked away in the dungeons, a threat hanging over his head, a threat that would see his life ended if Yvaine were to go back on the deal she had made with her father: to see Caelen's life saved and him set free, she would enter into the union her father had planned for her and marry Malcolm Morganach, leader of Clan Morganach.

The thought alone made her feel sick, and yet what was she to do? Even if Caelen were a stranger, she could not sentence him to death. She could not bear the burden of knowing that she could have saved him and had done nothing to do so. Only Caelen was not a stranger, was he? Nay, despite being the son of the MacLeòirs' greatest enemy, despite the fact that they had only met a few months ago, despite having spoken no more than a few words with one another, he had somehow, inexplicably won Yvaine's heart.

It was a simple truth, and a devastating one all the same. More than anything, Yvaine wished to return home. Day and night, her heart ached for the family she had lost, for her parents and her three older brothers Duncan, Keir, and Magnus. Aye, they could all be exasperating at times, Duncan with his condescending streak, Keir with his teasing humor, and Magnus with his adorable thoughtlessness. Aye, she loved them all and she longed to see them again.

Now, though, there was this part deep inside her that conjured an image of Caelen whenever Yvaine thought of returning home, as though to hold it against her, to throw the image in the balance and make her doubt. And she did doubt, did she not? All of a sudden, what Yvaine wanted no longer led her in a straight line. Nay, the road ahead now forked into two directions, and she no longer knew which one to take, wanting both and neither at the same time.

"If what ye say is true," Yvaine remarked, her gaze once more fixed upon her mother's face, "then why the secrecy? I heard what Father said to ye. I saw the expression in his eyes, and I ken that he urged ye to keep something from me. If 'tis not about Caelen, then what is it?"

Again, her mother shook her head, and Yvaine understood in that moment that there was nothing in the world that could persuade her to speak out against her husband. Nay, fear held her in a tight grip, ensuring compliance.

Anger surged through Yvaine's veins, and she felt her hands clench and ball into fists, the urge to drive them into something hard and painful almost overwhelming. Feeling powerless was such a crippling feeling that Yvaine barely knew how to handle it. She knew she needed to remain in control, and yet with each day that passed it became increasingly difficult. Never before had she needed to rein in her emotions like that. Always had she worn her tongue on her sleeve, speaking her mind with no fear of repercussions. Now, every word could spell doom, and Yvaine felt exhausted by the need to think everything through before voicing a thought.

"If I marry the Morganach leader," Yvaine asked tentatively, a shiver of fear crawling over her skin, "will Father keep his word? Will he release Caelen?" Deep down, Yvaine could not shake the feeling that as soon as she was married, as soon as there was no going back for her, her father would no longer feel bound to the deal they had made. Instead he would execute Caelen in order to get back at his greatest enemy and finally see the blood feud between the two clans settled once and for all. After all, with Caelen dead, the future of Clan MacCarmaig would be in great peril.

Sadness rested in her mother's eyes. "Ye'd be wise to guard yer heart, Child," she murmured softly, her voice barely audible. "Those who care are easily broken in this world. Harden yer heart, and perhaps..." She closed her eyes, and a silent tear ran down her cheek.

Staring at her mother, Yvaine wondered about the life she had lived. In truth, she knew very little about the woman who had birthed her. The conversations they had had over the past few months had rarely gone deeper than fancy gowns and appropriate etiquette, clan loyalty and familial obligations.

"Why did ye marry Father?" Yvaine asked abruptly. "Did ye care for him at some point? Or was it nothing more than an arranged union?"

Her mother's eyes remained closed, and yet her head turned away from Yvaine and toward the landscape flying by outside the window. Not a word fell from her tongue, her lips pressed into a tight line as though to suppress emotions that burdened her despite the advice she had only just given to her own daughter.

Harden yer heart, and perhaps...

Aye, perhaps hardening one's heart was not as simple as that. Perhaps her mother had tried and failed as well, knowing from her own experience how devastating this life could be.

Now am I to follow in her footsteps? Yvaine thought desperately, outrage simmering in her veins, making her hands once more curl into fists, testing her self-control yet again. *Am I to be trapped in a union to a man who expects my complete obedience?*

Yvaine clenched her teeth against the roar of fury that threatened to tear from her throat. *Nay, I will do what I must but no more. I willna bow my head or cower in fear. I willna. This willna be my life.*

As they continued on their journey, the rolling hills turned to mountains and the sky overhead darkened as the sun set. They traveled in near silence, and Yvaine found herself lost in her thoughts as the miles passed by. She thought of Malcolm Morganach, the man she would be forced to marry, and a chill ran down her spine.

Only a few days ago, Yvaine had first laid eyes on the man. He stood tall, his hair as dark as Caelen's, yet there had been no kindness, no laughter in his eyes when he had looked upon her. Half his face bore the marks of fire, which had touched him at some point in his past, giving him an almost monstrous expression. Yet it had been the hard and commanding tone in his voice that had sent outrage through Yvaine's blood. He had spoken to her the same way her father spoke to her mother, without respect, expecting to be obeyed.

Perhaps this simply was the way of the world. Even in her own time, Yvaine knew that many unions were not based upon love, were not entered into willingly. Yet on MacKinnear Island, the place Yvaine called home, life had always been different; and somehow, Yvaine had always expected the rest of the world to be the same. Perhaps her mind had known better, her heart, though, had found itself shocked beyond all measure at the discovery that it was not.

The night grew colder as the family party continued onward. Finally, when the sky was black and stars were blazing above, Logan called to make camp until morning, and soon everyone was busy setting up tents and gathering wood for a fire.

While the others worked, Yvaine found herself drawn to the edge of the camp. She had been so wrapped up in her own thoughts that she had not even noticed how far away they had traveled from home, away from the coast and the island Yvaine longed to return to. Before, her mind had been so occupied with only one thought: to get away, to return home. Over the last few days, though, it had not even entered her mind once. Not in the way it had before. Nay, all she had been able to think about had been saving Caelen's life as her future loomed threateningly in front of her.

And now, all of a sudden, here she was, out in the wilderness, far from the walls that had kept her locked in. She stood looking out into the darkness beyond their campfires, unable to shake the feeling that something out there was calling to her.

More than anything, Yvaine simply wanted to melt into the darkness and slip away, find her way to the coast, and reach the island without delay. She wanted to go home.

Home.

The word made Yvaine sigh with longing, and she wrapped her arms tightly around herself, fighting to hold back the impulse to simply run out into the night. "Think of Caelen," she murmured to herself. "Ye canna leave him to his fate."

As though out of nowhere, Rory appeared at her side, his eyes searching hers with an intensity that made Yvaine's heart flutter with both fear and anticipation. "Yvaine, there's something I needa tell ye," he murmured, casting a furtive glance over her shoulder, his voice no more than a whisper.

Yvaine's heart almost paused in her chest, the feeling painful and frightening as though she stood upon the edge of a cliff. "What is it?" she gasped, turning to him, and grasping his little hands. "Do ye ken what Father's trying to keep from me?"

Rory nodded, the expression in his eyes almost desperate; however, before he could say a word, their father's voice echoed across the small clearing. "Rory, come and help yer brother with the horses!"

Brother and sister both spun around, eyes wide as they stared at their father. He stood illuminated by the campfires, dark shadows dancing across his features and twisting his expression into a ferocious snarl. He glared at them, his approach slow and yet determined, as though he feared what Rory might say in the few seconds that remained.

"Tell me," Yvaine hissed urgently.

"Rory, now!" Their father thundered, his booming voice disturbing the quiet peacefulness of the night. Two more steps and he stood beside them, his right hand settling firmly upon Rory's slender shoulder. "Go."

With an apologetic gaze in his eyes, Rory bowed his head and turned away, slow footsteps, made heavy by disappointment and failure, guiding him across the clearing, past the watching warriors and toward his elder brother.

"Dunna test me," Yvaine's father snarled as he glared down at her. "Ye will do as I say, is that understood?"

Yvaine frowned, regarding her father's face most carefully. Indeed, there was a hint of concern there, and she wished she knew why. Clearly, Rory did. As did her mother. Yet both were forbidden from saying anything. "I simply wish to speak to my brother," Yvaine replied, struggling to keep the taunting tone out of her voice. "Why would ye object to that? What do ye fear he might tell me?" Her brows rose in challenge even though she knew it to be unwise.

Yet her father said not a word, his gaze stern as he looked at her before stepping away, leaving her alone on the far side of the camp.

Yvaine sighed in frustration as she gazed after him, for she could not shake the feeling that what she did not know was of the utmost importance.

About Bree

BREE WOLF is a USA Today bestselling author and award-winning word wizard, who is rarely seen without a book in hand or fingers glued to the keyboard. Searching for her true calling, Bree valiantly battled the hallowed halls of academia, earning a BA in English, an MA in Specialized Translation, and countless paper cuts. After wandering abroad and toiling at translation agencies and law firms in Ireland, she realized her heart belonged to one place only: the pages of a good romance novel.

With over 50 published works, Bree has crafted a myriad of intricately woven worlds where resilient heroines find once-in-a-lifetime love with complicated heroes. Through tales of heartbreak and triumph, her characters persevere to hard-won happily-ever-afters, taking readers along on the poignant journey.

Whether in Regency England, medieval castles or the drama of Highland lairds, Bree's gift is capturing romance's full emotional spectrum. Her stories sweep across landscapes and centuries but always promise hard-fought hope for heroes and heroines to find that magical blend of laughter, sorrow, passion and partnership that is true love.

A lifelong bookworm and language enthusiast, Bree is devoted to love stories that linger in a reader's heart long after the last page. Her own heart beats through every tale promising romance as the greatest adventure.

If you're an avid reader, sign up for Bree's newsletter on www.breewolf.com as she has the tendency to simply give books away. Find out about freebies, giveaways as well as occasional advance reader copies and read before the book is even on the shelves!

Connect with Bree and stay up-to-date on new releases:

facebook.com/breewolf.novels
x.com/breewolf_author
instagram.com/breewolf_author
amazon.com/Bree-Wolf/e/B00FJX27Z4
bookbub.com/authors/bree-wolf

Printed in Great Britain
by Amazon